BELOVED ANGEL

"You can't talk about my friends like that," Celeste said. She kissed Fox playfully on the lips as she brushed the damp hair off his forehead.

"And if I do?" He lifted a dark eyebrow comically. "How will you punish me?"

She laughed sensually as she took his hands in hers. "Let me take you upstairs and show you."

Celeste led Fox up the stairs and into her room. Inside the doorway she faced him and wrapped her arms around his neck. She pulled him closer and was rewarded by the hard, hot sensation of his hungry mouth against hers.

"Celeste," he murmured in her ear.

"Fox." She stroked his cheek with her palm as she studied his suntanned face. His eyes were half-closed, his voice thick with desire for her.

She kissed an invisible path down the center of his chest, caressing the hard, muscular flesh, teasing the crisp mat of dark hair. Playfully, she tugged at one of his nipples with her teeth and laved it with her tongue. He pulled the tortoise hairpins from her hair, and it fell in a thick wave of red over her shoulders and down her back.

"You have the most beautiful hair, Celeste." He pushed the heavy locks over her shoulders so that he could see her face. "Like an angel's."

They kissed again . . . a long passionate kiss that whispered of the need they had for each other.

Books by Colleen Faulkner

Forbidden Caress
Raging Desire
Snow Fire
Traitor's Caress
Passion's Savage Moon
Temptation's Tender Kiss
Love's Sweet Bounty
Patriot's Passion
Savage Surrender
Sweet Deception
Flames of Love
Forever His
Captive
O'Brian's Bride
Destined To Be Mine
To Love a Dark Stranger
Fire Dancer
Angel In My Arms

Published by Zebra Books

ANGEL IN MY ARMS

Colleen Faulkner

Zebra Books
Kensington Publishing Corp.

http://www.zebrabooks.com

ZEBRA BOOKS are published by

Kensington Publishing Corp.
850 Third Avenue
New York, NY 10022

First Printing: April, 1998
10 9 8 7 6 5 4 3 2 1

Printed in the United States of America

Prologue

February, 1869
Carrington, Colorado

Celeste sat lightly on the edge of the iron bed and smoothed the crisp coverlet. Her friends filed quietly into the room and surrounded the bed. She heard nothing but muted footsteps, the swish of starched petticoats, and the hiss of the gas lamps that lit the room. For once, the lively group was subdued.

"John," Celeste whispered, half-fearing he was already dead. "John, love. It's Celeste. Can you hear me?" She took his bony palm and smoothed it between her two hands. His skin was gray and transparent. Cold. "John," she persisted as she willed herself not to cry. "They're all here, as you asked; Sally, Kate, Titus, Ace, even the Reverend."

John MacPhearson's eyelids fluttered. He inhaled a whistle of air and his chest rattled like a stove pipe. He coughed and struggled to catch his breath.

Celeste lifted his worn hand to her lips. "It's all right," she soothed. "Take your time."

John sucked in another labored breath and opened his eyes. "C . . . Celeste?"

She put on her best smile and leaned closer. Before his illness, John had been a strikingly handsome man with sparkling black Indian eyes and salt and pepper hair. The sparkle was gone from his eyes, the luster gone from his hair. "Here, you old codger. Where else do you think I'd be?"

Another cough wracked his body, and everyone in the room seemed to struggle with him to gain the next breath. The air smelled not of a cloying sickroom, but of sunshine and herbs. Celeste wouldn't have it any other way.

After a long, tense moment, John managed to smile. A decent smile for a man dying of tuberculosis at fifty years old. "Thought you'd be playing cards at Big Nose Kate's. It's . . . it's Sunday, ain't it?"

Celeste's heart swelled with sorrow, but she gave a little laugh. "Ah, we've got hours yet. Still time to get in some Black Jack before supper."

He closed his eyes. "Put a chip in for me, will you, sweetheart?"

"I'll do that."

He closed his eyes, then opened them again. "Silver?"

"Right here on the end of your bed," Celeste assured him.

The yellow dog lifted its head and whined pitifully, as if already in mourning for the death of his master.

"I—" John started to speak, but a fit of coughing seized him.

Celeste helped him lift a bloodstained handkerchief to his lips and held his shoulders as his frail body fought to gain another breath. He exhaled with a rattley *whoosh* and everyone in the bedroom exhaled with him in sympathy.

It took so long for him to inhale again that Celeste wondered if this would finally be John's last breath. The thought of losing her friend twisted painfully in her heart, but he had suffered too long. No man as good-hearted and full of life as John MacPhearson deserved to suffocate to death.

For a long moment everyone stood and stared at John and Celeste, probably wondering if he were dead. There was Big Nose Kate, the madam of Kate's Dance Hall, dressed in her Sunday best red crinolines, and Silky Sally in her silk sheath gown as shimmering as a drop of water. Titus, the washed-up gold miner, stood to the rear in his dirty denims, smelling of cheap rye whiskey. Ace, the young deaf and dumb half-breed, stood at Titus's side, perhaps to catch the miner if he began to sway. The last visitor was the good Rev. Joash Tuttle, who hovered on the far side of the bed, dressed in a tight, cheap black suit, a worn Bible cradled in one arm. Celeste knew every man and woman in this bedroom would mourn the loss of John MacPhearson, a man they called their friend.

"Celeste," John whispered hoarsely.

"I'm here. Right here." She gently dabbed at the bloody corners of his mouth with the handkerchief.

"Knew you'd stay with me 'til the end . . ."

"Why wouldn't I? You'd do the same for me."

Sally sobbed and Kate handed her a lacy handkerchief from the sleeve of her gown. "Straighten up or get out," she hissed as she elbowed her young charge.

Sally dabbed at her painted lips and sniffed. "I'm sorry."

John struggled to sit up in the bed, and Celeste reached behind him to fluff the goose down pillow. "Called you all here to—" he gave a hacking cough "—to witness my—" cough "—signature." He pointed to the carved rosewood armoire on the far side of the room. "Fetch my box, Celeste. You know, the tin one."

Deftly, Celeste retrieved the battered tin box painted with Indian symbols from the clothing cabinet and returned to John's side. "Here you go."

With a shaky hand, he opened the box and rifled through papers and a few photographs. "Got it." His head fell back on the pillow and another fit of coughing wracked his body. When he could breathe again, he held out his hand to the reverend. "Gimme your fancy fountain pen, Joash. I know you got it inside that funeral suit of yours."

The reverend handed his friend the pen. "Not my funeral suit, I'll have you know, John. It's my lucky card-playing suit."

The joke, though weak, was enough to make everyone in the room laugh and crack the veneer of awkwardness.

"Hell, you ain't gonna win, lucky suit or not," John teased.

Sally poked the reverend playfully in the side. "I was hoping to win enough off you to buy myself that new pot of rouge, Joash."

The reverend laughed with them.

John uncapped the pen and squinted to focus his eyes. "I want you all to witness that I'm of sound mind. This here's my will and last testament." He sucked in a breath. "I won't bore ya with the details, 'cause I know you got a card game to git to, but I don't want no one contestin' my words after Fred hauls my body off in that new glass hearse of his." He paused. "I'm givin' the house to my Celeste."

Celeste's gaze met his. "John, your son—"

"Let me speak, will you, girl? I ain't got much breath left in me," he panted.

Celeste folded her trembling hands in the lap of her pearl gray sateen gown. "I'm sorry, go on."

"I'm leavin' what's left of my bank account to her, too. Hell, it would have been hers anyway if the stubborn tart would have married me."

Celeste smiled, taking no insult from his words. She was a tart.

"And . . . and the mine claims I bought up," John wheezed. "I'm leavin' half to Celeste, half to that rich son of mine back in California." He tapped on the tip box. "There's a sealed letter for him inside, Celeste. All you gotta do is post it."

She nodded, afraid to speak. She didn't want John's fancy house with the gaslights and flush commode. She didn't want his money. She didn't want his worthless gold claim. She wanted John. She wanted him to live.

"That's all I got to say." John signed the crinkled document with a trembling hand.

Celeste caught the pen as it fell, while John was seized by another coughing spasm. "That's enough visiting," she told the group as she eased his frail shoulders back onto the pillow. "Go on back to Kate's."

John's eyes flickered open. "Bye to ya, friends. It's been a wild ride."

One by one the men and women filed out of the bedroom, each stopping to touch John's hand or kiss his cheek. Each said goodbye in their own way, then left the room. Celeste closed the door behind them, and returned to John's bedside.

"You still here"—cough—"Celeste, love?" John didn't open his eyes.

"Still here." She took his hand once again.

"Tired," he murmured.

"Then sleep."

"More tired than that."

A lump rose in Celeste's throat. Doc Smite said John should have been dead days ago. He didn't know what was keeping him alive. Celeste knew. *She* was keeping him alive. John was staying here for her sake.

"So go," she said softly. She brushed a lock of his hair off his forehead, fighting tears. "Go find that mother lode you've been looking for all your life."

"Think I might"—cough, hack—"do that. First, a kiss."

She smiled. Tears ran freely down her rice-powdered cheeks. "I thought you'd be wanting something more than that," she teased.

As she brushed her lips against his cheek, he lifted one hand to caress her breast. "Maybe after a nap, eh, sweetheart?"

She kissed him again. "Whatever you say, John."

He opened his eyes, his mouth widening into a grin, and for a moment John looked like the handsome man who had swaggered into Big Nose Kate's Dance Hall and into Celeste's life a little more than a year ago.

His eyes drifted shut and the smile faded with a sigh. It was a full minute before Celeste realized he was no longer struggling for breath.

John MacPhearson was dead, and she was once again alone in the world.

Chapter One

Fox MacPhearson stepped off the train with a leather satchel in his hand and a strange sense of hope in his heart.

The Baldwin locomotive's whistle wailed and the wheels screeched as it pulled through the station behind him. In a puff of smoke the train was gone, and Fox was alone on the wooden platform.

So what now? Fox brushed his hand over his bare chin. He'd worn a beard and mustache for years, but on impulse had shaved it the morning he'd left San Francisco. A cleansing ablution. As he washed the facial hair down the drain, he'd washed away his past. Here, in Carrington, he hoped he would find the start of a new life.

He removed his father's letter from inside his dusty wool tweed overcoat. Plum Street. That's where he was headed. That was where his new life would begin. Number 22 Plum Street.

Fox deliberated on the platform and stared at the rickety

depot steps that led to the street below. For some reason he was hesitant to go. Not just because in going to his father's home he would have to deal with the emotional baggage of words left unsaid, but because . . . because . . . He sighed. Hell. He didn't know why he was standing here.

Fox took the warped steps two at a time. He reached the wooden sidewalk that kept pedestrians' shoes out of much of the mud of Carrington's rutted street, and made a decisive right turn toward the false-fronted stores lining both sides of the road through town.

It was mid-afternoon, but there were few people on the street. Many of the stores' window shades were drawn shut. The community did not appear to be the bustling gold mining town that, in his letters, his father had led Fox to believe it was.

A creaky sign, hanging by a nail from a corner post, read: *Apple Street.*

Fox nearly laughed aloud. After the bustling city of San Francisco with its port of call, opera houses, and art museums, Carrington was little more than a crossroads, a slum near the docks of the bay city. From the look of the loose shingles and broken windows, Carrington hadn't seen gold in years. Maybe that was why Fox had been forced to wait two days in Denver for a train passing through.

He passed a boarded-up storefront. *Smythe's Emporium* the peeling painted sign stated over the door. He walked past several private homes. Tinny piano music filtered through the open door of The Three Caballeros Saloon. He passed the saloon, though his heart pounded and his palms broke out in a sweat at the thought of a shot of rye whiskey. But he no longer drank. Drinking was one of the vices that had brought him to this pathetic one-horse town to begin with.

A half block ahead, Fox spotted the first humans he'd seen in Carrington. So it wasn't a ghost town, after all. There was a big woman dressed in waves of red crinolines. She had a rather prominent nose, but pretty blue eyes and a come-hither smile. Her rouged red lips and cheeks gave evidence of her profession. The woman standing beside her, laden with brown paper parcels, was barely more than a girl, with a fine mane of wheat-blond hair. A whore, too, but a natural blond whore. Fox had known enough bleached women in his life to recognize a natural one when he saw her.

The blonde was dressed in a shimmering sheath, not the billows of skirts and protruding bustle common to the day. The gown met tightly at her ankles, so that she had to take tiny steps to walk. On anyone else the outfit would have been ridiculous, but on this woman, it was exquisite. Up until a few months ago, she would have been just the type he would have taken for a tumble in bed.

"Good afternoon, ladies." Fox swept off his bowler hat and gave a slight bow.

"Afternoon to you," the woman with the big nose responded warmly. "Just come to town on the four-thirty, I see." She offered a gloved hand. "Kate Mullen, but my friends call me Big Nose Kate."

He hooked his thumb in the direction of the train depot. "Guess the stop's not long. The conductor nearly pushed me out the door as the train passed through."

The young blond woman laughed shyly. Her heavily rouged cheeks and the thick blue shadow on her eyelids detracted from her ingenuous beauty. "Have business in town, sir?" She shifted the weight of the bulky packages from one slender arm to the other. Her steady gaze made no excuses for her appearance, nor for her vocation.

"Um. Yes." Fox hedged, hesitant to say why he was here, just yet. "I suppose I do. I'm looking for Plum Street."

Big Kate's blue eyes lit up as if she were privy to some secret. "Plum Street? Expected there, are you?" She studied him more carefully.

"Yes, as matter a fact, I am."

The wooden sidewalk creaked under her weight as Big Nose Kate took a step toward him. "We could show you if you want. Not that this sniveling town is so big a fine, smart man like yourself couldn't find your way on your own."

For a moment Fox thought she would reach out to stroke

his coat, or perhaps his cheek, but she didn't. For a whore, she had a touch of class. He replaced his black wool hat on his head. "Just point me in the right direction and I'll be on my way. I don't mean to trouble you."

"Wouldn't trouble us a bit if you stopped by Big Kate's Dance Hall tonight," the blonde said in a finely textured voice. "I'm Sally, Silky Sally." She managed once again to blush beneath her heavily rouged cheeks.

"I just might do that." He smiled and winked. He had no intentions of frequenting a whorehouse. That fragment of his life was gone, washed down the drain with his beard. "Plum Street?" He lifted his brow.

Kate pointed a red lace-gloved finger. "You're headed in the right direction, handsome. Two blocks south. If Petey, the town drunk, is passed out on Plum and Peach, just step over him. He's harmless."

"Thank you. I'll do that." He tipped his hat and passed the two women on the plank sidewalk.

"Big Nose Kate's is on Peach Street," Kate called after him. "Can't miss it. It's one of the few places still open on that side of town."

Fox waved over his shoulder, but did not turn back. Two blocks down, he turned right onto Plum Street. The wooden sign at the corner had a plum painted beside its name, only the purple had faded to a pale blue. The street seemed to be mostly residential; white clapboard houses with varied roof lines, elaborate porticoes, and gingerbread moldings. Each home was trimmed in a different confection color; bright pink, seafoam green, lavender. The houses appeared to have been no more than ten years old, built during the town's short gold boom, no doubt.

Plum Street was a pleasant, tree-lined street, out of place in the desolate, muddy town. He smiled to himself as he passed an empty porch swing shifting in the breeze. No wonder his father had liked it here.

At Peach and Plum, Fox did not encounter the town drunk. He read the numbers on the houses as he walked, amused that the townspeople would actually anticipate the need to give the houses numerical addresses, as if they had expected the town to grow to the size of Denver or Colorado Springs. But the practice served his need.

Number 22, Plum Street. He halted on the wooden sidewalk to study the white frame house, trimmed in sunshine yellow. It looked almost identical to the other houses, except that while some of the others appeared abandoned, this one was definitely occupied. While many of the others had been left to deteriorate, someone had obviously taken care of this house. The clapboard walls had been painted recently. The shutters hung straight. The glass of the windows were squeaky clean and unblemished by cracks or breaks. A stone walk had been laid and flowers planted on either side of the walk. It was like a house out of a child's fairy tale.

Fox halted on the stone walkway feeling somehow undeserving. Would his father be disappointed that he intended to sell the home? Surely he hadn't expected Fox to live here in Carrington. Fox, who had traveled the world, Fox, who had once owned town houses in San Francisco and New York City at the same time.

Fox chuckled. Maybe the joke was on him. Who in their right mind would buy this fairy-tale house in the middle of a ghost town?

He walked up the painted white steps and across the porch. A swing drifted back and forth in the breeze at one end. To his left were a row of flower pots filled with dirt, zinnias or daisies yet to be planted in them. A trowel lay beside the pretty clay pots, as if recently abandoned.

His father's cryptic letter had said he would leave someone to watch after the house. Apparently he'd had the good sense to hire a man as caretaker, or perhaps a spinster nurse had stayed on after his death to watch after the house and gain a roof over her head for a few months. Fox wouldn't evict whoever it was immediately. He would give him or her a few days to find lodging elsewhere.

Fox's first impulse was to walk right into the house. After

all, it was his inheritance. One of the few things his father had ever given him. But he didn't want to startle the caretaker, or worse, be shot for an intruder. He rapped his knuckles firmly on the paneled oak door, his leather satchel still in his hand.

A dog barked wildly, and he heard the padding of the animal's four paws as it approached the door from the inside.

Fox heard footsteps behind the door. Light footsteps; confident, yet feminine. It swung open and his gaze met with the clearest green eyes. *An angel.* A green-eyed angel with a halo of red gold hair.

Fox had never before experienced such an immediate attraction to a woman. It wasn't his way. If he'd been asked only a moment before if he believed in love at first sight, he would have denied its existence with a cynical chuckle. Suddenly he believed otherwise.

A large yellow mutt thrust its black nose through the open door and growled. Obviously a guard dog, it kept its hind end pressed into the young woman's billowing skirts.

For a moment Fox didn't know what to say. This had to be Celeste, the woman his father had mentioned in his final letter. *Celeste, the heavenly angel.*

A whore. The moment Celeste's gaze met Fox's—for surely this could be no one but Fox MacPhearson—she wished desperately that she was not a whore. She wished that she was once more the young socialite of Denver, her reputation unblemished. For the first time in her life, she desperately wished she could turn back the hands of time.

"Mr. MacPhearson?" she asked with a catch in her voice.

Silver whined.

Celeste smiled at the stranger as she dropped her hand to her dog's smooth head to let him know the man was welcome. Silver had been John's dog, only now he was hers. "You are Mr. MacPhearson, aren't you?" she asked when he didn't respond immediately.

"Uh, yes. Yes, Fox MacPhearson."

He seemed older than his thirty-some years, but not in a negative way. His handsome, angular face had the look of a man of experience. She was pleasantly surprised to see that he was clean-shaven, unlike most of the men that passed through Carrington. He didn't even have long side-whiskers, which were popular with city gentlemen of the day. He had the same black Indian eyes as John, the same smile that could make a woman swoon. Even a whore.

"Come in." She stepped back, self-consciously smoothing her cotton day gown. She'd been gardening and felt rumpled. She nearly stumbled over the dog as she stepped back into the foyer. "Silver, back, boy."

"How . . . how did you know it was me?" He followed her into the marble-floored foyer.

"Well, we don't get a lot of strangers here in Carrington, not since the gold petered out in the gulch," she answered, trying to get past her silly embarrassment. "And you look just like John, I mean your father, I mean Mr. MacPhearson." She stumbled over her words, not understanding her reaction. She had been expecting John's son for weeks. Why was she suddenly so clumsy?

He laughed, his smile radiating a warmth of sincerity. His voice was deeper than John's had been, rich, heady, like the oak of a good Chardonnay wine. "No, I don't suppose you do get a lot of visitors."

He removed his hat, and she hung it on the oak hook over the mirror in the foyer. Unlike his father's black hair, his was dark brown, and without a sliver of gray.

"I'm sorry, I . . . I didn't introduce myself," she stumbled, still feeling awkward. "I'm Celeste—"

"Celeste Kennedy. Yes, John told me in his letter."

She felt a strange sinking in her heart. She also noticed that she referred to his father by his first name. It sounded so impersonal and uncharacteristic of the man that stood before her. "He . . . he told you . . . about me?"

"Not exactly." Fox set down his leather bag and pushed back a thick lock of hair that fell boyishly over his forehead. "You know John, he could be vague when he wanted to be."

She smiled hesitantly, and met his gaze. He doesn't know

who I am . . . or at least what I am. John didn't tell him, the sly old bird . . . And Fox hadn't guessed. Otherwise it would have reflected in his dark eyes. It always did with men and women, though the look was different. With women it was accusing, bitter, a little envious in some bizarre way. With men it was lust, pure lust, and lack of respect. The lack of respect had always bothered Celeste more than the lust.

"I'm sorry. How ungracious of me to keep you standing in the foyer. I was making myself a cup of tea." She motioned down the hallway, toward the kitchen. "Would you like one?"

"I would love a cup of tea." He removed his overcoat and hung it on the hook beside his hat before Celeste could take it for him.

She liked a man who could fend for himself. She walked to the kitchen, Silver leading the way. Never once in her life had she seen a man hang his own coat, not even John. "I . . . I was planting flowers. Summer's going to come early to Colorado this year."

"Is it? To San Francisco, too. That's where I came from."

"I know." She indicated a white kitchen table where he could sit and retrieved an extra teacup, saucer, and white damask napkin.

Silver circled Fox, watching him with curiosity.

"Lay down, Silver."

The dog obediently slid to the floor and rested his muzzle between his front paws, but kept his gaze fixed on the stranger.

Celeste turned her attention back to Fox. "John . . . your father, talked about California often. He used to say he was headed back that way."

Fox chuckled, but his dark-eyed gaze reflected a shadow of pain.

"Always searching for that mother lode, wasn't he?"

She smiled at the memory of John. This was just small talk. Something she'd gotten good at in the last few years, but Fox was easy to converse with. He made her comfortable. Maybe it was just because she liked the idea that he didn't know she was a whore. Of course she would have to tell him the truth, but the fantasy was so pleasant that she let it go a little longer. It had been a long time since she'd felt this kind of freedom with a man—the freedom to just be herself and not have to worry about saying what he wanted her to say . . . or doing what he wanted her to do.

She watched Fox study the bright white and yellow kitchen. Sun poured in through the west window and cast golden light across his face.

"You've taken excellent care of the house," he said.

She lifted a kettle of hot water off the black, cast-iron stove and crossed the kitchen to fill the flowered china teapot. "It's a beautiful house. All the modern amenities. Gaslights and a flush—" She blushed as she replaced the lid on the teapot and walked back to the stove. "John loved modern conveniences. He was always reading the newspapers to me, telling me what's been invented. He used to swear we'd be riding in horseless carriages in another ten years."

Fox chuckled with her and reached for the teapot. Celeste reached out at the same instant. Their fingertips brushed. She lifted her gaze to meet his across the kitchen table, feeling a connection with him that went beyond John. A strange tingle arced between their fingertips.

Celeste pulled back in amazement. *Must have picked up static electricity on the hall carpet,* she thought. But she knew better. The moment he had touched her, her reaction had been emotional as well as physical. In her line of work, emotion was dangerous.

"I'm sorry," Fox apologized. "I thought I would serve you." He studied her warmly. He was such a true gentleman. "May I?"

Celeste couldn't take her eyes off Fox. This felt so strange. She had cared for John deeply, perhaps even loved him on some level. She had shared a bed with him many times, but she'd never felt this way about him. Never felt this immediate attraction that she felt for his son. A little frightened by the thought, she glanced away. Celeste had worked hard to isolate herself from men, to protect herself, even from John. She'd never felt like she was in danger of cracking before . . . before now.

She watched as Fox poured the amber tea into her teacup with the expertise of a parlormaid. ''You do that well,'' she said as he poured himself a cup.

''Thank you.'' He smiled. ''Thought I might find myself a job in a London teahouse serving crumpets sometime.''

He doesn't take himself too seriously, she thought. That was admirable in such a successful man.

She laughed at his silliness and he laughed with her as he reached for the cream and sugar on the table. He had large, broad hands, clean and steady. Celeste had always thought a man's hands told much about him. She could see that Fox had not worked manually for a living, as most men who passed through Carrington had. And judging from the newsprint stains on his fingers, he read a great deal.

''I seem to have upset your dog. I don't think he cares for me.'' Fox indicated the big yellow mutt with a nod of his chin.

Celeste glanced at Silver. ''No, he likes everyone. John used to take him wherever he went. He used to say Silver had seen every saloon west of the Mississippi and east of the Nevadas.''

''Silver?'' Fox raised an eyebrow. ''The dog is as yellow as a nugget of Colorado gold.''

She chuckled. ''Silver was John's; I'm surprised you didn't know about him. Surprised you never saw him. They'd been together for years. It seems John won him in a poker game. Originally his name *was* Gold, but John said he wasn't a prime dog, not worthy of the name, so he called him Silver, after the lesser metal.''

Fox nodded. ''Sounds like something he would do.''

They both sipped their tea in a comfortable silence.

''Oh.'' Celeste glanced up at him. ''I'm sorry. I just don't know where my manners have gone today.'' She rose from her chair, feeling a little unsteady on her feet. It had never occurred to her that she might be physically attracted to John's son. It had been a very long time since she'd been physically attracted to anyone. Whoring did that to a woman.

"Would you like a slice of cake? Mrs. Tuttle sent it over with her husband. He's the reverend here in town. Joash keeps an eye on me."

Fox took a sip of his tea and pushed back in his chair, casually propping one ankle on the other knee. "I'd love a piece of cake."

"It's angel food." Celeste sliced off a piece and placed it on a china dish she drew from the cupboard overhead. "Light as a cloud in the heavens, Joash says." She took a fork from a drawer and set it and the plate in front of Fox before retreating to her chair on the far side of the table. She felt safer there.

"You're not going to have any?"

She shook her head.

"What? Another woman who doesn't eat?" He cut off a bite-size piece of white cake with his fork and brought it to his mouth.

Celeste watched him part his lips, mesmerized by their full sensuality. "Uh . . . no." She laughed, the spell broken. "It's not that I don't eat, only that I've had three pieces today already."

He laughed with her again, and their voices echoed off the punched-tin ceiling.

Fox took another bite of the cake and Celeste sipped her tea, watching him over the rim of the teacup, fascinated by how in some ways he was so like John, and in other ways so different. Many of his mannerisms were the same as his father's, like the way he slipped the fork out of his mouth, his lips pressed to the tines. But while John had often been crude in his table manners, Fox was smooth and obviously comfortable with the silver plate and the fragile china. She had no doubt he had been served tea in London. While John had been a simple man, Fox was obviously a worldly one. He reminded her of the men she had known in Denver, men who had wooed her. That had been more than eight years ago. It felt like eight centuries.

Fox finished the cake and wiped his mouth with the linen napkin before taking a sip of his tea. "Well, Miss Kennedy, this has been very pleasant, but I suppose we should get on with business.''

Celeste set down her teacup with a slight clatter. ''Business?''

He made a motion with his hand meaning to get on with it. ''Of John.''

That sinking feeling came back again. For a half an hour's time she had been a woman sharing a cup of tea with a handsome man. In a moment she would just be a whore again. ''Your father, you mean,'' she said softly. ''You haven't called him your father, only John.'' She didn't mean to criticize but, to Celeste, it seemed disrespectful.

For a split second Fox looked uncomfortable. ''Y . . . yes, my father. It's just that I never called him that. Only John. We both preferred it that way.''

''Even when you were a little boy?'' She was amazed by his confession. It seemed so unlike John. And there was the way Fox explained it. He said he had preferred it that way, but their was something in his voice that expressed otherwise. ''John never told me that.''

Fox uncrossed his legs and pressed both hands to his thighs, leaning forward slightly. ''Miss Kennedy, you seem to have known—or think you knew—my father quite well.'' There was an edge to his voice now. ''Will you tell me exactly what your relationship was with him?''

Chapter Two

Celeste sat perfectly still, her hands clenched in her lap. "My relationship?" Stalling, she repeated Fox's phrase as if she hadn't heard him correctly.

"Yes, your relationship." He slid back his chair, making a wood-scraping-wood sound.

Silver looked up in response to Fox's movement, and Celeste dropped her hand to the dog's muzzle to reassure him.

The kitchen seemed darker than before. A cloud must have passed over the sun. She watched Fox pace with swinging arms and a long stride, the identical way John had paced the same floorboards.

"I don't mean to be rude but what is . . . *was* your relationship with John MacPhearson? Why are you in his house? Why do you speak of him in such a familiar way?" He paused, seeming dread to ask the next question. "You weren't his wife, were you?"

She blinked, surprised by his possible conclusion. Who would marry a whore? Even a whore with a good reason for her fall from grace? But then she remembered that Fox didn't know she was a lady of the evening. "N . . . no. We weren't man and wife."

Celeste could have sworn she saw relief wash over Fox's face. She got the distinct impression that he was pleased that she and John had not been husband and wife because Fox himself was attracted to her.

"So you were . . . ?" He raised a dark eyebrow, making a motion for her to complete his sentence.

Only Celeste didn't know how to finish the sentence. She wanted to be honest, but didn't want to just blurt out that she had been his paramour. Nor did she want to say that the first night she'd met John, he'd been nothing more than a well-paying customer who, to Celeste's good fortune, bathed. But their relationship had quickly changed. She had become more than that to him, and he more to her. To say she was only his whore would have trivialized their relationship . . . even John's life.

"I . . . I was his friend," Celeste said finally. "His very good friend."

"I see." Fox appeared even more relieved. "You watched over the house?"

"I took care of John during his illness." She lowered her lashes, softened her voice. "I moved in with him when he could no longer care for himself. I bathed him, dressed him, read to him. Sang his favorite songs to him."

Expecting further grilling, Celeste was surprised to look up and find Fox standing beside her.

He rested his hand on her shoulder. "Then I thank you."

Though Celeste had shared many intimate acts with men, his touch seemed more personal. She was so confused by how Fox was affecting her. By her reaction to him.

"I appreciate your doing what I couldn't," he said with a gentleness she had never realized a man was capable of.

She wanted to ask why he hadn't come to Carrington sooner . . . why he hadn't been here for his father's last days. Yet she wasn't sure she wanted to know why.

"He was never any trouble. Not even in the end." She

smiled, feeling a catch in her throat and tears welling behind
her eyelids. She wanted to cover Fox's hand with her own
because she felt the need to comfort him in return, but she
didn't. "Even in the end. He was still laughing and teasing. It
was a gentle death . . . for a gentle man."

For a moment both Celeste and Fox were silent, each lost
in their own private memories. The silence seemed to bind
them together as two people who had both lost a great deal
when John MacPhearson had died.

Fox lifted his hand from her shoulder and stepped away from
her. "Would you mind taking me to his grave, Miss Kennedy?
I'd like to see it."

It amused her to be called Miss Kennedy. It had been a long
time since she'd heard the phrase. "Now?"

He glanced at the window. The room had turned bright again.
"There's still plenty of daylight left. If you don't mind, I'd
like to go now. And then, if you'd be so kind as to indulge
me, I'd like to take you to supper."

She rose from her chair. Silver moved with her. "You don't
have to do that."

"It's the least I can do, considering how well you cared for
John."

She gave a nod. "I'll be right back then. Just let me grab
my bonnet."

Upstairs in her bedroom, Celeste closed her door and leaned
against it. Her heart beat erratically, her breath was irregular,
and for once she wasn't faking it. She stared at the yellow-
rose vined wallpaper that covered three walls of the bright
room. On a fourth wall, behind the white iron bed, the paper
was yellow striped. John had had the wall coverings sent from
Boston just for her, because he said the yellow had reminded
him of her, of everything that was good and bright. Of an angel
come down from the heavens.

Comforted by the familiarity of the room, she went to her
chiffonier and removed a straw bonnet.

Silver leaped onto the bed and lay down.

Celeste studied her own reflection in a floor-length oval

mirror as she tied the bonnet to her head with the wide, pale green ribbons.

"It's wrong not to tell him who you are," she whispered to herself. "*What* you are." But there was another man in her life who didn't know the detestable truth either. She turned away from the mirror and her own admonitions. "Stay, Silver. I'll be home directly."

Celeste found Fox outside on the front porch, seated on the swing, his bowler hat in his lap. "Do you want your coat?" she asked as she tossed her sage green cape over her shoulders. "It gets rather cool quickly here in the mountains, and it looks like rain. I could fetch it for you."

He shook his head. "No, thank you. I think I'll be warm enough without it."

She stood at the steps leading down off the porch and waited for him, but he seemed in no hurry to leave the swing. "It's nice here, isn't it?" she asked.

"Peaceful," he murmured.

She wrapped her arm around a white pillar and stared off into the mountains beyond the tiny town. Carrington was situated in a bowl, surrounded by mountains with a river running through the valley. It was that river that had brought the town its success in the form of gold, until it had eventually played out and produced nothing but fresh water again.

Celeste glanced at Fox from around the pillar. The air was cool and fresh and the scent of the surrounding pine trees mingled with her neighbor's apple pie, and a hint of rain. Though the sun was bright, somewhere in the distance a thundercloud rumbled. "I suppose after your city life in San Francisco, you would find the beauty of nature rather boring."

Warmth spread from her ears to the tips of her toes as his gaze met hers.

"I have never been a man to find beauty in anything or anyone boring." He emphasized the word *anyone* in such a way that she knew he was referring to her.

For sweet heaven's sake. John's son was flirting with her!

She turned away. Celeste knew that by a man's standard she

was beautiful. Her thick, wavy hair was a natural red gold, her eyes bright green, her porcelain skin flawless, save for the sprinkling of freckles on her nose. She had full breasts and a narrow waist and legs—a gentleman had once told her—that stretched to the moon. But Celeste despised her appearance. Perhaps if she'd been moon-faced and bucktoothed like her younger sister, she would not be selling her body to make enough money to keep her secret safe in Denver.

Fox rose. "Well, shall we go?"

They walked side by side down the wooden sidewalk, through the residential part of town, past storefronts and saloons, many closed and boarded up. Celeste took the long way through town, so as to avoid Peach Street and Kate's Dance Hall. She wanted Fox to herself a little longer, the truth about her safe from him just a few more hours.

As they walked, they chatted amiably, as if they had known each other a very long time. Celeste told herself that she was comfortable with Fox because he was John's son, but the truth of the matter was that she was insanely attracted to him. His flirtation on the porch seemed to be evidence that he was attracted to her, as well. It wasn't that he had done or said anything obvious, it was just that after all these years, if there was one thing Celeste knew, it was men. What was truly charming about Fox's interest in her was that he wasn't blatant, at least not compared to the fellows that passed through her life at Kate's.

Fox and Celeste reached the grave site just as the sun was setting in a ball of fire beyond the crests of the snow-sugared mountains to the west. The small, whitewashed clapboard church was surrounded by dozens of graves marked mostly by wooden crosses, but a few headstones.

Most of the men who rested here had died in mining accidents, either by cave-ins or runaway ore wagons. A few had died of gunshot wounds in bar brawls. There were no female graves, to Celeste's knowledge, save for Lottie's. She'd died last year of the clap.

Celeste led Fox to his father's grave, weaving her way

between the many burial mounds arranged in orderly rows. The Reverend Joash Tuttle kept a neat graveyard, as neat as his church on the bluff, as neat as his parlor with the horsehair settee.

Grass had begun to grow over the mound of earth that covered John's grave, and the wildflowers Celeste had planted were beginning to spread with bushy green leaves and buds. By midsummer, the daisies and bluebells would be in full bloom.

Fox halted at the foot of the grave and stared at the polished granite headstone. *John L. MacPhearson,* it read. *Loving Father.* The inscription was followed by his dates of birth and death. He had been a few months short of his fifty-first birthday.

"*Loving Father,*" Fox read sarcastically. "Yeah, right, John." He turned away.

Celeste was as surprised by his bitterness as she was by the pain in his voice. John had painted a verbal portrait of devoted father and son, telling Celeste that he didn't see Fox often because his son was so busy traveling the world as a successful businessman. Had it been a deliberate lie, or perhaps just wishful thinking?

"How'd you get the stone so quickly?" Fox asked, apparently recovered from his emotions. He stood with his back to the grave, studying the whitewashed church with its cupola bell tower.

"He ordered it before he died." Celeste lifted her cotton skirts and sank down on one knee to pull a weed from the grave. "He looked at hundreds in a catalog before he chose just the right one. Had it shipped from Denver."

"How morbid."

"Perhaps to you or to me." She tossed the weed over her shoulder and reached for another. "But for John it was a way of preparing himself for the inevitable. He liked to make plans; it made him feel secure."

Fox turned back to the grave, rolling a small rock with the toe of his polished shoe. "He shouldn't have had to choose that headstone alone. I should have been here for him."

She rose and brushed the gray dust from her sprigged skirt.

"You should have been here," she agreed, "but he wasn't alone."

Their gazes met, and once again Celeste felt warm all over. Fox wasn't angry with her over her mild admonition. John had been right. His son was special. Fox was the first man in the last eight years to make her forget her shame, to make her feel pretty. This feeling inside that he created, allowed her to see hope for her own future where no hope had been. She didn't know what it was about Fox that made her feel this way. Maybe it was just the idea that she could spend time with a man, enjoy his company, and have him enjoy hers without the inevitable looming over them—sex on a squeaky bed. "Shall we go?" He bowed his arm out to her, and Celeste accepted.

As they passed the church and the rectory, Joash Tuttle walked out on the porch. "Evening to you, Celeste."

"Evening, Joash." She halted, knowing she'd not escape before she introduced Fox. "I'd like you to meet Mr. MacPhearson, John's son."

The reverend strode off the porch to greet Fox. In his mid-forties, Joash was tall and wiry, with a bulging Adam's apple. His head seemed too large for his body, emphasized by his receding hairline. Behind his silver wire-frame glasses, his gray eyes were kind.

"I'm sorry for your loss, Mr. MacPhearson." Joash did not shake Fox's hand, but folded his pale, beefy hands together as if he intended to pray.

"Thank you."

"I'm sorry you couldn't make it before he passed on. Your father was a good man. A friend to us all here in Carrington. *Appreciated* by us all."

Fox nodded.

Celeste sensed that Fox was trying to be polite, but that he wanted nothing more than to escape the graveyard and the reverend's incriminating gaze. Celeste never paid any mind to Joash. He'd been trying to save her soul for years, but she could understand how Fox could find that innocuous, yet accusing gaze unsettling.

"Mr. MacPhearson hasn't had his supper yet, and I'm sure he's tired from traveling," Celeste said. "We really should be going."

The screen door shut and Mrs. Tuttle descended the porch steps. She was a tall woman, as tall as her husband, with broad, sturdy shoulders and a plain, round, German face. Her graying hair was curled tightly in corkscrews at her cheeks, often singed from overindulgence with the metal rod of a curling iron.

"Miss Kennedy, did you enjoy the cake Mr. Tuttle brought you?" Despite Mrs. Tuttle's plainness she had a pretty smile. Celeste guessed that it was that smile that had first attracted Joash to her.

Celeste smiled back. She knew Mrs. Tuttle disapproved of her, but the woman always made it a point to be kind. Once when Celeste had been ill, Mrs. Tuttle had actually come to Kate's Dance Hall and nursed Celeste through the fever. "It was delicious. Thank you. No one makes angel food cake like you, Mrs. Tuttle."

"Mrs. Tuttle," the reverend said. "Let me introduce you to John MacPhearson's son."

Mrs. Tuttle fluttered her eyelashes as she always did with handsome, younger men, and she and Fox exchanged pleasantries.

Celeste glanced up at the sky as thunder rumbled across the sky. "We'd best be going, Mr. MacPhearson. I fear the storm is moving in quickly."

Celeste and Fox said their goodbyes and headed back through town, taking the same route they'd come. Dusk settled over the empty streets. A few stray dogs scuttled in the shadows. Piano music could be heard faintly, though from where, one couldn't quite tell.

"Creepy," Fox said.

"What?" Celeste strode beside him, her petticoat swishing, her arm brushing his.

"Mr. and Mrs. Reverend." He twitched his shoulders in a shudder. "They're creepy the way they look at you with that holier-than-thou air."

Celeste laughed. "They're really very nice, both of them. It's a minister's job to keep his sheep in the flock. They're harmless. Besides, Mrs. Tuttle is the best cook in Carrington. If you think her angel food cake is good, you should try her cherry cobbler."

"Speaking of food, I'm hungry." He glanced at her. "Is there a hotel where we can dine?"

She frowned. "The Green Glass burned to the ground last fall. It was a beautiful place, three stories high with a muralled ballroom and enough rooms to put up a hundred people, but Mr. Marvel didn't rebuild after the fire. No one came to stay any more, anyway. I hear he moved to Colorado Springs and opened a new hotel."

"Surely there must be some place to eat." They circumnavigated a battered rain barrel. The clouds overhead moved faster, and the rumble of thunder grew louder and closer as if pursuing them.

Kate's was the best place to dine, but obviously Celeste wasn't going to suggest they go where customers would constantly be attempting to buy her services. Celeste hadn't returned to Kate's Dance Hall since John died, and many of her regulars had been asking for her. Celeste knew she would have to return to Kate's soon, but she was trying to stretch what little money John had left her to delay the inevitable. "I have an idea," Celeste said brightly. "Come back to the house, and I'll cook you a meal better than any you can find in Carrington."

"I thought you said Mrs. Tuttle was the best cook in town," he teased. "Perhaps I should go there."

She laughed and looped her arm through his and stepped off the end of the plank sidewalk, crossed the rutted street, and stepped back onto the walk. "Rack of lamb with fresh mint— the last of Mrs. Tuttle's spring lambs—new potatoes, and buttermilk biscuits. Will that suit your palate, Mr. MacPhearson?"

He placed his hand over hers where it looped through his arm. "Fox."

She looked at him from beneath the rim of her straw bonnet. "Pardon?"

"Call me Fox."

She smiled. "Only if you'll call me Celeste."

"You took such excellent care of John. I feel like I know you well. Like you immensely."

She felt heat in her cheeks in response to his compliment. No one before had ever come right out and said they liked her.

"There's no need for formalities between us."

She said nothing. He was charming, this son of John's. She'd give him that. Charming enough to have coaxed the pantaloons off many a young lady, she guessed.

"Fox?"

"Celeste?"

"Have you a wife?" John said his son had never married, but she doubted he'd remained celibate. She wondered if he had a woman, perhaps even a fiancée.

He glanced at her sideways with sparkling dark eyes. "I do not. I'm quite available."

She felt a curl of pleasure in the pit of her stomach and she cut her eyes at him. His flirtation didn't pass unnoticed, and she felt a strange surge of anticipation.

"No fiancée, no woman you lavish with attention?" He glanced down at the plank walk caked with dried mud. "There was, but . . . she's gone. Dead."

"Oh." She knitted her brow. "I'm sorry."

He waved his free hand as if he could skim over emotions that she sensed weighed heavy on his heart. "Oh, I miss her, but it wouldn't have come to anything. We wanted different things. We had different values, shall I say."

"I see." She wondered what he meant by *values.* "How long has she been gone?" Celeste didn't know why she was being so nosy. She never asked her customers anything, not even their names. Many, though, were anxious to spill their life stories into her lap before lifting her petticoats, as if that could somehow justify their deed.

"A year," Fox answered.

"And there's been no one since then?"

"I suppose I was waiting for you."

Celeste felt a warmth rise across her cheeks. She was amazed to discover that she could still blush. "You're as charming as your father was, Fox."

"Hopefully more sincere."

There it was again, that dry sarcasm of Fox's. They walked the rest of the way home in silence.

Supper was all that Celeste had promised it would be. One of her best efforts. She had not learned to cook in her mother's home. There had been cooks and kitchen maids for that. It wasn't until Kate Mullen had taken Celeste in that Celeste had found the need to learn how to prepare meals. She had found it less laborious than scrubbing wood floors with lye soap, and far more rewarding.

After supper, Fox suggested that they take their sherry out onto the porch.

A light rain began to patter on the tin roof. Bright lightning cracked the skin of the dark sky. It should have been a full moon, but the black clouds obscured it from view.

Protected and dry in the shelter of the porch, Celeste sat beside Fox on the swing, safely at the far side. He pushed with his long legs, and she tucked her feet beneath her, enjoying the smooth motion. She sipped her sherry, wishing the evening would never end.

"Thank you for the supper and your company, Celeste. I can't say when I last had such an enjoyable evening."

She smiled at him. "Funny how people take to each other, isn't it?" She didn't know what made her speak so boldly of her own feelings, or to suggest she understood his.

The swing glided back and forth.

"Funny," he echoed. "I've been with women from all over the world, Paris, China, New York City, and I've never felt so comfortable with anyone as I do with you."

She could feel his gaze on her. "You're quite the popular man, Mr. MacPhearson."

She heard him slide his hand toward her and then felt its warmth on her arm. "I didn't say that to impress you with my manhood. I meant it as a compliment to you."

Over the years Celeste had become wary of men and their words, but for some reason she believed Fox spoke sincerely.

He took her hand in his and she squeezed it. "I know. I'm just not used to such lavish attention."

"John said you were unattached." He slid along the swing until he was beside her. "Is that still true? No rich miner has come to sweep you off your feet and out of this dying town?"

Celeste held her breath. She didn't know what to do. She'd spent so many years playing the game of seduction that she didn't know how to allow herself to be seduced. She was afraid of Fox and his advances, but at the same time she yearned for the attention. She longed to feel special.

"No," she answered in a small voice. If only he knew the truth of how desperately she had once wanted to be rescued. Before the resolution. Before the dull, throbbing acceptance of her lot in life. "No one has rescued me."

"I'm sorry. I've offended you."

"No."

"Frightened you, then, by my forwardness."

She felt so strange inside, like a young girl with her first flirtation. It was so odd to couple those feelings with her obvious experience with men. "A little."

He caught a lock of hair that had fallen over her cheek and gently tucked it behind her ear. "I want you to know I'd never take advantage of you or your virtue."

She almost giggled out of nervousness at his mention of her virtue.

He tentatively slid his arm around her shoulders. In a way, he seemed as shy as she felt.

"It's just that . . . I don't know how to explain it," Fox said. "I suppose I feel like I've waited my whole life for you, Celeste."

She knew she should jump up from the swing and retreat to her room, or just burst out with the truth. It was wrong not to tell Fox what she was, or what she had been to his father. But she couldn't help herself. John had lavished attention on her. He had made her feel secure. But John had never made her heart pound like this. He had never made her feel so alive.

Fox touched her chin with two fingers and gently turned her face toward him.

In the darkness she could only make out the outline of his face, but she knew he was going to kiss her. *A real kiss.* Something she'd not experienced in many years. Celeste never allowed her customers to kiss her; it was too personal.

Just one kiss, she told herself. Another moment of fantasy, and then she would go back to the harsh reality of life.

Though she was prepared for his kiss, Fox took her completely by surprise. His lips brushed hers in a warm, light caress. It was a chaste kiss, but one of promise if she dared part her lips. Did she dare?

She touched her finger to the corner of his mouth, and he kissed her fingertip.

"Marry me," Fox whispered.

Chapter Three

Celeste inhaled sharply, but felt as if she were suffocating. It wasn't that she'd never been proposed to. Customers were always asking her to marry them. John had made that request at least once a week for the last three months of his life. But somehow this was different. It cut into her heart and bled her. It made her want to cry, not just tears, but torrents. She wanted to cry for all that was lost, all she would never have.

Celeste pushed Fox away and jumped up from the swing, almost tripping as she made her escape.

"I'm sorry," he called after her. He made a move to rise from the swing, then settled back as if realizing how brittle her emotions were at this moment. "I shouldn't have said that." He sounded perfectly sincere as he brushed back the hair off his forehead.

Now that he was no longer so close, Celeste could think more clearly. She patted back the loose strands of hair that had fallen from her neat chignon. She had always hated her hair. Red as sin, her father had called it.

She laughed, feeling foolish at her reaction to Fox. *Treat him like a customer,* her survival instincts told her.

"Do you always propose to a woman the first time you kiss her?" she asked, hoping that he didn't hear the tremor in her voice. A woman could protect herself from a man as long as he thought she didn't care ... didn't feel anything for him.

"No. No, I don't." His voice held a serious tone, as if this had not been a boyish attempt to woo her into bed or at least to gain a peek beneath her petticoat. "I ... I've never."

"Never what?" She felt better now. More confident. She could breathe once more. *Celeste, The Heavenly Body* of Kate's Dance Hall could handle far more than little Celeste Kennedy, the Denver socialite. "Never kissed a woman?" She couldn't resist brushing her fingertips across her lips. "I find that hard to believe."

"Never asked a woman to marry me." He rose from the swing.

She took a step back. "I find that equally hard to believe, Mr. MacPhearson."

"So now it's Mr. MacPhearson again?" He extended his hand. "Look, I said I'm sorry. I didn't mean to frighten you. It's just that I'm very ... taken with you. My father was right when he said you were very special. I've never met a woman so beautiful, inside and out."

Celeste watched him in the darkness. Now was the time to tell him what she was. What would he have to say of her inner beauty, then?

She opened her mouth to speak, but couldn't form the words. Suddenly she was afraid, more afraid than she'd ever been in her life. For some reason she wanted Fox to accept her; she needed him to accept her. It was almost as if her soul depended on it.

"Celeste ... it wasn't a seduction line," he continued. "Perhaps a little premature, but ... I'm very attracted to you, and I know you share the same attraction. I see it in your eyes."

Celeste tried to speak, to blurt it out, but again her voice failed her. Somehow his eyes that seemed to reflect equal measures of hope and desperation tangled the words on her tongue.

"I've made so many mistakes in my life," Fox said. "Lost

so many chances at happiness. I just think that if there's a possibility for something between us, we should pursue it.''

"It's late," Celeste said shakily as she walked to the front door. "It's been a long day. I think I'll retire." Somehow the thought that Fox might turn away in disgust seemed unacceptable tonight. For tonight she needed to savor the illusion that she was a respectable woman. She needed to relish the hope that flamed from his attraction to her.

"I really am sorry. I don't know what came over me. I'll get my bag and go, but tomorrow I'd like—''

"Get your bag and go where?" She was feeling more steady, her old, practical self again.

"A hotel, of course.''

She paused, wondering if she should just let him stay. It would be easier that way. Safer. "This was your father's house. There are spare bedrooms. I expected you to stay here.''

He shook his head. "I couldn't. I wouldn't want to give the town gossips reason to question your virtue.''

Celeste nearly laughed aloud, her nerves were so raw. Her *virtue?* Her virtue had been gone eight years, gone since that beautiful summer evening in Denver. But she didn't laugh because she was touched. How considerate of him to think of her, rather than his own comfort.

She pushed open the door that led into the front foyer. She felt weary to the bone. "Fox, there's not a hotel in town. They've all burned or been boarded up. I told you most everything has closed." She held open the door for him. "So unless you intend to spend the night in a bordello, I suggest you come inside before I lock the door for the night.''

He hesitated.

"It's all right," she said with tired exasperation. "No one will think badly of either of us.''

He passed her in the doorway. "I don't want to be a bother.''

She walked away, headed for the sanctuary of her bedroom. "Then lock up." She tapped her thigh. "Come, Silver. Come, boy.''

The yellow mutt bounded from the shadows of the parlor and followed her up the steps.

"Take the room at the end of the hall." She ran her hand along the smooth, rosewood banister as she made her ascent. "There are clean linens in the armoire. You can make a bed, can't you?"

"Tightest corners in San Francisco."

She turned away, headed up the stairs. His face was too handsome. He was too kind. Her lips still tingled from his kiss. Fox MacPhearson was trouble.

Fox paced the bedroom in the darkness, listening to the boom of thunder and the patter of rain on the tin roof. Occasionally a bolt of lightning lit the room in eerie brilliance before enfolding him in darkness once again.

Fox removed his coat, but made no further attempt to undress. He was tired, but knew he couldn't sleep. He wished desperately that he had a cigar, but he'd given up that vice with the drink.

"I can't believe I asked her to marry me," he said aloud and thumped himself on the forehead with the heel of his hand. "Idiot. I find the perfect woman, and then I make an imbecile out of myself in front of her."

He sighed as he walked to the window and drew back the lace curtain to peer into the darkness. Lightning lit up the sky, and Fox caught a glimpse of himself in the reflection of the glass. He didn't like what he saw.

"A place to begin again," he whispered. "A new beginning. A second chance." He leaned forward and pressed his forehead to the cold glass windowpane. He couldn't sleep because he couldn't close his eyes. He couldn't close his eyes because when he did, he saw *her*. Dead. Wide-eyed, yet unseeing.

Guilt washed over Fox as he clenched a fist at his side. "*A new beginning,*" he whispered. He turned away from the window and pushed the thoughts of the dead woman out of his head, forcing himself to think of something more pleasant. Or someone.

Celeste.

He walked to the bed and sat on the edge. He studied the bedroom, sensing it had been his father's. When he sat still like this and closed his eyes, he could smell the scent of John's dusty miner's clothes. He could hear his voice as smooth as whiskey. "Hell, John," he murmured, "I've made a mess of things, haven't I? I never lived up to what you expected . . . what you thought I was." He shook his head. "I should take the money and go. I know you brought me here to Celeste for a reason, but you don't really know me or the things I've done. I should just get out of her life before . . . before . . ." He couldn't bring himself to say it aloud. But he thought it.

Before I kill her, too.

Sometime in the night Celeste stirred. She heard a sound. A door, but not her door.

Silver lifted his head off the end of the bed where he slept and stared at the closed, locked door.

"Just John getting up," she said sleepily as she rolled over and pulled the quilt over her shoulder. "Go back to sleep, mutt."

The footsteps sounded down the hall, past her room, down the stairs.

She drifted off to sleep again to the steady patter of rain.

"Rice flapjacks with molasses?" Celeste asked Fox as he entered the kitchen.

"Coffee," he said sleepily. His dark hair was damp and combed straight back over his head, his chin freshly shaved. His face had a boyish look, fresh, innocent.

She noticed that he had dressed in the same sharp, pinstriped pants and waistcoat he'd worn yesterday, though he wore a clean, starched shirt and a fresh cravat.

He hadn't brought much in the way of luggage. Obviously he didn't plan on staying long. A part of her was saddened by the thought. She'd been lonely since John died, and Fox's company had been good for her. But it was just as well that he was going. She had to return to her job at Kate's, and he had to return to his rich life in California.

"Coffee's on the stove." She walked around him and set a platter of steaming flapjacks on the table between the two place settings.

"Can I get you some?" He poured himself a cup of coffee.

"No, thank you." She waited until he joined her at the table, and then she closed her eyes and bent her head to silently say grace. Opening her eyes, she glanced up to find him watching her.

"I want to apologize again for last night."

She unfolded her napkin and placed it on her lap. She'd dressed carefully this morning in one of her Denver dresses. It was a very elegant sapphire blue with a rounded collar and vertical rows of velvet trim. She wore her grandmother's pearl earrings in her ears. It had been a long time since she'd worn them, since she'd felt worthy. Clean.

"You sorry you kissed me?" she asked pointedly.

He met her gaze and held it. "No, I'm not sorry I kissed you last night. I'm only sorry I made a buffoon out of myself afterward."

She smiled and reached for the flapjacks. "It's all right. I reacted childishly." She placed the three largest cakes on his plate, then two smaller ones on her own. It was so nice to speak civilly with a man. To actually hold a pleasant conversation. "It's forgotten. We weren't ourselves last night. Grief does that."

"Listen to me," he said passionately. "I know we've only known each other less than a day, but I don't want to lose you. I feel as if my soul depends upon it." He set down his fork with a groan. "Now, I've made a fool of myself again."

Tell him, she thought. *Tell him the truth. Don't lead him on like this. But once again, the words wouldn't form on the tip of her tongue.*

"You haven't made a fool of yourself." She smiled hesitantly. "I'm flattered. It's . . . it's been a long time since some-one showed me this kind of attention." *And look where that got you,* she warned herself.

"I find that hard to believe." He took a bite of the flapjacks and nodded approvingly. "Apparently John knew what a spe-cial woman you were. He told me so in the letter."

"He did?" She wanted to ask what else John had said in the letter, but she didn't. "John was a good man. He saw promise in everyone, even when it wasn't there."

"He certainly saw promise in you, and he was right." Fox took another bite. "So tell me about yourself, Celeste. What brought you to this town?"

Celeste nearly choked on her flapjack. She hadn't been pre-pared for his question.

"Nursing?" he probed.

She froze. What did she say now? Did she just blurt out the truth or did she—

Silver leaped up from the kitchen floor and raced down the hall. A moment later a knock sounded at the door.

"Excuse me." Celeste wiped her mouth with her napkin as she rose from her chair. She'd never been so thankful for an interruption in her life.

The knock came again, faster, more urgent.

"Coming!" Celeste called.

"Celeste! Celeste!" Big Nose Kate called from the other side of the door as she pounded with a heavy fist. "Celeste, we need you."

Celeste fumbled with the lock. Something was wrong. Terri-bly wrong. She'd never heard Kate so upset. "Just a minute," she called.

The brass lock finally relinquished its hold and Celeste threw open the door. "What is it? What's wrong?"

Kate wore a three-tiered, red velvet cape thrown over her sleeping gown. Her hair was twisted in rag rollers, her face, splotchy red and devoid of any makeup. Without her cream and paint she appeared far older than her thirty-five years—a fact that frightened Celeste. Was this to be her fate, too?

"What's wrong, Kate?" Celeste repeated.

"There's been a murder." Kate panted, trying to catch her breath, as she steeled herself in the doorway. Her cloak fell open and her large breasts heaved up and down above the neckline of her red and black satin nightgown.

"A murder?" Celeste took Kate by the arm. "Come in, sit down. You're winded." Kate was breathing so hard that Celeste feared her heart would give.

"No." Kate shook her head furiously. "You have to come. The girls are in such a fit, I don't know what to do."

"Who was murdered, Kate?"

"Mealy Margaret," Kate puffed.

"Margaret? Little Margaret?" The picture of a petite face and wispy, blond hair immediately came to Celeste's mind. Mealy Margaret was a working girl who plied her trade down the street from Kate's at Sal's Saloon. Celeste didn't know her well, except for the few times she had met her at Kate's on Sunday afternoons when they played poker.

"Oh." Celeste lifted her hand to her cheek, feeling oddly numb. "Not little Margaret. She'd nearly saved up enough money for her train ticket. She was going to Oregon to her aunt's farm."

"You have to come to the dance hall, Celeste." Kate wrung her swollen hands. "The girls are in such a way. I can't get them to stop wailing."

All the girls at Kate's had known Margaret, but none of them had been close with her. Unfortunately, like many of the young women who came to Carrington, she was just another lost soul passing through. It was a tragedy when any human lost his or her life, but Celeste knew that women like herself quickly hardened themselves to life's tragedies. It was the way they survived.

Celeste frowned as Kate's initial words caught up to her. "I can't believe Margaret was murdered. By a customer?" That would be reason for Kate's girls to be fearful. Carrington was a small town of less than two hundred. Working girls didn't get murdered by rough customers here, as they did in the bigger cities.

"We don't know yet. Sheriff Tate's at Sal's now. I only got a quick look at Margaret before Tate and his deputy shooed us out, but I'll tell you, I saw enough that I won't be sleeping any time soon."

Celeste still couldn't quite believe it was true. "What happened? A fight with a customer? Was she knifed?"

"She was knifed, all right." Kate's pale face turned a shade whiter. "She was tied up. Cut up." Tears welled in Kate's eyes. "Disfigured the way a woman shouldn't be."

Celeste's stomach gave a lurch. "Do they know who did it?"

"That's the strange thing. Margaret didn't see anyone last night. She . . . she was on her off week. She made gingerbread with one of the other girls at Sal's and then went to bed early 'cause she was cramping." Kate fished a handkerchief from between her breasts and wiped her nose. "No one saw or heard anything. They found her this morning." She wiped her nose. "I need you, Celeste. I'm tellin' you, the girls are in a way. They won't stop crying."

Celeste brushed Kate's arm with her fingertips. "Let me get my cape. I'll come now."

"What's wrong?" Fox appeared behind Celeste.

"There's been a murder. A woman friend." Celeste grabbed her cape off the oak rack on the wall. She tried not to think about the fact that Margaret was one of their own. Celeste could have been Margaret. "This is my friend Kate. I have to go with her."

"We've met." He nodded gentlemanly, giving no indication that he noticed she was standing on the front porch in her nightgown and rag rollers. "I'll go, too."

"No. Really." Celeste tossed her cape over her shoulders. "It's not necessary." She didn't want Fox at Kate's. She didn't want him to find out who she was that way.

But Fox already had his hat in his hand and reached for his

coat. "If there's a murderer about town, I don't want you ladies walking the streets alone."

Celeste made no further protest. What was the point? Perhaps it was better if he saw for himself what she truly was. If Kate and the other women needed her now, she had to go. She couldn't be concerned for herself.

Celeste put her arm around Kate and led her friend across the porch and down the steps, leaving Fox to trail behind them. The storm had passed and the rain had ceased, but there was still a light mist in the morning air. Celeste looked up to see that the sky was as gray and dreary as her heart.

Chapter Four

Funny how easily a sinner's blood washes from my hands. Somehow I knew it would. I am protected. I am unsoiled.

Watching my hands rinse clean and the water in the chipped porcelain washbowl turn a dirty red, I have to remind myself that I must remain humble. This is not my work, this slaying of sinners, but His work. It's through Him that I pass invisibly down the street, through doors, down hallways where I hear the whores laughing.

I can't resist a smile as I reach for a clean, dry towel and rub my thick fingers with the rough cloth. It was so easy . . . Easier than I had thought it would be. The little slut was so meek that she mewed when I gagged her and tied her to that filthy bed. She never cried out, not even when the knife sank into her pale, white breast. Not even when the blood splattered her dolly.

An omen. I know now that this is what I have been called to do. It is for this that I was born, have lived out this dull existence. It's for this work.

* * *

Celeste hurried up Peach Street, her arm linked through Kate's. "Everything's going to be all right," she soothed as they walked. The misty fog was cold and enveloping. "I'm sure Sheriff Tate will catch the bastard," she whispered in Kate's ear.

Fox walked behind the two women, remaining silent. Celeste felt comforted by his presence. She wasn't afraid of anyone in Carrington, but the idea that a mad killer was in town petrified her. She thought of Denver and a chill shivered up her spine. She hadn't gotten to know Mealy Margaret well, and now she regretted it. Had Margaret had her own Denver somewhere? Would someone weep for the loss of her life? Would someone's heart break when he or she received word of the tragedy. That was what frightened Celeste. Not fear of her own mortality, but fear for the one who waited for her in Denver.

The three passed Sal's Saloon on Peach Street where a crowd had gathered. Celeste resisted the temptation to stop. *Keep walking. Pretend not to see the stone-faced townsfolk. Pretend not to feel the tearing in your heart.* Just the thought that a woman she had played cards with last week had been murdered so brutally, so senselessly, made her want to scream in rage. It made her want to hit something . . . someone. It made her want to hug someone.

"That where it happened?" Fox asked as they passed the double swinging doors blocked by two of Sheriff Tate's burly deputies.

"Poor girl," Kate muttered. "I always told Sal he wasn't careful enough about who he let pass through his place. He don't keep a close enough eye on his girls. It's not right, just not right," she muttered.

Celeste wrapped her arm around Kate and patted her, comforting her as though she were a child. There had certainly been many a night Kate had done the same for her. Celeste couldn't help poor Margaret, but she could help Kate by consoling her. She could help Kate's girls by calming their fears. "I know, I know, but Sal can't be blamed. It's nobody's fault," she told her friend.

Halfway between Sal's and Kate's they passed Joash Tuttle, his black felt hat pulled low over his ears, his old Bible cradled in his arms.

Celeste nodded to Joash as they passed. He tipped his hat, mumbling as he passed her, reciting a prayer, probably.

No doubt he was headed for Sal's to give some Protestant form of last rites. Celeste didn't envy Joash having to see Margaret's body. Despite his constant warnings of what fate sinners met, she knew it must upset Joash to see one human being butchered by another. She mused how hard it must be for him to keep his faith through such incidents.

They reached Kate's and passed the front door used by customers that led to the dance hall's central room, turning instead at the end of the red, white, and blue painted false front and down the alley that ran alongside the frame building. Mud splashed up on her gown. She didn't care. What mattered was getting Kate inside, getting her warm.

Fox looked uneasy as the alley narrowed. "This isn't a good idea, Celeste. Not with a killer on the loose."

"Here's the door," she said. "See, we're here." She didn't want to admit to Fox that she didn't want him to see the dance hall with its nude women painted on the whitewashed walls, or the stage where she'd danced half-naked. She didn't even want to admit it to herself.

It looked like he was going to protest again, but then realized Celeste was bound and determined to get Kate home.

"See," she said. "This is the private entrance, where Kate lives."

Celeste turned the doorknob on the back door, but it was locked. She banged with her fist. The ruffled red curtain on the window parted and she saw Ace's face peering out. She didn't say anything because Ace couldn't hear and couldn't speak, but he could read lips. "Let us in," she mouthed.

Ace immediately opened the door. Ace was an orphan, of sorts, adopted by Kate because no one wanted a half-breed Indian who couldn't speak. He cleaned for Kate, kept bar in the days when the dance hall had been busy. Now mostly he hauled wood, scrubbed floors, and played cards. In many ways he was much like the girls Kate hired. They all worked for her and in return she fed them, clothed them, hugged them when they needed it, lacing it all with a cold splash of reality.

Ace slammed the door behind them, making an event of turning the lock as Celeste, Kate, and Fox stepped into the kitchen. His face and hands were freshly scrubbed, his black hair slicked back, still wet. He must have just risen. At Kate's they stayed up late into the night and slept late into the morning. Celeste noticed Ace's rifle leaning against the wall.

"Let me take off your cape," Celeste said to Kate, then touched Ace's sleeve to get his attention. "Stoke the fire," she said so that he could read her lips. "Kate's wet and cold."

Ace nodded and hurried to do her bidding. He was a great lumbering man with big feet, broad hands, a mane of long black hair, and coal black, hooded eyes. Ace wasn't smart, but he was caring and fiercely loyal to Kate, who had taken him in when he was only nine or ten. He'd been with Kate when Celeste met her in Denver eight years ago. Apparently Kate had found him in some kind of perverted house of ill-repute back East, and brought him west with her. Rumor had it she'd bought him. Celeste had never asked Kate for details, and Kate never offered them.

Celeste ushered Kate to a chair at the long wooden table in the center of the room. Here in the kitchen was where the cook prepared meals, where Kate hired and fired, where the girls met to eat and talk, and where Sunday poker games were played. It was the center of Kate's girls' lives and, until six months ago when Celeste had moved in with John, it had been the center of her life, too.

"Fox, will you fill the teakettle and put it on the stove to heat?"

Seeming relieved to have something to do, he moved away from the door. He glanced suspiciously about the room as he followed through on the task. He was probably wondering why Celeste was so familiar with the back room of a dance hall, as well as with everyone here. Thankfully, he knew this wasn't the time or the place for questions.

She prayed that when he did ask, she would have the chance to somehow explain, and that he would listen.

"You're here!" Her arms flung out, Silky Sally burst through the curtained doorway between the hallway and the kitchen. "I knew you would come."

Sally's pale face was streaked red from tears, her eyes bloodshot. Her satin sleeping gown and robe billowed around them both as she embraced Celeste.

Celeste hugged her tightly. Sally was her best friend. Her confidant. She and Kate were the only people in her life who knew about Denver, past and present. She'd never even told John.

"I just can't believe it," Sally breathed, patting her eyes with a handkerchief as she stepped back. "Little Margaret killed like that." She gave a delicate sniff. "She didn't deserve it."

"No one deserves it," Celeste said. Out of the corner of her eye, she spotted Fox making a pot of tea, digging through cupboards to find what he needed. That uncharacteristic male self-sufficiency again. "I'm going upstairs to see the other girls," she told Fox. "I'll be back in a few minutes." She patted Kate as she passed her. "I'll send down a robe for you. You sit here and warm yourself."

For once Kate didn't try to take over or tend to someone else. She sat there in numb silence and nodded.

Celeste, accompanied by Sally, went down the hallway and up the back stairway. The private rooms all faced an open balcony with the dance hall directly below. They found the girls huddled together in Sally's room in various states of undress, their eyes puffy and red from weeping and wide with the fear that any one of them could be the next victim.

Celeste spent half an hour with the girls, calming their fears, then returned to the kitchen.

Kate seemed more like herself again. She had removed her rag rollers and fluffed her hair. She'd even added a bit of rouge to her lips and cheeks and covered her sleeping gown with a ruffled red satin wrapper. She was flirting with Fox.

Celeste battled a sudden surge of irritation, even as she wondered why she should feel it in the first place. "I think you should consider remaining closed for a day or two," she told Kate. "Give Sheriff Tate a chance to catch the murderer. Give the girls a chance to calm down. They're pretty upset."

"That won't happen in my establishment," Kate said. "I'm careful who I let up those steps. I protect my girls."

Celeste leaned on the back of Kate's chair, eyeing her. "So, you're going to open tonight?"

"Of course. It's Saturday. Best night of the week. The boys from Odenburg'll be in cashin' their pay and wantin' a little fun." Kate winked at Fox. "Besides, the girls need something else to think about besides poor butchered Margaret."

Celeste winced. She liked Kate. No, she loved her. But Kate's bottom line was business.

"I'm going home," Celeste said, swinging her cape over her shoulders. "I'll check back this afternoon. Maybe the sheriff will know something by then." As she passed Fox she noticed that he was watching her, a strange look on his face.

"Coming?" Celeste asked Fox.

He stared at her with an accusatory gaze.

Celeste knew what he was thinking. She knew what he would say once they stepped out of Kate's door. The tension made her palms sweat. What was wrong with her? How could she have expected anything else out of Fox? "Coming?" she repeated.

"Coming." His voice was cool.

The minute they stepped into the alley, Fox brushed his hand against her arm. "How do you know those people?"

"Kate didn't say?"

"No."

She walked faster, wishing she could halt the conversation that was about to take place, wishing she could go back to the swing last night. "I told you, they're my friends."

"Friends. Did John know them?"

"Yes. They were his friends, too."

"That doesn't surprise me." Their shoes clacked on the wet, wooden sidewalk. They passed Sal's and the crowd of curious citizens still standing around. "My father made a lifetime career of passing time with whores, miners, and no doubt a few outlaws."

Celeste drew her cloak closer. The sky was gray. It was raining again, the drops falling lightly on the hood she'd drawn over her head.

"I know my father frequented every whorehouse, in every flea-bitten town this side of the Mississippi, but what about you, Miss Kennedy? How did *you* come to be associated so closely with that lot? I understand that in a town of this sort, the same rules of propriety don't apply, but surely you know the danger of associating with women like Kate."

Celeste ground her teeth as she rounded the corner onto Plum Street. She had become Miss Kennedy again. "Could we take this conversation inside?" she asked, walking faster. "I don't want to talk about this in public."

Silver bounded toward her as Celeste opened the front door of her house. She yanked off her cloak, dropped it over the wooden coatrack, and headed for the kitchen. Dog and man followed at her heels.

"Celeste!" Fox clamped his hand on her shoulder and spun her around in the kitchen doorway.

Silver pricked back his ears.

Fox eyed the dog, then fixed his gaze on Celeste. "Tell me how you know those women so well. Tell me how you knew my father. I have to know."

She felt her lower lip tremble. She'd make no excuses. She did what she did for a reason. For a damned good reason and not Joash Tuttle, Fox MacPhearson, nor the Holy Father himself would make her feel guilty for what she had done. "You know how I know everyone at Kate's," she said quietly. Firmly. She was surprised by how strong her voice sounded, how easily she met and held his gaze.

"No, I don't," Fox said softly. He released her shoulder

slowly, as if beginning to fear some type of contamination. "Tell me."

She looked directly into his eyes, choosing to speak simply. The words came so hard. "I'm one of them."

"You . . . you couldn't be that kind of woman!" He sounded so sure of himself.

Feeling suddenly bone-deep cold, Celeste marched into the kitchen and threw open the door of the blackened potbellied stove. She grabbed the coal shovel in the bin behind the stove and tossed a full load inside. Her anger flared. She knew it irrational to suddenly be upset with him. There was no need for her to take this personally. How could she have expected any other response but this one? "And just what kind of woman is that, Mr. MacPhearson?" She slammed the door shut.

Now he was beginning to anger. "An intelligent, attractive, capable woman."

She folded her arms over her chest. She was trying so hard not to feel the pain of disappointment. He wasn't going to ask why she did what she did, because the truth was, like everyone else, he didn't care. It was crazy of her to have ever placed a single grain of hope in this man. Dreams didn't come true and handsome, rich men didn't save women from prostitution.

"I am intelligent, attractive, and capable, Mr. MacPhearson. I'm also a whore. I was your father's whore, later his lover, then his friend when he could no longer *perform.*"

Fox tore off his wet bowler hat and threw it on the table.

Celeste didn't know why she shouted at him like that. Said it so crudely. Maybe she just wanted to shock him, make him hate her enough to leave now before he broke her heart any further.

"You slept with my father for money?" he spat.

"At first. Later because I cared for him."

"Because you cared for his money."

Celeste narrowed her eyes. "You son of a bitch," she said softly, too angry to shout now. "You have no idea what I shared with your father. You have no idea because you weren't here. You weren't here when he became ill. You weren't here

when he died. You couldn't even make it for the blessed funeral
because you were too busy with your fancy house and your
business in California!''

Fox blanched.

For an instant Celeste felt a pang of guilt. No matter what
he said to her, she shouldn't have said that. She didn't know
what his circumstances were, why he hadn't come, any more
than he knew why she sold her body for money. His cruelty
was no excuse for her own.

''Fox . . .'' she said softly. She took a step toward him. She
knew what she had said hurt him because she knew he cared
about her, just as what he had said cut her to the quick because
she cared about him.

He stood stock straight and stared at her with dark, accusatory
eyes. ''Miss Kennedy, I'm afraid I'm going to have to ask you
to leave.''

Her brow furrowed and she almost laughed. Her emotions
were such a jumble that they were all beginning to run together.
''Leave?''

''Leave my father's house. My house. John may have had
a weak spot for whores, but I don't. Not anymore.'' His tone
was so angry and condemning that it spurred her own fury
again.

''You can't make me leave.''

''I can. Private property. I can have the sheriff remove you
from my house.''

Who the hell did this man think he was talking to? Who was
he to judge her? She didn't owe him an explanation for why
she was a prostitute. He didn't deserve an explanation. ''Well,
you're right about the private property.'' She strode toward
him with Silver following the hem of her dress. ''You're even
right about calling Sheriff Tate.'' She stopped directly in front
of Fox, her gaze fixed on his face. ''What you're wrong about,
Mr. MacPhearson is who has the right to have whom removed.''

He stared at her blankly. ''Pardon?''

She gave a small, triumphant smile. ''John MacPhearson's
will and last testament was read and authenticated three days

after he passed away. It's been filed legally in Denver. Here's how it goes according to John's wishes.'' She paused and then began to count on her fingers, pinky first. ''I, sir, Celeste Ann Kennedy am the sole owner of this property at 22 Plum Street in Carrington, Colorado.'' She bent the next finger. ''I am also owner of Mr. John MacPhearson's bank account.'' She touched her middle finger. ''And lastly, sir, I am half owner of the old land claims now known as MacPhearson's Fortune, some one and three quarters of a mile northwest of this fine town.''

Fox stared at her, apparently trying to decide if she was telling the truth. A flicker of emotion crossed his face. Was he so shocked that his father had left this little house, a few dollars, and half a worthless gold mine to a whore who had been kind to him when his own son wasn't here to comfort him? Fox was already rich beyond her dreams or those of his father. He didn't need the money or the property.

Was Fox really such a petty person?

No, it wasn't shock that she saw. It was hurt.

Now Celeste was confused. Was this about her or John? She couldn't tell.

''Who did he leave the other half of the land to?'' Fox asked quietly.

''You.'' Then she gave him a smile that mixed sarcasm and a plea for a truce. ''Whether you like it or not, it seems we're partners, Mr. MacPhearson.''

Chapter Five

"Son of a bitch," Fox murmured. He sat on the edge of the bed covered with the white candle-wicked bedspread. "You son of a bitch. How could you have left a whore my inheritance?" To a cultured whore with a voice as smooth as honey and lips that are sweeter, he thought. He propped one elbow on his knee and brushed back the long locks of dark hair that fell over his forehead.

Rain pattered on the window glass. A gaslight hissed on the wall beside the bed. The room smelled faintly of wildflowers, of Celeste. Downstairs he could hear her banging pots, talking to herself or that mutt of hers.

"Even in death you couldn't do me a good turn, could you, John?" Fox said aloud. "She welcomed me into your home, her home, drew me like no woman has ever drawn me before." *And what is she,* he thought bitterly. A whore. A woman who sold her body, not just to men, but to his father. His father's whore. A whore like Amber, like . . .

"Damn it! What have you got to say for yourself now?"

Of course his father didn't answer.

He dropped his head to his hands. "I don't know why I'm

expecting anything out of you now,'' he muttered. ''Learned my lesson long ago, didn't I?''

He sighed. There was no use going over and over in his head the ways his father had wronged him. That was all in the past and nothing could change that past. So, *what now?*

The business man in him tried to analyze his situation. In half a day's time he'd fallen in love with a whore. Just what he needed in his life, another whore. And he was penniless. He had nothing but the clothes on his back, his toiletries, and two spare shirts. He had less than twenty dollars in greenbacks and nowhere to go.

His plan had been to sell the house, take what money his father had left him, and start a new life. He had wanted to go back to California, but not to San Francisco. There was a pretty little valley in northern California he'd visited with Amber. He wanted to buy some land there and start a winery. She had laughed at his dream and Fox had let the subject drop, but he'd never forgotten that valley. At night he dreamed of it. But he hadn't had the courage to leave his business, the house, Amber, and buy the land when he still had the money. In those days all he could think of was the amount of cash in his bank account. He'd wanted to be rich. He'd wanted John to be proud of him.

Now he had nothing. Nothing but some worthless land claims. Hell, he didn't even have that.

Fox stared up at the striped green wallpaper. All he had was *half* a land claim. First he'd had a liar and a cheat for a business partner, now he had a whore.

He rose and walked to the window, thinking of the woman downstairs. How could he have been so foolish? With all his experience, how could he have fallen so fast? He should have known that his father couldn't have actually been friends with a decent woman.

But there had been no indication of what Celeste was. No war paint of red rouge, no revealing clothing. More importantly, she didn't carry herself like a whore. Celeste walked with her head held high, a self-confidence in her stride. He had never known a whore who was so educated and well mannered.

Amber made a good appearance, but inside her fancy clothes, beneath the jewels, she had been just another San Francisco dockside strumpet.

Fox pulled back the curtain and stared outside. The sky was gray; the horizon was gray. Though he knew there were mountains just beyond the town, they were invisible in the gray sheet of rain. The water ran in rivers on each side of the muddy street below. Only the crown of the dirt road stood above the water.

A black hearse with frosted glass sides rolled by, the horses struggling in the mud as a sheet of dirty water sprayed the frosted glass of the vehicle. No doubt, it was bound for Sal's place to pick up the dead girl.

"So what now?" Fox said aloud. He tapped on the window with his knuckles. The glass was cold and damp with condensation. He let the curtain fall.

The first thing he needed to do was to apologize to Celeste. He shouldn't have spoken to her that way, treated her that way. He shouldn't have taken her declaration so personally. She'd not become a whore to hurt him. She'd not lured him into her house and into her arms. He'd entered her home and her arms of his own free will. He was the jackass who had asked her to marry him without realizing she was just another woman out to get what she could from a man, like every other blessed whore he'd ever known. Fox knew he'd acted irrationally. It was just that he had been so disappointed to discover what she was ... what she had been to his father. He was hurt and disappointed that again his hopes had been shattered by a woman who would never have the capacity to love him.

He didn't know why he was so surprised. His father had spent his whole life moving from one whore to another. Like father ... like son, he mused grimly.

Fox paced the floor. Silently, he cursed James Monroe, his business partner. The man had been brother to his mistress, Amber. He and James had gotten along well; they drank together, played cards together, whored together in the early days. Eventually they had made a great deal of money in the commodities together. Then the cheating bastard had stolen every penny from him and fled to Europe.

Fox had had to sell his town houses in San Francisco and New York City and empty his own personal bank account to pay off Jamie's debts. Because their company had borne the name Monroe & MacPhearson, Jamie's debts had become Fox's. Fox knew now that this had been Jamie's plan all along. Most likely Amber had been in on it as well.

He thought of Amber, but pushed her image from his mind. He didn't want to remember the thick dark hair falling over her face, or the chill of her skin in death. If he thought about the regrets, the could-haves, the should-haves, he'd drive himself mad.

Fox stared at the closed bedroom door. He didn't want to be alone right now. As angry as he was with Celeste for deceiving him, he wanted to be with her. To see her green eyes dance with amusement, to hear her laugh and speak his name. The thought that his father had slept with the same woman he was so attracted to felt very strange. For the first time he wondered which disturbed him more—that she was a whore, or that she had been his father's private whore. Or was it the fact that John had obviously cared more for her than for his own son. John had been old enough to be her father. Fox told himself he shouldn't care. She was just a whore. And his father was dead.

Now he had more to worry about than a woman who had lied to him by omission. He shouldn't have expected anything from his father. He shouldn't have counted on an easy way out. He'd been on his own for a long time. No one could solve his problems but him.

He walked toward the door, needing to see Celeste again, to talk to her and either confirm or refute his initial impressions of her. He needed to know that desperation hadn't made him into a blind fool. The truth was he just needed human comfort.

Fox found Celeste still in the kitchen. She was making something in a bowl, stirring furiously with a wooden spoon.

She didn't turn to face him as he entered the room.

The dog woke and lifted his head. When he saw that it was Fox, he relaxed again.

"You leaving?" Celeste asked. Her tone was neutral, neither warm nor cold. Fox walked to the coal stove that had been stoked and radiated a comforting heat. He put the teakettle on to boil. "I'll buy the house from you, the worthless land." He didn't know why he'd said that. He had no money. He doubted anyone would loan him any either. And what was he going to do with a house in godforsaken Carrington, Colorado? Maybe he wanted it because it was his father's. Maybe he just wanted it because John had given it to Celeste.

"If the land your father staked is worthless, why do you want it?"

"It might not be completely worthless." He gave a noncommittal shrug. "Might be able to get some type of ore that's salvageable."

She dumped the bowl upside down on the wooden worktable. Bread dough. She pushed up her sleeves with floured hands and began to knead the dough, releasing a yeasty scent into the air. The woman was domestic for a whore.

"I don't want to sell the house." She paused. "Or the land."

He reached into the cupboard for a teacup. He pulled down two, wondering if his father was the one with the good taste in fine china, or if Celeste or one of his other whores had helped him pick out the pattern. "You'd be foolish not to take money offered." *What money?* he thought. "What are you going to do with the worthless claims?"

Her response came in a split second that seemed to surprise her as much as it surprised him. "Mine them."

Fox chuckled. "Mine them?" He set the teacups on the table and went back for the teapot and loose tea. "You? How?"

It was her turn to shrug. "How does everyone else mine? Pick a good spot and dig. John was certain there was gold in that area; he said he just hadn't found the placer yet."

"From what I heard on the train, this area has been mined out. I seriously doubt there's any gold here."

She flipped the dough on the table with capable hands and

punched it down. "We'll just see about that, won't we?" She looked at him over her shoulder for the first time since he'd entered the kitchen. "Of course, I could buy *you* out." She lifted an eyebrow. Her green eyes were more hazel now. Stormy.

"Buy me out?" He gave a little laugh. *Take the money and run,* a small voice inside his head encouraged. "Why would I want to do that?"

"If it's worthless, Mr. MacPhearson, it would be an excellent deal for a wise, wealthy businessman like yourself."

"Look, Celeste, you slept with my father. We're sharing an inheritance and presently a house. I think we're on a first-name basis here."

She nodded. "All right, *Fox.* If the land is worthless, why not sell it to me?"

Why not? he thought. He filled the teapot with hot water from the kettle, taking his time to respond. "I'd like to have a look at the land first." She looked out the window. "Once the rain stops. It'll be a day or two, I suspect."

Fox didn't know why he was stalling. If she'd give him money for his half of the claims, he could take it and return to California. He could be done with reminders of John and visions of a red-haired beauty who had been his father's mistress. But, of course, she couldn't pay him enough to get his vineyard started. And somehow the idea of getting on a train and returning to California was not very appealing. The ride here had been lonely. He'd had enough of loneliness to last a lifetime.

"All right. I can wait a day or two." He pulled back her chair. "Tea is served."

She glanced at him over her shoulder again. "I suppose you'll want to stay here in my house?"

He was hoping she'd offer, so that he wouldn't have to ask. "If you'd be so kind."

"You're John's son," she said simply. "I'd not turn you out."

Fox felt shame for the tone of voice he'd used with her. She was more a lady than he would ever be a gentleman.

"Celeste, let's call a truce," he said quietly. "Come have tea and let me apologize for my earlier behavior."

She dropped a clean linen towel over the mound of bread dough, and turned toward him. She had covered her dress in a white ruffle kitchen apron. It was feminine and very becoming. He smiled as she crossed the room toward him, her dog at her heels.

"All right, Fox." She took the seat he offered. "I'm ready for those apologies." She looked up at him and smiled sweetly. "And will you please pass the cream?"

"You told him you were going to what?" Sally's pretty eyes widened.

"Shhh," Celeste hushed through a mouthful of straight pins. "Turn around and keep your voice down. He's upstairs."

Sally turned on the small wooden stool she stood on in the middle of Celeste's cozy kitchen, as Celeste pinned up a new gown Sally would wear on Big Nose Kate's stage.

"You told him *what?*" Sally repeated.

"I told him I intended"—she pulled a pin from her mouth and slipped it through the jersey fabric—"to mine the land John left me."

Silky Sally burst into a fit of girlish giggles. "Why, that's the silliest thing I done ever heard, Celeste. You can't dig for gold!"

"Why can't she?" Rosy, in her mid-forties and Kate's oldest girl, took a bite of fresh bread covered with blackberry jam.

Rosy was large, with melon breasts and a sagging stomach, but she was one of the most popular women at Kate's. Rosy always said it was because some men didn't really want sex, they just wanted to rest their cheek on a mother's breast.

"Celeste's a smart girl," Rosy continued. "She could mine that land just as well as John MacPhearson could, probably better, because she don't nip at the bottle."

Sally giggled in retort and covered her mouth with a delicate hand. "Really, Rosy. Can you see our Celeste dressed in a man's breeches with a pick ax over her shoulder, traipsin' about the mountains?''

Rosy eyed Celeste. "Reckon I could."

"You're not serious, are you?" Sally turned her attention back to Celeste. "You're not really going to become a miner?"

Celeste slipped another pin into the hem of the dress. "Entirely serious. I didn't realize that's what I was thinking until Fox asked me."

"Fox is it, already?" Rosy gave a wink. Her eyes were made up heavily with arcs of blue face paint.

Celeste ignored Rosy's insinuation. "John and I talked about that land. He said he thought there was gold there, riches beyond his dreams; he just hadn't gotten lucky enough to strike the vein."

"Johnny was a miner his whole life, Celeste." Sally turned back. "What makes you think you can find gold when he couldn't?"

Celeste plucked the last few pins from her mouth and stabbed them into a pin cushion on the table. "I don't know," she said softly. "Desperation?"

"Desperate? You ain't desperate, woman." Sally gave her a playful push. "When you set your mind to it, you can make more money in one night than me and Rosy put together, and you know it."

Celeste offered her hand to help Sally off the stool. "I can't do this forever, Sally. I can't dance and bed men."

"Sure you can't do it forever. Once you get to be a woman of Rosy's age," she glanced at Rosy, laughing so Rosy knew she was teasing, "you got to start thinkin' about savin' for your own place, but you, Celeste, hell you got another twenty years left in that pretty tail of yours."

Celeste spun Sally around and began to undo the long row of buttons down her friend's back. "You *know* why I can't stay here," she said meaningfully. "You always knew I didn't intend to do this for the rest of my life."

"I hate to tell you this, sweet pie, but that's what we all say." Rosy bit into a second piece of bread and jam. "You

think we was all little girls who used to think that we wanted
to be tarts when we grew up?''

Celeste tugged the gown over Sally's slender shoulders. ''I
didn't mean to insult you, Rosy. You know how much you all
mean to me.'' She sighed. ''It's not you. It's me. I just can't
do it anymore.'' She shook her head, feeling as if she were on
the verge of tears.

''That's what happens when a decent man passes through
your life,'' Rosy soothed. ''Don't worry about it. Young Mr.
MacPhearson will take what's his and move on soon enough.''
She reached across the table and brushed Celeste's cheek. ''Just
don't let 'im take your heart with 'im when he goes. Promise
me that?''

''I have no intention of *dancing* with Mr. MacPhearson.''

''No?'' Sally strutted across the kitchen naked but for high
heels, stockings, and garters. ''Well, if you say you ain't interested.'' She reached for the gown she'd worn to Celeste's.
''Then I might just invite him over to Kate's. One look at me
in my gown and he'll be emptyin' his pockets on the end of
my spring bed.''

Celeste had to smile at Sally's innocent confidence. Although
Sally was only five years younger, sometimes it seemed to
Celeste that it was fifty. For a whore, Sally had led a very
sheltered life. She didn't yet understand how having sex with
men could eventually take its toll on a woman's body and her
heart.

''Cover yourself, sweet pie,'' Rosy chastised Sally. ''You
want Celeste's man to come down those stairs and see you
bare-assed?''

''He's not my man,'' Celeste hissed through clenched teeth.
''Please don't spread that all over town.''

''Wouldn't mind a bit if he saw my bare tail,'' Sally said
flirtatiously.

Rosy heaved herself out of the chair. ''Get your silly, shameless bare butt over here and cover yourself.'' She took Sally's
silver and gold gown and held it over the younger woman's
head. Sally slithered into it.

Silver lifted his head off the kitchen floor and whined.

"Here he comes," Celeste warned with a wave of her hand. "Get her buttoned up."

"Oh good," Rosy said. "I can meet this man I've heard so much about."

"Heard what? From whom?" Celeste asked, annoyed. "He just—"

"Good evening, ladies." Fox appeared in the kitchen doorway.

Celeste's heart fluttered at his good looks, and then she was irritated with herself for her reaction.

Fox smiled, all charm and good teeth. "I hope I'm not disturbing you."

"Not at all," Sally cooed, sliding closer to him.

"We was just leavin'," Rosy said as she linked her arm through Sally's. "Wasn't we?"

"I guess we'd best get to work." Sally pouted prettily. "But if you'd like to come by the dance hall later, Mr. MacPhearson, we'd love to see you."

Rosy scooped up Sally's new silky gown and ushered the girl toward the door. "Thanks a bunch, sweet pie." She blew Celeste a kiss. "I knew if I pinned up Sally's gown it'd be crookeder than the Snake River."

"I wish you wouldn't work tonight." Celeste rose from the chair feeling tired to the bone. "It's not safe. You said yourself Sheriff Tate doesn't have any idea who might have killed Margaret."

Rosy lifted a meaty shoulder. "We'll be careful. 'Sides, chances are he's long gone by now. Moved on to a more prosperous town." She turned to go, then turned back. "Oh, I forgot. The girls over at Sal's is taking up a collection so's they can bury Margaret in a decent coffin. Fred already come and got her, but he says someone has to pay for the box." She adjusted the feathered purple hat on her head. "Over at Kate's, we thought we'd toss a few dollars in. Margaret would 'ave done the same if it had been one of us."

"Could have been one of us," Sally said softly.

Celeste gave Sally's arm a squeeze. "It's all right. You're all right." She looked at Rosy. "Of course I'll contribute. Let me run upstairs and get my pursestring. I'll meet you in the front hall."

"Wait," Fox called.

All three women turned back to him. He had his hand inside his well-cut waistcoat. He hesitated a heartbeat before he spoke. "Let me . . . I want to contribute, too."

"You didn't know Margaret, did you?" Sally asked.

Fox unfolded an expensive French wallet and peeled off ten one-dollar greenbacks. "No," he said as he held out the cash. "But I knew too many like her."

Rosy took the cash, turned away, and headed down the hallway with Sally in tow. Celeste just stood there and stared at Fox. "That was a very nice thing to do," she said softly, truly touched.

He smiled a distant smile as he tucked his lighter wallet back into his coat. "It's the least a man can do."

Chapter Six

"Thank you for helping with the dishes," Celeste said, acutely aware of her proximity to Fox.

With rain still falling, they'd spent a strangely domestic afternoon reading several Denver papers that Celeste received weekly through the U.S. mail. Then, while Celeste prepared an evening meal of pea soup and biscuits, Fox had read a book he'd brought with him.

It was not unlike many evenings Celeste had shared with John after he became ill and she'd moved in with him. But there was one distinct difference. John's presence had been comforting, like the feel of a worn pair of bed slippers on a chilly night. With Fox, there was a tension in the air, an electricity as undeniable as the bolts of lightning that lit the shadows of the parlor. Each time a casual comment passed between them, she sensed the tension with every fabric of her being. She knew he felt it, too.

Celeste understood that Fox was angry with her for not telling him who she was the first evening he'd set foot on her doorstep. But she also realized that a part of him was disappointed in her. It was that disappointment that hurt. She was no different now as Celeste the whore than she'd been when he thought she was the attractive Miss Kennedy, his father's nurse. Only now he saw her differently.

That first night in Carrington, Fox had liked Celeste for the person she was inside. He'd been physically and emotionally attracted to her, so attracted that he'd actually asked her to marry him. Now he saw her as nothing more than another commodity, like his gold investments. Celeste knew men well enough to know that he was still sexually attracted to her, but his attitude toward her had clearly changed. Like any other man, he thought she was merely a warm body, for a price, and it angered her.

"I never knew a man who could make tea, hang his own coat, and dry dishes." Celeste glanced up to find Fox watching her.

He passed her a dry plate to return to the yellow painted cupboard. Their fingers touched through the cotton dish towel. "I've lived alone since I was fourteen." He lifted one shoulder. "I learned to take care of myself, dishes included."

Celeste felt as though she was walking a tightrope. They were talking about dishes, but she could see the way he looked at her. She knew he wasn't just thinking about dishes. He was thinking about her—about her body. About the way he'd like to touch her. He passed her a fork and once again their fingertips brushed, this time bare skin against bare skin. Invisible sparks arced between them.

Celeste wondered how this man could affect her the way he did. After all the years of men climbing in one side of her bed and out the other, she had thought herself numb of sexual feelings.

"Fourteen is young to be alone. If you don't mind my asking, where were your father and mother?"

Fox scowled. "I mind. It's not something I like to think about. Let's just say unavailable."

She wanted to question him further, to ask about his mother, who even John had been tight-lipped about, but the look in Fox's black eyes warned her that she'd trespassed far enough.

"Tell me something," Fox said after a moment. "Were you serious when you said you intended to mine John's land?"

"Completely." The dishes dry, she moved to a safer distance from him, where she couldn't see the flickering light in his eyes. "Your father was positive he was going to get rich off that claim. He just hadn't found the gold before he got sick."

"I don't mean to offend you, but why would a whore want to become a miner?"

She didn't flinch. This was the type of behavior she expected out of men. "So she won't have to be a *whore* for the rest of her life."

He exhaled as if trying to comprehend. "I don't understand how a woman gets herself into such a position to begin with. What happened to you, Celeste? You obviously come from a good family. You're educated, you cook, you're well read."

This could have been her opportunity to tell Fox about her father, about Gerald Marble, but it didn't seem the right time. The damage was already done. Fox would never look at her as he had looked at her that night on the swing, so what was the point? "I'd have been an excellent catch for a man like yourself?" she intoned with a taste of his own sarcasm.

He didn't answer her.

"Is that what you were going to say?" she prodded.

He leaned against the sink stand and crossed his arms over his chest. "I suppose it was what I was thinking," he admitted softly. "Seems a waste."

"You don't know anything about me." Her temper flared as she pointed a finger. "You don't know where I came from or why. You have no right to judge me, Fox MacPhearson."

He lowered his head to stare at his polished shoes. "No, I don't suppose I do have the right to judge you, or anyone else for that matter."

She took a deep breath. He had disappointed her again. She'd given him another chance to ask why she had been forced to sell her body, but he hadn't taken the opportunity. "Don't you see? That land, the gold that might sit just below the surface, could be my way out. If I struck gold, I'd never have to set foot in Kate's Dance Hall again.''

He nodded. "There are probably easier ways for a pretty woman like yourself to get out of the business.''

She gave a little laugh. "What? A man?'' She looked him straight in the eye. "No, thank you. A man is what got me into this in the first place.'' She strode toward the kitchen door, her head held high. She wasn't ashamed of herself because she knew she'd had no other choice.

"Celeste—''

She ignored his voice that beckoned her back. She sensed that he was struggling with his own demons. "I think the rain's stopped. I'm going to take Silver out. If it's still dry in the morning, we can borrow Kate's wagon and ride out to the claim. Good night.''

Outside Celeste breathed in great gulps of the cool, damp air. The rain clouds had passed and the sky was clear. Stars were just beginning to appear in the black bowl of the sky, piercing its surface with pinpricks of white twinkling light. Celeste sat on a bench in the backyard and drew her wrap tighter around her shoulders. She knew her dress would be damp from the wet bench, but she needed to remain outside a few minutes longer. She needed a reprieve from Fox and her own feelings for him.

"Can you believe it?'' she asked Silver softly. "After all these years, I still haven't learned my lesson.''

The yellow dog looked up from a hole he was digging in the wet soil of one of her flower beds, and cocked his head.

"You know, the truth about males and their worthlessness,'' she said.

The dog whined.

"Present company excluded.''

He returned to his task in the muddy hole.

Celeste sighed as she glanced up at the dark house. Only one window was lit, the large wallpapered bathroom that had been John's pride. It had a flush commode, running water, and even a hot-water tank for bathwater.

A shadow passed on the back wall and Celeste thought she heard the sound of pipes banging as water rushed through them. *Fox. He must be taking a bath.* She looked away, wondering if he realized he needed to close the frilly white drapes. Not that it mattered. The back of the house faced the mountainside. There was no one but the coyotes to see his bare bottom if he was about to undress.

She couldn't resist. She glanced in the window. Sure enough, he was disrobing. From her vantage point on the bench, she could see him perfectly through the large, uncurtained window to the left of the back door.

He slipped out of his pin-striped waistcoat and leaned to hang it on one of the wooden pegs that ran half the length of one wall. His shadow danced on the papered wall behind him.

Slowly he untied his cravat, staring straight out the window, his gaze unfocused. Though she knew he couldn't see her in the dark, she felt guilty for watching him, but not guilty enough to look away.

He slipped the white cravat from his neck and reached down to unfasten the tiny buttons of his starched shirt. A V of skin and curly chest hair appeared.

Celeste moistened her lips. She'd never seen a man disrobe so slowly. The men she knew rarely took off their clothes. Mostly they just dropped their dirty trousers, which was fine with her. John had slept in a red union suit; it wasn't until he was in the last stages of his illness that she ever saw his bare chest, and then he had been embarrassed.

Silver barked and Celeste glanced up. She knew she probably shouldn't be alone outside in the dark like this. What if Margaret's killer was lurking about?

Silver barked again as he chased a mole or some other creature that had come out of the hole he was digging.

"Shhhh!" she warned. "Silver, hush."

The yellow dog ran around the side of the house, his nose pressed to the ground.

She glanced back at the window. Either Fox hadn't heard the dog bark, or he paid no mind to the sound. His shirt fell open to bare his broad, planed chest sprinkled with dark hair.

Celeste exhaled softly, mesmerized as he peeled the shirt off muscular shoulders, slipping it over strong forearms. He undressed so slowly that it seemed like a dance. She knew by the expression on his face that his thoughts were faraway. Where? With the woman he had mentioned? Was he remembering the feel of her skin against his? Her burning kisses?

Surprised by the wave of jealousy that washed over her, Celeste reminded herself that the woman was dead, for heaven's sake. And it wasn't as if Celeste could have ever competed with her. The woman, whoever she had been, had surely been a lady. Men like Fox and Gerald only become involved with ladies.

Pushing thoughts of Gerald from her mind, Celeste glanced at the window again. Fox had discarded the white shirt. He lowered his hands to the waist of his pin-striped trousers.

"You should be ashamed of yourself," she said softly to herself. But she couldn't look away. She just couldn't.

Fox's fingers found the button of the waistband and unfastened it.

Celeste held her breath, though why, she couldn't imagine. She'd certainly never been interested before in what lay beyond that button.

Fox turned away just as he slid the trousers down and Celeste caught a full view of muscular male buttocks. Her breath caught in her throat. His back was broad and planed with muscle, his buttocks firm and powerful. As he walked away from the window toward the porcelain tub, she caught a glimpse of long, lean legs.

Celeste raised her hands to her lips as he disappeared from view. "Oh," she murmured.

Something touched her knee and startled her.

"Silver!" she breathed as the dog pushed his dirty muzzle into the folds of her gown. "You scared me." The dog panted as she patted his head. "Are you ready to go inside, boy? Had enough?'' She rose, feeling a little out of breath, and headed for the back door. "Good, because I think I've had quite enough night air as well."

Sometime in the middle of the night, Celeste stirred and rolled over in her bed. She heard the sound of heavy footsteps in the hallway. Silver lifted his head from her feet and whined. Celeste opened her eyes, unsettled by the sound in the hallway.

John's dead. It isn't John.

Then she remembered Fox.

The footsteps halted directly outside her door. Celeste lay still, now fully awake. What was he doing? Would he dare come into her room?

Then she heard his footfall again. He walked to the end of the hallway and down the stairs.

Silver whined again, and Celeste sat up to stroke his smooth head. "It's all right, boy. I guess he's not much of a sleeper, just like Johnny."

By the light of the moon that spilled through her window she saw the dog stare at her with big, liquid brown eyes. He licked her hand and laid his head down, as if the mention of his old master soothed him.

Then Celeste heard the sound of the front door opening.

The dog lifted his head off the bed again.

"I hear it, too," she said softly. "Strange he would go outside. It must be two or three in the morning." Curious, she climbed out of bed and padded barefoot across the cool floor to the window. The flannel of her high-necked, white sleeping gown brushed her toes as she walked.

Celeste parted the curtains to look down on Plum Street. The window was locked. She had checked it twice before she went to bed, fearful of the killer.

A shadow moved from her porch onto the street, cloaked in black. It had to be Fox. She watched until he disappeared into the darkness, headed toward town.

Celeste let the curtain fall. "What do you think he's doing?" she asked Silver as she climbed back into bed.

The dog didn't answer.

Celeste laid her head on the embroidery-edged pillow and stared up at the punched-tin ceilings. "Strange," she said sleepily. She closed her eyes and snuggled under the flannel blanket. "But then, aren't all men?"

"Good morning." Fox walked into the kitchen.

"Good morning." Celeste turned from the stove, hoping her embarrassment didn't show in her cheeks. The moment she saw Fox's handsome face, she thought of the sight of his bare chest and buttocks. One seemed to be as aesthetically pleasing to her as the other. Of course he had no way to know she'd been watching him, but she felt guilty and embarrassed just the same. "Coffee?"

"Please." He was carrying the same book he'd been reading yesterday.

"I see you're reading about wine." She cracked an egg in a spider skillet.

"An interest." He set the book on the table and reached past her to pour himself a cup of coffee.

She smiled dreamily. "Mmmmm. I always thought I'd like to live in a vineyard, walk the rows of grapevines, watch them grow and produce."

He halted in mid-stride between her and the table, the cup of coffee poised in his hand. "What did you say?"

She felt self-conscious around him this morning. *Sweet heaven,* she thought, *maybe Sally is right. Maybe I do need to get back to work. This life of domestication is making me lamebrained.* "I just said I used to think I'd like to live in a vineyard. Own one," she confessed. The minute the words were out of her mouth, she regretted them. Women didn't own vineyards.

He continued to the table and sat down. "I once thought the same thing," he responded with a wishful tone.

"Well, why don't you?" She carried the hot pan of eggs to

the table and scooped a portion onto each plate. "A wealthy man like yourself, it could be an investment." She added several strips of fried pork to his plate.

"You sound like a business woman, yourself." He picked up his fork.

She returned the skillet to the stove and came back to the table with a cup of coffee for herself. "You have to be in my line of work." She reached for a slice of toasted bread on a serving platter between them.

He looked at her as if he failed to see the humor of her statement.

She laughed. "I'm sorry if I make you uncomfortable referring to my occupation, but I live with it every day, and I won't be ashamed of myself or pretend I'm something I'm not." She took a bite of the toast. "Try the eggs. Mrs. Tuttle sent them. She has a whole henhouse full of eggs. I keep trying to pay her for what she sends me, but she refuses. She's a nice woman."

"Maybe she thinks that if she stays on your good side, you won't service her husband." This time he laughed.

And Celeste had the good humor to laugh with him. "Joash Tuttle? That's funny. I doubt he even has relations with his own wife." She chuckled again at the mental picture of Joash in his red union suit climbing into bed with Mrs. Tuttle, nightgowned to her ears.

Fox laughed with her and it made Celeste smile. She'd always preferred female company to male, but Fox was so easy to talk to. To get along with. When he wasn't angry with her, at least.

"So, shall I borrow Kate's wagon this morning?" Celeste asked. "I think the road should be dry enough to make it to the claim. We can walk around a bit. You can tell me what you see with your educated eye."

"I'm not saying that I'll be able to come up with any better idea than John had," Fox confessed. "But if you and I are going to be partners, we should work together."

Partners, is it, now? Celeste thought. But she didn't say anything. Fox was a complicated man.

There was a knock at the front door and Celeste rose. "Who could that be? Sally and the girls are never up this early."

It was Ace with a note for her. A telegram. She thanked him with a warm smile and closed the door with a shaky hand. The telegram had to be from Denver.

She unfolded the sheet of paper from the telegraph office.

> *I need you*
> stop
> *Adam*

She refolded the paper on the crease with a shaky hand. Her stomach was doing flip-flops. *Oh, heavens what's wrong?* she thought. *Is he sick? Hurt?*

"Is everything all right?" Fox appeared in the hall doorway. "Celeste?"

She looked up from the telegram. "I have to go to Denver."

"Denver?"

"Now." She made a dash for the staircase. If she ran, she could catch the nine o'clock train. Otherwise she'd have to wait for the four-thirty the day after tomorrow, or get a stagecoach to Odenburg and catch the train there.

"Wait a minute," Fox called after her. "We were going out to look at the claim. We should discuss this. Can't it wait?"

"It can't wait," she called over her shoulder as she took the stair steps two at a time.

"Celeste! Celeste!" Fox called after her. "Hold on!"

But Celeste didn't hear another word. All she could think of was Adam, as she turned at the top of the stairs and ran for her bedroom to pack her carpetbag.

Chapter Seven

"How she could do that? Just walk out on us?" Brushing the hair that fell annoyingly over his forehead, Fox paced the kitchen.

Silver sat on his haunches by the stove and watched Fox walk back and forth across the room.

"Without so much as an explanation." He shook his head. "Damned flighty woman."

Silver gave a whine, thumped his tail on the floor, and followed Fox's movement with big brown eyes.

"All right. All right. So she doesn't owe us anything. Me." He touched his chest. "I made it clear I was no longer interested because . . . well, you know."

The dog stared as if he didn't know.

"Because she's a . . . she was my father's . . ." Fox paced faster, turning sharply on the imaginary corner. "Women like that, they can't have a . . . they can't . . ." He took a deep breath. "Silver, they just can't love a man and they can't be trusted. Not as far as you can toss them. If anyone knows that, I do."

The dog panted.

"But hey, look, just because she left us—you—that doesn't mean you're stuck here. We're stuck here. We could go out to the claim ourselves." Fox halted and looked at the dog. "After all, we don't really need her, do we? We know as much about gold mining as she does."

The dog loped over and sat down beside Fox, resting his body against Fox's leg. His tongue lolled from his mouth and he looked up in anticipation of the trip abroad.

"Should I take that as an affirmative?" Fox crouched and scratched the mutt behind his ears. "Tell me something. Why is it that now she's gone, you're my best buddy?"

The dog whined and rubbed his head under Fox's hand.

"Were those eggs from breakfast I fed you sufficient bribery?" He rose. "If so, you're cheap, old boy. Which is good, because I'm just about broke now that I gave that cash for the whore's funeral."

The dog continued to stare, seemingly unimpressed with Fox's generosity.

"Yeah, just money. I know. Doesn't mean much to either of us these days, does it?" Fox halted in the kitchen doorway for a moment and sighed. "So, you with me or not? Want to go for a ride in Kate's wagon and check out our worthless land?" He patted his leg and the dog leaped up and bounded toward him.

Hours later Fox rode back down the dusty path he and the dog had followed earlier in the day. He was tired, but felt a strange, floating sense of contentment.

Fox had easily located the tract of land he and Celeste had inherited. Kate's directions had been good and the dog's instincts had been better. Fox guessed the dog had probably walked the land with John many times.

As best as Fox could tell, John's land gave no indication of gold beneath its surface, but neither did it deny it. The river ran with fresh, cold water directly through the center of the hilly plot. There were several abandoned mine shafts where

John had dug for gold and come up empty-handed. Truthfully, the land looked barren to Fox, at least barren of gold ore.

Fox lifted the leather reins in his hands and urged the horse south toward town. "I don't know about you, boy," he said to the dog, "but I'm parched. I could use a drink. You?"

Silver sat up on the bench seat beside Fox and stared straight ahead at the storefronts and buildings that loomed ahead. At the mention of a drink, the mutt cocked his head inquisitively and thumbed his tail eagerly.

"I suppose we could stop at Kate's Dance Hall." He looked at the dog. "No?" He grimaced. "Doesn't sound like a good idea to me either. How about Sal's? I could get you a big bowl of water and a nice sarsaparilla for myself. What I really want is a good kick of whiskey, but I don't imbibe anymore. Got me in too much trouble. Made me too trusting."

Fox chuckled as the dog licked his arm where he'd pushed up his dusty sleeve. Surprisingly, he'd enjoyed his day out on his father's land. It had made him feel closer to him. He had remembered some of the good times they'd spent together, rather than the feelings of loneliness and abandonment that he usually associated with John MacPhearson.

Fox remembered sailing wooden boats with canvas sails on a stone-lined pond in a Boston park. He remembered riding his first horse, a palomino, at a livery stable in St. Louis. He remembered his first whore, a gift from his father on his six-teenth birthday. Her name had been Antoinette and she'd been a redhead. Maybe that was why he was partial to redheads.

Fox glanced at Silver. Surprisingly, the dog had been good company. Better than Celeste would have been. The dog was comfortable with him, and he with the dog. Neither expected anything from the other, so neither could be disappointed. Celeste made him uncomfortable, not because she was a tart, but because he knew she was a tart and he was still insanely attracted to her. Hadn't he learned his lesson with Amber? Apparently not well enough.

Fox returned the wagon to the livery where Kate Mullen stabled her horse, and then he and the dog walked down Peach

Street, past Kate's Dance Hall to Sal's. While Kate's was not yet open for business, Sal's was a saloon and, therefore, always open to a thirsty man with a coin in his pocket.

Fox entered Sal's through the swinging doors, carrying his coat and waistcoat on his arm. It had gotten warm out on the claim, and he'd shed them hours ago. It was the only suit of clothing he owned, and he knew he had to take care of it. Only a week ago he'd been heartsick at the loss of all his French suits and German leathers. Today, though, one suit seemed plenty for any man.

With Silver trailing behind him, Fox walked up to the bar and took a seat on a cracked wooden stool. It shimmied when he lowered his weight onto it, and for a moment he wondered if it would hold him or send him crashing to the floor.

Fox looked up and groaned inwardly at his reflection in the mirror that ran the length of the bar. *Sal's Saloon* was written with a flourish in gilded gold paint across the top. Fox always hated mirrors, hated being forced to look at himself. He glanced away.

No one sat at the bar or the tables that were scattered in the hall. The red and gold velvet drapes were pulled shut on the small stage constructed at one end of the bar. There wasn't a soul in sight. It was quiet. Too quiet.

"Hello? Anyone here?" Fox's voice echoed off the crumbling plaster walls and high ceiling, sounding tinny.

After a moment a curtain of fringe rustled over a doorway to the far left behind the bar. A man with a handlebar mustache and a balding head emerged. "We're closed," he grumbled.

"You don't look closed. Door's open." Fox didn't mean to be argumentative, but he didn't feel like going back to the house on Plum Street. It was too strange being alone in his father's house. Too strange to be there without Celeste.

The man looked up. "I said, we're closed," he barked.

Fox threw up his hands defensively. "Sorry. Sorry. I didn't meant to ruffle your feathers, I just wanted a drink of water for my dog."

The bartender peered over the bar at Silver. "That ain't your dog. 'At's John MacPhearson's.'' He lifted a pitcher from the bar, poured water into a large glass, and slid it across the polished but scarred bartop.

Water sloshed onto Fox's hand as he caught it. ''John was my father.'' He lowered the glass to the floor and Silver began to lap it up greedily.

''Still ain't your dog. Now he's Celeste's. You ain't got no right to claim that dog, same as you ain't got no right to that claim of John's.''

Fox frowned. ''Who might you be, sir?''

''Sal,'' the bartender grunted. He pulled a cloth from the strap of his green suspenders and wiped at a drop of water on the bar top.

''So this is your place.'' Fox indicated the room. ''I heard about the woman who was killed. I'm sorry.''

Sal continued to wipe the bar despite the fact that the water was gone. '' 'Bout put an end to my business. Who wants to come drink, play cards, dance in a place known for dead whores?''

Fox gave a nod of empathy, thinking it ironic that he was the one at the bar doing the listening, rather than the talking.

''Not that it matters,'' Sal went on. ''I'm about ready to close up anyway, move onto another place where I can make a decent living.'' He continued to rub the same dry spot. ''I'll miss her, though, little Margaret. She was right cheeky. Nice girl. Wanted to go to Oregon and catch herself an apple farmer.''

Fox glanced over his shoulder as the hinges of the swinging saloon door squeaked behind him. A man wearing a ten-gallon hat and a badge in the shape of a star approached. ''Afternoon, Sal,'' he said in a Texas drawl.

''Afternoon, Tate.''

Sheriff Tate took the stool beside Fox. ''A double rye,'' he ordered.

Sal had said that the saloon was closed, but apparently it was never closed for the town sheriff.

''Afternoon,'' Fox said. ''I'm Fox MacPhearson, John—''

''I know who you are,'' the sheriff cut in, then accepted his double whiskey, and threw back half the shot in one gulp. "Already know who you are, 'cause it's my business to know strangers in town."

Fox glanced uneasily at the sheriff, then back at Sal. The sheriff was almost too stereotypical to be real. Who did he think he was, a Texas Ranger? "Well, thanks for the water for the dog. Appreciate it, Sal." Fox started to rise off the stool, and the sheriff tapped the bar with one hand.

"Not so fast."

Fox stared at the sheriff, not liking the way Tate looked at him. He didn't like the man's accusatory tone of voice either.

"Have a seat, Mr. MacPhearson. I got a question or two for you."

Fox hesitated for a moment and then settled on the creaky bar stool again. He didn't know why he was feeling so defensive. If the sheriff wanted to ask a few questions, he supposed he could answer them. After all, what could the questions possibly be? Why was he here? When was he leaving?

The sheriff finished his whiskey and wiped his mouth with his bulging forearm. Fox wondered if he'd been a blacksmith in a former lifetime.

"Did you know the girl?" Tate asked. He stared at Fox with pale blue eyes.

"The girl?" Fox cocked his head. "What girl?"

Tate looked at Sal and then back at Fox. "If yer gonna be difficult, Mister, I can haul your fancy white ass down to the jail and see how difficult yer feelin' after a few days on Deputy Garner's pork and beans. Give you gas something ferocious."

Fox would have laughed at the man's ridiculous statement, but he knew Tate wasn't kidding. He really would throw him behind bars, and what could Fox do about it? Telegraph his lawyer? How would he pay him? Hell, he barely had enough cash to pay for the telegraph.

"I've only been in town a few days," Fox said as he looked the man straight in the eye. "You'll have to clarify whom you speak of."

"Have to clarify whom you speak of," Tate mimicked. "The dead girl, that's who the hell I speak of!"

Fox didn't flinch. He'd been to hell and back on more than one occasion in his lifetime. Men like Tate didn't scare him. "No. I didn't know the dead girl, though I believe I heard her name was Margaret. Miss Kennedy knew her."

Tate's eyes narrowed. "You bunked up with the Kennedy hussy, now, are you?"

Fox ground his teeth, suppressing his urge to knock the sheriff off the bar stool with one well-placed punch. It had been a long time since Fox had been in a brawl, but not so long that he'd forgotten how to swing. He knew what Celeste was, but he didn't like hearing it come out of this jackass's mouth.

"Miss Kennedy has offered the hospitality of her home to me while my father's estate is settled," Fox said icily.

Tate looked away, backing down a notch. "So you didn't know Mealy Margaret?"

"No, sir."

"But you came in on the 4:30 the night she was murdered?"

"Coincidence."

Tate didn't say anything. Fox took that as his opportunity to depart. He slid off the bar stool that wobbled and picked up the glass Silver had used. "Thanks, Sal. What do I owe you?"

"For water?"

Fox hooked his thumb toward the bar stool. "You ought to get that thing fixed before someone falls off it."

Sal frowned and leaned his elbows on the bar. "John Mac-Phearson used to do the repairin' 'round town. Never charged nothin' but a rye or two."

Fox nodded and glanced at the stool again. "Well, I may be around a few days. Might come by and take a look. Once upon a time I was good with my hands."

For the first time Sal met his gaze and something twinkled in his eye. "That'd be nice of you, Mr. MacPhearson."

"Fox." He tipped his bowler hat and walked out of the saloon with Silver on his heels. "Have a nice day, gentlemen."

Back at the house, Fox and the dog ate what was left of the angel food cake, bread and jam, and some peas he found in the icebox from the night before. Silver wouldn't eat the peas, so Fox gave the mutt the last slice of his bread. Their meal finished, they went into the parlor as twilight settled. It was too early to go to bed, but Fox didn't know what to do with himself.

He missed Celeste's light footsteps, the delicious smells that came from the kitchen, her voice.

He sat in a chair with a newspaper on his lap and scratched Silver behind the ears. Fox had never had a dog, not even as a child. He had never thought himself the kind of man who would like a pet, but honestly, he enjoyed the dog's company.

"So who do you think is in Denver?" Fox contemplated as he stared at the gas lamp that flickered and cast shaky shadows on the floor and far wall. "A man? A client?"

The dog licked Fox's fingers.

"She doesn't seem the type to be in a place like Kate's. Maybe she's working on her own, trying to build business in Denver. Or maybe . . ." He stared without seeing. "Maybe she has a wealthy, married man. He beckons; she runs to him."

The dog stared with big, limpid brown eyes.

Fox sighed. He couldn't believe it. He was jealous. He was jealous that Celeste might be lying in bed with some fat, balding businessman at this very moment, while Fox sat talking to a dog. The truth, though hard to admit, was that Fox wanted to be in Celeste's bed.

He wondered what it would be like to stroke her hair, to nuzzle her breasts, to make her sigh with pleasure. Of course Amber had always faked her pleasure with Fox. All whores did. Would Celeste be the same, or could he crack her veneer? He liked to think he could arouse her. But more importantly, he liked the idea that maybe he could make her feel—really feel. She had certainly unsettled *him* emotionally.

Fox groaned and lunged out of the chair, letting the newspaper fall.

The dog started.

"Want to go for a walk, boy? I can't stay here. I can't just sit here and think about her." He walked into the foyer and grabbed a sturdy coat made of denim that he'd found in his father's armoire. In the same dresser he'd discovered denim pants and a durable brown shirt. From under the iron bed he'd retrieved a pair of work boots. They had all been his father's, and though Fox had never worn such common men's attire, he liked the feel of it against his skin. He liked the smell of the washed clothing. Probably because it smelled like *her.*

Silver bounded toward the door. "We'll go for a walk and then hit the bed early."

Silver followed him out the door.

"I figure she's got to be back in a few days, but we might as well keep busy while she's gone. Let me go over my plan with you."

Six days after she left Carrington, Celeste returned on the 9:30 A.M. train. It had been a tiring trip with the train passing through little towns, sometimes stopping to pick up passengers, other times sitting for hours while coal or supplies were loaded into cars. Still, Celeste returned calm. Everything was all right in Denver. She'd taken care of the problem, which turned out to be minor.

As Celeste walked up Plum Street, she wondered what she would find when she reached home. Would Fox still be there? All week she had tried to think of nothing but the problem at hand. She'd tried not to remember the way his hair fell boyishly over his forehead, or the way he laughed in his rich baritone voice. Mostly she tried hard not to think about the one kiss they had shared.

But once she had solved the issue in Denver, all she'd been able to think about was Fox and returning to Carrington to see him. Logic told her it would be better if he'd returned to San Francisco never to be heard from again, but she hoped he'd still be here. Even knowing nothing could exist between them, she liked having him around.

Celeste came into sight of John's house and spotted Fox sitting on the porch, swinging, the dog beside him. She felt a heat flush her cheeks at the sight of him. Fox was dressed in his father's denims and a leather miner's cap. The sturdiness of his attire was complimentary to his own rugged good looks, the clothes as becoming as the pin-striped suit had been.

"I see you didn't harm each other while I was gone," she called, hoping he couldn't tell how glad she was to see him.

Fox looked up, his face breaking into the most engaging smile she'd ever seen on a man. His dark eyes crinkled with laughter and her heart gave a little patter beneath her breast. She didn't understand what was happening between them, but he seemed to be as happy to see her as she was to see him.

Silver bounded off the swing and ran down the walk toward her, barking and leaping. Fox rose to take her bag.

"We were beginning to worry about you."

"We?" She untied the wide azure ribbon of her bonnet as she climbed up the porch steps.

Fox looked sheepish. "Silver and I."

"Don't tell me you changed masters again?" She halted on the porch to pet the dog that bounced up and down around her and nipped at the hem of her azure taffeta gown.

Silver dropped to his haunches and huffed and chuffed with pleasure as she scratched his back with her blunt fingernails.

"You were gone so long." He swung the carpetbag in his hand, trying to seem causal. "I was . . . afraid something might be wrong. You didn't say why you'd gone."

She gazed up at Fox, not certain if she was flattered by his concern or disturbed by it. Something had changed between them in her absence. It was almost as if they had both forgotten who the other was, and they were on the porch swing for the first time again. Of course Celeste knew they couldn't go back, not ever. "I didn't tell you where I was going because I didn't want you to know."

He sighed and pushed back his hair. "I know. I'm sorry. I didn't mean to pry. I'm just . . . we're . . ."—he indicated the dog—"glad to see that you're all right. With a killer on the loose, you never know," he finished lamely.

He walked around her and backed toward the door with her leather satchel still in his hand. "Hungry? I made flapjacks. They're not as good as yours, but decent. Or tea." He glanced up, as eager to please as the dog was. "I could make you tea."

She stood and pulled off her bonnet. "I'm not hungry. Just tired."

Fox gestured. "You want to sit on the swing. Rest? It's a beautiful day. Has been all week."

Celeste took a seat on one side of the swing, flattered by his attention, charmed by his awkwardness.

She gave the swing a push with one toe of her black button shoe. "So what did you two do to keep busy all week?"

He set the satchel by the door and joined her on the swing. The dog immediately jumped up and sat between them.

Celeste didn't know who was acting more peculiar, Fox or the dog. The dog had never sat in the swing with her before. Not even when John had been alive.

"We . . . uh, the dog and I, we checked out the claim." Fox said it so casually that she knew there was more meaning behind his words than he let on.

"Oh?" She scratched Silver behind his ears. "And?"

Fox pushed Silver off the swing impatiently as the dog turned and tried to lick his face. "Enough all ready." Fox's eyes met her gaze. "And . . ." He gave a noncommittal shrug. "We panned a little in the river. Didn't find anything, but I think digging is worth a try. We might hit gold. Who knows?"

Celeste lifted an eyebrow. She didn't know what she expected from Fox, but this wasn't it. Did he mean they should mine the land together, as business partners? Would he be willing to do that? Could she trust him?

But that would mean he would stay, a little voice whispered in her head.

Celeste halted the swing with her foot. *"We?* When did my idea of a mining operation become a partnership?" She crossed her arms over her chest. "I think you've got some explaining to do, Mr. MacPhearson."

Fox took his time in responding. "I just thought it would be a decent business venture for us both. You could make the kind of money you would need to get yourself out of Carrington—"

"And whoring," she offered tartly.

"You could do what you wanted to do, Celeste, whatever that might be. Set yourself up as a rich widow in California. Open a mercantile store in Boston. You could do anything you set your mind to."

She pushed the swing with the toes of her boots and they glided backwards. The warm breeze kissed the dark hair at his temples and sent it fluttering. His rugged good looks and earnest, dark eyes made it difficult for her to concentrate on the subject of the claims John had left her. "I understand the advantages for *me* of making money off the claims, should I strike gold." She looked straight ahead, focusing on the painted white rail on the far side of the porch. "My question is, what's the advantage to you?"

"What advantage does any businessman see in a business proposition, but money?"

She glanced at him. "You want to form a partnership so we can mine the claims together?"

"The land was left to both of us. My understanding is that it can't be divided, but must be shared. I don't know what the hell John was thinking when he wrote the will like that, but what's done is done. We could split the profits straight down the middle." He made a cutting gesture with one hand. "Fair and square."

"If there are profits," she amended. "But if we don't find gold?"

"We can work the details out later." He rose from the swing and offered his hand to help her up. His tone was all businesslike, yet relaxed.

Celeste climbed out of the swing without his assistance, a feeling of desperation tight in her chest. Suddenly she saw this venture as her only chance to survive whole. There had to be gold on John's land. There just had to be.

Her satchel in his hand, he held the front door open for her. "But if there is no gold, I ... I'd just have to return to San Francisco without the riches."

She passed him in the doorway. *And I'll have to return to whoring,* she thought. *An impossibility.*

Chapter Eight

"Five-card draw, ladies and gents." Celeste dealt the cards with the ease of a riverboat gambler. "One-eyed jacks and the man with the ax are wild. Cost you two bits to play."

Coins clinked in the center of the table in Kate's kitchen. It was Sunday afternoon and the usual gang was gathered. They had been meeting in Kate's kitchen on Sundays since the first week she'd opened the dance hall in Carrington six years ago. Back then, the town had been bustling. Gold had been found at Albert's Fork, and men traveled from as far as California to try their luck in the little gold-mining town. Like most gold booms, this one had not lasted long, and Carrington was soon just another occasional stop on the Colorado L&M Railroad.

Celeste picked up her hand, but did not smile. No one really seemed to be interested in the game today; they played out of habit. It had been three weeks since Mealy Margaret's death, but a pall still hung over the usually jovial poker game.

Celeste glanced over her dog-eared cards to Ace across the table. He was usually her greatest competition. He was studying his cards; the tip of his tongue hung out in concentration.

Celeste often wondered what went on in Ace's head. The

deaf-mute spent all of his time around half-dressed women, and yet, to anyone's knowledge, he'd never had a tumble. He had to be in his early twenties. Wasn't he attracted to women? Didn't he have the same urges other men did? Or had his sordid past left him unable to perform?

Rosy threw down her cards. "Fold," she declared as she rose from her chair. "Say, Joash. You bring some of that cake your wife bakes?"

"Gingerbread on the sideboard. Fresh whipped cream beside it." Joash sat arrow-straight in the chair beside Celeste, his fanned cards held tightly in his hand. "I'll take three." He discarded carefully.

Celeste dealt from the top of the deck. "Tell me something, Joash." She moved on to Kate, who wanted three new cards as well. "Isn't there something in the Bible that warns against gambling?"

"Excess. The good Lord warns us against excess in almost anything." He gazed at her over the rim of his wire-frame glasses. "But there are other sins, *fleshly sins,* that the Lord is quite clear upon."

Celeste laughed good-naturedly. "You never give up, do you?"

"I cannot. After all, it is your soul, all your souls"—he eyed the other women—"that I must be concerned for."

"Never heard a man say he was interested in my soul before," Sally giggled from behind her cards. She was robed in a silky pink dressing gown with her hair pulled back in a pink ribbon. Without rouge or hair pomade she could have been someone's socialite daughter.

"Pearl, what can I do for you?"

Tall Pearl gave a sigh. "A redeal?"

Celeste smiled. She liked Pearl. The woman was honest and earthy. She had been with Kate since the days in Denver. "Not a chance."

"All right, then, if you're going to play like that, I'll take three." She started to discard and then raised the cards. "But good ones, mind you. I'll have no trash. I've been dealt three limp hands in a row.'' She tossed down her cards. ''Which is better than three limp you-know-what's.''

The women and Titus all laughed. Ace never heard the joke. Joash sat stiff as always, his lips puckered. ''Straight to hell,'' he murmured under his breath. ''Straight to hell you'll all go.''

No one took offense to Joash's warning. They were used to his admonitions of doom. They were as much a part of the Sunday afternoon as Rosy's silk dressing gown, Mrs. Tuttle's cake, and Tall Pearl's risqué jokes.

''Ace?'' Celeste looked the young man directly in the eye so that he could read her lips. She had a soft spot in her heart for Ace.

He tossed down two cards.

Celeste passed him two fresh ones. Ace's gaze held hers for a moment, and she wondered once again what he was thinking. He seemed to be watching all the girls a lot lately.

''Five,'' Sally said, slapping down her cards. ''I'll take five. Say, where's that handsome man of yours? I mean, I understand why you don't let him out during the week, but why don't you bring him to play on Sundays?''

''You can't have five, only four, Sally.'' She waited while Sally picked up her cards. ''And he's not *my man.*''

Sally pouted prettily as she rearranged her hand. ''I know that's what you say.'' She batted her eyelashes. On anyone else it would have seemed a silly gesture, but on Sally it was charming. ''But everyone's buzzin' about the two of you headin' off in Kate's wagon every morning and sometimes not comin' home 'til past dark.'' She peered over the fan of her cards. ''You two gotta be doin' something all that time. 'Course I wondered what you did with the dog.'' She scrunched her forehead. ''Does 'e watch?''

''We've been walking John's claim and panning the stream, and you know it. We think we may have found a place to run a shaft.'' Celeste dealt Titus three cards. ''That was what I wanted to ask you about, Titus. You've got experience in the gold mines.''

''South Platte, Clear Creek, Gilpin County.'' He spat a stream

of brown tobacco into a tin at his feet. "Mostly done pannin'."
He wiped his mouth with the back of his tobacco-stained hand.

"But you have done some mining. Digging." As the two conversed, the players bid on their hands.

"Done a shaft or two in my day. Never hit gold on my own, but I seen others hit it."

"So you know what equipment we would need. You know the procedures."

He tossed down his coins to stay in the hand. "Hell, if it's tools you want, John left his 'quipment in a stall at the livery. Just sittin' there, best I know."

Ace called, and his full house beat Celeste's two pair. She passed the cards on to Kate, who had once again taken her seat, a dish of gingerbread and whipped cream in each hand. She licked her fingers and began to deal. Ace hauled in his coins.

Celeste tucked a lock of freshly washed hair behind her ear. Since Fox's arrival, she'd taken great care with her appearance. He was the kind of man who noticed a new dress or a new hairstyle and complimented her. Celeste liked his attention; it made her feel feminine. It gave her back some of the confidence she had lost in the arms of strangers. "To tell you the truth, Titus, I was looking for more than just the equipment. I'm interested in your expertise."

Titus cracked a broad grin, showing off his two gleaming, gold front teeth. "Is you, now?"

They were playing seven-card draw. Kate passed out two cards down, a third up. Celeste bid her ace high. She had a second one laying face down in front of her. "I want to hire you to dig the shaft. I don't have a lot of cash, but if . . . *when* we hit gold, I'll offer you a percentage. My partner and I will."

"Partner, is he?" Sally giggled. "Guess I heard every word in the book for it now."

Celeste glared as Sally clamped her hand over her mouth.

Celeste turned back to Titus. "The weather's good. You could get started tomorrow."

"And what's yer partner say on this?"

"We're in agreement. We need to hire someone. We'll pay you enough to hire a helper. I know you like to throw work Petey's way."

"When he's sober."

"That's up to you. We just want to get to work right away."

"Tell you the truth." Titus chomped on his tobacco. "I was su'prised to see that fancy pants stay as long as he has. Thought fer sure when he found out there weren't no money for him, he'd hightail it back to Cal-i-for-ni-a."

Celeste was amazed as well that Fox had stayed this long. Surely he was bored with life in Carrington, as compared to the one he'd led in San Francisco. Of course, she liked to fantasize that he stayed because of her. "He says he needs to stick around and protect his interest in his father's land."

"So 'e wouldn't sell it to ya?"

The bid went around on the reverend's pair of deuces.

"No. I tried, but he wouldn't sell."

"He's smitten on you," Sally injected. "I just know he is. I can see that look in his eye."

Celeste gave Sally a half smile. "Nonsense. He pays more attention to the dog than he does me. Of course he's full of opinions." She tossed a coin to the center of the table. "He didn't want me to come here today."

"Just like a man." Kate took a big bite of the gingerbread, leaving whipped cream at the corners of her painted mouth. "Always wanting to control a woman. Any woman will do, even if he ain't got rights to her."

They made their final bids. Celeste won two and a half dollars with three aces. As she swept the money up, she glanced at Titus. She didn't want to push him into doing something he didn't want to do, but she felt a sense of urgency. The longer she spent away from the dance hall, the more she knew she couldn't return. She just couldn't. "So are you in?"

"Don't think I got anything on my social calendar come tomorrow." He spat. "But I'll check just the same and let you know, Missy." He winked.

Celeste smiled. "I'm sure you can borrow Kate's wagon to

haul the gear. How about we meet you out on the claim tomorrow morning, say nine?''

"Guess I ought to be chargin' for that horse and buggy,'' Kate chided. "I'd be making better money than I am on these girls. I got more of a demand for wheels than heels.'' She chuckled at her own quip.

Celeste pushed away from the table. "Hate to empty your pockets and run, but I'm off.''

"Would you like me to walk you home, Celeste?'' Joash questioned. "I'm not sure that it's safe, a woman walking alone at night on these streets. I told Mrs. Tuttle she wasn't to go alone anymore after dark on her nursing visits. It's just not safe.''

Celeste smiled appreciatively. "I'll be fine, Joash. Really. Good night.''

"Good night,'' the poker players echoed as she stepped out the door.

"You're a bald-faced liar.'' Celeste leaned back against the scrub pine and laughed merrily. "She didn't really swallow flaming swords.''

Seated beside her, Fox stretched out his long legs, covered in dusty denim. His arm brushed hers, radiating a tingling warmth. "Juggled lap dogs, too.''

"Sounds like she belongs in a circus instead of a whorehouse.'' Celeste was laughing so hard that tears ran down her cheeks. It wasn't that funny. She just couldn't help herself. She was so happy. It had been such a wonderful week.

For six days in a row, each morning, Fox and Celeste had met Titus at John's claim. All day they walked the land and searched for likely places to tap for a gold vein. Titus had dug in three prime spots. So far they'd come up with nothing, but Celeste wasn't discouraged. Fox was such good company that the days flew by. Mostly they just talked and laughed together as they explored the land. Fox told her about his adventures in faraway countries, and Celeste told him about the interesting characters that had passed through the dance hall's swinging doors over the years.

The attraction between Fox and Celeste was obvious to them both, and at some point during the week, they had come to some unspoken agreement. They had begun to touch each other in innocent ways. Fox would tuck a lock of her windblown hair behind her ear; Celeste would remove a smudge of dirt from Fox's cheek. They did little favors for each other, fetching a canteen of water, or a necessary tool, retrieving a bonnet from the wagon.

Celeste knew the flirtation was dangerous. She knew what Fox ultimately wanted, and wanted for free. But the truth was, for the first time in her life, she wanted the same thing. Just once she wanted to make love with a man of her own choosing. She wanted to make love with a man she knew and cared for.

True, she had known and liked John, but that hadn't been the same. The feelings hadn't been the same, nor so intense. He had never made her heart flutter or her pulse quicken the way Fox did.

Fox lifted Celeste's hand in his and smoothed it. Both their hands were dusty. *Funny how they fit together so well,* Celeste thought.

"I kid you not," Fox went on, still laughing about the juggling prostitute in the Parisian whorehouse. "And the dwarves. You should have seen them."

Celeste laughed again and playfully pushed him with her shoulder. "There were no dwarf women."

"Were too, honest, hope to die." He crossed his heart with his free hand.

Still chuckling, Celeste shook her head. She liked this side of Fox, carefree and laughing. The other side of him she knew, the dark, brooding man, made her uncomfortable. Made her wonder how much John hadn't told her about his son.

Fox looked out at the rolling, rocky terrain they shared. "Guess I'd best get back to work. Titus and Petey shouldn't be hauling that drill bit on their own." He kissed the back of her hand as if he did so often, and stood and pulled her up with him.

Celeste's hand tingled where his lips had touched her skin.

Instead of walking away, he lingered, standing in front of her, looking into her eyes.

Celeste's stomach felt queasy, full of butterflies. Fox's hair was windblown, his face and hands dusty from the hard work of digging in the rock-hard Colorado soil. His sleeves were pushed up to bare muscular, suntanned forearms. The outdoors was so becoming to him that it was difficult for her to imagine him sitting at a desk in an office in San Francisco. It was difficult for her to imagine him returning there . . . leaving here.

"Ah, Celeste," he breathed. "I swore to myself I'd resist your charms." He brushed his knuckles against her cheek. "But I—"

"I'm the kind of woman that makes a man hard-pressed to resist," she said softly. "That's the intention."

His dark eyes, flecked with green in the sunlight, studied her face, searching . . . searching for something in her eyes. "I didn't mean it that way."

"Pretending I'm not a whore doesn't change the fact," she said.

"I know."

"But just because I've been with other men doesn't mean I can't feel or care."

He exhaled slowly and she felt his warm breath on her lips.

"It's just that I swore to myself after Amber—" he said. "That was her name. I swore that I wouldn't become involved with another—" He cut himself off.

So Amber had to be the dead woman. It was the first time he'd mentioned her name, except in his sleep. Was he implying that Amber had been a prostitute? Celeste was astonished, then realized she shouldn't be. Like father, like son.

"Fox," Celeste whispered. "This is very complicated, not just for you, but for me. A woman like me . . . we're careful not to allow ourselves to become too attached."

He stroked the corner of her mouth with his thumb. She inhaled the scent of him carried on a hot breeze.

"Hard life to lead, never becoming *attached*."

Celeste looked up into his dark-eyed gaze as she thought about Denver and who waited for her there. Tears clouded her eyes. *Just the wind,* she thought. She was wrong to want more than she had, but she wanted it just the same. "Let's stop trying to rationalize and just kiss me, Fox. I don't want to think, I don't want to—"

He clamped his mouth down hard on hers, silencing her.

Celeste raised her hands and slipped them around Fox's neck. Instinctively she pressed her body against his and her dusty skirts tangled around his feet.

He tasted of lemonade and sunshine. Of promise.

Celeste parted her lips, felt the flick of Fox's tongue against hers. A sound came from her throat at the sensation she'd thought herself past feeling. *Passion.* She was overjoyed that it was only buried deep inside her rather than stolen, as her virginity had been all those years ago.

"Celeste," Fox whispered, and she melted deeper in his arms.

They kissed again. Their tongues delved deep as they explored. He ran his fingers through her hair, sending rivulets of sensation down her spine. Reluctantly, she drew back for breath.

"Wow." He brushed back his forelock of thick hair.

"Yeah," was all she could manage.

Their gazes locked.

"Ah, Fox, what are we doing?" She glanced away, focusing on a rock in a grassy patch. "This is a bad idea. For both of us."

His tongue darted out to touch his upper lip, and she wondered if he could still taste her.

"I don't know what the hell I'm doing." He tugged on his earlobe as he always did when he was uncomfortable. "All I know is that I'm attracted to you," he continued. "I keep

telling myself no good can come of it. I just don't want you
to—''

"Hurt you like she did," she finished for him. She was
beginning to understand now that it wasn't for moral reasons
that he was troubled by her occupation. It went deeper.

He didn't deny her words. "Look, I know you don't understand this. Me."

She exhaled, expelling his breath with her own. He was right.
She didn't understand how he could run so hot one minute,
then cold the next. She had a feeling that it wasn't just because
of Amber though. "I could try to understand," she said softly.

"MacPhearson!" Titus appeared at the edge of the stand of
trees where Fox and Celeste had been taking their lunch. "Me
and Petey, we could use your help over here, if yer done with
your dinin'.''

"Coming." Fox picked up the battered felt hat that had once
been his father's. It fit him nicely. He avoided eye contact as
he spoke to her. "You rest in the shade. I'll give the men a
hand." He strode away.

"Wait." She scooped up his leather work gloves from the
Indian blanket they'd been sitting on. "You'll need these."

Their fingertips brushed as she passed the gloves to him.
Their gazes met again, and Celeste knew that Fox would
become her lover. Perhaps not tonight, nor tomorrow night,
but soon. It was as inevitable as the west wind that blew through
the canyon.

Fox rolled over in bed and stared at the punched-tin ceiling
tiles. The full moon lit the room almost as brightly as the gas
lamps that his father had strategically placed in the bedroom.

Fox couldn't sleep, only for once it was not Amber who
kept him awake. It was not her face he saw when he closed
his eyes. It was Celeste's.

Why had he kissed her today? Because she'd asked him to
and he was just being polite? He chuckled aloud. He kissed
her because he'd been dying to all week. There was something

about the mountain air and hard work that made him forget his past troubles, made him think that maybe he deserved a little happiness. Celeste made him laugh. And her mouth was so damned kissable. All he could think of was covering her entire body with kisses, tasting her . . .

He groaned, yanked the goose down pillow out from under his head, and covered his face with it.

Damn. Damn. Damn. Don't you ever learn? Women like her are a curse. A curse on your life. They were a curse on your father's, too.

Fox tossed the pillow on the floor and climbed out of bed. It was warm tonight and he slept naked. Or rather, he tried to sleep.

He pulled on a pair of dusty pants and a shirt. He slipped his feet, without socks, into his father's boots that had become his own. Maybe a walk would tire him. He just wished he had the dog with him. Old Silver was good company for a man shadowed by demons.

Fox opened his bedroom door, glad it didn't squeak. He didn't want to wake Celeste.

Celeste rolled over on her side, then after a moment, rolled to her other side. She tossed off the quilt. She was hot. She couldn't sleep.

Silver stirred on the end of her bed, his form illuminated by the bright light of the full moon. He lifted his head to stare at her, groggy with sleep.

"Sorry, old boy," she apologized. "Can't sleep." *Can't stop thinking about him.*

Lying on her side, Celeste touched her lips and remembered the passionate kiss she and Fox had shared beneath the aspen tree today. She couldn't stop thinking about his kiss, about what it would be like to feel his mouth on her breasts . . . lower.

"Shameless hussy. Tart," she said aloud and grimaced at the absurdity of it.

The dog whined and rolled away from her, expressing his displeasure at having been awakened in the middle of the night.

''All right, I'll be quiet. I'll suffer in silence so you can sleep.'' She punched her pillow down and rested her head on it again.

The dog laid his head between his paws and closed his eyes.

Celeste sighed and forced herself to shut hers. Sleep. Sleep. It was her escape. If she could just stop thinking about Fox, she knew sleep would come. But of course, even then, she wouldn't really escape. Lately he had not only haunted her days, but her nights as well. She dreamed of him not here in Colorado, but in a warm place with rolling green hills and rows of grapevines.

Celeste heard footsteps in the hallway and opened her eyes. This wasn't the first time she'd heard him leave in the middle of the night. She wondered where he went, what he did.

She held her breath, half-hoping he would stop at her door. She exhaled as his footsteps passed and faded down the stairs. Something told her that his night wanderings had something to do with his past and the woman who now had a name. Amber. That was why she hadn't asked him about his nighttime jaunts. Aside from that brief mention of her, he'd made it clear he didn't want to talk about his past.

She closed her eyes again. Maybe she'd bring it up tomorrow. Maybe they'd go to church and then share a picnic lunch out on the claim. She snuggled deep into the down mattress. And maybe, just maybe, he'd kiss her again.

Chapter Nine

It's the moon. The moon that calls me ... commands me tonight. Blood. Only the blood spilled upon the sinner will make her see her sin. Protect others who would fall into her web of flesh and lust.

But I must be careful. There are those who would not understand, who don't know these women as I know them. They wouldn't see why this has to be done. They'd question my judgment and time would be lost.

The weight of the knife is a comfort to me. The ropes. The black cloth. The needle and thread. It gives me the strength I need to do what I must. The confidence. I wish that another could be responsible, but I must accept my responsibilities. I must do as I am told, for I am judgment.

Celeste lifted the meat cleaver and brought it down hard on the worktable, slicing a thick slab of bacon. She raised the cleaver again and her hand shook. Hot tears blurred her vision. She sniffed, wiped her eyes with the sleeve of her new gingham dress, and lifted the cleaver again, trying to concentrate on the bacon and nothing else. She wanted to make breakfast for Fox. He'd slept in late this morning, because he'd been up late last night, no doubt. She had to make him breakfast. A man who worked hard needed a decent breakfast to start the day.

Celeste heard footsteps behind her. Man and friend. Fox's boots clunked on the hardwood floor. Silver padded past her on his way to his water bowl.

"Good morning, Celeste." Fox groaned and must have stretched his lean, hard body. "I can't believe it's raining again. I was hoping we could take a walk this afternoon after you got back from church."

She heard the legs of a chair scrape on the polished wood floor.

"I thought we'd have a look at the places where John already drilled. Maybe we can figure out what his reasoning had been. Where *he* thought the gold was."

Celeste held the meat cleaver in the air, but couldn't bring it down.

"Celeste, are you all right?"

She heard him rise from the chair and approach her.

Still she didn't turn.

"Celeste?" He placed his hand on her shoulder.

Slowly she lowered the meat cleaver. The bacon didn't cut, because she didn't use enough pressure.

"Celeste." He grasped her shoulder and turned her toward him.

Tears brimmed in her eyes. She held the cleaver in a death grip, her knuckles white.

"What's wrong?" he whispered.

"Tall Pearl," was all she could say.

"What?" Gently, he took the knife from her and lifted the corner of her apron to wipe the bacon fat from her left hand.

She stood unmoving, her arms hung at her sides, like a rag doll. "Tall Pearl," she repeated. She didn't want to cry. What good would tears do? What good had they ever done? she thought miserably.

"Tall Pearl? Who's Tall Pearl? One of your friends at the dance hall?"

"Dead," she whispered. "Murdered."

His gaze met hers and he swore under his breath. "I'm sorry."

Celeste's lower lip trembled. Tall Pearl had moved out of Rosy's room into Celeste's when Celeste moved in with John. *It could have been me,* was all Celeste could think. *Maybe it should have been me.*

Fox led Celeste to the table and pushed her gently into a chair. "Murdered like the other woman?" He crouched so that he could look into her face. His mouth was pulled tight in genuine concern. His eyes reflected the pain he felt vicariously through her.

"Yes." She swallowed the lump that stuck in her throat. "Brutal. Blood everywhere," Celeste said as she fought a sob that would render her speechless. "M . . . mutilated in some horrible way. The s . . . sheriff wouldn't say." Celeste squeezed her eyes tight and fat tears slipped down her cheeks.

Fox wrapped his arms around her and pulled her against him. "Shhh," he hushed. "It's all right. It's all right, honey."

Celeste clung to him, to his warmth, to the scent of his clean hair and shaving soap. At this moment, he was the only solid thing in her crumbling world. "I . . ."—sniff—"knew her for years," she whispered. "She was my friend when no one else would . . ." A shudder stole the last word from her.

"Ah, Celeste." Fox stroked her back in soothing circles. "I'm so sorry."

She pressed her face to his shirt, her flood of tears soaking the clean denim. The shirt smelled of yesterday's sunshine and his own distinctly masculine scent. "I'm sorry," she whispered. "Sorry I'm being so—"

"Shhh." He kissed her forehead and smoothed her hair at the crown óf her head. "It's understandable that you'd be upset."

"She's just a whore," Celeste whispered bitterly. "No one loved her; no one cared about her. It doesn't really matter."

"You cared about her," Fox reminded her gently. "And I know that she knew you cared. You're that kind of person, Celeste. You care for us all."

Fox's arms felt so good around her, so comforting. She wanted to stay in the warmth, forever protected from the outside world. "I just can't believe it," she whispered. "We played cards Sunday. Tuesday I saw her at the dry goods. She was so excited. Her French stockings came in on the morning mail wagon."

"I know, I know. It's so hard to believe someone you care for is gone, especially in such a brutal manner." He smoothed her temple and kissed the place where his fingers had been.

Celeste sighed. All this attention from Fox. His touch. This wasn't how she wanted it to happen. She didn't want to seek a man's arms out of desperation.

Still, she couldn't help but turn her face up to his.

He lowered his lips to hers. His first kiss was gentle. Almost brotherly. But Celeste wanted more. She wanted to replace the sickness in her heart with another emotion. She wanted passion.

"Fox," she whispered. "Please take me away from this." She pressed her mouth to his in a kiss that was not sweet and soft, but hard and searing. Her tears fell on their lips. "Just for a few minutes. Make me forget," she moaned desperately. "Love me?"

"Ah, Celeste." He sounded as if he was in as much agony as she was. His mouth descended hard against hers, forced her lips to part, and Fox filled her mouth with his tongue. She clung to him and dragged her fingernails down his broad back. Thoughts of Pearl, of John, even of Denver, slipped from her grasp. All at once nothing mattered but this man and the physical urgency she felt in her loins.

He tugged the ribbon from her hair and let it fall in a bright red curtain over them. "Celeste . . . Celeste . . ."

She buried her face in his chest. "Fox . . ."

He swept her into his arms, moving so quickly that Silver yelped and sidestepped them. Fox turned on his heel, strode through the kitchen and up the long staircase. Celeste held tightly to his neck and rested her cheek on his chest to hear his heart pound as rapidly as her own.

This didn't make sense. She'd regret it later. She'd been his father's whore. But at that moment Celeste didn't care. She wanted Fox, needed him, and consequences be damned.

Fox halted at her bedroom door. "Did you ever . . . with my father here."

Her gaze met his. "No," she whispered. "Not here. Never in this house. He was too sick by then."

"Good." He kicked open the door and carried her to the bed. He set her down gently and kissed her mouth. "Out," he commanded.

The dog, who had followed them up the steps, hightailed it into the hallway. Fox slammed the door shut, and unbuttoned his shirt as he approached the bed.

Celeste lay on the edge of the bed, her head on the pillow, her skirts around her knees. She watched him, the desire for her burning in his dark eyes. She held out her arms to him. He kicked off his boots and leaned over her.

She caught his shoulders and pulled him down on top of her. His tongue was like velvet in her mouth. His weight felt good against her breasts and the ache between her legs.

Fox rolled onto his side and cupped one breast through the cotton of her gown and undergarments. She groaned with pleasure. This was the first time in her life that a man had touched her breasts and it actually felt good. It was an epiphany. So this was what sex was supposed to be . . .

He fumbled with the tiny buttons at the bodice of her gown. She nipped at his earlobe. He kissed the pulse of her throat. She stroked his bare chest through the folds of his open denim shirt.

She breathed deeply, inhaling the intoxicating, musky scent of his skin and his desire for her. It smelled so good. Another first.

He whispered her name in her ear as he found his way through the obstacles of her dress, petticoat, and corset. She arched her back with another moan of pleasure as flesh met flesh, and he brushed her puckered nipple with the rough pad of his thumb.

Fox's businessman's hands had roughened in the last month. But instead of being too harsh, they only added to the sensation of his stroke. She gasped in wonder as his lips brushed her nipple.

"Fox," she groaned in disbelief. How many times had she committed this act and felt nothing? Nothing.

He nuzzled his face between the valley of her breasts, and then opened his hot mouth over her nipple that swelled in anticipation. Celeste threaded her fingers through his thick hair, in awe of the sensations that rippled, no, *coursed* through her body. She felt as if she was on a runaway train. It didn't matter that the train would end in the bottom of a chasm. All that mattered was this moment of sheer, unadulterated pleasure. For this moment, she was willing to risk everything, even her soul. Instinctively, she parted her thighs as Fox ran his hand up her stockinged leg, his fingers burning a trail of molten pleasure as they drew closer to the source of her heat. He tugged at the drawstring of her pantaloons, all the while showering her face with sweet, tantalizing kisses.

His warm hand grazed her bare belly beneath the layers of clothing, and she wished that she had undressed. She wanted to feel with every inch of her flesh. Just once, she wanted to feel.

He lowered his hand to the apex of her thighs and she arched her back and moaned. Even through the cotton of her pantaloons, she could feel the heat of his hand.

She throbbed for him and instinctively lifted her hips to meet his rhythmic stroke. "Now," she told him. "Do it now."

He kissed her tenderly on the mouth, but did not cease the heavenly stroking. "Not now," he whispered. "Just relax. Let me touch you. Let yourself enjoy it."

"But—"

He silenced her with a kiss that left her breathless.

Celeste didn't understand. What was this touching for if not to lead up to the act? The thought was absurd. Intriguing . . .

Then, all thought slipped out of her head and Fox's insistent stroking carried her higher and higher up the weaving path of some remote mountain she had never climbed. She felt as if she was floating, and yet there was still that burning desire, that ache that yearned to be quenched.

Celeste rode the waves of pleasure, losing herself to Fox's touch, his scent, the press of his body. Higher and higher until suddenly, shockingly, she felt a surge of pleasure so intense she cried out. Fox stilled his hand, but left it there, warm and wet between her legs.

Hot tears trickled down her face. She panted, her eyes squeezed shut. Oddly, she was embarrassed, though it had been the most wonderful thing she had ever experienced. Then she came to the disturbing realization that Fox had not had his own pleasure, and that he had to be lying here beside her still hard and swollen.

"It's all right," she said, trying to draw her skirt up and her pantaloons down. "I'm ready for you."

He laughed—but it was a teasing laugh—and pushed down her skirt. "There'll be plenty of time for that later."

She opened her eyes. "You mean you don't want to—" She made a gesture with her hand, completely confused. What man climbed into bed with a woman and didn't want to satisfy his own need to rut?

"I'd love to," he whispered, gently kissing her cheek. "But not now. Not like this."

She closed her eyes again. "You don't want to because of John. Because I . . ." Tears burned behind her eyelids.

"I don't want to right now because you're overwrought. I want you to want me, Celeste, but not like this. Not when you're overcome with grief."

She opened her eyes. "I'm really confused."

He smiled and brushed a luck of tumbling hair away from her face. The shadows were long and dark in the room. Outside, rain fell rhythmically on the windowpane. For the moment it seemed as if they were alone together in the world.

"It's simple." His voice was warm and still husky with

desire for her, but comforting. "I want to make love with you, but I shouldn't right now because it would be taking advantage of you."

She smiled. His words almost moved her to tears, not because he said them, she'd learned long ago that a man would say anything, but because she felt that he meant it. No man had ever treated her like anything but a whore for many years. No man had ever cared how she felt, what she felt. John had come close, but it wasn't the same. "I swear," she choked, her voice thick with emotion, "I think that's the sweetest thing that I've ever heard come out of a man's mouth. You even sound sincere."

He gave her that boyish grin of his, sounding sleepy. "I am sincere."

Suddenly she felt tired, too tired to sort out the confusion of what Fox had done, what he'd said. She had lain awake half the night thinking about things, about Denver, about Fox. She closed her eyes, content to feel his warm body next to hers. Before she knew what was happening, she drifted off to sleep.

Fox woke sometime in the afternoon to find the bed beside him empty. He touched the hollow in the down mattress where Celeste had been. She was gone. The dark room was empty. Rain still pitter-pattered on the window. He breathed deeply. He could smell Celeste in the room. Her desire. It had taken all his will not to make love to her this morning. If he got a second chance, he doubted he could resist her charms.

In a way he was relieved that she was gone. He didn't know what he could say to her. He needed time to think. He stared at the ceiling and wondered what the hell he thought he was doing. He'd almost blown it. He had sworn not to become involved with another whore, another woman like Amber, like—

He pushed that thought from his mind. No sense dragging up the past. The present was what mattered, and he was backing himself into a hell of a corner.

Celeste was a whore. Knowing that, he didn't understand how he could feel tenderness for her. He didn't understand what it meant. Women like that had no loyalties. They couldn't love, not really. And they couldn't be trusted. It wasn't their fault. It was just the way they were. He didn't know if being a whore made them that way, or if women like that became whores. It didn't matter. What mattered was that he needed to insulate himself.

The smartest thing he could do right now was to pack his meager bag and go as far as the last five dollars he owned would take him. He should leave that worthless land to Celeste. Hell, she deserved it more than he did. Maybe she could sell it to some other gold-digging fool and make a small profit.

But where would he go? And what if there really *was* gold out there, as John had believed? The smartest thing Fox knew he could do was bide his time. If he could just keep his emotions in check . . . his father's gold claim was his best chance to get enough money to start his vineyard. If he could just keep his distance from Celeste, at least emotionally, he'd be all right. He threw back the coverlet and climbed out of bed. His stomach rumbled with hunger.

Barefoot, Fox padded down the steps. The house felt empty. "Celeste?" He was hoping to smell coffee brewing and maybe some soup bubbling on that magical stove of hers. Now that he'd had a moment alone he wanted to see her; he needed to see her. "Celeste?"

Silver met him at the kitchen door, whined, and thrust his head beneath Fox's hand. "Where is she, old boy?"

Silver whined again and looked up as if he could apologize for his mistress's actions.

"Celeste!" Fox's voice echoed hollowly off the ceiling and walls. He checked the parlor and the bathroom, even the front and back porches. She was nowhere to be seen. He went upstairs and checked the three bedrooms, the dog following him from room to room.

"That's strange," he said as much to the dog as to himself. He stood in the doorway of her bedroom.

Something caught his eye. The door on her armoire was ajar. He lit a gas wall light and opened the closet door. Something was obviously missing. Clothing. He pulled open several drawers. She must have been rifling through them fast. Lacy undergarments had been unfolded, stockings tossed here and there. He sensed things were missing and felt queasiness in the pit of his stomach. Didn't she understand that he needed her?

He slammed the drawer shut. He couldn't deal with pity for himself, but anger, now there was an emotion he knew well. "Son of a bitch," he whispered, feeling his ire color his ears. "Guess she's run off to that man in Denver again."

Chapter Ten

Celeste sat on the train seat, her leather satchel clutched in her lap. She stared out the window at the darkness as they pulled into Denver, wishing she could see the glorious mountains or the lush green grass and tall timber.

It had been hours since she'd left Carrington by stagecoach and caught a train in Odenburg, and she still couldn't stop shaking. *Fox.* It was his fault she felt this way. This was all his fault. He had made her care about him. Worse, he had made her *feel.*

She squeezed her eyes shut, her nerves on edge. She wished fervently for the comforting numbness she had known for so many years; but no matter how hard she prayed for it, it would not come. In the past, it was in that numbness she'd found sanctuary, if not happiness. The numbness had protected her from the men at Kate's. It had protected her from her past— a wound that was suddenly fresh and bleeding again.

Once before she had cared for a man. She had allowed herself to feel. What a fool she'd been, seventeen years old and full of herself and her womanhood. How she had enjoyed those stolen kisses and the few bold caresses through the layers of her ruffled, starched clothing. He had been young and handsome, so refined. The son of a bitch.

She opened her eyes and set her jaw. Only one good thing had come out of that nightmare.

"Next stop, Den-verrrrr," called the conductor as he swayed down the aisle with the motion of the train. The train exhaled in a great *whoosh* of steam. "Den-verrr."

Denver. She'd had to come. It was the only way to get her feet planted firmly on the floor again. Here in Denver she could gain control of her frazzled emotions and figure out how the hell she was going to get Fox MacPhearson out of her life.

Against her will, she recalled the taste of his mouth on hers. Hot and so utterly masculine. He had desired her, truly wanted her. It had been as if she were a virgin again, anticipating every brush of his lips, every caress of his hands. Just thinking about lying in his arms made her stomach flutter, her breasts tingle, and her cheeks grow warm. She patted her flushed face with a handkerchief and glanced around to see if any of the passengers were looking at her.

Everyone was gathering their belongings. Women yawned, patted their coiffures, and smoothed their wrinkled traveling suits. Men stretched and slipped into their coats and fumbled for their bags. It was nearly midnight.

Celeste sighed. What she couldn't understand, what frightened her, was why Fox had made her feel so good. How had he been able to break through the wall she had so carefully built stone by stone, man by man? How had he been able to make her feel anything? Why him?

She'd been having sex with men so long that she'd thought herself beyond feeling. Even with John, with whom the act had at least been pleasant, she'd never actually felt anything profound. The act of intercourse had never been sexual for her. It had just been . . . work.

"Den-verrr," the conductor called again.

The train slowed and the wheels squealed against the track as the passengers were pushed forward and then back against their leather seats by the braking motion. The train came to a stop and passengers rose and filed down the aisle. Celeste peered out the window, but it was dark outside but for bright lanterns, and she couldn't see anything but a jumble of people moving on the station platform.

She rose and hurried down the aisle and craned her neck to see over a woman's large hat with a peacock plume. She still couldn't see Adam, but she knew he was there, waiting for her. Self-consciously, Celeste smoothed her gown. Miss Higgens would be with him here, so Celeste had a certain image she had to maintain. One hand on her satchel, she nervously checked her hat pin. Once she saw Adam, she would feel better. All that had happened between her and Fox would make more sense. She would know what to do.

Celeste stepped off the train onto the wooden platform and spotted him at once. She broke into a proud smile that, against her will, threatened to become teary. "Adam," she called, taking care to pronounce his name carefully so that he could read her lips.

Adam grinned, raised a small hand, and signed. "Mama!"

All afternoon Fox paced the shadowy kitchen. When he thought he'd worn down the floorboards sufficiently, he tried out the carpet in the hallway. Then the parlor. He even ventured into the dining room that had never been furnished.

"I can't believe she'd just run off like that again," he told the dog who had given up pacing with him hours ago. Instead of his anger abating, it grew stronger with every hour. He was damned pissed.

Silver sat in the doorway, lazily scratching.

"You would think that after"—he glanced at the dog—"after what happened upstairs, she'd at least have stuck around to say something. I mean personally, I thought it was pretty nice." Just thinking about Celeste in his arms made him break out in a sweat. "Damned nice," he amended. "Not like the others. I mean, with them I could always go through the motions, but I never felt anything. Really felt it." Even though he'd not found his own physical satisfaction in Celeste's arms, he'd still felt a sense of completion that he couldn't explain.

Silver cocked his head.

"Hell, I don't know what came over me. When I carried her up those steps I fully intended to make love to her, have my own pleasure. It's what I should have done. It was what she expected. What she offered."

Fox paced more furiously. "But somehow it didn't seem right," he agonized aloud. "She was so vulnerable. It's not that I didn't want her. Hell, the desire was there. I wanted her more I think, than, I've ever wanted any woman. I just didn't want to hurt her. I didn't want her to think I'd changed my mind . . . about her. Us."

He yanked a red handkerchief from his denim pants and wiped his damp brow. "She probably thought I'd lost my mind. Women like her, they probably laugh when a man doesn't . . . well, you know. Perform."

Silver's tongue lolled and he panted.

"This is going to sound stupid." Fox paced faster. "But I wanted her to care about me. Just a little. Of course, if she'd cared about me, if I'd been something more than a little morning indulgence, she would have stayed, wouldn't she? Before she ran off to that man—whoever he is—she'd have stuck around long enough to share a cup of tea and a biscuit."

Fox groaned and struck the wall with his palm. "Hell. I'm losing what little sense I have left—talking to a dog about my sexual escapades."

Silver whined, slumped to the floor, and closed his eyes as if he couldn't stand another minute more of Fox's rambling.

Fox halted in the center of the empty dining room. "I know. I'm boring the dog bones out of you." He ran his hand through his hair. Even talking to the dog seemed to relieve some of his anger and frustration. "What's say we pack up our tool bag and head down to Sal's, eh?" He tapped his thigh.

The dog bounded up.

A short time later Fox and Silver walked into Sal's Saloon through the back door. Being Sunday the saloon was closed for regular business. Fox took the stool that had become his own since he'd repaired it the week he'd come to Carrington. This was where he and Silver spent time when Celeste was busy with her friends. On Sundays, when she was attending her poker games at Kate's, he and Sal and the mutt even passed a few hours playing cards themselves.

"Hey, Sal," Fox called.

Sal crossed the saloon pushing a broom.

Sal nodded his head in greeting. "Hear about Pearl?"

Fox dropped his tool bag on the bar. "That the girl that was murdered?"

"Kate said it wouldn't happen in her place." Sal spat into a brass spittoon as he passed the bar. "Said Mealy Margaret was my fault. Guess she didn't know what she was talkin' about, did she?"

Fox watched Sal sweep. There was no dirt on the floor. He swept out of boredom. "Tate think it was the same guy?"

"Sounds like it. He's keepin' his lips pretty tight, but word is, the killer left some kind of writin' in blood on the wall over her bed."

Fox grimaced. He wasn't weak-stomached, but the thought made him queasy. "So it wasn't just a drifter?"

Sal shrugged his thin shoulders. "Still could be. We got enough small towns scattered through the hills around us that 'e could be comin' in at night, doin' his dirty business, and hightailin' it home. There's plenty of men that come to Kate's outta Odenburg—could be any one of 'em." He passed the spittoon again and spat a stream of brown tobacco.

Fox leaned both elbows on the bar. "What about someone in town?"

"Reckon it's possible. There's about two hundred of us left here. We got a few shady characters."

Someone pounded on the back door and Fox heard it open. Sal looked up apprehensively, seemingly put on edge by their discussion.

Sheriff Tate appeared in the back hall doorway. "Evenin', Sal."

Sal began his track across the saloon floor again, pushing his broom. "Hey, Tate. Help yourself."

The sheriff walked behind the bar and poured himself a double, eyeing Fox. "Been lookin' for you."

Fox didn't glance at him. "That right."

"Went by your father's house. You weren't there."

Fox glanced over his shoulder. He didn't like Tate. The man was cocky, and with a woman-killer roaming his streets, he had little reason to be. "I guess because I was here."

Tate slurped his whiskey. "Didn't run into you on the street."

"Silver and I took the long way around. Rain stopped. The dog needed a walk."

Tate came around the bar to stand in front of Fox. Sal pushed his broom around him and back on course.

"That right?" Tate took another sip of the amber drink.

Fox frowned. "Is there a point to this conversation?"

Tate flashed a cool grin. "Just trying to be friendly-like."

Fox gave an unamused laugh. "What makes me think that's not your intention?"

"Don't know. Maybe you're nervous."

Fox didn't appreciate the direction this conversation was taking. Tate was out to get him. He had been since the day he came into Carrington. "You said you came by the house. What do you want?"

"Miss Kennedy seemed to be in quite a hurry. She had Clyde Perkins hold the coach so's she could get on it."

Fox didn't say anything.

"The girls at Kate's said they didn't know nothing about her makin' one of her trips to Denver. Said she just went a couple of weeks ago. You say something or do somethin' to scare her?"

Fox ground his teeth. "Such as kill a whore?" He lifted a dark eyebrow.

"I didn't say that."

Fox slid off the bar stool. "So what the hell is your point, Tate? You want to take me in for questioning? Take me in. Otherwise, leave me the hell alone." He grabbed his bag off the bar. "I'll be back tomorrow, Sal, when the company's improved. Tell Emmy Mae I'll fix that hinge on her door then, all right?"

Sal stood near the front where he'd been watching the exchange between Fox and the sheriff. "I'll do that. You take care walkin' home. You never know, with that bastard roamin' our streets."

Fox pulled his wool hat down over his ears; the dog followed him toward the back door. "You kidding? I'll be fine with my trusty killer-dog, here. 'Night."

Fox didn't look back as he left the saloon through the back door. He knew Tate was watching him. He could feel his beady eyes on his back, and they made him just a little nervous.

Three days later Celeste returned to Carrington on the 4:30 train. She'd had a wonderful visit with Adam. He was progressing so well in school, not just according to her son, but according to the headmistress, Miss Higgens.

Not only did Adam excel in his academic lessons, but he made friends easily and was popular among the students and staff. He missed his mother, as did all the young ladies and gentlemen, Miss Higgens explained, but he had adjusted well to boarding school. There in the pleasant surroundings of brick buildings, hills, and trees of the exclusive school, Adam had not only taken well to his lessons, but was learning to live deaf in a speaking world. He had even learned to speak a few words, and had delighted Celeste by saying them over and over again.

The three days with Adam had done wonders for Celeste. She was so happy to see her son happy that no problem seemed insurmountable, not even her problem with Fox.

Celeste stood outside her dark house, staring up at the windows that reflected the waning moonlight. Putting off the inevitable confrontation with Fox, she'd spent the late afternoon and evening at the dance hall. Remaining in the back so as not to encounter customers, she passed the hours with Kate and whichever girls were not occupied in their rooms upstairs.

Celeste learned from Kate that Tall Pearl had died the same way Mealy Margaret had. Sheriff Tate confirmed that the killer had used the same or a similar knife, and that the murders had been identical, except that Pearl's had been even more brutal. The truly chilling thing about the latest murder was that the killer had left a message in Pearl's own blood. The sheriff refused to reveal what the message had said, but he had implied that it had been righteous in nature. Sheriff Tate was conducting numerous interviews in Carrington as well as the surrounding towns. So far, he had no clues.

Celeste took a deep breath and walked up the steps and onto the porch of the house. She wondered why the windows were so dark. Had Fox left? She couldn't blame him after the way she had run off. It would be the best thing for both of them.

She placed her hand on the door. *Please let him still be here,* she thought, even at the same instant realizing how ridiculous the wish was.

Celeste opened the door and was greeted by Silver, who bounded at her out of the darkness.

"Hello there, old boy." She set down her satchel, removed her hat and cloak, and scratched the mutt behind the ears.

"Have you been a good boy? Have you? Did he feed you while I was gone? Huh?"

The dog panted and rubbed his head beneath her hand as they walked toward the kitchen. The house was dark. It was eerie.

"Fox?" she called tentatively.

Moonlight had shone through the windows framing the door in the front foyer, but the hallway was dark. Celeste had never been afraid to be in the house alone, not even right after John died, but she was suddenly uncomfortable. The thought of Pearl lying dead, tied to her bedpost, had her spooked.

"Let's just get one of these lamps lit, shall we?" she said loudly to the dog to comfort herself.

She walked across the shadowy kitchen to the stove, which was warm to her touch. With a broom straw, she lit a gas lamp.

"There, that's better, isn't it?" She turned, blowing out the broom straw. "I— Oh!"

Celeste took a step back, startled to find Fox sitting in the kitchen.

She pressed her hand to her pounding heart. "You scared me half out of my wits. What on God's green earth are you doing sitting here in the dark?"

He took so long to answer that she began to feel uneasy. He iust stared at her with some unfathomable emotion in his black eyes.

Finally he spoke, his strong jaw set, his dark gaze fixed on her. "Welcome home. Three days. You mind telling me where the hell you've been?"

Chapter Eleven

"Where the hell have I been?" She dropped her hand to her hip, narrowing her eyes. No man had a right to speak to her that way. She was her own woman, dependent on no one. That had been her vow the night her father had thrown her into the street in the pouring rain, without so much as a cape to protect her from the downpour.

And Fox had no right to demand any information in that tone of voice.

Especially since her trip to Denver had been so wonderful. It had felt so good to hold Adam in her arms. She'd not been able to tell him about the claims or her intention to mine them, of course, because Adam thought she was a widow and ran a ladies' clothing shop in Colorado Springs. But seeing him, eating with him, taking a long walk with him, had strengthened her determination to find gold on that land. Being with Adam had made her realize just how badly she wanted a real life.

Celeste stared Fox down. "Where have I been?" she repeated. "I've been in Denver."

"I know that," he snapped. "I want to know why you went to Denver, who you went to see. A man, I assume?"

''That's none of your business,'' she flared. The good feelings she had carried home from Denver ebbed. Of course she had expected a confrontation with Fox on her return, but the man just sounded so . . . so possessive.

He glanced away and then back at her. ''I was worried about you. I didn't know where you'd gone. What happened to you. I kept thinking you were tied to some bedpost with your throat cut.''

She crossed her arms over her chest. She supposed she should be flattered that he was concerned for her well-being, but her anger prevented it. ''That's certainly a pleasant thought.''

He scowled. ''It's the truth. The only reason I knew you went to Denver was because Sal saw you chase down the stagecoach to Odenburg. He said you were in an awful hurry. Was that to get away from me, or to get to someone else?''

She ignored his question. That was none of his damned business either. ''I've a right to come and go as I please. I don't have to tell you what I'm doing or *whom* I'm seeing. You made it clear when you found out who I was that you had no intention of pursuing any kind of permanent relationship with me. You reneged on that charming marriage proposal rather quickly, remember?'' Celeste didn't know what made her say that. To push him away, she guessed. To hurt him so he would go. Leave. Leave Carrington, leave her and her pathetic trollop's life.

He flinched.

If her intention had been to hurt Fox, it worked. She could see it in his stormy eyes.

''I . . .'' He paused. ''No,'' he said quietly. ''I don't guess you owe me an explanation. I just thought that after the other morning . . .'' His sentence drifted into silence.

Celeste knew what he was referring to. Her bedroom. And he didn't just mean the kissing, the touching, the incredible way he had made her feel. He meant the emotional connection they made in each other's arms. It wasn't her imagination. He had felt it, too. Now she was really confused by her emotions, by what she wanted and didn't want.

Celeste didn't know what to say. She had planned this entire conversation. On the train from Denver, she'd gone over and over in her head what she would say to Fox. She'd intended to tell him he would have to move out of the house. Their partnership could be conducted at a distance; the further he was from her, the better. She'd intended to tell him that the morning in her bed had been a mistake. She'd been overwrought about Pearl and hadn't realized what she was doing.

She had intended to lie through her teeth.

Now that he stood before her in the flesh, it seemed somehow harder to follow her well-thought-out script. "Fox . . ."

He waited.

She felt as if a glass window separated them, and anything she might say or do would shatter the glass. She didn't know if she wanted to break it or not. She sighed, lowered her gaze, then glanced back at him. Silver sat beside him.

Fox patted the dog's head, but his full attention was on her.

"I . . ." She exhaled again. "The other day. It was a mistake."

He glanced down at her button shoes that peeked beneath her green and black taffeta petticoat and overskirt.

The dress was new. She'd splurged and bought it in Denver. The sales clerk had said the green matched her eyes. In the back of her mind, she knew she had bought the dress because she wanted to look good for Fox.

"A mistake?" he asked coolly.

"A mistake," she repeated. "You have no intention—I have no intention of getting involved with you, Fox. It was wrong for me to—"

"It was wrong for me to take advantage of you." He rose and turned, to lean against the back of his chair and face her. "I shouldn't have—"

"You didn't take advantage of me," she corrected, wanting to get it straight between them. She had been forced once. She'd let no man make that claim ever again. "I'm an adult woman. I know what I said to you." It seemed so strange for her to be dancing around the subject of sex, when sex was what she did for a living. But somehow it was different with Fox. It meant something now. "And *I* know and *you* know what I meant." She folded her arms, refusing to look away.

She'd gotten herself into this; she could at least have the decency to look him in the eye while she got herself out of it. "And I have to admit," she continued, "that it was sweet of you not to—" she lifted her hand lamely "—you know."

They both stared at each other for a moment, at an impasse. *What now?* Celeste thought. She knew he was thinking the same thing, because even as they mutually admitted their love-making had been a mistake, the attraction between them still existed against all logic. No matter what either of them said, the desire was still there, a hot flame burning between them.

"So what now?" He said it first. He scuffed his boot on the floor, which she noticed had been washed while she was gone. "You want me to leave?"

He didn't say if he meant the house, or Carrington.

No. The protest leaped into her mind. She didn't want him to leave. She knew it was crazy, but she didn't want him to leave her. She didn't want to feel alone anymore.

She studied his face. He appeared haggard, as if he'd been up all night. He hadn't shaved since she left and was beginning to look like a genuine miner. "Do you want to leave?" She wondered what had happened to her speech about him getting out of the house by morning.

He thought for a moment. "I think Titus may be on to something. He found an underground rock formation while you were gone. It's not a placer, but it looks promising."

Her eyes widened. "Gold?" In the back of her mind, she knew the idea of finding gold on the property was just a pipe dream, but the longer she stayed away from Kate's, the more desperate she became to keep it that way. Her visit to Adam had solidified that desire. Since she'd met Fox, the idea of returning to her old life seemed out of the question. Somehow he had given her the confidence to believe she could find a way out of the life she'd begun to hate. She almost believed that she deserved something better. "He thinks he found gold?"

"Well, no. He didn't find anything, but there's a certain pattern to the rock formation around a strike."

The talk of gold cooled the heat between them, both the anger and the desire.

He pointed to the stove. "You want some tea? Mrs. Tuttle sent some kind of berry pie. You look tired."

"Tea would be good." She sat on the edge of his chair. Suddenly the fatigue of traveling to and from Denver in three days caught up to her. She was tired and she was hungry. All she wanted to do was climb into her bed and sleep.

Fox put the kettle on the stove. "He wants to start drilling at first light."

"All right. I can be ready."

He leaned on the work table. "So I guess I'll stay a few more days. Just to . . . to see if anything comes out of the rock formation."

This was Celeste's chance. She could just tell him no. It was her house. She had a right to refuse him. He could go elsewhere. Sal might rent him a room. He could bunk up at Titus's, or he could just go back to San Francisco. "All right," she said. "You might as well stay here. We'll see what happens in a few days."

Celeste felt weak-spined, but she couldn't help herself. She didn't want him to leave. Well, she did, because she knew nothing could come of their relationship. Her head told her to kick him out the door, now, while she could still muster the strength. But her heart wanted nothing more than for her to be in Fox's arms once more.

Celeste stood on the back step, an old leather vest of John's in her hand. Fox was in the backyard, shoveling coal for the kitchen stove. Because it was already dark, he worked by the light of an oil lantern. They'd stayed out on the claim until sunset, and both of them were exhausted. After a quick meal, she knew they'd each go into their respective bedrooms for the blessed sleep they needed.

Since Celeste had returned from Denver last week, they'd followed the same routine every day. They were up at dawn, ate cold egg sandwiches for breakfast on the wagon ride to the claim, worked till noon, ate again, and worked until the sun set. It was hard on both Celeste and Fox, but there was something comforting about their routine. The animosity between them had faded somewhere between the egg sandwiches and the tons of useless dirt they'd moved. It seemed that they had both accepted themselves, each other, and the relationship that would never be. And yet . . . something was changing very subtly between them.

Now that they had admitted to each other and accepted that there was no permanent relationship, the tension between them had eased. Fox was warm to her, even flirtatious and charming. In her domestic style, Celeste cared for him in the small ways that she had once dreamed she would care for a husband. It seemed that they had parted a week ago, but were now slowly coming full circle to meet again.

Celeste watched Fox as he shoveled coal bare-chested. The yellow lamplight illuminated the perspiration that beaded on his broad chest and rippling muscles. As he swung the shovel and flexed his biceps, she couldn't help recalling what his skin had felt like beneath her fingertips. She shivered despite the heat of the summer evening as she recalled the feel of his hands on her body. Sweet God in heaven, he was a handsome man. Another time, another place, and perhaps things could have been different between them.

"Need something?"

Celeste blinked, startled. She'd been caught staring at him, and this wasn't the first time this week.

Fox leaned on the shovel, taking a breather. He smiled lazily at her, that smile that made her knees shaky.

She held up the vest lamely. "I . . . uh. I found this in my mending basket." She picked at one of the tin buttons. "It was John's. I wondered if you want it. I could find a new button."

Fox's gaze shifted reluctantly from her tired, pretty face to the vest. He felt his smile harden on his face.

The old leather vest brought an unexpected rush of memories, and the emotions that weighed them down. The gingerbread house, the coal bucket, the dog at his side, the beautiful redhead, all faded into the mists of the past.

He saw a little boy standing on a stone step. Where had it been? Boston, or St. Louis? The dark structure of the boarding school loomed over the boy, but the building wasn't distinctive. In his mind, they were all the same.

The boy cried silently, his hands pressed woodenly to his side.

John MacPhearson stood on the far side of the empty street, his hands thrust into his breeches. He was wearing the new leather vest.

"Don't go yet," the child murmured.

"Gotta go, the boys is waitin'," John answered. "Now you go on back into school. I'll be seein' you soon enough."

"Not 'til spring," the little boy said, trying to be brave. "You said not 'til the rivers thaw, and you can paddle your way back."

"With a ton of gold ore on my back," John promised with a grin.

The little boy's face brightened. "Then we could live together, sir? You and I?"

John plucked at one of the tin buttons of the leather vest. "We'll see. We'll see." His eyes downcast, he tapped the brim of his hat. "Well, you take care and do your studies. You get smart so's when you grow up you can be a rich man in a black suit."

Then John ambled away and Fox was left alone on the step. Alone again. Alone with his tears.

"Fox?"

Fox focused on Celeste's face again. She had moved closer, though he didn't recall her walking toward him. The vest was still in her hand.

"Where the hell did you get that old thing?" He picked up the shovel. His heart pounded in his chest and his eyeballs were scratchy. After all these years, he still felt the pain of his abandonment.

"I told you. My mending basket." She touched his sleeve. "Fox, are you all right?"

"I don't want the vest. Give it to Petey. Burn it. I don't care." He leaned on the shovel, knowing she couldn't have missed the tremble in his voice.

"Fox, if you would tell me——"

"I don't want to talk about it." He thrust the shovel into the pile of coal and picked up the filled bin by the handle. He headed for the kitchen.

She followed. "If you could tell me about your past, about you and John, you would feel better."

Damned perceptive, green-eyed woman, he thought. "Don't want to talk about it. No point."

She squeezed through the door with him, preventing him from passing her and continuing on into the kitchen. "Fox."

His gaze met hers. "Celeste, what's done is done. It can't be changed."

"You need to forgive your father for whatever he did."

He felt a chill deep in his chest, a chill that threatened to climb up his throat and strangle him. "And what if he doesn't deserve forgiveness?"

She reached up with one hand and caressed his cheek. Her touch made him want to close his eyes and bask in the nearness of her. The warmth of her.

"Maybe he doesn't deserve it, but you do."

"I don't know what you mean." He studied her green eyes, full of caring, sincerity. God in heaven, why did she have to be a whore? Why couldn't he feel as if he could trust her . . . love her. It would be so easy to love her.

"I think it's this bitter grudge that's tearing you up inside. It's why you pace the floorboards at night. It's what's keeping you here when you could have gone home to San Francisco."

You're who's keeping me here, he thought. He glanced away, the heavy coal bin still in his hands. "You don't understand."

"Make me understand."

He shook his head. "I can't talk about it." It came out as a whisper.

She studied him for a moment and then smiled gently. "All right. How about some supper?"

Their gazes met again, and for a moment he felt cared for, almost loved. He was grateful for Celeste's concern, but also grateful for her acceptance. What woman had he ever known who knew when to push and when not to?

"Thank you," he murmured.

Chapter Twelve

"Nothing?" Celeste asked despondently as she stared down into the dark mine shaft.

Fox pulled a red handkerchief from his pocket and wiped some of the dust from his face. "Nothing."

She watched his hand as he wiped his neck and the V of chest hair that protruded from his red flannel work shirt, and wondered what it would be like to touch him like that.

For over two weeks they had worked side by side from dawn until dusk. While Fox drilled and dug, Celeste ran for tools, hauled buckets of dirt, and kept the men fed. There had been nothing but business between her and Fox, just as they'd agreed. They spoke only of the land and the gold they hoped to find. But as the days passed, the nervous tension between them mounted, their attraction to each other stringing tighter and tighter, like a band of rubber, bound to snap.

"There's no gold here," Fox continued. "Hell, there's no gold on any of this land." He stuffed his handkerchief back into his pocket, sounding as disappointed as Celeste felt. "I sent Titus and Pete home. They've been digging for ten days straight, without even a Sunday off.'' His gaze met hers. ''I thought they could use the rest.''

Celeste stared at the pile of earthen rubble at her feet. The warm wind that blew through the aspens along the creek bed teased locks of red hair that had tumbled from her battered hat. ''Guess they could.'' She pushed back her hair impatiently. ''Guess we all could. You look worn out.''

Then, for the first time in almost two weeks, Fox touched her. He reached out and tucked a lock of her hair behind her ear. ''So do you,'' he said tenderly.

She was wearing one of John's old brimmed felt hats, a pair of denim breeches, and a man's white shirt, yet he made her feel feminine.

Without considering the consequences of her actions, she caught his hand before he pulled it away, and held it to her cheek. ''I suppose it's time to let the dream die. You were right from the very beginning. There's no gold here. John just hoped there was. You should go home to your nice house in San Francisco, and I should stop putting off the inevitable.'' She tried not to think about what their failure really meant to her or how hard it would be to go back to Kate's. She didn't want Fox feeling sorry for her. This was her life, and though she didn't like the hand she'd been dealt, at least she'd managed to remain free of a man's control. At least her bad choices were her own.

Still standing an arm's length from her, Fox smoothed her cheek with his palm. ''Ah, Celeste,'' he said, his voice filled with emotion. ''I wish I could—''

''What? Take me away from here?'' She sighed. ''Don't say it. Please don't say it, because we both know it's not going to happen.''

Guilt seemed to fill his eyes.

She looked down so as not to make it any harder for him . . . for herself. ''We should just say our goodbyes and you should go home.''

''Home,'' he mused. ''Hell, I don't—''

Something at her feet caught one of the last rays of the setting sun and reflected the light. "What's that?" she interrupted.

"What?"

She kicked the small chunk of rock near the toe of her men's work boot, afraid to touch it. "That. See the way the sunlight glimmers off it. It's black. It shouldn't shine," she said carefully.

"Odd." He leaned over and picked up a rock the size of a small pullet egg. He rubbed one of the craggy edges with his thumb, an excitement in his voice. "Celeste. Tell me something."

"Yes?" She stared at the rock and held her breath.

"Have you ever seen silver?"

"Silver?" she exhaled.

"Silver. White metal, not the dog. Not as precious as gold," he said, the excitement in his voice building, "but damned precious if you're a man, or a woman, in need."

She took the chunk of rock with its blackish matrix from Fox's hand and rubbed it vigorously with the corner of her white shirttail.

Fox stared at the metal. "What does the creek run off?"

"What do you mean?"

"It's a branch of some river, right?"

"A creek," she answered. "Clear Creek, I'd guess."

He kicked at a pile of dirt and rubble they'd brought up from their last hole, and picked up another rock. He rubbed it. "I've heard rumors about some old miner finding silver off Clear Creek."

Celeste's eyes widened. "Is it?" she asked softly, as though if she spoke too loudly, it wouldn't be so. "Is it silver?"

"I'll be damned," Fox whispered, a light passing over his face that she'd not seen since he arrived in Carrington. "I'll be damned, old man. You were right." He gave a laugh of amazement as he picked up another chunk of rock, and another. "Riches beyond your dreams, just not in gold." He thrust a handful of dirty silver ore at her. "Silver, Celeste. Silver."

Celeste squealed in delight and, without thinking, threw her arms around Fox. "Silver? Silver?" She kissed him on the lips, laughing with excitement. "It can't be!"

Fox let the silver nuggets fall from his hands to take her in his arms. "Silver!" He threw his head back and his laughter came from deep in his belly, his soul. "It's silver, all right. My father really did leave me something." He picked her up in his arms and swung her around. "Silver, silver," he whispered against her lips. "Enough for us both. The answer to our hopes, our dreams, Celeste!"

As he set her back on the grassy ground, he lowered his lips to hers. This time their kiss was not one of congratulations or excitement, but of passion.

Fox's kiss deepened and Celeste put up no protest. She parted her lips as he thrust his tongue inside, savoring the delicious taste of him.

Thoughts of the precious metal flew. All she could think of was the taste of Fox's mouth on hers, and the touch of his hand as he caressed her breast through the rough cotton of her shirt. Her nipples puckered in response to his caress, the brush of the cotton sheeting against her flesh increasing the pleasure.

"Celeste, Celeste . . ." He whispered her name in her ear as he nibbled her lobe.

Suddenly Celeste couldn't get enough of him, the taste of him, the smell of him, the feel of his hard, muscular frame in her arms. She swept her hands over his broad back and thrust her tongue into his mouth. It was as if a dam had been broken and her flood of feelings for him were all rushing by. She was in a frenzy to touch and be touched, and that frenzy swept through him as well.

Fox fumbled with the buttons of her shirt, and she helped him to unfasten them. The warm evening breeze caressed her skin as she pulled open the shirt, covering her breasts with prickly goose flesh.

"Fox," she whispered. "I swore I'd never become involved with a man I could care for."

"Swore I'd never love another whore," he muttered as he sank to his knees.

Celeste leaned forward, and he took her nipple in his mouth. She moaned with pleasure as she closed her eyes and welcomed the waves of sensation. "Swore I'd send you packing," she breathed heavily.

"Swore I wouldn't touch you," he answered. "No matter how badly I wanted to."

Celeste laughed and sank to her knees in the grass beside the mine shaft. The sun was just setting over the horizon beyond the hills and the forest of aspens. Golden light filtered through Fox's dark hair as she ran her finger through the silky, dark strands. He smelled of shaving soap, pine trees, and desire.

For her.

"Swore . . . swore I wouldn't," she protested weakly as she melted into his arms.

"Promised myself . . . promised the dog," he echoed.

She laughed as she unbuttoned his shirtfront, wanting to feel flesh against flesh. All these years she'd been doing this, and never once had she felt anything.

Until Fox.

"No good can come of it," Fox said, his voice husky. His eyes were half-closed as he stroked the slope of her breasts and buried his face in the valley between them.

"No good," she agreed.

His gaze met hers. "But what the hell."

She broke into a mischievous, sultry smile. "What the hell," she whispered.

Then he kissed her, the most delicious kiss a woman could ever hope for.

Celeste rolled in the grass with Fox; her shirt fell open, and her nipples hardened in response to his touch and the cool night air that blew out of the mountains. First she lay on top of him, then he on top of her. When he slipped his hand beneath the waistband of her breeches and pantaloons, her breath caught in her throat. "Oh," she murmured.

"Mmmmmm," he hummed in her ear. "So sweet. So perfect."

Celeste laid back on the sweet grass and closed her eyes.

She flung her hands back in total surrender. *Just once, she told herself. Just once, let me enjoy this.*

Fox covered her breasts with hot, damp kisses, burning a trail of molten desire from the pulse of her throat to her navel. Every flick of his tongue, every brush of his fingertips, sent her swirling higher and higher, making her dizzier by the moment.

Celeste's entire body was alive with sensation, and yet in some way she felt shy. She had gone through the act of making love many times, but she had never really made love. She had just gone through the motions. Now she felt as giddy as a schoolgirl, as bashful as a bride on her wedding night. She had never guessed a man and a woman coming together could be so wonderful.

He pulled off his shirt and flung it away. She pressed a kiss to his bare chest and then tentatively tasted the nub of his male nipple with the tip of her tongue. With her customers she had never taken any initiative, just laid there and waited for it to be over, reading recipes in her mind. Tonight there were no recipes, only waves of burning, building desire.

She felt her heart swell as Fox moaned with pleasure. For the first time in her life she felt as if she were a participant rather than an observer.

Fox kissed her above the metal button of her breeches and she lifted her hips in encouragement. She threaded her fingers through his thick hair. "Yes," she whispered. "Yes, kiss me there."

He unhooked the button, rested his cheek on her belly, and slid his hand beneath the rough, dusty fabric.

"Ohhhh," she moaned.

"Here?" he whispered.

His fingers found the warm folds of her womanhood, and she sighed and moaned again. "There," she encouraged. "Yes, there."

Celeste wiggled her bottom to escape the confines of her tangled clothing as he pulled off her breeches and the pantaloons she wore beneath them. She never gave a thought to the idea that they were in the middle of an open meadow, or that anyone could come upon them. For once, she was beyond reasonable thought.

The sounds of his heavy breathing filled her head. He kissed her again and again, moving his hand to the rhythm of her rising ardor. He kissed her throat, her collarbone, the cleft of her chin.

"Please," she whispered, so filled with a burning ache that she could barely speak. "Please, Fox . . ."

"Yes?" he said softly, teasingly into her ear. "A request?"

"Take them off." She tugged at his denims, too embarrassed by her own desire to open her eyes.

"Now?"

She giggled nervously and he kissed her mouth. "Yes, now," she whispered against his lips. "I won't let you get away this time."

She felt him shift his weight off her and she stretched out in the soft grass, her eyes closed. As his weight descended on her again, he was completely naked. His stiff phallus brushed against her bare leg and, instinctively, she lifted her hips.

"We don't have to do this," he whispered.

"We do. I . . . I do." She couldn't get up the nerve to touch *it,* but she wanted it, needed it. She kneaded his bare buttocks with the palms of her hands. "Please don't tease me now, Fox."

He kissed her tenderly. "I won't."

He parted her thighs with his hand and stroked her again. A most delightful, gratifying touch . . . Then, when she was warm and wet and swimming with that urgent need again, he guided himself inside.

Celeste arched her back and cried aloud with pleasure, shocked by her own reaction to him. Never before . . . never before had it been like this.

Deep inside her, Fox held himself perfectly still over her. She could tell by his heavy breathing that he wanted to move, needed to move, but he was giving her time to adjust.

She lifted her hips and pressed her hands to his bare buttocks. He lowered his hips to meet her first thrust.

"Celeste, Celeste," he whispered in her ear. "I feel as if I've waited for this, for you, all my life . . ."

Celeste didn't say anything because she'd spent years hearing men in the throes of passion say things they never remembered afterward. But a part of her was happy to hear those sweet words, even though he didn't really mean them. At a moment like this, men didn't know what they really meant and what they didn't.

She rose again and again to meet him, wanting it to go on forever, yet desperately needing to find fulfillment.

He kissed her face and throat. He laced his fingers through her tangled hair. Again and again they rose and fell, not as two separate people, but as one.

Her world exploded with pleasure into a thousand stars of twinkling silver light. Fox groaned and thrust, and together, wrapped in each other's arms, they drifted back to reality and the setting sun.

Fox rolled off her, onto his back, and drew her close. She snuggled against him, still drifting in the last pulses of ecstasy. She kept her eyes closed, wanting to prolong the moment of contentment.

He kissed her above her eyebrow. "I think we're being watched," he whispered in her ear, his breath still warm and husky.

Her eyes flew open and she bolted upright.

He laughed and pulled her down on top of him. "The dog."

She spotted Silver under a distant pine and she laughed with Fox. "Think he's been watching long?" She flung herself back into the warm grass and stared up at the darkening sky.

"At least he can't repeat any tales."

She laughed again, feeling warm and tingly all over.

Fox rolled onto his side, still stark naked, and propped himself up on one elbow to look at her. He traced a pattern on her stomach with his fingertip. "That was . . ."

She sighed. "I know."

He studied her face carefully. "You . . . really enjoyed it? You weren't just, you know . . ."

She rolled onto her side to face him. *"Faking my enjoyment?"* She lifted her eyebrow with amusement.

She could have sworn he blushed. "I just know that—"

"That whores fake it all the time."

His gaze met hers again, but he didn't say anything.

She threaded her fingers through his. "This was different," she said softly.

"Better," he offered. "Than the past. Different. For me at least."

She kissed his stubbled cheek. She didn't care if he was lying. It was a lie she could live with, at least for the time being. "So now what?" she asked.

He pressed his lips to hers in a lingering kiss. "Guess we ought to get dressed."

She pushed him back into the grass, playfully. "I mean a little more long-term than that. I mean the silver." She took a breath, feeling less confident. "I mean . . . you and I."

Fox sat up. "All right. Here's the plan." He handed her shirt to her. "We dress. We get some of these chunks of rock assayed by someone who knows what he's doing. My guess is that the silver is galena. It looks black because it's mixed with lead. As for us . . ." He hesitated.

"We make no commitment to each other. No promises that can be broken." Celeste slipped into her shirt and began to button up. "That way you're free to go. I'm free to go. No attachments." She spoke the words she knew he wanted to hear. A part of her felt as if this was truly best for her, but a part of her wanted to cry for what would never exist between them. "No expectations to be shattered."

He looked as if he wanted to say something, then changed his mind. He stuck out his hand, a boyish grin on his handsome face. "It's a deal, partner."

Celeste's heart sank just a little. For some foolish reason she had hoped he would say something else. Offer some kind of hope for something more between them. But who was she fooling? She was a whore; she'd been his father's whore. He was a rich Californian. They would enjoy each other's company while it lasted, and then he would move on. It was better this way. This way no one got hurt.

She stood to pull on her denims. It all made perfect, logical sense. So why did she feel so hurt?

"Kate says we ought to be givin' you a chunk of our earnings," Silky Sally chattered. "After all, if it wasn't for that silver strike of yours, Carrington wouldn't be boomin' the way it is. Miners are pourin' in by the day, all stakin' claims. I hear the train'll soon be running through here every day, since Garret struck silver farther upriver." She turned away from the mirror, dressed in nothing but silk stockings and heels, and held up a sheath gown made of gold lamé. "You like this on me, or do you think it makes me look like a hurdy-gurdy girl?"

Celeste sat on the edge of Sally's lace-trimmed bed, her arms crossed over her chest. "Sally, you are a hurdy-gurdy girl," she teased.

Sally rolled her eyes and turned back to the mirror. "You know what I mean." She studied herself critically in the oval free-standing mirror, turning her head one way and then the other. "It's not too cheap-looking is it? I hear Sal's got two new girls, come from Denver 'cause of the silver boom. Them city girls could be serious competition."

"There's no competition when it comes to your charms on the stage or on the bed ropes."

Sally turned to Celeste. "Aw, that's sweet of you to say." She tossed the gown over a straight-backed chair and sat on the bed beside Celeste. "I'm so glad you came by. I've missed you somethin' fierce." She gave Celeste a hug.

"I've missed you, too."

"Oh, you have not." Sally slapped Celeste's knee and reached behind them to retrieve a half-eaten box of pink candy confections. "You been too busy getting rich with that man of yours."

"He's not my man."

"No?" Sally bit into a piece of candy and pink frosting fell onto her small breasts. "Not what he says."

Celeste looked at Sally. "When did you talk to Fox?"

"Yesterday in Smythe's Emporium. I was buying some of that new orange toilet water he just got in. Your Mr. MacPhearson was tryin' to get Getty to order some book for him. Something about grapes."

Celeste threw up her hands. "And Fox just walked up to you out of the clear blue sky and declared I was his woman?"

"Well, no." Sally licked her finger and picked up the pink crumbs from her breasts, then popped her finger into her mouth. "I just asked how he was doin'. Polite conversation. I invited him here to Kate's."

"You propositioned him? Sally!"

Sally poked Celeste in the side with her finger, laughing. "You said he wasn't your man! What do you care?"

Celeste didn't answer because Sally was right. She and Fox were not a couple. They had both agreed that there were no strings attached. They were simply enjoying each other's company.

"Anyway, he thanked me kindly, but said he didn't think you'd approve."

"So he didn't actually say I was his woman."

"Well, no, but he was *practically* sayin' it!"

"Oh, Sally." Celeste rose off the bed and wandered to the mirror where a fur boa lay draped over it. She smoothed the white fur with a hand. "This is all so complicated with Fox and me." Though secretly pleased that Fox would say such a thing, she wasn't ready to admit it.

"Y'all being business partners and ownin' all that silver lode, you mean."

"It's not a lode yet. It's got to be excavated, hauled to the smelt, refined, and sold first. We're not rich yet."

"But it's only been three weeks since you hit the vein. It'll come," Sally encouraged.

Celeste sighed. "I suppose."

"You certainly don't sound happy, being a woman who's

not only struck it rich, but has caught herself a rich, handsome, manly man who's going to take her away from a life of whorin'."

Celeste spun around. "Don't say that, because it's not true. He's not taking me anywhere. He's going to take his silver and go back to California."

Sally scrunched up her pretty nose. "He's not takin' you with him?"

"No."

"Why not?"

"Because he's a handsome, rich, manly man and I'm a whore!"

"Not anymore you're not."

Celeste groaned. "Sally, once a whore, always a whore. A woman can't get away from that kind of reputation."

"Sure she can."

"No man like Fox MacPhearson is going to marry me or you, Sally. Men like that want decent women."

Sally lowered her gaze as if she'd been reprimanded. "I'm sorry."

"It's all right. I didn't mean to snap at you. I just don't want you to expect too much out of life. I don't want you to get hurt."

"So you never even thought of him askin' you to go with him, or had the idea of you askin' him?"

"No. I wouldn't go with him if he asked me," she added for good measure.

Sally looked up. "You saying that for truth, or so it won't hurt so much?"

Celeste didn't know how to answer. Silky Sally knew her well, too well.

Sally rose off the springing bed to fetch her dressing gown. "That's all right. You don't want that man anyway. There's some sayin' he's got a past."

Celeste dropped the fur boa over her neck to try it on before the mirror. "Everyone's got a past."

"A bad one." Sally tied the ribbon of her dressing gown

and picked through a bag of face paints. ''I hear the sheriff's questioned him.''

''Oh?''

''More than once.''

Celeste turned, an uneasiness coming over her. ''About what?''

''The murders, of course. Rosy said that Mad Mary over at Sal's said that Sal said that Sheriff Tate said that Mr. MacPhearson's been spotted on the streets of Carrington long after decent folk are abed. Something ain't right there.''

Celeste removed the boa and put it back over the mirror. Sheriff Tate was right. Fox did wander about at odd hours of the night, but it was because he had trouble sleeping. The cool mountain air and the walking tired him. ''Did they say that, now? And that makes him a murderer?''

''Talk is, Tate knows something about Mr. MacPhearson that the rest of us don't know. Something that happened in California.''

''Gossip.'' Could the sheriff really think Fox had something to do with those brutal murders? Celeste flipped her hand. ''People are jealous over Fox's silver strike, so they're gossiping. It's much more exciting to think that a rich Californian has come to town to kill whores than some stinkin', fish-bellied miner.''

''I don't know.'' Sally painted a broad streak of blue eye paint under one brow. ''Maybe you ought to watch your back just the same.''

''Fox is not a murderer.''

'' 'Course not.''

''He's *not.*'' She said it to convince herself as much as Sally. Of course Fox wasn't a murderer. There was a lot about him she didn't know or didn't understand, but surely she was a good enough judge of character to know the man didn't murder women.

Sally looked into her hand mirror at Celeste. ''I'm agreein' with you, for heaven's sake! Now help me do something with this hair of mine. Big Nose Kate expects me to be on stage in two hours to do the opening number, and I'm a mess.''

Pushing her uneasiness aside, Celeste picked up a hairbrush. ''I've only got a few minutes and then I have to go. Fox and I are going to supper at the place that opened in the old Crystal Hotel. The chef is supposed to be French.'' She pulled the brush through Sally's pretty blond hair. ''So what shall it be? Up and sophisticated, or down and girlish?'' Celeste looked into the mirror over Sally's shoulder, and both women broke into laughter.

Chapter Thirteen

Celeste stepped onto the dark street. After visiting with Sally, she was anxious to return home and dress for the evening. She and Fox were going out to dine, to be seen in public together socially for the very first time. She didn't mind that people would point her out as his mistress, or that she'd once been his father's woman. She was too happy to be with Fox and to celebrate their silver strike.

An assayer had come from Denver to determine the authenticity and quality of the silver on MacPhearson's Fortune, the name she and Fox had given the land claims. In the assayers expert opinion, the silver ore from the mine they called The Celeste would yield twenty-three thousand dollars to the ton. Even with the cost of equipment and labor to mine the ore, even splitting the profits with Fox, the strike meant Celeste was a rich woman. It meant she would never have sex with another man again, except by choice.

For weeks, Celeste had carried that joyous excitement in her heart. Only in the last two days had her feet finally touched the dusty Colorado ground enough for her to begin to make plans for her future. Right now her future involved getting the ore out of the ground, and protecting hers and Fox's rights to that ore. When she and Fox had made the discovery, she had immediately known what good changes the fortune would mean to her, but what she was just discovering, were the bad changes.

Within days of their initial discovery, she and Fox were hounded by miners seeking work, businessmen wanting to buy them out, and an assortment of men wanting to steal from them in one manner or another. And not only had Celeste's life changed, but the life of the town had changed.

She was astounded by the number of folks on Carrington's streets. Since the discovery of silver on MacPhearson's Fortune three weeks before, the population had increased nearly two-fold and more miners were pouring in every day. They came by train, by stagecoach, by wagon, and under the power of their own worn boots, each man hoping to make his fortune.

Along with the miners who staked their own claims, came other men eager to make a dollar or two off any silver that might filter through the town. There were laborers to construct the mine shafts and haul the ore from the depths of the steamy tunnels, and freighters with mules and wagons to carry the ore to be pulverized and shipped. Investors dressed in fancy suits with ready money appeared on every doorstep, willing to finance the entire operation at an exorbitant profit.

Both of Carrington's hotels had reopened this week, as well as a bank. Three mercantile stores opened their doors and several entrepreneurs on the outskirts of town had raised tents and were selling everything from mining supplies to prepared food. Miners filled the hotels, but most men threw crude shelters on the land where they had staked their precious one-hundred-square-foot claims.

On a Saturday night like tonight, the new arrivals were all in town, looking for a little companionship, a drink, a hot meal, and maybe a roll with one of Kate's or Sal's girls. And it wasn't only men who had flocked to Carrington. There was a laundress, several cooks, and a seamstress who was said to be staking a claim on the next miner who struck gold along the river. One enterprising hurdy-gurdy girl had apparently put up a tent near the train station, and hung a sign to advertise her wares. Celeste hadn't been down near the tracks, but she heard that on a Saturday night, there was a line of men eager to make her acquaintance.

Celeste walked quickly down the street, passing miners without making eye contact. There were so many strangers that it made her uncomfortable. Unfortunately, along with those seeking an honest living, came the riffraff from other towns. Two days ago there had been a knifing in a new saloon and gambling house on the far end of Peach Street, and a miner had been shot and killed north of MacPhearson's Fortune, when he'd evidently attempted to jump another man's claim.

To add to Celeste's discomfort over the town's new arrivals was the ever-present threat of the murderer who had killed Pearl and Margaret. It seemed as if everyone had forgotten their deaths in the commotion of the silver strike, even Sally and Kate. How sad that their lives could be dismissed so quickly. But Celeste hadn't forgotten. It seemed as if the happier she was, the more the murders haunted her. Maybe it was because for the first time in a long time, she truly valued her own life.

A wildly bearded man in a dusty overcoat passed her; his arm brushed hers. What if one of these men was the murderer? She met the miner's gaze as she passed and, spooked by the idea, she looked quickly away.

The more Celeste thought about the murderer, the more concerned she became. Apparently Sheriff Tate still had no suspects. Well, other than Fox, which was, of course, a ridiculous, unfounded notion.

Another miner passed her on the sidewalk and she averted her gaze.

The idea that Fox was the killer was preposterous. So what if he'd arrived the night the killings began? So what if he wandered the town at night? Did being an insomniac automatically make Fox a cold-blooded killer? These supposed bits of evidence were all coincidence, she told herself. Sheer coincidence.

Celeste turned the corner off Peach Street and found herself suddenly alone. There had been lanterns hung outside saloons and hotels on Peach Street, but Cherry was dark and vacant.

Celeste walked faster, gripping her cape. She wished she'd brought Silver along for protection. Her heels clip-clapped on the board sidewalk.

"Howdy there, Celeste."

A man stepped out of the shadows of a dilapidated livery stable, and Celeste took a step back in surprise. It was so dark that she squinted to recognize who had called her by name.

"What's a matter, girl? Don't know old Reb?" The man caught her around her waist with one large, dirty hand. He reeked of sweat and whiskey.

"Let go of me," Celeste intoned. She shoved his hand down. Just the thought of a man—other than Fox—touching her, made her skin crawl.

"Celeste, baby, it's Reb. Old Reb Cattleton." He reached for her again. "I know I ain't been through in two years, but I know you remember me. 'Member my *big reb* for certain." He grasped his groin.

Celeste swallowed the bile that rose in her throat. It had been months since she'd slept with a customer, but it seemed like another lifetime.

"I'm not in the business anymore, Reb," she said. She tried to push by him, but he grabbed her arm.

"What do you mean, *not in the business?*" His fingers pinched her arm tighter. "I walked my ass four miles in off that claim to get a taste of Celeste, the heavenly body, and I aim to have me that taste."

Celeste gritted her teeth as she tried to struggle free from his grasp. "Did you hear me, Reb?" She spoke loudly and firmly, trying not to let him hear any panic in her voice. "I'm no longer available. See Kate. She'll set you up with a pretty girl to your liking."

He grabbed her other arm and pulled her against him. "I want you."

She thrust her face into his. "Don't you understand, Reb? I don't want *you.*" She jerked both of her arms from his grasp.

She was so angry that she barely felt the pain. Free of his grasp, she spun on her heels and strode off.

He didn't follow her, but she could feel his eyes on her as she made her escape. Apparently he had the decency to know when his attentions weren't wanted after all. She lifted her skirts and walked faster, but she didn't run. Damn men and their crude, rough ways.

Abruptly, she heard footsteps pound behind her. "Get back here, bitch. I was willing to pay you good money, but now—"

Celeste broke into a run, but a moment too late. Reb's hand clamped her right shoulder and pulled her backward, hard against his solid, stinking body.

"Now I guess I'll have that piece of tail for free."

Celeste screamed, twisted around, and elbowed him hard in the soft pouch of his stomach. "Get your hands off me!"

Reb grunted with pain. "Bitch!"

He slapped her.

She swung her arm up and managed to hit him in the jaw with her balled fist. "Help!" she screamed to anyone who might hear her. "Help me!"

He wrapped his arm around her throat, and Celeste panicked as he cut off her breath.

"Who do you think you are, denyin' me? Filthy whore! You're goin' straight to hell for this, you know. Straight to hell for spreadin' your legs, tempting honest men like myself."

Oh my God, Celeste thought. *Is it him? Is Reb the killer?*

"So how's about we find ourselves a little private place?" Reb hauled her backward, off the sidewalk, and into the alley.

Celeste struggled and dragged her feet. She tried to twist in his arms, but he had her pinned against his body. The smell of his sour sweat and the bad whiskey made her want to vomit. She was dizzy from lack of air. Her head spun in black circles and her limbs felt weak. *Please don't let me faint,* she thought. *Don't let me faint and this man butcher me.*

In answer to her prayers, Celeste heard running footsteps. Reb turned to see who was approaching, just as Celeste spotted a man leap through the air.

Reb gave a grunt of surprise. He let go of Celeste and she fell to the ground, gasping for breath.

The dark figure hit Reb in the center of his chest and sent him hurling backward into the livery stable wall. Rotten boards creaked and splintered.

"What the hell?" Reb shouted. "Get off! Get off!"

Panting to catch her breath, Celeste looked up.

Fox MacPhearson shoved Reb to the ground, face first on the hard dirt between the stable and the sidewalk.

It was Fox! Fox had come for her. He'd saved her from rape at the very least, perhaps death.

"Looking for trouble?" Fox demanded, his voice so harsh and threatening that it frightened even Celeste.

"No. No trouble," Reb answered. Fox held him down, chest to the ground, his arms twisted unnaturally behind his back, his cheek pressed into a pile of dry horse dung.

"Celeste, you all right?" Fox called over his shoulder.

She pushed herself off the ground and brushed the grass and dirt from her lavender gown and matching petticoat. Her throat hurt and she still felt dizzy, but she was all right. "Fine. Fine," she managed. "This . . . this is Reb."

Fox grabbed Reb by a handful of his matted hair and sat on his back, his knees pressed into Reb's back. "You bothering my woman?"

"N . . . no. Did . . . didn't know she was taken. U . . . used to know her—in the biblical sense."

"Did she tell you to get lost?"

When Reb didn't answer immediately, Fox jerked up the miner's head and looked into Reb's bloodshot eyes. "I said, did she tell you she wasn't interested?"

"Y . . . yeah. Yeah."

Celeste was shocked by the intensity of Fox's rage, by his brutal behavior. It wasn't that she wasn't glad to see him, she'd just never seen this side of him.

The unwanted thought drifted through her mind that perhaps a man this full of rage really could be capable of murder.

"Then I'd suggest you take your sorry ass elsewhere!" Fox slammed his face into the dirt and climbed off him.

Celeste stood there and stared at Fox as he straightened his black jacket. She wasn't afraid of him, but she wondered for the first time if she should be. She was certain in her heart he wasn't a killer, but at the time she wondered if she could trust her instincts.

"You sure you're all right?" Fox asked. They stepped out onto the sidewalk where there was a little more light from the street beyond them.

Reb scrambled up and disappeared down the alley, running in the opposite direction.

"Yes. Yes, I'm all right." She patted her hair that had come down from its chignon in the struggle. "He didn't hurt me. Just scared me."

He took her arm possessively. "You shouldn't be out here alone." He escorted her back up the sidewalk toward Peach Street.

There was something in his tone that set Celeste off. "You mean I was asking for it?" She halted to face him.

His dark eyes were stormy, his hair ruffled. "I mean you shouldn't be outside after dark, alone. It's not safe. I don't want you doing it again. You want to go somewhere, I'll take you."

She gave a little laugh, but there was no amusement in her voice. "Fox MacPhearson, I'll come and go any damned time and any damned where I please."

He looked at her as if she'd just grown horns. "What?"

"You heard me! You can't tell me where I can and can't go."

"That's ridiculous. It's not safe for you to be on the streets at night. Not with all the strangers in town and a murderer on the loose. You belong at home."

She looked him straight in the eye. "And just how do I know I'm safe there?" she asked softly.

Before Fox could reply, she strode away, headed for Plum Street.

* * *

When Celeste heard the front lock click and the door open, she wiped her wet hands on her apron and crossed the kitchen to stir her stew. She and Fox had intended to go out tonight to celebrate their silver strike. After what had happened earlier, she'd assumed there would be no celebratory meal. He had been gone over an hour.

Fox entered the kitchen with Silver at his heels and Celeste felt a pang of jealousy. Lately it seemed as if the dog was more his than hers.

She heard him halt in the doorway. She could feel him watching her.

The stew no longer needed to be stirred, but she stirred it anyway, just so she wouldn't have to turn and face him. The kitchen was quiet save for the sound of the bubbling supper and the sound the light breeze made when it tickled the frilly curtains at the open window.

"Celeste, what just happened back there on the street?"

She took a deep breath. "Someone got rough with me. You came along, broke it up." She held the wooden spoon tightly in her hand.

"That's not what I meant and you know it."

She turned to him. "You can't tell me what to do. You have no right. No ties that bind, remember?"

"I have a right to be concerned for your safety." He strode into the kitchen.

"You can be concerned," she granted. "But you can't tell me what to do." She shook the spoon at him. "I vowed a long time ago not to ever let a man run my life again."

He raised one eyebrow. "So you didn't want me to pull that jackass off you?"

She knew he must think she was being irrational. Hell, she felt irrational. The point was that he couldn't have it both ways. He couldn't tell her that because she had been a whore he could never love her, and at the same time want to play the part of husband and protector. It wouldn't be fair. Celeste had to remain independent of him. It was the only way she could accept their relationship of sex without commitment.

She sighed. ''I'm sorry. I should have thanked you for saving me. He could have raped me.'' She stared at her button shoes. ''I just didn't like the attitude you took afterwards. It's as if you want me, but you don't want me.'' She lifted her gaze.

He was quiet for a moment as he mulled over her words. ''You're right. I don't make any sense to you because I don't make any sense to myself.'' He took a step toward her, his hand outstretched. ''Celeste, I care for you very much. I'm damned attracted to you. I love holding you in my arms, touching you, having you touch me. But—''

There was that knife in her heart again, twisting, wrenching. He loved her body, but not her. Never her. She struck out with the only weapon she had, her calm logic. ''Look, we've agreed on the ground rules. I expect nothing from you, but in return, you can't make demands on me. You can't tell me what to do. You can't control me.''

''I just want you to be safe.''

He spoke so kindly, so honestly, that Celeste put her arms around him and kissed his cheek. Even without love, this was the most fulfilling relationship with a man she'd ever experienced. It wasn't what she wanted, what she'd dreamed of, but she was a fool not to take what he offered. Any woman in Kate's would have given a limb to have a man say that he just wanted her to be safe. ''I know,'' she whispered. ''I'm sorry I'm acting so crazy.''

He encircled her waist and brushed his lips against her temple and the hair that curled in tendrils there. ''So what was that about wondering if you were safe here . . . with me, you meant.'' He pushed her back so that he could look into her eyes. ''You don't think I could be the murderer, do you?'' There was a flash of desperation in his concerned voice.

She remembered the rage Fox had expressed only an hour ago on Cherry Street . . . but when she looked into his Indian eyes, she didn't see a murderer. She just didn't. ''No,'' she said softly. ''I don't believe it; I just said it because I was angry. But,'' she traced the line of his jawbone with her index finger, ''there are others in town who are talking. Wondering.''

He kissed the tip of her nose, released her, and walked away. ''That damned Tate. He's had it in for me since I arrived in town.''

''There was some gossip about your past. Something Tate mentioned to someone.''

Fox whipped around. ''About my past?'' He strode toward her. ''What about my past?''

Unnerved, she took a step back, the spoon smelling of stew still in her hand. ''I . . . I don't know. Sally didn't say. She didn't know anything either. Only that Tate had mentioned you had a past.''

''There's nothing in my past that is anyone's business but my own,'' he flared.

Celeste thought of her own past and nodded. ''I'm certainly in agreement with that.'' She dropped the spoon back into the stew. ''I think you should just ignore Tate. Maybe he's passing the gossip around town in the hopes of drawing out the killer. Maybe if the killer thinks the sheriff thinks it's someone else, he'll make a mistake.''

Fox leaned on the back of one of the kitchen chairs. ''I sure hope so, because we don't need this right now. We've got a hell of a mess out on the claims. I had to hire two more men this morning to keep claim jumpers at bay. The workers are having a bad time keeping the walls up of that last pit we dug. The carpenters are supposed to be building the barn to house the equipment—'' He rubbed his hand across the back of his neck. ''And don't ask me how well the timber walls of the shaft are going up, because you don't want to know.''

She pointed to the table. ''Set the plates. I made stew and biscuits. We'll eat and discuss the operation. We've got to have a plan once the miners start hauling the ore from underground.''

His anger over Tate and the troubles with the mine faded, and he flashed a boyish grin. ''So we're moving onto another conversation. That's good. Does that mean I'm out of hot water now, and there might be a place for me in that bed of yours tonight?''

She smiled sassily. The way he watched her made her warm

all over. It wasn't that she could so easily forget the problems between them, only that she was desperate for every shred of happiness she could find. Life was too short not to enjoy; Margaret and Pearl were proof of that. "It's a possibility." She turned away. "Now get the bowls. The stew is ready and I'm starved."

After the meal and a thick piece of chocolate velvet cake, Celeste and Fox sat down with ink and pen and paper and began to write down what needed to be done at the MacPhearson's Fortune to get the first mine in full operation. People outside the mining business had the idea in their heads that a miner just dug a deep hole like a well and brought up ore in buckets on an ordinary windlass or some other crude convenience. The truth was, Celeste and Fox were quickly learning, that mining silver ore was far more complicated. The sides of the pits they had initially dug were already beginning to slump, and a timber shaft would have to be dug.

First a building had to be constructed over the shaft. The building, resembling a small factory, would house the shaft and housing works. If their first mine were as prosperous as the assayer guessed The Celeste would be, additions would have to be added to the main building to house carpenters, blacksmiths, and machinists. Once the five foot by twenty foot shaft was dug, cages would have to be set in place to hoist and lower men, ore, and supplies. A pipe would have to be set in place to pump water from the depths of the mine, and fresh air would be blown in to keep the miners alive. Then there were steam-hoisting engines and hoisting spools and a myriad of other equipment to be put into place.

It was near midnight when Celeste finally laid down her pen. "Who ever thought getting rich could be so complicated?" she said, as she stared at the stacks of paper and columns of numbers.

"Who'd have thought it?" Fox echoed, sounding equally grim.

"We've got to get some of that silver out of that hole so we can buy more equipment, hire more men." She glanced at him, not sure how to approach the next subject, yet knowing she had to. "But we need the equipment and the men to bring the ore up."

Fox leaned back in his chair and tucked his hands behind his head. "Doesn't put us in a good position, does it?"

"Fox?"

He leaned forward, scribbled another number, and rocked back in the chair again. "Mm hm?"

"I . . . I know this is a joint effort. Half and half, straight down the middle, but do you think—" She moaned silently. It was so hard for her to ask anyone for anything, but this was even more difficult. "Do you think you could put a share of your money into the operation and loan me an equal portion? Just to get started?" His face was suddenly expressionless. "I . . . I'd pay you interest of course."

"No." He let the chair rock forward and hit the hardwood floor with a bang.

She was completely taken aback by his curt answer. "No?"

"We'll have to make do." He rose from the chair and grabbed his coat off the back. It was the same coat he'd worn when he'd first come to Carrington. He'd never bought a single piece of clothing since he'd arrived. "We'll have to start out using manual labor to do the hoisting. We'll take the cash from what we've sold, and sink that into the operation and buy the engines when we can."

Celeste didn't know what she'd said wrong, but he was obviously upset with her. And even though she tried not to be, her feelings were hurt by his response. "All right," she said quietly. "We'll make do." She got up from the table to clear away the dishes. As she turned her back, he walked out of the kitchen. Celeste heard Fox's footsteps as he ascended the staircase.

Hastily, she wiped away the silly tear that had gathered in the corner of one eye. It wouldn't have been a good idea to borrow money from him anyway. Just another tie to bind . . .

Chapter Fourteen

They think this silver strike will bring life to the town. Fools, stupid, mindless fools. It will bring nothing but filth. It will spread nothing but the filth that already eats away at mankind.

Duty. It is my duty to cleanse, to purify, to teach by deed, not just by word. I cannot sit by and watch the filth spread.

The blade is sharp. The time is right. I must follow my calling; put an end to their wretched lives and save the souls of the men they lure with their silken hair and lovely breasts.

I cannot rest until my duty is done. I cannot rest until they are gone. All gone, and godliness reigns again.

Celeste walked into the kitchen the following morning to find Fox standing at the window sipping a cup of coffee. He hadn't come to her room last night, but he looked as if he hadn't slept either.

His face was pale. He took a sip from the delicate teacup that looked so strange in his broad, callused hand. She wondered if he was feeling guilty for his refusal to put up his own money for the mining operation. *He should,* she thought.

"I didn't do it," he said softly as she entered the room. "I want you to know I didn't do it."

She froze in the doorway, her hands falling to grip the knot of the tie that held her dressing gown closed. She felt light-headed. Thoughts of the mining operation and the encounter they'd had last night slipped out of her head. A chill crept from the floor to her knees, making them weak. "Another?" She looked up anxiously; her legs felt wobbly beneath her sleeping gown. "Someone I know?"

He nodded gravely. "Another, but no one you knew. The new girl who set up business in a tent by the station. They called her Lacey."

Celeste was immensely relieved that it wasn't one of her friends, but at the same time her heart ached for any woman like herself. What if *she* had had an Adam waiting somewhere for her? "How do you know?"

"I took Silver out for a walk just before dawn. There was a big fuss on the street. Someone had found her. One of Tate's men was just heading over to get him out of bed."

"So you were out again when it happened?" She stood where she was. She knew in her heart he wasn't the killer, and yet . . .

There was an edge to his voice. "I was walking the streets like I do. Silver was with me."

Sometimes men said the most ridiculous things. "Walking a dog doesn't exclude a man from killing, Fox."

He had lifted his cup to take another sip of coffee, but halted to stare at her over the rim. "I'm not a murderer and you know it, damn it!"

She moved to the stove. He had already put tea water on for her. She reached for her china teapot. "Did anyone see you on the street?"

"No. But I'm sure Tate will be here before we're done with breakfast. He's dying to throw me into jail."

"Maybe you should go to him first, or . . ." she hesitated as she poured boiling water from the kettle into the teapot. "Maybe I should just say you were with me all night."

"I don't need you to lie for me," he snapped. "I didn't kill that woman by the tracks. I didn't kill anyone."

"Maybe you should tell me what Tate thinks he has on you. If I knew, maybe I could talk to him myself." She added tea leaves to the pot and carried it to the table. She was too sick to her stomach to think of food. She needed hot tea and a chair.

"I—I don't know what he thinks he has on me. It doesn't matter, Celeste." He came around the table to her. "It doesn't matter because I haven't done anything wrong. I need you to believe that."

Silver shot out from under the table a second before a knock sounded at the front door.

Celeste started to rise, but Fox laid his hand on her shoulder. "I'll get it," he said tersely. "Probably a pair of handcuffs for me anyway."

She eased back into the chair. It was so easy for her to let Fox be the strong one for a moment. Too easy. She was growing weak. Her veneer was cracking. It felt so good to have someone she felt she could depend on, lean on. But Celeste knew she was making a mistake. She knew she couldn't really depend on Fox. At some point he'd turn the mining operation over to someone else, or he'd sell his share, and he'd be gone.

Celeste stirred her tea and listened at the door. It was Kate. Celeste knew she should get up and go see her, but she just couldn't bring herself to do it. She couldn't bring herself to hear the details of that poor woman's murder.

The door closed and Fox walked back into the kitchen. He halted and brushed back a long lock of hair over his forehead. He was sadly in need of a haircut. "Kate thinks you need to get down to the sheriff's office right away. She says she'll meet you there."

Celeste half rose from her chair. "Tate's office? Why me?"

"Ace needs you. One of Tate's deputies just hauled him in for questioning."

She jumped up to go dress. She had to get to the sheriff's office as quickly as possible. She knew Ace had always been both frightened and intimidated by Tate. "Questioning? Questioning for what?"

As Celeste passed Fox in the doorway, he brushed his fingertips against hers. "For the murder of the whore."

"Not another one." One of Tate's nameless new deputies stood in the jail house doorway, a toothpick protruding from his mouth. "That boy's already got a room full of visitors."

Celeste pushed her way past the deputy, leaving Fox no choice but to follow. "Ace has a right to have someone present when he's questioned. Truth is, he ought to have a lawyer, and you know it." With one hip, she pushed open the swinging half door that led to the rear of the jail.

"Lawyer? That half-wit don't need no lawyer!" The deputy followed Celeste and Fox. " 'Sides, 'e ain't been charged with nothin'. Sheriff Tate just wants to question 'im."

Celeste hurried down a shabby, narrow corridor, through another door that led to the cells. She spotted Ace inside a small cell that resembled a straw-strewn cow stall with bars. The young man clung to the iron bars with white knuckles, pathetically staring out into the room.

He reached for her with one hand.

"Tate, what the damnation do you think you're doing?" Celeste couldn't see the sheriff because he was blocked from her view by Kate, Reverend Tuttle, and Rosy. Everyone was talking at once, but appeared to be accomplishing nothing.

Fox remained in the doorway. Celeste had only allowed him to come to serve as personal protection. She was still angry with him about last night, but after another murder, she had welcomed his escort.

"Ah, Miss Kennedy. I wondered how long it would take you to git here." Tate's cheek protruded from his wad of chewing tobacco.

"Expecting me, were you?" She walked to the barred cell and took Ace's cold hand. To her horror, she could now see that his face was beaten and streaked with dried blood, his shirt spattered as well. An icy shard of fear crept up her spine. Surely Ace couldn't have . . . wouldn't have . . .

"I was expecting you because the half-wit won't speak."

"He *can't* speak," she answered tartly.

"He won't even talk with his hands the way I seen him do. Just stares at me with that mule-stupid look on his face."

Celeste stared into Ace's black Indian eyes. The young man was scared out of his wits. "How did he get this blood all over him?" She directed her question to Kate.

"Don't know. Sheriff's right. He won't talk. Not even to me. He just keeps signing that he wants you. Wants Miss Celeste."

Reverend Tuttle approached the jail cell and thrust his face in front of Ace's. "Save yourself and confess if you have, indeed, committed this sin, son." His Adam's apple bobbed. "Confess and save your immortal soul."

Celeste glared at Joash. "Really, now. Do you think that's going to help Ace get out of here?"

Joash lifted his chin haughtily. "My first concern must be for our dear friend's afterlife; you know that, Celeste."

"Well. Let's get him out of here and then deal with his soul, shall we?" Celeste turned on the sheriff. "Let Ace out of here. He's hurt. His wounds need to be cleaned."

Sheriff Tate sauntered up to the cell, the keys jingling on a key ring on his belt. "And what if he's the murderer, Miss Kennedy. What if he intends to make you his next victim?"

Celeste never flinched. It wasn't that she hadn't considered the possibility that the killer might come after her, she just refused to be intimidated by Tate's bullying. "Ace didn't kill anyone and you damned well know it! Let him out!"

"You look into that Reb character I told you about?" Fox questioned from the doorway. "I told you last night that he attacked Miss Kennedy on the street."

Tate turned slowly to Fox as if he barely deemed him worthy of a response. "Yeah, I looked into it. Talked to Reb. He says he was just funnin' with Miss Kennedy. Besides, he was at Kate's most of last night. I've got witnesses."

Kate gave a nod of her fleshy chin. "Aye, Reb was at my place all right. Nearly drank me dry."

Celeste glanced at Ace, who still held her hand tightly, and then back at Tate. "You going to let him out or not?" she demanded.

"First some questions." Tate studied his prisoner. "Ask the half-wit where he was last night. How he got the blood all over him?"

"Don't let that blubber wind scare you," Rosy said, approaching Ace's cell from the other side. She looked directly at him so that he could read her lips. "Tate don't really think you killed that poor girl. He just wants the town to think he's doing something about these murders, only we all know he ain't."

Ace looked anxiously into Celeste's eyes.

Celeste gently took her hand from Ace's. "What happened?" she asked. She touched her own face. "The cuts on your face." She touched the bodice of her striped blue and green morning gown. "The blood on your shirt."

Ace looked anxiously at the sheriff, then back at Celeste. He drew back his fist, punched the air slowly, and then pulled his head back as if he'd been struck.

Celeste glanced at Tate. "He got in a fight."

"When? Where? Who are the witnesses? He was seen down by the tracks last night. He can't deny he was there."

Celeste met Ace's gaze again. "You were seen near the train station last night. A woman in a tent was murdered. Did you see the woman?"

Ace nodded adamantly.

Celeste's face went hot. "You saw her?" She wondered now if she was doing Ace more harm than good by questioning him in front of the sheriff.

Ace nodded again, and then drew his hips back and thrust them forward in an obscene gesture.

Celeste's eyes went wide with surprise. Rosy and Kate chuckled. Joash drew in a deep breath and began to mutter under his breath.

Celeste gripped the bars. "You were *with* the woman in the tent?"

Ace nodded and made the same gesture again.

"See that," Tate exclaimed. "Told you he'd seen her."

"Being with a whore doesn't make a man a murderer," Fox said, stepping into the room.

Celeste could tell by the look on his face that he'd been patient and quiet as long as he possibly could.

"You can't convict a man for murdering a woman on the basis that he screwed her," Fox continued. "Seems to me I heard that first one that was killed at Sal's was a favorite of *yours*."

Tate huffed and took a step back.

That was news to Celeste, but she didn't doubt Fox's word. She only wondered how he knew.

"You damned well know I didn't have anything to do with Mealy Margaret's murder," the sheriff sputtered.

"No. I don't think you did. Not any more than I think that Indian boy had anything to do with the whore's death last night."

"Then how'd he get that blood all over him?" Tate seemed to be taking the defensive now.

Fox's gaze met Celeste's. Celeste turned back to Ace and touched her bodice again. "Where'd you get the blood?" she asked.

Ace flung a fist in the air again.

"He got in a fight," Celeste said.

The sheriff moved his wad of chewing tobacco from inside one cheek to the other. "Before or after he was with the girl in the tent?"

"Before or after the woman?" Celeste questioned.

Ace blinked. He didn't understand. He was scared, and he was having a hard time following the conversation.

"The fight, before or after," Celeste repeated.

Ace shook his head in confusion.

"Wait a minute," Fox said. He stepped up to the jail cell, made a swinging motion with his fist, and then copied Ace's hip thrusting motion. Then he repeated the gestures in the opposite sequence.

A light seemed to go off in Ace's head. He broke into a grin. He thrust his hips, tipped back an invisible drink, then swung his fist.

Fox glanced at Sheriff Tate. "He was with the woman and got in a fight later after drinking at one of the bars."

"You got all that out of that half-wit?"

Just then the door to the cell room swung open and one of Tate's deputies, Addie Morris, walked in. He was sporting a black eye and a swollen lower lip.

"You're late. What the hell happened to you?" Tate barked.

Addie stroked his bruised chin. "Got in a little brawl at that new saloon at the end of Peach. Had to crack a man over the head a few times to get him to see things my way." The clean-cut deputy craned his neck. "Hey, what you doin' with Ace locked up?" He walked toward the cell. "You all right, boy? That was a mean lickin' those men gave you last night."

"You were with Ace last night?" Fox asked.

"Sure. Down to the saloon, like I told the sheriff." Addie hooked his thumb in Ace's direction. "The boy get into more trouble this morning?"

Celeste lowered her hands to her hips in relief. "The woman who set up shop near the tracks was murdered last night. Our good sheriff brought Ace in for questioning."

The deputy scrunched his nose. "How the hell is Ace gonna kill that hurdy-gurdy girl when he was with me all night? We slept together in a livery stable stall."

Everyone's gaze was fixed on Tate.

"Hell," the sheriff muttered under his breath. "You understand I got to bring people in for questioning." He glanced up meaningfully at Fox as he turned the lock on the cell door. "Anyone I might be suspicious of."

"We understand that perfectly, sheriff," Celeste said as she stepped back to allow the door to swing open. "Carrington's just glad they've got a sheriff as fine and upstanding as yourself."

A few minutes later out on the street, Fox, Celeste, Ace, Rosy, and Kate all stood in a tight knot. Joash had reprimanded Ace for his participation in fleshly sins, and then tottered off to see what arrangements he could make for the poor dead woman who no one knew except by the name Lacey.

Celeste laid her hand on Ace's arm. "You all right?" she asked.

He nodded and made a sign with his hand, thanking her.

Celeste knew she had a soft spot for Ace and guessed it was because of her own dear Adam. She understood how frustrating it could be to try and communicate without the benefit of hearing.

"Joash is right, though," she told Ace. "You should stay away from women like that. Stay away from bars. You belong at Kate's, not rippin' up the town with men like Addie. You understand me?"

Ace nodded and hung his head.

She patted his arm again. "Now go on home with you and let Kate or Rosy clean you up."

"Thanks, Celeste." Kate took Ace by the arm. "Now don't be a stranger our way. Just because you're gonna be a rich woman, don't mean you don't have to call on old friends."

"I'll be by." Celeste waved.

Rosy stayed put as Kate and Ace walked away. She appeared dressed to travel in a becoming gray gown with a black overskirt and a black and gray hat. It was probably the most conservative gown Rosy owned.

"Now that Ace's taken care of, Celeste, I gotta say goodbye."

"Goodbye?" Celeste stood beside Fox and stared at Rosy in disbelief. "What do you mean?"

"I mean I'm getting the hell out of here while I still got any life left in me. That's what I mean. And if you had any sense, you'd do the same."

"You're leaving Carrington?" Celeste breathed.

"Aye, and I'd guess Sally won't be far on my heels if that miner of hers is willing to take her away."

"What miner?"

"Didn't she tell you? Sally's found herself a live one. Proclaimed his love and wants to take her out of here once he makes his fortune."

"Don't they all?"

"No. I think Sally's right. This one's different. Anyway." Rosy took Celeste's gloved hand. "I wanted to say goodbye, but I didn't want to make no fuss."

"Oh, Rosy. I'm going to miss you." Celeste released Rosy's hand and flung her arms around her friend's neck. They hugged and she stepped back. "Do you know where you're headed?"

Rosy lifted one meaty shoulder adorned in gray ruffles and grinned. "Far as my change purse will take me, I reckon."

Celeste smiled sadly. "I wish I had some money to give you, but I don't have any cash yet. It takes time to bring up the silver and have it processed."

"I wouldn't take your money anyway."

"Good luck and please let me know you're safe. Get someone to write a letter to me for you, will you? And if you get into money troubles, you send me a telegram. The telegraph office here in Carrington reopened last week."

Rosy nodded, her eyes filled with tears. "If I need you, I'll let you know. Take care of yourself. Good luck with the silver mine."

Celeste stood on the dusty sidewalk and watched Rosy walk away.

"She's wise to go," Fox said. "Tate doesn't know who the murderer is. I'm afraid more women may die before the killer's caught."

Celeste's eyes brimmed with tears as she watched Rosy fade from sight and from her life.

Fox leaned down. "Ah, sweetheart, don't cry." He pulled a handkerchief from his pocket and offered it awkwardly. "She'll be fine."

Celeste didn't know why she felt emotional. "Oh, it's not just Rosy. I know she'll be all right," she sniffed.

"Then what's wrong?" They started back toward Plum Street and home.

It was still early enough that there were few people on the street. Stores were just beginning to open their doors. A man swept the sidewalk in front of his general store. A horse and wagon filled with barrels rolled down the street.

Celeste dabbed at her eyes, hating to show her own weaknesses with tears. "It just seems like nothing is turning out the way I thought it would." She gripped the handkerchief. "I thought hitting silver would be the answer to all my troubles, but it isn't. Someone's killing my friends, we can't get the damned silver out of the ground, you—"

He placed a hand on her shoulder. "I won't put up the money to finance the operation."

She fluttered his handkerchief, damp with her tears. It wasn't just the silver, of course. It was Adam, too. Now that she would be financially secure, she didn't know what she would do with Adam. She had always thought that someday they would live together as mother and son, but now she was having second thoughts. No boy deserved a whore for a mother, even a retired whore. He would probably be better off at school with decent folk.

"I understand about the money," Celeste said, once again tabling her worries over Adam.

"You don't."

They walked under the trees that lined Plum Street, past white picket fences. It was warm, but there was a breeze blowing out of the mountains that made the loose strands of hair that framed her face flutter. "I understand that you don't trust me with that kind of money."

"Celeste—"

She held up her gloved hand. "It only makes sense that a man like you wouldn't loan money to a woman like me. I understand completely. And you're right. You're absolutely—"

"Celeste!"

She halted on the front steps of her porch. "Yes?"

"Will you listen to me for a minute?" He tugged at his

earlobe. "I'm trying to tell you why I won't— why I *can't* loan you the money. Why I can't put any money into the operation myself."

She met his gaze. "Yes?"

"Celeste . . ." He glanced away as if he couldn't look her in the eyes. "Celeste, I can't finance the operation because I don't *have* any money."

Chapter Fifteen

"It's all right, really." She walked up the steps and slipped her key into the lock. "It only makes sense to have your money safely invested. I'm not so sure I would trust banks either." She pushed open the door, and Silver bounded out onto the porch and down the steps.

Fox groaned. "Celeste, you're not listening to me." He closed the door behind them. "I have no money. None. Anywhere. About a dollar and a half in my pocket."

As she lifted her fanchon bonnet from her head, she turned to face him, taken completely by surprise. What did he mean he had no money? Did he mean he *really* had no money? "I don't understand."

He stared at the polished hardwood floor of the foyer. "Hell, I feel so bad about this." He took a deep breath as if struggling for air, and started again. "I mean I'm a poor man. I lied to you, or at least allowed you to believe what wasn't so. I have no cash, no investments, no property, but what you and I share."

She lowered the bonnet to her side, trying to comprehend what Fox was saying. "No money?" she murmured. Fox wasn't the rich San Francisco businessman that John had said he was?

"But what about all those successful business ventures John told me about? What about the homes in New York and San Francisco? What about the investment in the China shipping company?"

"It was all true." He swept his hair off his forehead, sounding defeated. "Once."

"What happened?"

"My partner stole from me, left me with bad debts." He scuffed his boot. "James Monroe was my partner . . . and Amber's brother. I was a fool." He raised his palms lamely. "I trusted him completely, and he was a liar and cheat. Her, too."

"Oh, Fox." Celeste held her hat with both hands, the tulle ribbons dangling to the floor. She wanted to touch him, but she didn't want him to misconstrue her sorrow for him as pity. "Did John know?"

He shook his head, studying a pattern of the wallpaper somewhere beyond her. "No. I didn't tell him. It only happened last year. James took off right after . . . after Amber died."

She hung her hat on an oak hook. "So that's why you didn't come to Carrington before."

"It was a mess. I was trying to keep creditors at bay until I could liquidate what little I had left and pay what James owed them. Because we were partners, his debts became my debts." Fox spoke faster than before, as if he needed to get the confession out while he had the nerve. "And John never said he was dying. He . . . he told me not to come, Celeste." His gaze met hers, his stormy eyes filled with tears. "In the last letter I received before he died, he said he was feeling under the weather but that an angel had come from heaven to care for him. I thought it was just more of his drunken, babbling nonsense. You know he always talked nonsense when he imbibed."

"I'm so sorry." She took the two steps between them and wrapped her arms around him to hug him tightly. "So sorry."

"Oh, it's all right," He spoke nonchalantly, though there was still a catch in his voice. "It was just money. After James and Amber did what they did, the money didn't really seem to matter anymore.''

"I mean about your father." She drew back to look into his eyes. She knew how difficult this must have been for him to share with her. "I'm sorry you weren't here with John. I'm sorry for him. For you both."

"It would have killed him to know I failed him." There was that tremor in his voice again.

She shook her head. "No."

"It was all that ever mattered to him," he argued. "My success. My wealth. The clothes I could pay for, the kind of men and women I could entertain."

"It's not true. He was proud of your success, but he loved you, Fox." She forced him to meet her gaze. "I know. I was here with him. I know the things he said."

Fox brushed his lips against her cheek. "I wish I could believe that. My whole life he pushed me, demanded achievement."

"Because he loved you. He said he always wanted more for you than he ever had."

Fox stared at her through a forelock that dipped over his eyebrows. "Maybe. Guess I'll never know now."

Men just didn't make sense to Celeste. Why was it so easy for them to believe they were unloved, and so hard to convince otherwise? "You need a haircut," she told him. Now she realized that he'd let it grow so long and shaggy because he didn't have the money to pay a barber to cut it. "Want me to do it?"

He seemed relieved that she had changed the subject. A little color returned to his face. "Know what you're doing?"

"I've done a hundred haircuts." She caught his hand and led him down the hallway to the kitchen.

"I don't know if I trust you with a pair of shears in your hand. What if you go mad and stab me to death? I die, and you inherit all the claims and the silver rights."

In the kitchen, she pushed him into one of the kitchen chairs. "Guess you'll have to trust me, won't you?"

He laughed.

"Be right back."

A minute later Celeste returned with a pair of shears and a tortoiseshell comb. She could hardly believe that Fox had lost everything he owned and kept it a secret from her. But she wasn't angry with him. She understood why he did it. As difficult as it was for her to comprehend, he saw his misfortune as failure. *Just like a man.*

She dropped a frilly, white apron over her dress and carried a small bowl of water to the table. The fact that he felt he could tell her the truth made her feel good inside. Maybe there was a chance for some sort of permanent relationship between them. But she didn't dare think about it. Hopes only led to heartbreak. She of all people knew that. "Ready?" She opened and closed the scissors rapidly.

"I suppose." He drew his head back as she brought the shears dangerously close to the tip of his nose. "Just watch those things."

She dipped the comb into the water and combed his hair down straight over his ears and forehead, completely covering his eyes. "Hmmm," she said as she made the first snips. "I wonder if this is how it's done?"

"I thought you said you knew what you were doing?"

Snip. Snip. "I lied," she told him cheerfully.

"Fine. Another business partner who's a liar. I can really pick them, can't I?"

Facing him, she bent over to see if she'd cut a straight line. "I'd never lie to you, or cheat you out of a copper penny," she told him seriously.

"Mmmmm, this is nice." He encircled her waist with his hands and pulled her a little closer to nuzzle her breasts.

She noted that he hadn't responded to her declaration of honesty, but she decided not to press the issue. He'd talked more about himself and his feelings in the last five minutes than he had since he arrived two months ago. She didn't want to push him.

Celeste pushed his hand away as he tried to fondle one of her breasts. "Fox. Stop. Hold still, I'm almost done."

Obediently, he released her, and she sat on his lap to comb his hair to one side. "Much better." She gave a nip here and there. "I can actually see your eyes again."

He rested one hand possessively on her thigh. "Do you shave, too?"

She looked down at him as she smoothed his silky dark hair with one hand. "You really are a trusting soul to put a razor in my hand."

He laughed with her, but then his expression grew serious. "Ah, Celeste," was all he said, but his dark-eyed gaze was filled with emotion.

Her heart swelled. He cared for her. He really did. Celeste knew he was fighting it, but he cared.

She rested her hand on his shoulder and lowered her head to kiss his mouth. "Mmmmm," she sighed. "Best lips this side of the Rockies."

"This side? Both sides," he teased as he licked her lower lip with the tip of his tongue. "Want to see how talented this tongue is as well? I'd have to take you upstairs to show you."

As Celeste lowered her head to kiss him again, she caught a glimpse of a shadow at the back window. She stilled on Fox's lap, and stared at the window and back door. Someone was outside, watching them.

Fox glanced in the same direction. "What is it?"

"Someone looking in the window over the sink."

"Where's Silver?" He slid her off his lap and rose from the chair.

"I don't know." She followed him to the back door. "I think I left him outside."

"He should have barked." Fox drew back the lacy yellow curtain that partially covered the door. "I don't see anyone."

Celeste peered through the window as he drew back. "I could have sworn—" Celeste was startled by a face that appeared only inches from hers on the opposite side of the glass. She jumped back and gave a little squeak of surprise.

Fox turned to her. "Is someone there?"

Celeste touched her hand to her bodice where she could feel her pounding heart. Mrs. Tuttle staring in her window? "Just Mrs. Tuttle," she told Fox. Recovering, she opened the door. "Mrs. Tuttle, you startled me." Celeste couldn't figure for the life of her why the reverend's wife had come to the back door.

"I knocked at the front, but there wasn't an answer." The prim woman with her tight blond curls stepped into the house and placed a cloth-wrapped basket on the worktable. She was dressed in a gray, old-fashioned gown with a square-cut bodice and a diagonal ruffle that emphasized her broad hips and thick waist. "I brought dried apple muffins," she said, keeping her eyes cast downward so as not to look at Fox. "The reverend is waiting for me in the wagon. I . . . I didn't mean to be a bother."

"Oh, it's no bother. Thank you. Thank you so much."

Silver bounded through the door. Celeste was surprised the dog hadn't barked a warning when Mrs. Tuttle walked around the house to the back, but maybe it was because the reverend's wife was no stranger to the dog.

"Would you like to stay for a cup of tea?" Celeste brushed back a lock of red hair that had escaped from her loose chignon. Her cheeks grew warm as she wondered just how much Mrs. Tuttle had seen through the window. It was funny how a woman who had once made her living having sex with men could be embarrassed by the thought of having someone see her kiss a man.

"Oh, no. No time for tea today." Mrs. Tuttle backed her way to the door, her gaze still downcast. The immense ruffles on her bonnet nearly obscured her face, save for the curls that protruded stiffly from each side like bag worms hanging from a tree branch. "Busy, busy, no time. The good reverend has another funeral to do."

"That poor woman. I never met her, but I'm sad just the same." Celeste followed Mrs. Tuttle onto the porch, thinking of Adam. "Did she have any family?"

Mrs. Tuttle lifted her gaze to meet Celeste's for the first

time since her arrival. "I don't know," she said softly. "But considering the circumstances of her death, it would be kinder if they didn't know, don't you think?"

Celeste smiled grimly and nodded. Mrs. Tuttle had a point. She would never want Adam to know what she had done to pay his tuition to the deaf school. "Well, thank you for the muffins. I'm sorry you can't stay for tea. Another time, perhaps."

"I must go." Mrs. Tuttle bustled down the wooden walk that led around to the front of the house. "The reverend's waiting."

Celeste waved, walked back into the kitchen, and closed the door behind her.

Fox grabbed her around the waist and spun her in his arms. "Is the Mrs. Rev. Creepy gone?"

She laughed and pushed on his shoulders to make him put her down. "I don't know what got into her, staring in my window like that. Do you think she saw me sitting on your lap kissing you?"

He pushed her gently against the floral wallpaper and kissed the pulse of her throat. "Serve her right if she saw worse." He kissed a particularly sensitive place on her neck. "She had to be standing in your flowers to look in that window over the dry sink, the old badger."

"You can't talk about my friends like that." She kissed him playfully on the lips as she brushed back the damp hair off his forehead.

"And if I do?" He lifted a dark eyebrow comically. He acted as if his earlier confession had lightened him by ten years and twenty pounds. "How will you punish me?"

She laughed sensually as she took his hand in hers. "Let me take you upstairs and show you."

Enjoying being the seductress without having to fake it, Celeste led Fox up the stairs and into her room. Inside the doorway she faced him and wrapped her arms around his neck. She pulled him closer and was rewarded by the hard, hot sensation of his hungry mouth against hers.

In the last few weeks since they had begun having intimate relations, she had been careful to remain passive for fear that he would think she was playing the same part she had once played with customers. This morning, however, she wanted to make love to him the way she did in her dreams. She didn't just want to accept his attentions, but return them, initiate them.

Fox sighed as she ran her hand over his clean denim shirt, then lower to the button of his denim jeans. She could feel his muscles relaxing beneath her touch. His hair was still damp; he smelled of shaving soap and sunshine-dried clothing. She breathed deeply, delighting in the masculine scent that was his alone.

Sighing, she parted her lips as Fox thrust his tongue into her mouth. The taste of him, the smell of him, the feel of his hands pressed into her back sent shudders of warmth throughout her body. For the first time in her life she felt truly cared for . . . almost loved.

Of course she didn't know exactly what it would feel like to be loved, because no one had ever loved her. John had come close; he had worshipped her, coveted her, liked her, but never truly loved her.

Celeste's and Fox's tongues tangled in a sweet, wet dance as he found the pearl buttons of her blue and green polonaise gown. With nimble fingers, he unbuttoned the row to reveal her lacy nainsook camisole. Feeling secure in his arms, she found the courage to open the button of his pants.

Fox moaned with encouragement. ''Yes,'' he whispered as she tentatively slipped her hand beneath the waistband. ''Touch me, Celeste. It's all I think about. Touch me . . .''

Fox pushed Celeste's gown down over her shoulders and tugged the camisole over her head. She broke from a deep kiss to step out of the dress, her red petticoat, and crinoline. She stood in the bright sunshine of the morning in nothing but shoes, embroidered stockings, pantaloons, and her corset. Strong summer light poured through the open panes, and dust motes fluttered in the warm rays.

Celeste had never entirely undressed for her customers. She

preferred the lamp out as well. But with Fox, she wanted to share herself, all of herself. She instinctively knew that she would never care for another man as she cared for him. This was her one chance at happiness, no matter how brief it might be.

Celeste kicked off her shoes as she unhooked the horn buttons of his shirt. She caressed the hard, muscular flesh of his chest, teasing the crisp mat of dark hair. Playfully, she tugged at one of his nipples with her teeth and laved it with her tongue. She found his moan of pleasure—and the idea that she could bring him the same physical responses that he brought her—delightful.

"Celeste," he murmured in her ear.

"Fox." She stroked his cheek with her palm as she studied his suntanned face. His eyes were half-closed, his voice thick with desire for her.

She kissed an invisible path down the center of his chest, lowering herself to her knees on the cotton rag rug she'd sewn from old clothing. He pulled the tortoise hairpins from her hair, and it fell in a thick wave of red over her shoulders and down her back. It felt so good to feel his fingers entwined in her hair.

"You have the most beautiful hair, Celeste." He pushed the heavy locks over her shoulders so that he could see her face. "Like an angel's."

"I thought angels have blond hair," she whispered, basking in his poetic compliment.

"Not the angels in my head. They're all redheads with green eyes."

They kissed again, a long passionate kiss that whispered of sorrow and forgiveness.

Celeste could have sat all morning in the sunlight and kissed and been kissed, but there was a heat inside her that was building, fanning out. She wanted more than to be cuddled. She needed Fox in a way she was just beginning to understand that women needed men.

Boldly, Celeste tugged his denims down over his hips, and he sprang magically from the worn fabric, thick and pulsing.

Hesitantly she took his shaft in her hand, surprised by how warm and soft the skin was. He moaned aloud.

She stroked him, taking her time to study the male part of him in the bright sunlight. All those other men in her past seemed meaningless now. Suddenly she was in a world all bright and new and fascinating. She tested the length of him for sensitivity, first with the pad of her thumb, then with the tip of her tongue.

Celeste felt Fox sway and press his hands on her shoulders to steady himself. A sound came from his lips, half groan, half moan. He breathed heavily, panting indistinguishable words of encouragement.

She looked up at him. "Is this all right?" she whispered, half-teasing, half-unsure of herself. "Do you like it?"

"Oh, Celeste," he said thickly, his eyes closed. "More. Don't stop now."

She lowered her head, roused by his words. With a mixture of surprising inexperience and age-old instinct, she stroked him with her hands and with her tongue, taking her time to discover what he found most pleasurable.

Finally her attention brought him to his knees, so that he knelt facing her, his pants tangled around his ankles. "You want me to stop?" she whispered against his lips.

He opened his dark-pooled eyes to look into hers. "I want to make love to you, Celeste." He pulled her close to him and released the laces of her corset. "Now," he insisted urgently. "Right now."

As she unbuckled and slipped out of her corset, his hands found her swollen breasts, and it was her turn to sigh with pleasure. Ripples of white hot desire coursed through her. Touching him the way she had, had not only excited him, but her as well. She was damp and throbbing with longing for him.

Fox kissed her deeply and Celeste thought to suggest they move onto the bed, but the idea was gone in an instant as his lips found the puckered tips of her nipples and sent intense pulses through her torso.

Fox pressed Celeste back onto the soft, twisted rag rug, and she lifted her hips to allow him to remove her pantaloons and shoes and stockings. She laid back on the rug unashamed of her nakedness and watched as he shed his own clothes. She reached out to him and spread her legs, wanting him, needing to feel him deep inside before she burst.

Fox lowered his body over hers and slipped inside her. She rose in sweet anguish to meet his first thrust and closed her eyes that filled with tears of joy. Fox caught her hands with his and pushed them back onto the rug beside her head, their fingers laced. He thrust urgently and she rose to match his rhythm, almost frenzied in her need for fulfillment.

"Celeste, Celeste," he whispered in her ear as he panted and pressed fervent kisses to her perspiration-dampened cheek.

Celeste was so filled with the excitement of Fox's touch and the feeling of his caring, if not love, that she thought she would burst with happiness. And yet still she was not satisfied. The heat of desire was still inside her, building, scorching, demanding release until she thought she couldn't stand another sweet, tortured stroke. And then, her muscles contracted and shards of shiny white ecstasy fanned from the center of her being, outward. Shivering, shuddering, she clung to Fox and rode the waves of fulfillment. Fox gave a final thrust and groaned as he spilled his seed into her.

Celeste held Fox in her arms and stroked his bare back. After a moment he rolled beside her. Both stared at the white punched-tin ceiling for a moment. Then she giggled.

"What?" he said, his voice still warm and husky.

Her giggle burst into laughter.

"What?" he insisted. He rolled onto his side so that he could see into her eyes. He rested one broad palm on the flat of her belly. "What's so funny?"

"Me," she giggled. "You. The two of us, rolling on the floor." She laughed until tears came to her eyes.

Fox glanced at the doorway where Silver sat, his head cocked. "Makes you wonder what the dog is thinking, doesn't it?"

She laughed again as she rolled onto her side to face him.

Fox rested his head on his arm and stared into her eyes.

"Celeste?" he said when their laughter subsided. "Can . . . can I ask you a question? And you have to promise you won't get angry."

She had an idea what the question would be. She tucked a lock of his damp, dark hair behind his ear. "Only if I can ask you one."

"All right." He stroked her bare arm. "You go first."

She shook her head. "Oh, no. You started it. You go first."

He took a deep breath, but didn't break eye contact. "This . . . here . . . now . . . when we make love . . ."

"Yes?"

He brushed his knuckles against her chin in a gentle caress. "Is it . . . different? Different than with my father, with all the others that came before me?"

Chapter Sixteen

Celeste rested her head on the rug and stared at the ceiling. "I'm sorry. I shouldn't have asked. Never mind. It . . . it was childish."

She turned to gaze into his eyes. "No. It's never been like this for me before. Not with anyone," she said firmly. "And certainly not with your father." Her hand itched to touch him, but she kept it at her side, feeling very fragile. She understood now how truly difficult it had been for Fox to tell her about the loss of his fortune, because suddenly she felt the same way. Her stomach tightened in a knot. "All those men, they never meant anything." She brushed her left breast with her fingertips. She knew she was taking a chance by saying this, by revealing what she felt, what she was afraid of feeling. "Because I never cared for them here," she whispered. "I never cared about them at all. It was money. A job. Survival. Nothing more."

He was silent for what seemed to her like an eternity.

"Do you believe me?" she asked.

He lowered his chin in a half nod. "Yes."

She smiled and slipped her hand into his. "No one has ever cared how I felt before. What pleased me. Not even your father.

You have to believe that. He was a customer and then a friend, but never really a lover.''

Fox brought her hand to his lips and kissed her knuckles. ''Thank you for telling me what I needed to hear.''

''I'm glad it's what you wanted to hear, but that's not why I said it.''

''I know.'' He kissed her hand again. ''All right. Now your question.''

She studied the ceiling. ''Did you love Amber?''

''Yes,'' he answered without hesitation.

She couldn't resist a twinge of jealousy. She wanted to know the truth and he'd told her. She had no right to be upset, but the idea that he had once loved a woman hurt deeply. She wished she could have been that woman.

''I loved her in the same superficial way I think she loved me.'' He held her hand in his, but didn't look at her. They both studied the ceiling intently. ''We enjoyed each other's company. I liked her beauty. She liked my money.''

''Apparently she liked it very well, if she was in on her brother's plans to steal from you and leave you with all those debts.''

He rubbed his face with his free hand. ''I was an idiot, looking for the wrong kind of person to care about me.''

She felt a tightening in her chest. ''The wrong kind of person? What do you mean?''

He faced her, still on his back. ''I met Amber in a saloon in San Francisco. She was a dancer and a whore.'' He grimaced. ''Ah, I didn't say that right. I shouldn't have—''

Celeste closed her eyes and groaned. ''No wonder you're gun-shy. She took you for everything you had.'' She hesitated for a moment. ''But we're not all alike you know. You can't take a dozen whores, throw us in a bag, and not know the difference between us. We're just like everyone else. Some good, some bad, some a little of each.''

He didn't say anything.

Celeste knew she couldn't change his opinion overnight when the woman had used him so badly. A part of her hated that woman, hated what she had done to Fox, hated the way she had altered all their lives. "I would never cheat you out of any of the money that will come from the silver mine," she said softly, fiercely.

He kissed her shoulder and gently disengaged himself from her. "Climb into bed and I'll bring you some tea and bread with jam. I'm starved. We'll have a picnic."

So he didn't trust her. Not quite, though he was gentleman enough not to come out and say so.

"Bed?" Suddenly Celeste felt shy, naked in front of him, but resisted the urge to cover herself. "It's mid-morning. We need to get to the mine. Titus can't run the entire operation on his own."

"I sent word to Titus that we'd be there this afternoon. Now go ahead. Get into bed"—he winked—"and I promise I'll make it worth your while."

Celeste watched him leave the room, his firm buttocks flexing as he walked. Then she climbed into her bed to wait for him and his promise.

"Afternoon, ma'am."

Celeste glanced up from under her bonnet tied beneath her chin with a tulle scarf. Her attention shifted from a piece of fabric she was considering in the mercantile store, to a dapper man tipping his bowler hat to her.

"Good . . . good afternoon." She had become careful about speaking to strangers in Carrington. It seemed as if everyone knew she was the female partner in the MacPhearson Fortune strike, and everyone wanted something out of her. Miners approached her on the streets wanting jobs. Bankers offered to invest her money as they sat in the church pew behind her on Sundays. One enterprising young man, wanting her to see his new silver detecting device, had found his way into her backyard and approached her as she hung her pantaloons to dry.

The man replaced his hat on his head. He appeared to be in

his late thirties, well groomed, with clean hands. He spoke like an educated man. "Brent Trevor, ma'am."

She smiled, nodded, and glanced back at the pinstripe fabric. She had a little cash still in the bank from her inheritance, and she was considering having a suit made for Fox as a surprise.

"I . . . I was wondering if you might help me, ma'am," the stranger continued. "Which gloves would you suggest?" He held two pairs of ladies limeric gloves, one black, one ivory, both with fine stitching and flower ornamentation at the wrists.

She lifted an eyebrow. "For yourself?"

He laughed. "No. For my mother, actually. I've just arrived in Carrington. I've bought several old land claims near the MacPhearson strike. I intend to be here a while, so I thought I might send my mother a gift."

Celeste glanced at the gloves. His question seemed innocent enough. He apparently didn't realize who she was. "Would they be for travel, or dress?"

"Travel, I should think. I'm hoping that once I'm settled in the house I've just purchased on Plum Street, she'll come and stay with me."

Plum Street. He had to have bought one of the vacant houses near hers. They would be neighbors. "I would definitely go with the black then, shows less dust, and you know how dusty the trains and stagecoaches can be."

He smiled handsomely and tipped his hat. "Many thanks Miss . . ."

She hesitated to give her name, but the man was so pleasant, and he was buying gloves for his mother. "Kennedy, Celeste Kennedy."

"Very nice to meet you, Miss Kennedy, and thank you for your assistance." He started to turn away and then turned back. "Heavens, don't tell me you're *the* Miss Kennedy, half owner of the MacPhearson Fortune?"

She gave a quick smile, looking up to see if anyone had heard him. She was hoping to get in and out of the store without having to turn down any miners. Was this man going to ask something of her as well? "I am."

"Well, I'm very pleased to meet you. Good day." He smiled, tipped his hat, and walked away.

Celeste watched as he carried the gloves to the front of the store to make his purchase. Her fame was making her suspicious of everyone. He was a nice gentleman simply looking for a woman's opinion on gloves, nothing more.

Celeste bought the pinstriped fabric for Fox, and a nice brocade for herself. Fall would be coming and winter right on its tail. Despite the heat, she knew that, all too soon, she'd be grateful for a warm gown and woolen stockings. She also purchased a sturdy pair of boots she could wear beneath her dresses out on the claim. After making a few more small purchases, she left the store, balancing several boxes and brown paper parcels tied with string in her arms.

"Heavens, how can you see where you're going? A clerk should have carried these home for you." A man took a box and a large package from her hands so that she could once again see the sidewalk ahead of her. It was Brent Trevor, the man she'd met in the store.

"Mr. Trevor, thank you."

"Let me walk you home."

She hesitated. He didn't act like the others who offered to do her favors. He just seemed like a gentleman. Still, she was cautious. "That's really not necessary."

"It's no trouble. I'm going in the same direction."

"You are?" She thought for a moment. Truthfully, he was right. She would have a difficult time getting all these parcels home without dropping any into the muddy street.

"I'm headed for Plum Street."

She must have given him a strange look, because he went on quickly. "The gentleman at the bank, from whom I purchased the house, said Plum Street was very quiet and that I'd be well pleased with my neighbors. He mentioned your name in passing."

"Oh." She nodded as she walked beside him. "No harm in that, I guess."

Mr. Trevor glanced sideways at her. "It's all right, I understand your uneasiness with me."

"You do?"

"I suppose with the silver strike you've been pestered by all sorts of people."

"Sometimes."

"Everyone wants a job. A piece of your interest in the mine."

She sighed. "Exactly. I've been hiring, but I just don't have enough work yet. I can't hire everyone who comes to the site."

"Well, I'll be hiring shortly as well, so feel free to send some of the miners to me. I've opened a small office on Apple Street. We should be set up by week's end."

"Thank you. I feel badly turning away men who've come so far. It will be nice to send them packing with a little encouraging information."

As they turned onto shady Plum Street, Celeste found herself talking easily with Mr. Trevor. He knew a great deal about the silver mining industry. Apparently he hadn't heard of her sordid past and spoke to her with respect. He obviously found her attractive by the way he looked at her, but he was nothing but polite and considerate.

Celeste stopped at her front porch and held out her arms to accept the remainder of her packages. "Thank you so much for your help."

"You're welcome. Have a good day." He didn't ask to come in or indicate he expected any further contact with her. He tipped his hat with a slight bow and started back the way they'd come.

Celeste slipped into the house where Fox and her dog would be waiting for her.

"Seven-card stud, ladies and gents," Big Nose Kate said as she dealt.

"Wild?" Celeste asked as she picked up her cards.

"Nothin' but me, sweetheart."

Kate laughed and Sally, Titus, Celeste, and Sheriff Tate

laughed with her. Ace didn't laugh because he didn't hear the joke. Reverend Tuttle pretended not to hear.

"So how's life in the big silver mine?" Tate asked, his words slightly garbled by the wad of chew in his mouth.

Celeste retrieved another card. "Hell. Nothing is as easy as it sounds. We've got a tunnel that keeps flooding. We can't get the ore up and out of the shaft as quickly as we need to. The freighters won't haul it overland, and we need to have men guarding the claims twenty-four hours a day to keep claim jumpers away."

"Oh!" Tate moaned dramatically. "The troubles with bein' rich. We all feel so sorry for you, dear."

Celeste frowned. "You're right, I ought to count my blessings." She studied her hand. "So, Sally," she said casually. "What's this I hear about you gettin' yourself a man?"

Silky Sally giggled. She was dressed in a slim lilac gown with her hair tied up in tiny rags all over her head. "Name's Noah. Noah Patterson." She peered over the edge of her cards. "Says he wants to marry me." She giggled again. "Brings me presents. Pays for my whole night come Saturdays."

Celeste arched her eyebrows. "Goodness. Is he serious?"

She lifted one delicate shoulder. "I'm hopin'."

"Well, ain't that sweet?" Kate complained as she folded. "I won't have any of my old crew then, unless I'm plannin' on putting Ace here in silk stockings."

Everyone at the table laughed but Ace and Joash.

"Now, Kate." Celeste tossed in two coins. "I understand you've brought in two new ladies just this week to go with the three that came last week."

"It's not the same." Kate took a big bite of Mrs. Tuttle's peach turnover. Flaky crumbs clung to the corners of her painted mouth. "Not the same, and you know it. It'll never be the same without you, and Rosy, and if Sally goes and—"

"And Tall Pearl dead," Sally said softly.

Everyone turned their gazes on Sally.

"I got me a mind to get out of this town while the gettin's good," she continued.

Celeste touched her friend's arm and wondered if Sally had a premonition. The killer was preying heavily on Celeste's mind these days, keeping her up at night, as Fox's ghosts did. "Are you afraid, Sally?"

"Not really." She folded. "I just decided I want to change my occupation. I want to be the wife of a wealthy miner."

"Because if you are afraid, you should get out," Celeste said. "Get out now."

"Hey!" Kate glared at Celeste from across the table, half in jest, half-serious. "That's my livelihood you're shoo-flyin'. Sally's my most popular girl."

Celeste glanced back at Sally. Titus had taken the pot with a sweet pair of kings. "I'm serious. If you want out, you pack up today. Bunk with your man or come to my house."

"Aw . . . that's sweet of you." Sally smiled her angel smile. "But I ain't ready to go anywhere yet. I got my Noah, but I still got my regulars, too. I want to leave this place with some money of my own. I don't want Noah ever throwin' it in my face that he rescued a poor girl from makin' a livin' on her back."

The sheriff chuckled as he shuffled the cards. "A man willing to marry a whore." He shook his head with a sneer. "What's this damned world coming to?"

Chapter Seventeen

With a sigh, Celeste sank into the settee in the parlor and put one dusty boot up on the arm, not caring if she soiled the emerald velvet. She rubbed the persistent ache in the small of her back. She'd been working at the mine since dawn.

Fox was still there. There'd been a problem with the pumps that brought the water out of the tunnel, and it had to be repaired before mining could be resumed. The mine had had to be evacuated twice because of the near boiling water that kept rising from the rock.

She sighed and brushed back the stray hair that fell from her chignon and over her face. She rubbed her itchy nose. She was filthy. Even though she rarely actually went down into the mine, she came home each night covered in a thin layer of dust. It was in her hair and up her nose. She could taste it in her mouth. Celeste appreciated the financial security the mine would provide, but she was quickly discovering that she didn't care for the business itself.

The work was filthy and dangerous to the miners. Though she and Fox paid their workers very well, she still felt guilty for sending them down into that steamy black hole. Twenty-four hours a day, they worked in nothing but cut-off long johns, digging and hauling her silver ore in temperatures that sometimes rose five degrees with every thousand feet of tunnel. Last week Fox had ordered that ice be shipped in each day. A room had been built off one of the veins of the tunnel to hold the ice. Men could go there to cool off, get a drink, and find their breath.

Silver wandered into the parlor and Celeste patted her thigh. "Come here, boy. Come on, old boy. Are you as tired as I am?" Though she and Fox took the dog with them to the mine each day, if Celeste left first, Silver always accompanied her home for safety. Fox insisted on it.

The dog licked her hand and wagged his tail with delight as she stroked his back.

"You poor thing. You're as dirty as I am. Better stop riding those buckets down with Fox."

The yellow mutt slumped against the settee as she scratched behind his ears.

"Better stay up above with me," she crooned. "Too hot down there, and dirty. Don't you know those men have explosives? A doggy like you ought to have better sense."

Silver's ears perked and he turned away from her to look toward the doorway that led into the foyer.

Celeste glanced up. Maybe Fox was home. He had said he wouldn't be much longer, but he'd sent her home because she looked so tired.

"Someone there?" she asked the dog.

Silver rose off the blue and green carpet sprinkled with roses. A knock sounded at the door.

Celeste frowned. Who in heaven could that be? It was too late for anyone from Kate's to be calling. They were working. And Fox didn't knock. He had a key.

"Coming," she called out as she dragged herself off the settee. She hoped it wasn't another miner looking for work, but she knew it was. Not only did they come to the mine, but now that it had been operating for three months, they were finding her home as well.

"I'm sorry," she said as she unlatched the door. "We're not hiring. I can give you the name of a gentleman who—" As she swung open the door she was surprised to see Brent Trevor standing on her porch with fall flowers in one hand and his hat in the other. She wasn't really in the mood for a visitor, but at least it wasn't another man looking for work.

"Good evening, Miss Kennedy."

She leaned on the doorjamb.

Silver stood beside her in the doorway and growled deep in his throat.

Celeste lowered her hand to the dog's head. "It's all right, boy." She smiled tiredly at Brent. "Good evening."

She'd run into Mr. Trevor often in the last few weeks. Occasionally, he came by her office or stopped by the mine. She saw him at church, in the stores, and on the street. He was always pleasant and friendly—a little friendlier than Celeste thought was perhaps appropriate. Surely he had heard by now that she lived, and no doubt slept, with her business partner, Fox MacPhearson. Surely he knew by now that she was a tainted woman. What would his mother think?

"These are for you." He thrust out the flowers.

She took them. "Well, thank you. How kind."

He glanced up at the sky. "Beautiful night tonight. Cool air coming out of the mountains. I think winter may come early."

She glanced up at the starry sky. It was a beautiful night. "Um, would you care to come in?" She didn't really feel like company. She felt like a cup of tea and a biscuit, a warm bath, and bed, preferably in Fox's arms. But she didn't want to be rude.

"Well, just for a moment. I wanted to stop by and see how that piece of equipment I sent over was working out."

She stepped into the foyer and Trevor followed. Silver backed up, his ears pricked, his teeth bared. Though he made no sound, it was obvious he didn't care for Mr. Trevor.

Celeste thought it strange that he hadn't contacted Fox about the equipment. After all, Fox had made the arrangements. Celeste had only heard about it through him. "I appreciate you sending us the bit. We've got another one coming by week's end.'' She set the flowers down on the shelf beneath the mirror that hung in the foyer and smoothed her dusty gown. "You'll have to excuse my appearance. I've just now arrived home. Would you care to sit down?'' She motioned to the parlor, half hoping he'd decline.

"I'd be charmed.''

He followed her into the parlor and took a seat on the settee, making an event of leaving room for her.

Celeste chose the horsehair chair opposite the settee. There was something about Brent Trevor that made her uncomfortable, though she had no idea why. He was such a pleasant man. Once upon a time she would have welcomed such a man's attention. A benefactor like Trevor could, in her working days, have made a woman like her quite comfortable. Occasionally a whore even caught such a man for a husband. But after knowing Fox, after caring for him as she did, Celeste knew she could never be happy with a man like Trevor.

"Working at the mine again today, you say?'' Trevor removed his thin leather gloves. "A pretty woman like yourself has no business at a mine. What kind of man is Mr. MacPhearson that he demands such of you?''

Celeste looked up through a veil of lashes. "I choose to go to the mine each day, Mr. Trevor.''

"Oh, please.'' He raised a palm. "Call me Brent. And I'd be flattered if you'd allow me to call you by your Christian name. Celeste. How heavenly.''

Celeste had spent too much time with men not to know when they crossed the line between a genuine compliment and false flattery. That was what annoyed her about Brent. He didn't seem quite genuine. Celeste smiled coolly. "As I was saying, *Brent.* I go to the site because it's half mine, as is half the responsibility. It would be unfair to my partner if I didn't accept that responsibility. And you know yourself that the operation always runs smoother when the owner is there.''

"True. True.'' He set down his hat and gloves beside him on the settee. "But a woman in such a filthy, crude environment.

Why Mother hasn't been to my mine once since her arrival in Carrington.''

"And how is your digging going? I saw that you sank a shaft the first week . . . very close to my property line.''

She could have sworn he flinched.

He smiled grandly and chuckled. "Now aren't you the clever one, Celeste? And so knowledgeable about the business. A refreshing quality in a woman so beautiful. So . . . engaging.''

Celeste glanced at the clock that ticked over the mantel. It was after nine and she was exhausted.

He looked at the clock. "Oh, goodness, it is late, isn't it? And I suppose you are tired after your long day.''

She rose. "I'm sorry not to be good company, but I'm rather worn out.'' She walked toward the foyer, leaving Trevor with no choice but to politely follow.

He caught up to her at the door. "It was so nice to see you, Celeste. So nice to spend a few moments with an educated woman like yourself. Since my arrival in Carrington, I've not had the pleasure of the company of women like yourself, except for Mother, of course.'' He sighed. "And I do so yearn for an evening's respite from the work at the mine.''

Celeste opened the door for him. In her boots, she was two inches taller than he was. He halted in the door very close to her. Too close to suit Celeste.

"Which brings me to my actual reason for this call.''

Ah ha! she thought. *At last the reason.* "And that is?''

"Why, to ask you to the show and dinner Friday night. I understand The Grand Hotel has brought in a fine troupe of actors and that the comedy is quite amusing.'' He tried to take her hand, but she was too fast for him.

Celeste tucked her hands neatly behind her. "I'm sorry, Brent, but I can't possibly.'' She smiled sweetly. Never give a reason, her well-bred mother had taught her. Simply decline a gentleman's offer with a sweet smile.

He glanced down at his shiny black shoes. She had taken him unaware. The little twit had apparently expected her to melt in his arms.

"If you have another engagement—"

"I'm sorry, but I'm"—she cleared her throat delicately and then looked directly into his eyes—"unavailable." She could see that he was obviously annoyed with her now.

"Mr. MacPhearson?"

"Yes."

He pressed his hand to the doorjamb. "Might I speak frankly, Celeste?"

She crossed her arms over her chest. "Please."

"It is not that I have not heard of your . . . past. I know full well where you once worked and what your vocation was."

She made no response.

"I've come as an honest, humble man. Your past is unimportant to me. Unlike Mr. MacPhearson, though, my intentions are honorable. Do you understand what I'm trying so delicately to say?"

Celeste wasn't sure whether she was annoyed or amused. "No, I don't think I do."

"I'm saying that I'm interested in courting you . . . with honest intentions. I would not expect any display of your *affection* without proper . . . without marriage, Miss Kennedy."

She almost laughed aloud. "I'm sorry, Brent. I'm flattered by your honesty and your interest, but I can't accept this invitation or any future invitations." She smiled. "I hope you understand."

He forced a smile in return and dropped his hat on his head. "I . . . I see."

"But thank you for the flowers," she called after him as she crossed the porch. "And do call again, when Mr. MacPhearson is available to visit as well."

Brent's head was down so low that he nearly collided with Fox at the end of the sidewalk.

"Trevor!"

Started, Brent glanced up. "Mr.—Mr. MacPhearson." He tipped his hat nervously as if he'd been caught with his hand in the licorice jar. "I . . . I was just calling on Miss Kennedy. Good to see you." He passed Fox. "Good evening."

Fox met her in the foyer and closed the door behind him. "What the hell was he doing here?" He glanced at the flowers on the shelf. "And why's he bringing you flowers?" He yanked off his hat and tossed it onto the hook. He was as dusty and tired as she was.

Celeste smiled, secretly pleased. Fox was jealous. Celeste had always despised any sign of jealousy in a man in the past, but this was different. Maybe because she'd never before wanted to be possessed. "Oh, he just wanted to see how the drill bit was working out."

"And he couldn't have asked me when he came by to see me an hour ago?" He rubbed his temples tiredly. "He must have hightailed it here to beat me."

So Trevor had known she would be here alone. How interesting. "Oh," she said casually. "He also came by to ask me to The Grand."

"He what?" Fox's head snapped up.

"He asked me to the show and to dinner. He was quite gallant." She batted her eyelashes.

Fox glared. "You accept?"

She laughed. "No."

"Good. Because the man is an imbecile, and I don't trust him as far as I can toss him. His ore is coming up awfully clean and his shaft is awfully close to ours."

"You think he's stealing from us underground? Could he have tunneled that far already?"

"I don't think he could make it that far, but my guess is that he's considering it. He's been too nosy about what's been coming out of our shaft, and which direction we're tunneling next."

She sighed, reached out, and rubbed his shoulder. Fox often worked with the men in the mine, shoveling ore beside them. Occasionally he set the blasts of dynamite that drove a tunnel deeper. The danger of the work constantly worried Celeste, but Fox felt that he couldn't ask the men to do anything he wasn't willing to do himself.

"Want something to eat before you bathe?" she asked, still rubbing his tired shoulders.

He shook his head. "Nah. Too tired to be hungry." His gaze met hers. "I can't believe he asked you to go to The Grand with him!"

"He said I was an engaging female."

"Right. What the flea was thinking was that you were about to become a *rich* female," he said sarcastically.

"Why, Fox MacPhearson, I think you're jealous."

He grasped her around the waist and pulled her roughly to him. "Damned right, I am." He kissed the pulse of her throat where he knew she liked to be kissed.

"Oh, don't, Fox. I'm filthy."

He kissed a trail along her collarbone as he pulled her double-breasted bodice down over her shoulders. "Not any dirtier than I am."

"I know." She struggled, but only halfheartedly. "But I don't like you to see me like this. I probably smell as bad as those miners."

"I can remedy that." He took her hand and led her down the hallway.

"You can?" She wondered what had gotten into him now.

"Water heated in the hot storage tank?"

"Yes. I was getting ready to take a bath when Trevor stopped by."

He pushed into the bathroom that was as modern as any in Denver. It had been John's pride and joy.

"I *must* be dirty if you're this insistent on seeing I get a bath."

Inside, Fox took her by the arms and backed her into a chair. He went down on one knee. "Give me your boots."

With a button hook, he unhooked the long row of buttons and eased the black and brown leather boot off her tired foot. He rolled off her stocking and tossed it over his head.

She sighed with pleasure as he massaged the arch of her foot. "Oh, that feels wonderful." She leaned back in the chair and closed her eyes.

He removed the other boot and stocking, and rubbed the top of her bare foot and then the bottom, moving upward to her calf. As he kneaded her tired muscles, she began to relax.

"You shouldn't spoil me like this," she teased. "I'll expect it every night."

He took her hands and pulled her to her feet. As he undid the buttons on the bodice of her gray and blue work gown, he kissed the bare skin above her muslin camisole. She rested her hand on his broad shoulders and stepped out of the gown.

Next came the camisole and French-buckled corset. She sighed as the restraint was removed and her breasts fell free in his warm hands, not caring that his hands were dirty. His attentions were exquisite.

Fox removed her underskirt and crinoline and tossed them on the floor with her soiled clothing. He turned the faucet that ran from the hot water tank to the porcelain claw tub, then the knob that brought cool water from a holding tank hand-pumped from the well.

Fox helped Celeste to step out of her pantaloons and into the tub. The warm and cold water swirled at her feet. She started to sit down, but he stopped her.

"Not yet," he said quietly, a hint of mystery in his voice. "Stand and I'll pour the water over you."

When she looked at him doubtfully, he added, "Just wait, you'll like it."

He filled a small china washbowl with water from the tub and drizzled it over her breasts. She sighed as the heated water streamed over her nipples and down her belly. Her nipples puckered in response to the warm water and cooler air. It felt strange to stand here in front of him and let him bathe her as she had bathed Adam when he was a baby. But it was a good strange. It made her feel pampered. Almost *loved*.

There was that elusive word again. That word that floated in her mind. The word she'd sworn she would never associate with a man again.

Fox poured water down her back. He took a cotton washrag and soaped it with a perfumed bar of soap. With the wet, frothy rag he scrubbed first her arms, then her neck and breasts, her legs. He asked her to turn around and he scrubbed her back and buttocks. The rough, wet rag and slick soap sent shivers of sensation through her body. Every inch of skin he stroked tingled with warmth.

Covered in a soft film of perfumed soap, she turned at his urging to face him again. "Now the most important part," he murmured.

The small room smelled of perfumed soap, damp clothing, and of him. She reached out to caress his bare chest with one soapy hand, but he pushed it down. "Keep your hands to yourself, lady. I'm busy." He seemed to sense how erotic it was to stand and be touched without being permitted to touch.

He spread her legs gently with one hand, dipped the rag into the warm tub water, and bathed the bed of red curls at the apex of her thighs.

Celeste closed her eyes and moaned softly. The water, the washrag . . . his hands felt so good. She was so relaxed, and yet a spark of warmth glowed in her belly. A spark of desire.

Fox filled the washbowl with clean water and slowly rinsed her off.

"Can I sit down now?" she asked, her eyes closed. Her knees felt pleasantly weak.

He plugged the drain so that fresh water began to fill the tub. "You want to?"

"If I don't, I'm going to fall over."

"Can't have that, can we?"

He took her in his arms and helped her ease into the tub. The water that ran off her breasts splattered his bare, dirty chest. She laughed as she sat down, wiping suds off one of his nipples. "Want to join me?" she asked, feeling sultry.

"In a minute. Now your hair."

Before she could say anything, he poured a washbowl of water over her head.

She laughed and sputtered as the warm water ran in her eyes and ears and mouth.

He dumped another bowl of water over her head.

She pushed back a thick hank of wet hair. ''Trying to drown me?''

''Never.'' Fox dropped to his knees, leaned over the tub, rubbed the bar of soap between his hands, and began to wash her hair.

Celeste closed her eyes again. His fingers felt so good on her scalp. As he moved his fingers in small circles moving outward, she sank further in the tub.

Celeste could have laid in the tub with Fox touching her like this forever. Here she felt insulated from the world. Here there were no worries about the silver mine or the wealth it would bring or what she would do with the money. Here she didn't have to worry about where she would go or if she would take Adam with her. Here there was no murderer stalking her friends. Here there was just Fox and her and the warmth of their companionship.

''Ready for a rinse?'' he asked too soon.

''Mm hm.'' She was too comfortable to speak.

Fox poured several bowls of water over her head and then moved away from her.

She opened her eyes to see him disrobing.

''Going to join me?'' she asked, catching bubbles of soap that floated by.

''If you can make room.''

She smiled at him over the rim of the tub. He had just slipped his dirty denims down his long, muscular legs. He wanted her . . .

''There will always be room for you here.'' She leaned back in the tub. She hadn't meant to say it that way . . . to make him think she was looking for anything permanent between them. That she wanted him to stay forever.

But she did.

As Celeste watched Fox cross the bathroom, she realized she did want him here in her tub for the rest of their days. Here in her life.

''Slide forward.''

She did as he said and he slipped into the tub behind her.

She was glad that John had insisted they order the largest tub he could find in Denver. How ironic that she would share it with his son.

Celeste sat up for a moment as Fox dipped the washrag in the water and scrubbed his chest and arms. Then she took the rag from him and leaned back against his chest. He raised one knee out of the water and she scrubbed his leg.

As Celeste washed his legs leisurely, she could feel his engorged member pressed against the bare skin of her lower back. The feel of him made her warm and tingly there below the water.

"This is the life, Celeste." He leaned back and she rested against him. "Lazing in a tub of perfumed water with a beautiful woman on my lap."

"Beautiful, smart woman," she corrected.

"Beautiful and smart." He slipped his hands around her waist and held her against him, his chin resting on her shoulder. "Far more than any man could ask for." He kissed her earlobe and closed his eyes again. "Makes a man think he could stay forever."

Celeste's heart gave a little flutter. She didn't know what to say. Did he mean he wanted to stay? Here with her? She'd tried not to consider the possibility, because she knew it would never happen. There was no sense getting her hopes up for what would never be. Yet, suddenly, there was a spark of hope. These were words straight out of Fox's mouth, not just her own wishful thoughts.

How wonderful it would be to have a man like Fox for her own. To care for her, pamper her as he did.

Of course the idea brought up a problem Celeste had never considered until this moment.

What about Adam?

Chapter Eighteen

Fox walked along the dark street, disoriented. He didn't know where he was or why he was here. He could smell the stench of the harbor. It was close. The stinging salt smell of the sea mixed with an assault of familiar scents; rotting fish, open sewage, vermin. Somewhere a boat whistle wailed, a long and lonely sound . . .

He was searching for something . . . someone. He didn't know who or why. He didn't know how he'd gotten here.

Fox was wearing his good coat, the black wool one with the ermine collar. He felt the weight of his gold pocket watch hanging on a fob from his shirtwaist. Why did he still have them? Hadn't he sold them, along with his silk shirts, the Italian shoes, and German boots? Hadn't he sold them with the French watercolors and the Egyptian statues? All sold to pay James's debts.

Fox rubbed his eyes and kept walking. It was foggy tonight. The darkness was illuminated only by thin light from the moon and its reflection off the dirty water. A cat snarled and darted in front of him, startling him. He nearly tripped over an abandoned wooden crate with broken slats.

He gave the crate a kick. Damn . . . Where . . . where was she?

What was he looking for? Who?

Fox could feel his heart pounding in his chest. His hands were cold yet sweaty inside his thin leather gloves. He could feel the dampness of his brow beneath his wool felt bowler hat, the one Amber had bought him on their last trip to Chicago. He had told her he didn't need another hat. He had at least two dozen, but she didn't care. She insisted and he let her buy it.

Amber? Where was Amber? His mind churned as he struggled to remember.

Missing. Gone two days. He had to find her . . .

"Amber?" he called in a shaky voice. Now that he knew who he was looking for, panic seized him. He cut into an alley between two wooden structures that appeared to be stores. A shutter creaked. A rat darted in front of him, but instead of racing for cover, it scurried directly in front of him, leading him . . .

"Amber?" Fox called. He could hear the desperation in his hollow voice. He remembered now. He had looked everywhere for her, the saloons, the hotels, even an opium den.

"Amber, are you here?" he called again. He didn't know why he was so afraid. She'd disappeared before. She'd always turned up. But this was different. He could feel it in his heart.

He followed the rat. It knew. Fox knew that it knew he was looking for Amber. Beautiful, pitiful Amber.

The rat turned the corner and crept over a twisted gutter pipe. It perched on a shattered half barrel and twitched its long whiskers. There was debris everywhere. Surely Amber wasn't here.

Then Fox spotted an elongated shadow. Something was lying on the ground, shrouded in blackness.

Fox hesitated. But he had to look. "Amber," he said, only this time no sound escaped his lips. He could hear his heavy breathing and the pounding of his heart in his ears.

As he drew closer the shroud took shape. A woman . . . a

woman with long dark hair. Asleep? In a dockside alley? No.
Dead.

Fox wanted to turn away. He wanted to run. But he couldn't.
His footsteps led him to the dead woman, and he crouched so
that he could lean over her and see her face.

Fox rested one hand on her slender arm. She was cold.
"Amber?" he managed. He rolled her over.

There was blood everywhere.

A slit throat. Blood ran in rivers from the pulse of her slender,
pale neck.

No. No.

He tried to scream, but no sound came out. He wanted to
let go of the body. Release it. Run. But he was paralyzed by
terror. He couldn't move. He couldn't speak.

Not Amber. It wasn't Amber. Amber was already dead.

It was Celeste.

"No!" Fox screamed, and bolted upright. He covered his
ears, shaking his head madly. "No, no, no, not you, too."

"Fox . . . Fox . . ." Celeste said. She reached through the
darkness to where he sat upright in her bed, stiff with the fright
of a nightmare. "Fox, wake up. It's just a dream."

He was cold and shivering, yet bathed in clammy perspiration. His heart was pounding as if it would explode from his
chest. His eyes were wide open, and yet he didn't seem to see
her.

She shook him, first gently, then, when he didn't respond,
she shook him harder. "Fox!"

"Celeste?" he croaked as if he had crawled a thousand miles
through the desert without water. "Celeste?"

"Yes. Yes, it's me. It's all right." She crawled behind him
and wrapped her arms around his shoulders. She hugged him
tightly, her bare breasts pressing against his back. "Shhh," she
soothed. "It's all right. Just a dream."

He ceased shaking. She could feel his body relaxing, enve-
loped by hers.

"It's all right," she whispered. "I'm here with you. It was
just a bad dream."

"Oh, God," he murmured. It was his own voice now, weak, but definitely Fox. "Oh, God."

Celeste smoothed his hair with her palm and kissed his shoulder. "Shhh, you're safe now," she soothed as she had once soothed Adam. "You're safe in my room. You're awake and safe."

"Oh, Celeste."

"Tell me," she whispered.

He shook his head wildly and swallowed. "No."

"It might help."

He hung his head. He was still panting, but not as hard. "I . . . I was dreaming I was in San Francisco . . . not now, *then,* but now, too."

"Mm hm."

"I was looking for Amber. She hadn't come home. She just disappeared."

Celeste brushed his hair over his forehead with her fingertips. They hadn't been asleep long. It was still damp from their bath . . . or the arduous lovemaking afterwards. "Yes?" she encouraged. "You were looking for her."

"Down at the docks. I don't know why."

"Did you really look for her there?"

"No." He shook his head. "Someone else found her there. In an alley. Dead."

"I'm so sorry," she whispered, genuinely so.

"In the dream I was looking for her. There was this rat." He paused.

Celeste waited in the darkness, letting him catch his breath. She heard Silver move from one spot in the room to another and lay his head down again.

"I followed the rat," Fox finally continued. "It knew where she was."

"You found her?" Celeste whispered. "In the dream."

"Yes." He rubbed his face with his hand. "Only . . . no. No, Celeste, I didn't find her." He took a deep breath as if afraid to say what came next. "I found you."

She smoothed Fox's silky hair over one ear. "It's just a

dream. I'm not dead. I'm alive." She rose on her knees behind him and wrapped her arms tighter around his neck. "I'm alive and as happy as I've been in my life . . . because of you," she dared.

"You don't understand," he whispered. "I killed her."

Involuntarily she stiffened. A chill ran up her spine. "You killed Amber?"

He exhaled. "No. She . . . she smoked opium. She bought some in a den. Someone followed her out. Slit . . . slit her throat."

"Oh, Fox." She relaxed against him again. "I'm so sorry."

"It was her own fault. She knew better than to go to a place like that. My fault . . ." he finished softly.

"Your fault?" She crawled around him so that she could see his face in the moonlight that poured through the paned glass. It was cool in the room. Gooseflesh rose on her arms and across her chest. "It was your fault she bought opium and was murdered?"

"My fault she smoked it, maybe?" he said harshly. "My fault because I made her unhappy."

"Nonsense," she declared firmly. "You didn't hold the pipe to her lips. You weren't responsible. Women make choices. We all have our own heads about us. We make our own choices and then we must live by them . . . or die."

For the first time since he'd awakened her, he met her gaze. "Not my fault?" he asked. "But her brother James said it was. My fault. I made her unhappy. I drove her to it."

He looked so lost, so forlorn, that her heart ached. "The same James, your partner, who stole from you and left you with debts? That James?"

Finally she seemed to be reaching him. There was a light in his eyes that indicated he was listening, that he heard what she said and that he was absorbing her words.

"Yeah, that James," Fox said.

She rose on her knees and kissed him on the mouth. "You dreamed it was me lying in that alley because you still feel guilty about Amber's death. But you didn't kill her, and you're certainly not going to kill me.''

He lifted a hand to stroke her cheek. ''I would never hurt you,'' he whispered.

His voice was so passionate that it brought tears to her eyes. She hugged him so that he wouldn't see her tears and think her foolish. ''I know you wouldn't.''

''But there's something else.''

''Yes?''

He pushed her back to face her squarely. ''The sheriff. He took me in.''

She grimaced. ''For Amber's death?''

''Questioning. I think . . . I think James put him up to it and that was when he cleared out of town.''

''It's only logical that the authorities would question the man she lived with, Fox. She did live with you, right?''

He hung his head. ''It was stupid. I knew she was trouble. I knew it from the start. Then the opium. I should have put her out the day I found out.''

''The past,'' she told him. ''You can't change it. Give it up. You have too much to live for to bathe in the tragedy of days gone by.''

He clasped her hands and gazed into her eyes meaningfully. ''I do have a lot to live for. I have you.''

He hugged her and tears threatened to spill from her eyes onto his shoulder.

''There,'' he said finally. ''Now you know my sordid past. Now you know what kind of man I really am.''

She kissed his cheek. Fox had revealed so much of himself recently that she wondered if she should tell him about Adam. Just blurt it out. But she wasn't ready to do that. She wasn't ready to complicate their relationship. And she was still ashamed of the circumstances.

''I've always known what kind of man you were. Even before you arrived.''

''And how's that?''

She sat back on her heels on the mattress. ''Your father.''

He scowled.

"Everything he said was true," she insisted. "He said I would like you. That you were a fine, honest, handsome man."

Fox was still for a moment. "He said that to you?" He acted surprised, but pleasantly so.

"He did. He bragged about you all the time. He was so proud, not just of your accomplishments, but of you."

He laid back on his pillow and stretched out his arms to her. "Well, what's say you come a little closer to this honest, handsome man, and I'll show you a trick or two I bet my father never knew."

She laughed, her voice light and airy in the dark room. The words *I love you* were on the tip of her tongue. But she didn't say them because if she did, she knew what would happen. She knew what had happened before. This wonderful spell would be broken forever.

Sally stood on the parsonage steps and took a deep breath to calm her pattering heart. She'd dressed carefully for the visit. She'd borrowed a plain, metternich green traveling gown from one of the new girls at Kate's, pinned her hair up under a modest bonnet, and scrubbed her face clean of red paint until her cheeks stung. She didn't have a strand of blond hair out of place or a hint of color on her lips. This call was important to her, and she wanted to look her best.

Sally made herself rap on the door before she lost her nerve, turned, and hightailed it back to the whorehouse. Before she could exhale again, the door creaked open.

Mrs. Tuttle appeared, nearly as tall and as wide as the doorway. "Afternoon," she said kindly.

"Good . . . good afternoon." Sally smiled hesitantly at the reverend's wife, a little intimidated by her size. She must have doubled Sally in weight. But she had always been pleasant to her on the streets of Carrington, unlike most of the matrons. "I . . . I've come to see the reverend. Is . . . is he in?"

"Could I ask why?"

Sally glanced at the hem of the woman's gray gown. "P-personal, ma'am. Preacher business."

Mrs. Tuttle stepped back. "Please come in. We weren't expecting guests, but our home is always open to the reverend's lambs."

Sally stepped into the front hall that was dark and smelled peculiar. She tried not to wrinkle her nose. It smelled like rat poison to her.

"Would you care to wait in the parlor, Miss . . . I'm sorry, I don't know your true name."

Sally had to think for a second to remember her surname. She'd been Silky Sally for so long that her old identity was nearly lost. "Jenkins. Sally Jenkins, ma'am."

"Would you like to wait in the parlor, Miss Jenkins, while I fetch the reverend? He's in the kitchen doing a chore."

Sally glanced into the dark parlor off the front hall. The furniture was draped, just to keep out the dust, but it looked eerie.

This was where Sally'd come to pay her respects last year, when poor Anne had died of the clap. Joash had had the mortician lay her out here because she'd had no parlor of her own. It had been kind of Mrs. Tuttle to allow a dead whore in her parlor, but Sally would just as soon not go in. It made her think too much about Anne . . . about her own mortality.

"If'n it wouldn't be a problem, ma'am," Sally said softly, "I'd just as soon see him in the kitchen."

"This way."

Sally followed her down a hallway into a small, cozy kitchen.

"Miss Jenkins to see you, Reverend."

Joash Tuttle turned from a wooden worktable, a triangular butcher knife in his hand. The last of the afternoon sunlight glimmered off the blade. "Good afternoon, Miss Jenkins." He smiled in his preacherlike way. "Mrs. Tuttle, I think this knife will slice far more evenly now that it's sharpened properly." He ran his finger along the shiny blade carefully so as not to cut himself.

"Thank you, Reverend. A woman does appreciate a man's

effort in her kitchen.'' She smiled at Sally and backed through the doorway. ''I'll just go out and catch that hen while you speak with the Reverend.''

''I won't take much of his time,'' Sally said.

Mrs. Tuttle lifted her big hand, unadorned but for her platinum wedding band. ''Please, Miss Jenkins, take as much time as you need. The Lord's work cannot be measured by time.''

Sally gave her a half smile, not really understanding what she meant, but wanting to get on with her business. ''Thank you,'' she called after the woman disappearing down the hallway.

''Now what can I do for you, Sally?'' Joash wiped the blade of the butcher knife with a clean cloth and slipped it into a wooden block that held two other knives.

Sally watched the blade slide into the wood and licked her dry lips. It was the biggest butcher knife she'd ever seen. She thought about the dead women. They'd been killed with a knife. Brutally murdered, Sheriff Tate said. Thank God she was getting out of Carrington before it was too late.

''I . . . I wanted to talk to you on a matter.''

''Do sit down.''

She glanced at the wooden kitchen chair he indicated. ''I'd rather stand. Makes me humble.''

He nodded and smiled the barest smile as he folded his hands neatly at his waist. ''I'm pleased you came to me. I'm always pleased when one of my stray lambs comes to call. Now tell me how I can help you, dear Sally.''

She took a deep breath. She'd practiced what she was going to say on the walk over, but now she forgot the words. ''I . . . I want to know if . . . if someone, a woman, can be forgiven for her sins.''

''Christ died so that we might be forgiven of our sins,'' he answered.

She squeezed her eyes shut and then opened them again. ''I . . . I know that's what people like you say. But what I mean is . . . is, can I *really* be forgiven? If . . . I say I'm sorry for what I done and I'm really sorry and I won't do it anymore—'' She exhaled. "Hell, Joash." She glanced up him. She was trying so hard to be a lady her Noah would be proud of, but a thing like this took time. "I want to get married and be a wife . . . maybe even a mother. If I don't spread for no more men, and I'm sorry for what I done in the past, I won't be punished, will I?"

His smile was serene. "All you must do is accept Christ as your savior, confess your sins to His ears alone, and repent."

She heaved a sigh of relief. "You mean if I don't do it no more, if I stay true to my husband, and I go to church every Sunday, I won't go to hell?"

He chuckled. "It's the glory of Christ, Sally."

She smiled. "I . . . I never knew it would be so easy."

"It's easy to give yourself to the Lord, difficult to follow Him. Remember that."

She fluttered her gloved hand. "Thank you. Thank you so much." She started for the door. "I can't tell you how much better I feel. My Noah, he says he doesn't care what I've done, but I was worried about Jesus. Worried something fierce. I didn't want to die like those other girls—punished."

Joash followed her down the hallway to the front door and out onto the parsonage's front porch. "Go home and pack your things, and take yourself from that den of sin, Sally. That's the first way to begin your new life."

She tugged on the ribbons of the itchy bonnet she'd borrowed. "Oh, don't worry. I plan to get out of there soon. My Noah's hit silver." She broke into a wide grin. "We're going to get married." Happy beyond words, Sally fluttered off the porch. "Thank you. Thank you much."

Joash waved. "Go in peace, child, and do not sin again."

"Don't worry," she called back. "I'm not even lettin' Noah in my drawers again until I've got that ring!"

Chapter Nineteen

Celeste sat on a high stool behind a makeshift desk sketching a cross-section view of the progress being made by the laborers below her. Carefully she began to draw the timbers already in place to shore up the earthen ceiling and protect the workers from cave-ins.

The first vein of silver ore they had discovered beneath the ground was at least sixty feet long and thirty feet wide. With a vein of that tremendous size, and the discovery of three more ore bodies, Fox had made the decision that for safety reasons, they would have to change the structure of the wall supports. They were now building three-dimensional boxlike supports called square sets, rather than the typical post and cap method that looked like door frames. The square sets, shaped like timber boxes, took longer to build and twice the lumber, but made cave-ins far less likely. Slowly the square sets were being built to form the hollow cubes, one interlocked to the next, fanning out in the direction of the digging to resemble underground honeycombs.

Celeste sketched the west wall of the shaft that had been dug on an incline to follow the apparent tilt of the lode. On impulse, she added a miner with a pickax, digging where the ore was so crumbly that dynamite wasn't necessary to dislodge it. A smile played on her lips as she added a dog.

"Good afternoon, Celeste."

She glanced up from her desk. Seeing that the visitor was Brent Trevor, she covered her sketch with a sheet of figures. She didn't want him to know any more about their operation than what he had already bribed out of some of her miners. She was even less anxious to share the sketch of Fox and Silver.

"Good . . . good afternoon." She climbed off the stool.

"No, no, don't get up for me."

He raised a gloved hand and she wondered how he always managed to remain so clean in the midst of all the filth of the mine.

"I just stopped by to say hello and to see if you'd gotten that pocket of hot water up out of the tunnel."

She walked around the desk, rubbing the small of her back. It was mid-afternoon and she'd been here since dawn. "I needed a break anyway. I've been sitting for hours."

"Oh, you poor dear woman, worked liked a slave." He shook his head. "I keep telling MacPhearson that it's not seemly, a woman like yourself working amidst these men." He pointed with his silver-tipped walking cane.

Celeste watched a bare-chested miner pass through the open machinery room with a length of rope coiled over one shoulder and a bucket in both hands. The man tipped his battered hat cordially as he went by.

"I like to keep an eye on my investment," Celeste said. "Besides, even with the foremen, there's too much work for Fox to do alone. I try to keep track of the paperwork, the number of loads of ore we ship a day, and information like that." She came to stand in front of him. "It keeps the miners and my neighbors honest."

He smiled, apparently amused. "I should hire you to work for me." He brushed at an invisible fleck of dirt on his lapel. "My men are stealing me blind."

"Perhaps you should spend more time at your mine and less time making social calls." She smiled prettily.

Trevor laughed. "Oh, I do love a clever woman. You're certain you won't change your mind and allow me to escort you to supper one night? Just supper."

She tried to speak, but he went on.

"The more I see the two of you together"—he took a step closer—"the more I see that a woman like yourself could do much better than MacPhearson. He's a strange egg. Spends too much time in those pits with those filthy men. A woman like yourself deserves better. Deserves me."

Finished with his little speech, he appeared pleased with himself. He really was a laughable little man.

She tucked a lock of hair back under the linen cap she wore to cover her chignon and keep her hair clean. "Brent, we've been over this. I thank you kindly for your invitation and your compliments, but—"

Celeste felt a sudden shift on the flooring beneath her and, startled, she grabbed for the corner of the desk. It wasn't just the floor that seemed to move; it came from deeper below. A rumble from the earth accompanied the shifting ground and she looked up in fear at Brent. This wasn't typical of the sound the earth made when the men set dynamite to clear a wall of ore. This was . . .

"Oh, God, *a cave-in,*" she whispered. As the words passed her lips she unclenched her hand from the desk and ran for the shaft.

Fox.

All she could think of was Fox. He was down there. He and Silver had ridden down over an hour ago to settle a dispute between two men.

Celeste tried not to panic as she raced out of the equipment room into the main room that had been built around the shaft. There was no need to panic. Panic wouldn't help Fox; it wouldn't bring him out alive.

By the time she reached the square-cut hole that was the mouth of the main mine shaft, great clouds of dirt were puffing from it. The dirt mixed with the ever-present steam made a thick cloud that clung to her face and clothes.

A hoisting cage clambered up filled with men all talking at once.

"What's happened? What's happened?" she demanded of the half-naked, dirty-faced miners.

"Cave-in," a man whose beard was encrusted with dirt said. "Somewhere against the back, north wall, second level."

As they climbed out of the cage, she pushed her way in.

"Miss Kennedy!" Trevor called from behind. "Heavens, woman. You can't go down there!"

Celeste had forgotten his presence. She squeezed into the cage, yanking her petticoats in behind her. "Take me down, Joe," she yelled above the din of the clanking engine and the confusion of the men. Another bucket of men came up as she spoke.

"Miss Kennedy, you shouldn't go down there," the engineer called to her. "Ain't safe."

"Damn it, Joe, you send me down or you find work elsewhere."

The engineer pulled the lever, knowing full well the job as engineer at the MacPhearson Fortune was too sweet to give up. He also knew better than to question Miss Kennedy. Here, her word meant as much as Mr. MacPhearson's. "Yes, ma'am."

The iron-framed cage with open walls descended and Celeste grabbed a pole for support, taking care not to allow her arm to hang over the cage, where it would be smashed by the timber frame of the shaft as she was rapidly lowered. She passed the first level where she saw a flash of men with candles and lanterns and heard voices and the clank of machinery.

The cage hit the bottom of the second level of the shaft they had just begun constructing. Before the cage came to a complete halt, she bounded off.

"Where is he?" she demanded of the closest miner.

They were all standing around bare-chested in naught but

boots and breeches. Lanterns swung in their hands, illuminating their weary faces.

"Where's Mr. MacPhearson?" she repeated.

"Don't know, ma'am," one of the gravelly-voiced men offered. "Ain't seen him."

"How many hurt? Anyone killed?" She pushed her way through the crowd, shoving when they didn't move out of her way fast enough. "You." She pointed to a young man who couldn't have been more than sixteen. "Light my way."

"Foreman says stay back," another black-faced man said. "Stay back 'til they know ain't no more ore gonna shift."

"Light my way," Celeste repeated. "If you fear for your life, give me the lantern." She thrust out her hand.

"No, m . . . m . . . ma'am," the boy stammered. "I a . . . a . . . ain't scared. I'll light ye."

Celeste followed him through a newly constructed square-set into another. She heard men shouting, but she couldn't tell if any of them were Fox. Someone was calling orders, his voice echoing off the rock walls. Steam hissed from a gully, and she heard the grinding of rock being shoveled.

"Hurry," she whispered. She followed the boy through a narrow passageway joisted up with fresh lumber. "Fox?" she called.

Her voice echoed off the black walls streaked with silver ore. He didn't answer.

"Fox?"

She was rewarded by a sharp bark.

"Silver?"

The dog bounded out of the shadowy darkness and nudged her with his wet nose. She reached down to brush his head and found it covered in a thin coat of grime. "Where is he? Where's Fox?" she murmured.

They entered the last honeycomb supported by timber. Directly in front of her was a pile of rubble six feet high. The room was so full of dust that it stung her eyes and made it hard to breathe. "Fox!" she called sharply, the filth in the air so thick that it was like fog.

"Celeste." His voice was rough, but it was definitely Fox. "What the hell are you doing down here?"

She slapped her hand to her pounding heart. Thank God he was alive . . . safe.

"I came to see what had happened. What I could do."

Fox emerged from the fog, his face so grimy that she barely recognized him. His breeches were torn, his hat gone from his head. One sleeve hung off his shoulder, nearly rent from the shirt. "You can stay up above and keep the men calm."

She grabbed his hand. She'd have hugged him if he'd let her, but he kept her at arm's length.

"Celeste, do you hear me? I want you up above." He pointed to the low ceiling that nearly brushed the top of his head. "This is unstable, a pocket of clay."

"Anyone killed?" she asked softly, knowing he wouldn't lie to her. He wouldn't lie to her.

"No. Two slightly injured, another with what looks to be a broken leg. He's still trapped under some rock."

She stared in the dim lantern light at the rubble; the miners trying to set the man free blocked her view of him. "You should come up, too. Let these men get him out. They know what they're doing."

His gaze was dark, his eyes pools of concern. "I won't leave an injured man down here. He works for me; he's my responsibility."

Somewhere close, the earth groaned and a puff of dirt billowed from the ceiling. Fox threw his arms to cover her head. "Go," he insisted.

"Not without you."

"It'll take five minutes. I'll get these men out of here until we can reassess the structure. I'll check on the rest of the men and be up before the hour."

The groaning of the unstable ground ceased, and he withdrew his hands. Celeste was now covered in the same film of dirt as the miners. She dropped her hands to her hips. It was so hot that beads of perspiration trickled down her temples and the nape of her neck. "I don't want to leave you. This is my responsibility, too."

Fox rubbed the back of his neck, obviously irritated. "Celeste!" he said sharply. Two miners turned to look at them, and he lowered his voice. "How can I help this man if I'm worried about you?"

"My responsibility for these men is the same as yours," she repeated.

He looked away, shaking his head. "You are the most stubborn . . . irritating . . . inflexible—"

"I'll make you a deal." She yanked off her linen cap and shook it, sending dust and bits of dirt flying. "You get him out, I'll check the other men, up on the main level. This is the only area that's been affected, right? They can go on working in the other tunnels?"

He hesitated for a moment. She could tell this suggestion wasn't satisfactory either. The question was, would he waste any more time trying to convince her otherwise, or would he concede? With a sigh, he finally said, "All right. You check the other tunnels. Tell the men no one has been seriously injured. I'll meet you above ground as soon as we get the man out and close off this tunnel."

She nodded and turned to go. "Agreed."

"Celeste?"

She turned back. Even with torn clothes and covered in dirt and sweat, he made her heart give a little trip. "Yes?"

"Take Silver with you. These miners are rough. I think they know enough to keep their distance from you, but just in case—"

"I'll be fine." She smiled reassuringly as she tapped her thigh. "See you up above. Come on, boy. Come on, Silver."

Nearly two hours later, Celeste stood in the equipment room and watched Fox drink another cup of cold water. He was so exhausted he could barely stand.

"You all right?"

He leaned against her desk, covered his mouth, and coughed. "Better than poor Danny boy. The bone broke clean through. Doc says he's lucky it didn't break through the skin."

From a pitcher, she refilled the cup he set on her desk and added another splash of water to Silver's crock bowl on the floor at Fox's feet.

In the last two hours the tunnel with the cave-in had been closed off, the other areas checked, and the men were now back to work. The emergency had passed, but Celeste still felt edgy. She was upset that a man had been injured in her mine, more upset that it could have easily been Fox. He had been right there when the wall had caved in.

"So what caused the cave-in? Could you tell?"

He wiped his mouth with the back of his hand, smearing dirt. "It's the strangest thing. I checked the square set yesterday; it was solid. Today it caves in."

"Will rebuilding the square set eliminate the danger?"

He looked away, his face etched with worry. "I don't know, because I don't know why it didn't hold. Was the lumber weak? Was it notched incorrectly?" His gaze met hers. "Did someone purposely sabotage the supports?"

"Who would do something like that? Certainly not any of the men in the mine. Any one of them could have been killed."

"I know." He crossed his arms over his chest, moving slowly, as if he barely had the energy. "I'm just skittish about cave-ins. I feel like a damned rat when I'm down there."

"So what do we do about the new tunnel?"

"Keep it closed off. It's close to the north line of our property anyway. We'll just dig in other directions. There are so many veins we could easily fan off another way. We might lose some money but—"

"It's not worth someone getting killed over."

He nodded. "I knew you would feel the same way."

Celeste walked up beside him and slipped her arm around his waist. "I was proud of you today. I don't know any other owner who would have stayed down there with that man."

He didn't say anything.

She gave him a squeeze. "I say we've had quite enough excitement for today. Why don't we go home, eat, and try out that bathtub again?"

He glanced at her sideways, that boyish smile she loved turning up the corners of his mouth. "I've been waiting all day for a proposition like that, ma'am."

She lifted up on her toes and pressed a kiss to his lips. "Race you home."

Filth. Nothing but filth and stench. You can smell it. Hear it. Taste it in the air in Carrington these days. Sin is what brings it. Gambling. Swearing. Drinking. Whoring. The filth is everywhere, seeping into every crack of man's existence.

It has to be stopped. Silenced. Here. Now.

There is only one way. Only the blade can wipe the sin clean. Only blood can wash it from the sinner's hands and face.

Blood. Blood. Blood.

The metallic smell of it. The stickiness of it on my hands. The warmth that flows with it . . . It is an elixir.

Celeste's hands shook as she lit the gas lamp and sat down on the corner of her bed. She'd left the door open for Fox, hoping he would join her. Most nights he did. Since his confession to her about Amber, he had been sleeping much better. He rarely wandered the streets at night with the dog. He said it was because he slept with Celeste in his arms, but she knew that he was finally beginning to forgive himself for Amber's death.

Celeste stared at her hands in her lap. She'd bathed alone tonight and changed into a flannel sleeping gown and robe. A cold wind tore at the window shutters outside, and a branch scraped eerily against the window.

Another murder.

The killer had struck again. This time it was one of Sal's new girls. Her name had been Emma. Fox had just been to Sal's. He hadn't told her what happened. He'd just passed her in the hallway. He said he'd be up, after he bathed the day's sweat and dirt from the mine from his body.

She threaded her fingers together and waited, trying not to think. Not to feel.

Four women. Dead. Butchered. In less than five months. The idea terrified her. Rosy had been smart to get out while she could. She wished Sally would do the same, but the girl was still trying to save money. She intended to leave by Christmas; that was her plan.

Celeste felt guilty for feeling so relieved that she hadn't been the victim. After all, she'd not lain with a customer in almost a year. When John had fallen sick, she'd left Kate's to care for him. She wasn't a whore any longer. True, she slept with a man who wasn't her husband, but that wasn't the same thing. The killer only murdered women who slept with many men. That excluded Celeste—it made her safe. She told herself that at least once a day.

A sound in the doorway startled Celeste. She jumped up. "Oh—it's you. You scared me."

"I'm sorry." Fox walked into her bedroom, a white cotton towel tied around his middle. He'd just bathed, and his hair was wet and slicked back over his head. He'd shaved and smelled of fresh soap and clean skin. "I didn't mean to startle you."

She sat back down on the bed. "It's all right. I was just daydreaming."

Silver wandered into the bedroom and stretched out in front of the coal stove that burned warmly in the far corner of the room.

Fox sat on the edge of the bed beside her and ran an extra towel over his wet hair. "Long day. It's hard with it being so cold above ground and so hot below."

She rested her hand on his bare knee. "We could hire another foreman so you wouldn't have to work so many hours."

"No." He laid back on the bed. "I need to be there. It's only right."

She stretched out beside him and propped her head on one

elbow. "I wish I could say that I didn't understand." She smoothed his wet hair with her hand. "But I do."

She adored this time of evening, when they were close and talked about the day. She wondered if this was what it felt like to have a husband who loved you. Was this what husbands and wives did in the evenings?

He turned his head to stare into her eyes. They were so close that their noses nearly touched. Apparently, by silent agreement, they weren't going to discuss the murder tonight. They were both too physically tired, too mentally exhausted. Here, safe in the cocoon of John's house, they could find a moment's respite and just be together.

"I miss you when I'm down there," Fox said thoughtfully. "I think about you. I wonder what you're doing."

She smiled as a lump rose in her throat. He was so kind to her. So caring. If only he could accept her past . . .

"Ready for bed?" she asked, turning away so that he didn't see the tears that gathered in her eye.

"Yes, I'm ready for bed." He tossed the towels onto the floor and crawled beneath her down quilt. "Just not to sleep."

She blew out the gaslight and padded barefoot across the floor, her laughter mingling with his.

Running, running, running. Celeste was running, but she wasn't going anywhere. She could hear the footsteps behind her. She could feel the murderer pressing closer. Yet, when she turned around, she couldn't see him. When she turned around she saw nothing but the streets of Carrington. She heard nothing but the wind.

Celeste was out of breath, near exhaustion, and yet she couldn't stop running. If she stopped he would kill her. Her precious Adam would be an orphan. She couldn't let that happen. She wouldn't.

Peach Street seemed to go on forever. She kept on the same street, and yet she never reached the end.

She had to get to the train station. Celeste lifted her skirt to her knees and ran faster.

She could feel the killer growing closer. Her terrified heartbeat pounded to the rhythm of the killer's footsteps. She had almost reached the end of the street!

Then she felt the cold hard steel of the blade. She screamed as her knees buckled and she fell, white hot pain radiating from her back. She heard the killer's voice and she knew she knew him.

Fox shook Celeste harder. "Celeste, wake up. Celeste."

She sat upright, panting. The quilt fell away, uncovering her bare breasts. Her heart was beating so hard that she felt as if it was going to explode from her chest. "Oh," she sighed. "Oh."

"You awake?" came Fox's voice out of the darkness. He rubbed her arm.

"Yes."

"Good. Now why don't you tell me who Gerald is?"

Chapter Twenty

Celeste's mouth was so dry that her tongue stuck to the roof of her mouth. "Gerald?" she whispered. It was as if he had spoken the name of a ghost or goblin.

"Gerald."

She could feel Fox's piercing gaze through the shadowed darkness of the bedroom. He was so close to her that she could touch him, yet he seemed as distant as the stars in the night.

"Yeah, Gerald," he repeated. "You called his name."

"Gerald . . ." she murmured numbly.

"He the man you see in Denver?" Fox's tone was cool.

She shook her head, feeling numb from her toes to her hair. It had been a long time since she thought about Gerald. Handsome, blue-eyed Gerald.

"Then who is he? You can't expect me not to ask. To not need to know."

Celeste lifted the quilt to cover her breasts. She was suddenly cold to the bone. "He . . ." Her voice sounded strange in her ears. "He . . . um . . . he was my fiancé."

"Fiancé?"

She felt as if she was floating half in the present, half in the past. Images flashed in her head. She heard her own girlish laughter and Gerald's deep, charming voice.

"Was? You were engaged to be married?" he asked sharply.

She clutched the quilt to her breasts as if she could protect herself from those events long past. "A long time ago."

She heard him sigh and then felt his hand on her shoulder. "You want to tell me about it?"

"No." Her lower lip trembled. "Yes."

He was silent.

Celeste had never told anyone about Gerald, not even Sally. Sally knew about Adam, but not Gerald. Celeste had never intended telling anyone again, but somehow it seemed right that Fox should know.

"He was my father's business partner," she said so quietly that he leaned closer to hear her. "I was seventeen." She smiled bittersweetly at the memory. She remembered her mother's rose garden, and Gerald kissing her beneath a trellis. "He was older. So charming. So handsome. So well mannered. Everyone liked him. I loved him."

She thought she heard Fox inhale sharply. "He asked you to marry him, and your parents wouldn't allow it?"

"Oh, no." She turned to him. In the darkness she could only see the outline of his face. "My parents adored him as well. They gave me permission to wed. There was a great engagement party at our home. Everyone in Denver came."

"What happened?"

"We danced and drank champagne. Gerald took me into my father's dark office and kissed me and told me he loved me more than the moon loves the stars." She brushed her lips with her fingertips, remembering how much she had enjoyed that kiss. "Then he tried to touch me. He said he loved me too much to wait."

"Oh, Celeste," Fox said softly, as if he knew what she would say next.

"I said no. We could wait. We were marrying in six months. Surely a man and woman who loved each other as much as we did could show some restraint and wait six months."

A tear trickled down her cheek. "But he got angry. He said I'd gotten what I wanted, and now he was getting what he wanted." She cried silently, too ashamed even now to cry aloud. "He . . . he did it anyway. He raped me."

"Celeste." Fox tried to put his arm around her shoulder, but she shrugged him off. Just talking about it made her feel the shame. The anger. She should have fought harder. She should have hollered and brought the guests into the office. She should never have let him take what was only hers to give.

"What happened?" Fox asked.

She lifted one shoulder. "I told my father. He called me a liar. He brought Gerald into the office where the bastard raped me. The two of them stood there and smoked a cigar and drank brandy. Gerald said he didn't do it. He said it was someone else, but that he'd take me soiled just the same."

"Son of a bitch," Fox said quietly. "So what did you do?"

"I refused. I wouldn't marry a rapist. My father put me out of the house. It was raining. I had no place to go. Kate took me in. First I cleaned, but I couldn't make enough money to keep myself."

"So you took to the profession."

She nodded; hot tears ran down her cheeks. "I vowed the night my father put me on the street that no man would force me like that again. I would make the decision. It would be on my terms. I became the whore my father accused me of being."

"Ah, Celeste."

This time she allowed him to cradle her in his arms. She couldn't bring herself to tell him about Adam, but even a partial confession felt good inside. Now maybe he wouldn't think she was such a bad person. Maybe now he would understand why she had chosen to have sex with men for money, or at least not hate her for it.

"Celeste, Celeste." Fox stroked her forehead and she rested her cheek on his chest. "I'm so sorry. So sorry. If I'd been your father, I'd have killed the bastard right there."

"But he didn't believe me." She took a deep, gulping breath.

"He called me a whore. And then . . . then I showed him he was right."

"No. No. You can't blame yourself. Women are forced into these things. I know that. I never blamed you for what you've done."

She gazed into his eyes. In the darkness they glimmered. "But you never asked me why I sold my body. Not in all this time."

"I knew you had your reasons." He squeezed her tightly.

"But a whore is still a whore, and you could never love a whore." There. She'd said it.

When he didn't respond, she closed her eyes. Of course she couldn't expect him to just forget about the eight years she had sold her body to men. He could care for her and still not forget. It was more than any woman could ask of a man.

After a long sigh, he said, "It's complicated, Celeste. And it's not you; it's me. I don't know how to explain it, because I don't understand it myself."

"Amber did you wrong," she said softly. "You loved her and she did you wrong. No one could blame you for being wary."

"Celeste, it wasn't just Amber, it was—"

Celeste realized he had been about to say something very revealing, but then he cut himself off.

"Who?"

He set his jaw and shook his head. "Never mind," he said sharply.

She felt a wall lower between them. She knew it was as thick as any stone wall in the mine, so she let his comment go.

For a long time Fox held her. He didn't say anything, he just hugged her and stroked her hair. Finally she began to drift, and sleep came to them both.

Celeste clutched the leather handles of her valise as she stood on the train station platform, her face to the wind. Emma's death had scared her. She needed comfort. She needed to feel Adam in her arms. Nothing was working out as she thought it would. She was beginning to care about Fox too much, depend on him too much. The more she thought about him leaving to return to California and the vineyard he dreamed of, the more fearful she became. If she let him get any closer to her, if she fell in love with him, God forbid, she'd never survive his leaving. She'd crumble.

"I have to go," Celeste said.

"You don't *have* to do anything but pay taxes and die." Fox stood behind her in the same long overcoat he had worn the day he arrived in Carrington. On his head perched a new wool hat she'd bought him at one of the general stores in town.

The wind was cold on her face. It gave her the stamina she desperately needed. "I have to go to Denver," she repeated firmly. "I need to."

"You going to see *him?*"

"Him who?"

"Gerald," he said softly.

She turned around, grimacing. "Certainly not. If I see him at the gates of hell it will be too soon."

He glanced away. "You're not going to hell, Celeste," he said dryly. "He is, but you're not."

She turned her face back into the wind, saying matter-of-factly, "Whores go to hell."

"Damn it, Celeste," he swore behind her. "Tell me who you're going to see."

She shook her head. "Can't."

"I could find out myself. I could follow you or have you followed."

"You won't."

"No?"

"No. Because you respect my privacy."

He frowned. "You put me in a tight spot here."

Her gaze met his. "I know. I'm sorry," she whispered. She touched the arm of his wool coat with her gloved hand. "I can't tell you. I just can't. I'll be back in a few days. This changes nothing between us.''

"And just what is between us?" he asked under his breath, more to himself than to her.

She barely caught the words on the wind. "You tell me."

He shook his head and stared broodingly out over the small station that was under construction. "Never mind."

Celeste wanted to ask him again what he had meant by that. Did he mean it was more than she thought . . . or less. But she knew better than to try to get him to talk when he was in such a foul mood. She didn't blame him for his temper either. If their roles were reversed at this moment, she'd be angry, too.

Although neither seemed to be sure these days what their relationship was, both knew by silent agreement that one didn't go somewhere without telling the other. It had started out innocently enough. Fox would often leave for the mine before she was up and would call up the stairs to let her know he was leaving. She would go the store, or to visit Sally, and tell him, just out of common courtesy for someone else in the house. Now they checked with each other before making plans. They were beginning to behave the way Celeste guessed a married couple would. He picked up food stuffs she needed at the general store on his way home from the mine. She starched his Sunday shirt without him asking. She warmed his side of the bedclothes with a warmer before he climbed into bed; he always started her water for tea before she came down in the morning.

The sound of the train whistle brought Celeste out of her reverie. "I'll be back in three days."

The train chugged into the station with a wail and a whine of its brakes.

"Fox?" She laid her hand on his sleeve.

He turned his head. "Three days." He paused. "I'll miss you."

She almost smiled. It felt so good to hear him say that. She kissed his cheek. "I'll miss you, too."

* * *

"What do you mean you don't like it here?" Celeste signed, and then ate a bit of piecrust off her fork. She and Adam had taken a long walk and then stopped at her hotel for dinner in the dining room. Adam was on his second slice of apple-cranberry pie.

"I don't like it," Adam signed adamantly.

"Use words, please," she said gently. Adam's school mistress reported that he was speaking very well now, and needed only to be reminded to use his new-found voice.

"I don't like it here anymore." He spoke precisely, but still signed with his hands. His voice was low and guttural, but she understood every painstakingly pronounced word.

"Why? Isn't Miss Higgens kind to you?" She gave up signing and simply looked directly into his eyes so that he might read her lips. "She tells me you're her favorite student."

"I miss you," he grumbled, not bothering to sign.

She almost smiled, but knew he might have misconstrued her meaning. She didn't want him to think she was trivializing his homesickness. It was just that Celeste was so proud of her handsome son with his sandy blond hair and his brilliant blue eyes that resembled her father's.

When Adam had been small, the doctors had told her he would never learn to speak, that he was addlepated, and that she just ought to abandon him in an orphanage. But Celeste had refused to accept their diagnosis.

She had found Miss Higgen's school for the deaf, and Adam had learned to speak. He wasn't addlepated. He was a bright healthy young man. And his presence in her life was worth every agony she had ever suffered—every man she had ever bedded. Celeste didn't regret a single thing she had done since the night Gerald had raped her. The money she made provided Adam with the opportunity he had needed at the time. Now with her money from the silver mine she could slip into an acceptable place in society, and be the kind of mother her son would be proud of.

"I want to go with you." Adam set down his fork and stared at his plate. He was dressed in a pin-striped black suit she'd bought him yesterday. She only realized now that it was identical to the one—down to the wool hat—she'd had made for Fox in Carrington.

"I told you, Adam, there's no place in my shop." She had told him she was a merchant, that she sold ladies' dresses for a living. He thought his father was dead and that he had been a kind man. Celeste felt that there was no need for Adam to know the truth about his father. Ever. It would only harm him.

"I don't care where I have to sleep." He was becoming upset, so his spoken words were more difficult to understand. "I don't want to stay here anymore. I want to go with you."

"Shhhh," Celeste soothed as she slid her hand across the table to cover his.

The patrons at the next table, a man in a black suit and a woman with a feathered cap, glanced at them and then away.

Celeste glanced down at the pristine linen tablecloth and then at Adam. The candlelight twinkled off the red highlights in his hair—her mark on the beautiful child. "I don't know if that's possible."

Adam looked up from his pie plate. "Please, Mama?" he signed.

Celeste thought her heart would break.

She had convinced herself that Adam would be better off in boarding school, even if he was able to move to another school not specifically for deaf children. Even now. He would be better off with friends his own age, visiting their families on holidays. She was afraid she would taint his life with her past. What if someone who knew her from Kate's came along? She couldn't do that to Adam.

"Please," Adam whispered, his blue eyes beseeching.

She squeezed his hand. "I'll think about it. My situation has changed. I've . . . a new occupation, so there is a possibility," she heard herself say.

His eyes widened with interest. "Are you going to move?

Would you have room for me? I could sleep on the floor, ma'am. Really I could.''

He signed so quickly that she was having a difficult time following what he was saying.

"Wait. Wait," she said as she signed, laughing. "You're going too fast. Talk to me. I want to hear your handsome voice."

He repeated his questions, his speech remarkably good.

"Just give me some time," she said. "We can talk about it at Christmas."

"You're coming?" He ate a mouthful of his pie.

"Of course I'm coming for Christmas. We're going to have that plum pudding you love, and we're going to go skating, and we're going to the opera—"

"Op-er-a," he groaned.

Celeste laughed. "And if you're very good, I just might bring you a present."

He rose from his chair and walked around to hers to throw his little arms around her. "Oh, Mama, if you come for Christmas, that will be my present. I don't need any other presents but you."

Adam kissed her cheek, and she had to brush away her single tear with her fingertips.

Fox sat on the high stool, a row of figures in front of him. He stared at the numbers, knowing they would show that the productivity of the mine this week was excellent, but he didn't really see them.

Machinery clanged around him, and the pain in his head pulsed to the beat. He dropped his pen and lowered his head to his hands in frustration.

The mine was producing excellent silver ore. He was going to be rich again. He could buy that land in California and start the vineyard he had always dreamed of. So why wasn't he happy?

Celeste.

He hadn't wanted her to go to Denver. He had practically asked her not to. She had known he didn't want her to go, that he wanted her to stay here with him. But she'd gone anyway . . .

Fox ran his fingers through his hair and lifted his head. He stared blindly at the far wall of the equipment building. How could he have done this to himself again, damn it? How had he allowed himself to care so much?

He didn't know who Celeste went to see in Denver. As she had reminded him, it wasn't his business. But her gallivanting off was proof that he was right to be wary of her. Whores couldn't be trusted. They didn't have the capacity to love as other women did. His theory had been proved once, twice . . . now a third time with Celeste. If she really cared for him, she wouldn't have gone. She'd have stayed here and made the effort to be loyal to him. Of course she had never told him she loved him, so who was he kidding? No one but himself.

There was no future with Celeste here or anywhere else, and the sooner he accepted the fact, the better off he'd be. Where had he ever gotten the idea that he could have more from her than her laughter and her touch in his bed? He'd probably be better off to move on soon, to sell his half of the mine and get out of here. He didn't like the mining business anyway. With the cash now coming in from the silver ore, he could hire someone to begin looking for land in California. He could be gone by spring.

Fox stared at the column of figures again on the desk in front of him. They were in Celeste's perfect handwriting. He thought of her in Denver with a man, and anger bubbled up inside him. Anger was good. He could accept the anger. It was far easier to deal with than his breaking heart.

Chapter Twenty-one

Celeste stepped off the train in Carrington, disappointed that Fox wasn't there to greet her. Of course she hadn't really expected him to be here. It was midday; he was working at the mine. She'd not asked him to come. She didn't need his assistance to get home. She had only sent him her arrival time by telegraph as a courtesy—so he wouldn't be worried, not because she wanted him to be here.

She walked down the platform steps in her new black velvet redingote with its matching scotch cap and hair net trimmed in white aigrette. Adam had picked the gown out for her, and she had bought him a matching velvet coat. She'd been tempted to purchase the same coat for Fox, but she'd resisted—just another tie that bound.

Celeste held her leather valise tightly in her gloved hand.

"Take your bag, Miss Kennedy?" a miner on the street asked.

She shook her head. "No thank you," she said and kept walking. She didn't like the idea that everyone in this booming town knew who she was. Her visit with Adam and his plea made her long for anonymity. How was he ever going to live with her if everyone knew who she was, and what she had been before she struck silver? Even the manner in which she had acquired the land would be unacceptable in any decent circle of society.

Celeste knew she would have to move from Carrington, of course, but how far? Word of the MacPhearson lode was passing through the states and territories like a brushfire. Only two weeks ago another large vein had been hit half a mile south of the MacPhearson Fortune. The town was only going to grow larger, and her name become better known.

Celeste walked briskly down Peach Street, passing people she knew, nodding and smiling. She was thankful for the new black and gray wool cloak she'd purchased in Denver. The wind was cold and a few snowflakes drifted in the air. In the distance she saw the graveyard which had once been outside of town, but was now almost in the center of the growing town. She thought of the woman named Emma and felt a pang of sorrow.

The morning Celeste left for Denver, Fox had only given her a few details about the murder. The whore had been killed with a knife, tied and butchered like the others. She'd also been mutilated in some way. Fox refused outright to tell her the details. He said it made him sick to his stomach just thinking about it.

She smiled at the grim thought. Fox was as masculine a man as she had ever known, and yet there was a tenderness in him. He hadn't been hardened by his past as most men were. He seemed to feel deeper than other men and was less awkward in expressing those emotions.

She'd missed him while she was gone. She'd had a wonderful time with Adam, but damn Fox, she'd missed him. So much that it hurt.

As Celeste walked up the front steps to her porch, she sighed with frustration. What was she going to do? Adam wanted to live with her. She certainly couldn't bring him here. She couldn't bring him into a home where she was living in sin with a man.

But could she give up Fox for Adam? If she had to, she knew she could. The problem was, she didn't know what was the right thing to do. And she needed more money. She knew she could easily sell her half of the mine to Fox, or one of half a dozen other wealthy miners in town. But she had to bide her time. She needed to make sure that she had enough cash so that, with good investments, she'd never have to worry about money again. She didn't want to ever again be forced to sell her body to keep her child.

Celeste unlocked the front door and walked into the front foyer. The house was quiet. No one came to greet her, not even Silver.

She dropped her valise in the hallway and wandered to the kitchen, removing her bonnet as she walked. On the table she spotted a note; even from across the room, she recognized the handwriting. It was from Fox. He'd left her a note!

Anxiously, she picked it up.

> *C,*
> *Gone to the mine. Back late.*
> *No need for you to come.*
>
>   *F*

Celeste frowned. She had hoped for something more personal. Was he still angry that she'd gone to Denver? Of course he was. *No need for you to come.* Was he saying he didn't want her?

She let go of the note, written on the back of one of her lists, and watched it flutter to the table. Fox couldn't tell her not to come to the mine. It was hers as much as his. This was exactly why she didn't need a husband. All they did was tell women where to go and how to think.

Husband?

She laughed aloud as she climbed the staircase. Her voice echoed off the tin ceiling overhead. *Husband?* Where on earth had that ridiculous thought come from?

* * *

"You're sure he struck a vein and not a little pay dirt?" Celeste questioned. She'd changed from her traveling clothes to a simple brown gown and men's boots and come directly to the mine. She couldn't tell if Fox was glad to see her, or angry with her. She guessed it was a little of both.

"Petey swears he heard one of Trevor's miners at Kate's say Trevor hit a vein."

"When was this?"

"The night you *left*." There was a certain accusatory edge to his voice. "I didn't hear about it until the following day."

The two sat perched side by side on a wooden crate that had been used to ship a piece of machinery overland. Celeste's serge skirt brushed Fox's dusty pants. Their elbows touched. Fox had made no attempt to kiss her when she'd arrived. He'd said nothing of a personal nature in an entire hour. He'd been all business, and though she wanted to hear what was happening at the mine, she wished he'd say something about her, about them. Even if it was only to admit that he was mad that she'd gone to Denver. Something. Anything was better that this coolness that she couldn't shake despite the heat of the cast-iron stove in the middle of the room.

"Did he say where the vein was hit?" Celeste asked, trying to concentrate on the mine's problems rather than her own.

"His south wall."

She clasped her hands in her lap and stared at the light wool fingerless mitts she wore. "Right where our claim butts against his."

"You're on the mark," Fox said grimly.

He hadn't shaved in a day or two and he looked tired. Celeste wondered if he was roaming the streets at night again. She hoped he had better sense. There was no need to make Sheriff Tate any more suspicious than he already was.

"So do you think he honestly struck silver on his own property, or is he encroaching on ours?"

Fox ran his fingers through his hair. "I don't know. My first

impulse was just to ask him, but I didn't know if that was smart
or not. Maybe we should wait and see what happens. Keep an
eye on him.'' He lifted one shoulder. ''I didn't want to do
anything until I talked to you.''

Celeste brushed her knuckles against the back of his hand.
''Thanks. I appreciate your waiting for me to get back.''

''The silver's as much yours as mine,'' he grumbled.

''I know. I'm just saying I appreciate the fact that you recognize that. Most men wouldn't.''

He left his hand where it lay beside him, neither moving it
away nor touching her. The tension between them was so thick
in the air that Celeste thought she could hear it crackle.

''Fox, I'm sorry I had to go to Denver. I didn't mean to hurt
you. But I had to go,'' she finished firmly.

''Whatever. As you said weeks ago, we don't owe each other
anything.''

The words sounded so cold coming out of his mouth. She
wondered if they had sounded that way when *she'd* said them.
What kind of coldhearted woman would say such a thing? Only
a whore . . .

Celeste hung her head, suddenly feeling tired. She could feel
a wall building between them, brick by brick, she just wasn't
sure who was placing them there—her or him. Maybe it was
better this way. Maybe this was part of the answer to her
dilemma. If Fox left her, Adam would never know about him.

''So what do you want to do about Trevor? There's no way
for us to know for sure if he's on his own land, and that north
wall is the section of the tunnel we had to close off.''

''Had to close off,'' Fox echoed, pacing.

''You don't think he could have had anything to do with
that, do you?''

''I don't know. Seems like I don't know a hell of a lot these
days. I suppose we should start repairing that tunnel and wait
and watch.''

Fox's pacing made her nervous. He made her want to pace
as well. ''Should we call Sheriff Tate?''

''Let's hold off.'' He hooked one thumb in the pocket of

his denims. "He and I are not exactly the best of friends, and I understand that he and Trevor are."

She rose. "Agreed."

Fox shoved his hand into his pocket. "Guess I'll take a bucket down and see what needs to be done to the north tunnel to get it up and running. I'll get a crew on it as soon as possible." He walked away.

Celeste felt a tightening in her chest. Was this it? Were they drifting apart? Was this what Fox wanted? Was it what she wanted? "Hey," she called after him. "Want some company?"

"Nah."

He didn't turn back to see the tear she brushed away.

Petey appeared at her side as Celeste pulled the door shut at the assayer's office on Pear Street. "Miss Kennedy?" He yanked off his battered felt hat.

"Pete." The look on his face frightened her. There was something wrong at the mine. "What is it? What's wrong?"

"Titus said for you to come quick. I'm to take ye in the wagon." He pointed to the horse and wagon tied to a hitching post.

She hurried toward the wagon, and Petey had to run to catch up with her. "What happened?" she demanded. "Not another accident?"

He grasped her arm and helped her climb onto the front wagon seat. " 'Fraid so." He ran to the other side, unhitched the horse, and hoisted himself up beside her.

Celeste grasped the side of the wagon as it lurched backwards and then turned and lurched forward. "Where? Anyone killed? Injured?"

"It was a bad 'un. One man dead, Miss. Some broken legs. One poor hound gonna lose his arm."

"They'll need a physician. We have to find Doc Morris."

"Found 'im first. He went ahead in his own wagon whilst I came lookin' for you."

Celeste hung on tightly as they bumped over the rutted road, out of town and north toward MacPhearson's Fortune. She gripped the side of the wagon so tightly that she could feel her knuckles go numb. Petey hadn't said anything about Fox. Was he all right? Or was he the dead man, and Petey just didn't want to be the one who had to tell her?

The thought of Fox being killed was inconceivable. In the few short months that he'd lived with her in his father's house, he had become as much a part of her life as Adam, as vital to her as her own beating heart. It made her numb to think about him returning to California, but the idea that he might be dead turned her blood to ice.

"Pete?"

"Miss?" He stared straight ahead, the leather reins clasped in his hands.

"Mr. MacPhearson. You didn't mention him. Is he all right?"

When Petey didn't answer right away, she feared the worst. "No," she whispered, tears springing to her eyes. She wiped at them. She didn't want Petey to think she was a weak female. She'd worked hard for the respect of the miners who worked for her, and she couldn't afford to let them think her soft. Especially if Fox was gone . . .

She glanced up at the old miner. His face was as wrinkled as a dried apple, his hair as white as the snowcaps that had appeared on the mountaintops in the last month. "Tell me, Pete. Is Mr. MacPhearson dead?"

He looked sideways at her. "N . . . no, miss. He ain't dead, he . . ." He ended his sentence by letting the words dangle in the air.

"If he's not dead, then what?" She didn't mean to shout; just came out that way.

Pete cringed. "He . . . he's buried, Miss."

The numbness was creeping up on her again, from her feet this time. "Buried?"

"He went in to pull out the miner with the bad arm. Mousey Mike, we call him. Mr. MacPhearson, he pulled his shirt off and tied it around Mike's arm so's the blood would stop spurtin'."

Celeste could feel the blood draining from her face, not because she was squeamish, but because Fox has risked his own life, perhaps lost it, for a stranger. The sad thing was, she expected no less of him. "And?" she asked. "What happened then?"

He shrugged. They were pulling up to the equipment shed that covered the main shaft. "Rocks just started tumblin'. Mr. MacPhearson threw old Mike out of the way, and the rocks come tumblin' down. They was diggin' him out when Titus sent me to get you."

Before the wagon rolled to a halt, Celeste stood, raised her petticoats high, and jumped onto the ground.

"Whoa, there, Miss!" Petey hollered.

Celeste ignored him. She raced for the entrance to the mine shaft. A bucket was just coming up and dirty miners scattered to get out of her way. "Take me down, Joe."

This time the engineer seemed to sense he'd better not argue. Pete barely made his way into the cage before it lurched and began to sink into the shaft.

Celeste tried to stay calm as the iron cage hurled downward. "What level?" she demanded.

"It was the section we'd closed off, Miss. We was tryin' to put up supports."

"The injured men, where are they?"

"We took 'em to the ice room. I 'spect the doc is working on them there. Then the men'll bring 'em up."

"Did the dead man have a family?" she questioned softly.

"Wife. A kid in the Dakotas somewhere."

"We have to contact them. Send the widow condolences and money."

"Aw, you don't have to do that, Miss. Miners knows the risks. No one expects you to help nobody's family."

"Just do what I say, Pete."

"Yes, Miss."

She stared at her button shoes. *For money,* was all she could think. *We're doing this for money. Men dying, in accidents and of the coughing lung. Men losing limbs, their youth. Just for money.* The idea made her sick to her stomach. Hell, maybe whoring wasn't such a bad profession after all. People didn't get killed. She laughed bitterly to herself. At least they didn't used to.

The moment the iron cage hit the bottom, Celeste darted out. She didn't need anyone to lead her. She knew the way. Titus grabbed a lamp from one of the miners standing around and hurried after her.

It was so hot in the mine that sweat immediately covered her face and trickled in rivulets down her back. Her heart pounded. *Don't let him be dead. Don't let him be dead,* she prayed silently. *Please God, spare this man.*

Celeste spotted Titus standing knee-deep in chunks of rock and clay and splinters of silver ore.

"Found him yet?" she demanded.

"Almost got to him." A black-faced Titus pointed to a large pile of rubble against the north wall that appeared to have broken off from the low ceiling and fallen, despite the presence of the square-sets.

With her sleeve, Celeste wiped the sweat that stung her eyes. "Fox?" she called. "Fox, can you hear me?"

Miners were carefully hoisting fallen rocks and setting them down to make a new pile. It would have been faster to throw them, but she knew they didn't for fear the vibrations would cause another cave-in.

"Why don't you wait in the next section, Celeste?" Titus said quietly so that the other men wouldn't hear him. "No need for you to wait here. I'll call you the minute we find him . . . dead or alive."

She grabbed the closest rock, one the size of her head, and heaved it onto her shoulder.

"You don't have to do that." Titus tried to take the rock from her. "We got men—"

She yanked the rock from him and carefully set it on the pile the men were forming. "I can lift the same as these men," she said, surprised by how calm she sounded. "Let's get reinforcements in here and get these men to the ice room." She nodded to the three men working diligently. "They all look as if they're going to collapse."

Titus followed her orders and replaced the miners with a fresh crew. For five minutes they moved rock without saying anything.

Celeste's underclothing was soaked with sweat. She was dizzy from the heat, and her mouth and nostrils were filling with the fine film of dirt that clouded the air. But she kept moving rock. All she could think of was that Fox might still be alive and that she had to get to him. Somewhere in the back of her head she could hear the pounding footsteps of the killer in her dream. Only he wasn't coming for her, it was Fox he wanted.

Celeste heaved a rock over her shoulder, dropped it, and went back for another. "Fox?" she called. "You there?"

Nothing.

She leaned to grab another rock and heard something. "Shhhh!" she ordered. "Stand still. Fox?" she called again. "Fox, can you hear me?"

There was a long pause of silence, and then a sound that had to be human.

"Fox?"

"Some . . . someone going to get me out of here today?" came the weak voice from the pile of rocks.

She grinned, exhaling in relief. "Well, if you weren't laying around on the job, Mr. MacPhearson," she dropped her hands to her hips, using her best "boss" voice, "perhaps you wouldn't be in this mess."

The miners broke into laughter, easing the tension in the tiny alcove.

"Let's move faster," she told the miners. "Just be careful. We're this close. We don't want to injure him rescuing him."

It took another half an hour to reach Fox, but now that he was conscious and talking, the time moved quickly. When part of the ceiling caved in, he'd dove under a ledge that had been cut to expose the silver vein. That vein had saved his life.

When Fox's legs and bare torso were exposed, Celeste dropped on her hands and knees and crawled to him. "You're going to be late for dinner,'' she whispered, as she brushed his hair off his forehead.

He was laying flat on his back under the ledge, the silver vein touching his nose.

He chuckled. ''Sorry. I hope it wasn't pork roast. You know I love the way you make it with apples and that sauce.''

She smiled. He had a nasty gash on his forehead, but the blood had already congealed. ''You hurt anywhere?''

''Nah.'' Slowly he began to scoot out from under the ledge. ''Just scared half out of my wits. I couldn't breathe.''

''No, I don't guess you could.'' She lifted the hem of one of her petticoats and rubbed some of the dirt and sweat from his mouth and nose. She was so relieved that he was all right, yet suddenly she couldn't breathe. She felt as if she were the one trapped under the rock, suffocating.

He sat up and pushed his hair back over his forehead. ''Let's get everyone out of here, Titus, before we have another cave-in.'' He stood up, wobbly, but obviously unharmed.

The miners crowded around Fox, clapping him on his bare back and laughing with relief. Celeste knew that each man understood that it could just have as easily been one of them.

She watched the men pass into the safer section of the tunnel and pressed her hand to her chest. She was breathing so hard she was light-headed. Fox was all right. He was safe. Why did she feel like this? It was even worse than when she'd feared he was dead.

Celeste had a sudden, overwhelming need to see the sky, to feel the last rays of sun and the cold wind on her face. Unnoticed in the confusion, she pushed past the men and Fox. She climbed into one of the iron buckets, rang the bell, and rode up alone.

''Miss Kennedy?'' Joe called as she rose from the shaft. ''You all right?''

Celeste ran out through the covered building. She grabbed the side of the wagon, leaned over, and sucked in great gulps of fresh air. She was shaking from head to toe. *I can't do this,* she thought as she tried to calm her pounding heart. *I just can't live like this.*

Chapter Twenty-two

Celeste heard the front door open downstairs and Silver race through the hallway. His nails scraped as he slid on the polished wood floor, and she thought absently that she needed to clip them.

"Celeste?" Fox called. "You here, hon?"

The door banged shut and he turned the lock.

Celeste sat on the edge of her bed in the dark. She'd managed to bathe and get into her flannel nightdress. She'd mechanically brushed her hair, but had not made it beneath the covers.

She wanted to call out to Fox, but she couldn't find her voice. Her heart was still pounding, her hands shaking.

After she'd left Fox down in the mine, she'd taken the wagon and come home alone. She didn't know what was wrong, except that she had to get away.

"Celeste?" Fox's rich-timbered voice echoed up the stairwell as he passed down the hallway into the dark kitchen. A moment later she heard him come slowly up the stairs. "Celeste? Are you here?"

Her door was open. He halted in the doorway. Someone had loaned him a red plaid shirt.

"Celeste? Celeste, what's wrong, sweetheart?" He walked toward her. "You just disappeared. I didn't know where you were. Joe told me he saw you run outside, and then the wagon was gone. Why didn't you wait for me? I'd have come home sooner, but the doc insisted I come to his house, bathe and let him stitch my head."

She didn't answer. She couldn't.

"Celeste?" He stood in front of her for a moment, studying her. Then he sat on the bed beside her.

She felt his warm hand take hers.

"Ah, sweetheart, you're ice cold. Are we out of coal? You should have started a fire." He went to the stove, added a shovel of coal, and stoked it. "I told you, you need a maid. You can't work all day at the mine and take care of the house." He came back to the bed. "I'll have Petey look into hiring someone this week. Surely one of the miners has a wife who needs a job."

Celeste heard what he was saying, but it didn't sink in. *Fox was all right. He wasn't dead. He wasn't injured.* Why was she so paralyzed with fear?

She knew why. Somewhere deep inside she knew why. Because she'd crossed that line today. Maybe she'd crossed it months ago and hadn't realized it. She'd made a terrible mistake. She'd done what she swore she would never do again. She had fallen in love . . .

Fox crouched in front of her and took both her hands in his. "You're shaking," he said softly. He raised her hands to his lips and kissed them.

Close like this, she could smell that he was clean. He'd bathed and put on fresh clothes. Had he said something about the doc stitching him up?

"Celeste, I'm all right," Fox said softly. "You don't have to be afraid. I wasn't hurt."

"A man died," she whispered. Her lower lip trembled. "It . . . it could . . . could have been *you*." A sob rose in her throat and she choked it down, ashamed of her tears, ashamed that an experienced whore like herself could have allowed herself to care this much.

"Celeste." He rose and pulled her into his arms and held her tightly. "It's all right," he soothed. "It's all right. I'm safe. Wasn't my time to go."

Celeste fought to control her emotions as she melted into his arms. He made her feel so warm, so cared for, so loved.

Hell, there was that word again!

She knew now that she'd been fighting it for months. She should never have let Fox stay. Not even that first night. She was a fool. A fool.

Fox smoothed her damp hair and kissed her temples. He stroked her back with a soothing circular movement. He just held her until she relaxed a little.

"I . . . I don't know what came over me . . ." she said when she found her voice. "I shouldn't have run like that. What will the men think?"

"It's all right. You were strong when you needed to be. Titus told me you took over rescuing me." He rubbed her upper arms. "I hear you heaved a few rocks yourself."

"I was afraid you were dead." She looked up into his eyes. "I was afraid I would never see you again, and I couldn't bear it."

He pulled her hard against him. "Ah, sweetheart, I'm sorry."

"I hate this business," she told him. "I was never meant to run a mine. It's filthy and it's dangerous. I don't want men to die to line my purse."

Keeping his arms wrapped around her, he led her to the upholstered chair beside the coal stove that was beginning to heat up. He eased into the chair and pulled her onto his lap. "Me either," he said quietly.

She laid her head on his shoulder and traced the outline of the stitched gash on his forehead. "What?"

"I'm not cut of the cloth to be a miner. Call me weak if you like. I don't care for the business. I don't like the danger or the searing heat—or the enclosure. I feel like I'm climbing into a coffin every time I ride down in one of those buckets."

She smoothed his beard-stubbled cheek with her palm.

"I don't like the injustices," he continued. "Even paying the miners an exorbitant hourly wage, it's still a foul business."

"So what do we do?"

He traced the neckline of her sleeping gown. "Do? Sell it, I suppose. Hell, if Trevor is trying to steal our silver, why not sell it to him and make him an honest man? If not him, some other money-hungry wolf."

"Sell the mine?" He had taken her completely by surprise. "Sell it all?"

"Sell it," he repeated, firmer this time. He was toying with the long row of bone buttons that ran down the front of her gown. Then, hesitantly, "We . . . could sell it and go to California."

Celeste's breath caught in her throat. He had said *we,* hadn't he? *We,* as in both of them? "California?" was all she could manage.

"Sure. We buy land and we start that vineyard. I think I'm far better suited to planting grapevines than sending men into heated coffins, don't you?"

"And . . . and you want *me* to go?"

He was quiet for a moment, and then he turned his head to meet her gaze. White moonlight shone off his handsome, haggard face. "Once I became conscious, lying there beneath the rubble, waiting, all I thought of was you, Celeste. All I wanted was you. You're all I think about day and night. I'd be a fool to think I could walk out of this town without you."

Celeste was too shocked to say anything. He didn't want to leave her! He didn't want to go to California without her. He wanted to be with her as much as she wanted to be with him. She was suddenly so filled with excitement that she thought her heart would burst.

"Oh, Fox," was all she could say. She raised her mouth to his and kissed him.

"Celeste."

He pressed his warm mouth against hers and she parted her lips. He tasted clean and fresh; he tasted of promise.

She slipped her arms around Fox's neck and drew one leg up to curl herself in his lap.

He unhooked the buttons of her white flannel and lace nightdress. She sighed with pleasure as his hand found and cupped her breast. The thought that she could have this forever was beyond conception. It was what she secretly dreamed of, but never expected to have.

Fox brushed the rough pad of his thumb against her nipple and it hardened in response. With his other arm, he held her tightly against him, cradling her in his lap.

Over and over again, he brushed his tongue over her lower lips, teasing her, nipping at her tongue with his teeth. She threaded her fingers through his thick, glossy hair and arched her back, encouraging him to press his mouth to the pulse of her throat.

"Celeste, Celeste," he whispered. "What made me ever think I could leave you? I was doomed. Doomed from that first night in the swing."

She laughed, her voice husky in her ears. Everything really was going to be all right.

Fox kissed a burning path from her throat to the valley between her breasts. She slipped her hands around his head and gently guided his mouth to her aching nipple.

Fox tongued the pink bud and then suckled. She exhaled with pleasure. The room had been cold a moment ago, but now it seemed warm. Her flannel nightdress was hot and rough against her skin. Every inch of her flesh prickled with heat and sensation.

Fox sucked one nipple and gently squeezed her other breast with his hand. She covered his hand with hers, encouraging him, guiding him.

"I want to make love to you, Celeste," Fox whispered in the darkness. "I want to hold you in my arms and make love to you, tonight, tomorrow night, and all the nights to come." He raised his head from her breast, and the moisture in his eyes convinced her that he meant it.

"Will you let me do that?" he murmured. He kissed her

cheek, the tip of her nose, the faint cleft of her chin. "Will you let me make love to you?"

"Yes," she whispered, her heart bursting with joy. "Yes. It's what I want." *Always wanted.* She thought it, but she didn't say it.

Fox rose from the chair and carried her to the bed, never breaking from her gaze. He laid her gently on the bed, kicked off his boots, peeled off his stockings and breeches. He threw off his shirt and then climbed into the feather tick beside her.

"Brr . . . it's cold." Celeste scrambled under the bedcovers and he followed her.

"Too much clothing," he teased as he pushed the gown over her shoulders. "You've got far too much clothing on for my bed, woman."

She laughed with him as he pushed the gown over her shoulders and she wiggled out of it, leaving it rumpled somewhere at the bottom of the bed.

Fox pulled her against him so that they lay side by side, naked flesh against naked flesh. She could feel the prickly hair of his chest against her. She could feel his heart pounding as fast as her own.

"Much better," he whispered as he nuzzled her ear. "Just the way I like my business partners. Tough on the job, soft and"—he slipped his hand to the apex of her thighs—"and wet for me in bed."

A moan escaped Celeste's lips. He knew so well how to please her. He knew what she liked. He knew how to caress her. He knew how to tease her to the brink of fulfillment, only to draw her back again at the last moment.

Celeste ground her hips against him. She could feel his rod stiff and hot for her, pressing against her legs.

Fox rolled on top of her, his hand still stroking the sensitive folds of her womanhood. They kissed again and again, harder, until frenzied, she parted her legs and raised up to meet his first thrust.

"Please . . . now." Her voice was strained with desire, barely audible. Her heart was pounding, her breath coming in short gasps.

"You're always in such a hurry," he teased.

But as he kissed her shoulder, he slipped inside her.

Celeste rose to meet his thrust as hungry for him as she had ever been. "Fox," she whispered.

"Celeste." He lay still over her, deep inside. He kissed her closed eyelids. He brushed her lips in a butterfly kiss.

She sank her blunt nails into his buttocks. Drained of emotion, she needed physical fulfillment. She could concentrate on nothing else but her own burning desire and the only act that could fulfill it.

Celeste lifted her hips against his and pulled him down. Sensing her need, he thrust hard. She raised her hands above her head on the pillow, giving herself to Fox as she had never given herself to any man.

Ripples of hot pleasure coursed from the center of her being outward. Every vein in her body shivered with want of him. Again and again she rose to meet his thrust. He kissed her mouth and then lowered his head to take one of her nipples.

She strained against him, her pleasure surging. "Fox!" she cried out as she gripped his shoulders and her muscles convulsed. She felt as if she had climbed a steep mountain and flown off the edge. She was flying . . . flying in pleasure, flying in heat, flying in the comfort that she had finally found someone who could care for her . . . love her.

Fox spilled his seed inside her with a groan and both grew still. Tiny undulations of the aftermath of their lovemaking still rippled through her.

Fox slid off her and rolled onto his back, panting.

She rested her head on her pillow, her eyes closed, floating . . . floating.

Fox leaned up on one elbow, kissed her, and then pulled the cover over them both. The last thing she remembered before she fell asleep was the feel of his arms around her and the heady, musky smell of their bodies pressed close.

* * *

Sometime in the middle of the night Celeste's eyes flew open. Fox was asleep beside her, his breathing soft and even. He lay on his stomach, one hand flung possessively over her.

Her heart pounded.

"He didn't say he loved me," she whispered softly to herself. It must have come to her in her sleep and woken her.

"He said he wanted me," she said in a dazed murmur. "He said he needed me. But never once did he say he loved me. Never once did he say he wanted to marry me."

Ice filled her veins and she was chilled to the bone. Carefully, so as not to wake Fox, she slipped out of the bed. She grabbed her night robe off the bedpost and slipped into it, naked and shivering. Grabbing an extra quilt off the end of the bed, she sat in the chair by the stove and dragged the quilt up over her. The stove radiated heat; she should be warm enough, but she wasn't. Her chill came from a deeper place—from her heart.

Celeste sat in the chair, her knees drawn up, and rocked herself. *Fox has never been anything but honest with me,* she thought. *He said he could never love a whore again. How could I have ever thought I could change him? How could I have thought for a moment that a man like Fox would marry a woman like me?*

But somehow, deep inside, she knew she must have thought he might, else why would she be so disappointed? No, she wasn't just disappointed. She was heartbroken.

Silver whined, rose from the rag rug beside the bed, and padded over to her. She petted his head, scratched behind his ears, and the dog leaned against her and sank to the floor.

It was her own fault. She knew better than to fall in love. She knew better than to allow herself to get so close to a man that this could happen. She got what she deserved . . .

So now what? Did she go with Fox and live with him in sin as she did now? Wasn't it enough that he cared about her? That he needed her? She'd never find a better man to give her life to.

But what about Adam? She remembered the need she had heard in his voice when he said he wanted to live with her. Though she knew that he knew that she loved him, she also knew that he wanted more from her. How could she deny her son? Celeste didn't know what to do. She wanted Adam with her, but she wanted to do what was best for him, not what was best for her. Did she leave him at the school in respectable surroundings? Or did she take him with her, and let him see what kind of woman she was?

Tears slid down her cheeks.

And what about herself? Didn't she deserve to be loved?

The next morning Celeste stood at the stove, her back to the doorway when Fox entered the kitchen.

"Morning, sweet."

She heard him drop his boots by the chair and sit to put them on as he did every morning.

She spun around. "You didn't ask me to marry you," she blurted out.

Fox glanced up with a look of utter confusion on his freshly shaved face. "What?"

"I just want to understand." She raised her index finger. "You didn't ask me to marry you."

He looked down at his boot as he slipped his foot into it. "No."

"And you didn't say you loved me last night either. You just asked me to go with you to California."

He slammed his foot into the second boot. "Isn't that enough, damn it!"

"No." She dropped her hands to her hips. "It's not."

He rose out of the chair and slammed it under the table. "What do you want from me, Celeste? Just what the hell do you want?" There was a tremble in his angry voice. "I care for you. I need you. I'll take care of you. I'll give you anything the hell you want."

Her lower lip trembled as she fought back aching tears. She couldn't weaken now, she wouldn't. "But not your love."

He looked down at his feet, the hands she loved so much hung at his side. "No. I can't. Won't."

His words tore her heart asunder. She forced herself to be calm, her voice cool and unemotional. "I think you need to move from my house."

He strode from the kitchen and slammed the doorjamb with his fist as he passed into the hall. "I think you're right."

Chapter Twenty-three

"I can't believe you've done it and then stuck to your guns," Sally said as she poured Celeste a cup of tea from Kate's favorite china pot.

Kate's kitchen was quiet because it was only eleven in the morning on Sunday, and the other girls were still abed. Celeste and Sally had gone to church service together and then come back for tea.

"I just realized I couldn't live like that anymore, Sally. I've been so afraid something would happen to him. That I'd lose him. It was making me crazy."

Sally sat across from Celeste and reached for the sugar bowl. She wrinkled her nose. "But you have lost him."

Celeste shook her head. "It's not the same thing."

"It's not?" Sally added a third lump of brown sugar to her tea.

"No. It's not." Celeste stirred her tea, though there was nothing in it but tea to stir. "This is on my terms. If *I* give him up—if *I* send *him* away, it's different. It's my choice, and it's the right thing to do. I can live with that."

Sally licked her spoon. "Different, huh? So's you can live

with your conscience instead of the man you love.'' She sounded doubtful.

''Exactly.''

Sally dipped her spoon in her tea again. ''If you say so.''

Celeste unpinned her hat and placed it on the table beside her. ''If he doesn't love me, he won't stay true to me. You know he won't. That's the way men are. And if he loved me, he'd marry me. He'd make a home for my son.''

Sally poured thick cream into her teacup. ''But he don't know you got a son.''

''It doesn't matter,'' Celeste told her regretfully. ''What matters is that nothing could come of this relationship, so I might as well end it here before I get hurt.''

Sally poured tea into her saucer. ''Looks to me like you're already hurt,'' she said to her teacup.

Celeste watched Sally slurp from her saucer. ''I need you to help me here, Sally,'' she said softly. ''I need you to help me tell myself I've done the right thing. Even if Adam doesn't come to live with me, I can't continue to live in sin with men. I have to become respectable. As respectable as . . . your grandmother.''

Sally gave a snort of laughter. ''My grammy? She sold my mama's virginity to a mule driver when Mama was only thirteen!''

Celeste rolled her eyes. ''You know what I mean.''

Sally laughed and tossed her blond ringlets. ''I know. I'm just teasin' you because I hate to see you hurting like this.'' She slid her tiny hand across the table to take Celeste's. ''You know I give you a hard time, but I'd do anything for you. I love you as much as I love my Noah. More, because it's different with women.''

Celeste covered Sally's hand with hers and gave it a squeeze. ''Thanks. Now let's not talk about me. Fox has moved out and into one of those new boardinghouses on the end of Cherry Street. I imagine he'll be selling his part of the mine and moving on before Christmas. What's done is done.'' She lowered her hands to her lap and glanced up at Sally, forcing a smile. Her heart was crumbling inside, but she knew she was doing the right thing, the safe thing. "Now tell me some more about Noah. When are you going to get married?"

Sally giggled into her china teacup. "We was supposed to wait until Christmas, but Noah says he can't wait for me that long, else his *you know whats* going to burst." She lifted her lashes. "So we're talking about getting hitched the first of December."

"Why that's right around the corner! I'm so glad to hear it. I want you to get out of Carrington. I want you to have the life you deserve."

"Well, Noah says it's burning him up inside to think I'm still rollin' men, so . . ." Sally toyed with her spoon. "I'm going to tell Kate I'm done. If she wants to kick me out before Noah and I are married, she can, but this girl has asked Jesus to forgive her and I ain't doin' it anymore."

Celeste sipped her tea, truly delighted for Sally and only a little envious of her happiness. "The man sounds like he's worth his weight in silver. When do I get to meet him?"

Fox sat on the edge of the narrow cot and stared at the plain, painted white wall. The boardinghouse had gone up a short time after they struck silver at MacPhearson's Fortune, and the room still smelled of freshly sawed lumber and whitewash paint. The room was small, but clean, the walls thin, but it served his purpose. Fresh sheets and towels were provided weekly, clean water for shaving and washing daily, and the outhouse was only a short walk from the back of the building. What more could a man ask for?

Fox spent his long days at the mine and came here only to sleep, and then not every night. Tonight he'd returned only because Titus had insisted that if Fox didn't get some sleep, he was going to make a serious mistake in the mine and kill himself or someone else. Fox had reluctantly returned to his rented room, but he couldn't sleep. He missed Celeste. He missed her dog that had somehow become his.

Fox ran his hands over his unshaven face. Where had he gone wrong? What had he done? He had offered to take Celeste with him to California, to care for her, to provide for her. Why did women always want more than was offered?

She said she wanted him to love her. Of course she hadn't said anything about loving *him*. Women were like that . . . whores at least. They wanted to take, but they didn't want to give. Fox had to keep reminding himself of that. At some point in a man's life he had to stop laying his heart open. He had to stop trusting women that he knew, from experience, couldn't be trusted.

But then, what reason had Celeste given him not to trust her? He shared a house with her, a business, a bed, and not once in all these months had she led him to question her word or deed even once. So was he really afraid to trust Celeste because she had been a whore, or was he using this as an excuse? Maybe he was just plain scared to love a woman again, any woman.

Fox lifted his head from his hands and stared at the wall. Light from the lamp on the table beside the bed cast a distorted shadow of him against the vertical, painted boards.

Fox didn't honestly know anymore how he felt or what he thought. All he knew was that without Celeste, he was damned miserable.

He rose off the bed and began to pace. The room was exactly six paces by five. He knew from experience. He walked to the wall, turned and walked back, only to turn and go the other way again.

For two weeks he'd had no contact with Celeste except at the mine, and there it was strictly business with her. She treated him as if he were one of the damned workers. She smiled pleasantly, but coolly, and went on talking figures as if they had never kissed, never touched, never made love as they had that last night in her room.

Fox balled his hands at his side, so frustrated that he couldn't think clearly. He needed her. He wanted her. Why couldn't he have her?

Fox knew he couldn't continue to live like this. He knew he should just sell the mine, take his money, and go back to California. He'd even contacted Trevor about the possibility of buying his share. In the same conversation he'd threatened that if Trevor was stealing from him and Celeste, he'd slit his throat. Oddly enough, no more silver had come from the Trevor mine. It seemed as if he had hit a dry spot.

Going to California made sense. Fox would have enough money so that if he was careful, he could buy land and start the vineyard he'd always dreamed of. But for some reason the dream seemed to have turned as sour as a bad batch of wine. Truth was, he didn't want the vineyard without someone to share it with. He didn't want it without Celeste.

So why couldn't she be reasonable? Why couldn't she be content to take what he offered? They would be happy together in California. He knew they would.

But no. She didn't just want flesh, she wanted his heart.

Fox halted in the center of the room, squeezed his eyes tightly shut, and pressed his arms to his sides. For a moment he was a boy again. Alone. He remembered the ache in the pit of his stomach so fierce that he felt it now. "Why'd you let her do it to me?" he whispered to the lonely room. "Why . . . Papa?"

Fox's eyes flew open and he wiped at the moisture that had gathered there. It would be so easy to love Celeste. But could he do it? Could he take the risk again? He honestly didn't know.

Fox grabbed his woolen coat off the end of the rope bed and punched his arms into the raglan sleeves. Celeste must have worn it sometime. He smelled the scent of her on it.

Fox threw his new gray cloak over the coat because he knew how bitterly cold it was tonight. Then he blew out the lamp and reached for the new porcelain doorknob. It was late, almost midnight, but he had to get some fresh air. He had to think.

Fox walked the length of Cherry Street. It was dark and only a pale quarter moon shone. Its light reflected off the dirty snow and bounced up to illuminate his way. Somewhere a dog barked and he thought of Silver. Taking these midnight walks wasn't the same without the good old hound.

Somewhere a baby cried and then was hushed, perhaps by his mother's breast. The domestic thought made him smile to himself. He had always thought he might like to have a child. He knew he could be a better father than his had been. He'd just never known a woman he would want to share his blood with in that way—until maybe now.

Fox turned at the darkened railway station and started up Peach Street. There was still tinny music and drunken laughter coming from the saloons. Two miners, half-drunk, passed him on the wooden sidewalk and tipped their hats to him. Another man rode by in a wagon headed out of town, the buckboard bed filled with sleeping or passed-out miners.

Fox continued along the street, past Kate's Dance Hall, past Sal's Saloon. He thought about stopping for a drink at Sal's. Sal said it wasn't natural, a man who didn't drink. But Fox didn't want anything to interfere with his thinking. He was having a hard enough time making any sense to himself as it was.

Past the dance halls and saloons, Peach Street grew darker and quiet. The piano music and the laughter faded. Fox felt so alone in the cold silence.

The sound of pounding footsteps in an alley caught his attention, and he glanced over just in time to see someone running down the alley between a bank and a stable, away from him. Fox halted, took a step back, and squinted into the darkness. The shadow disappeared into the night.

Fox hesitated in the entry to the alleyway, the hair rising on the back of his neck. He smelled something odd, familiar, and yet not familiar. The scent was warm and metallic in the frosty air. Then his gaze fell to the ground and a crumpled shadow. A streak of light cast from the moon behind him illuminated a green fold of material. It was a cloak, perhaps. Celeste had just bought a new green cloak the very same color. He remembered how it had matched her eyes and made them sparkle when she'd modeled it for him.

''No,'' Fox whispered. It couldn't be . . .

He stood frozen for only an instant and then ran into the alley. He stooped to touch her, praying she lived and that he'd scared the killer off in time. She was still warm, but his hand was instantly wet and he knew that she was covered in blood. ''No, no, Celeste,'' he muttered under his breath as a chant. ''Not Celeste. Not my angel.''

He went down on one knee, oblivious of the muddy slush left by the last snow and men's boots, and lifted her in his arms. Her hair was long and dark, like Celeste's, but he couldn't tell what color. Her head fell back limply as he lifted her and pushed back the lumps of bloody hair that covered her face.

''No, no,'' he whispered, his heart pounding. He tipped her head so that the moonlight shone on her face. ''Please, please . . .''

Then he heaved a great sigh of relief, mortified at the same time that he could be so callus. It wasn't Celeste. *Oh, God, thank you, thank you, it wasn't Celeste . . .*

Fox touched the young woman's bloody throat, hoping to find a pulse. None. She was dead. He eased her back onto the cold ground and stood, heaving in great cold breaths of air, exhaling white frost. He had to get Sheriff Tate.

He stepped out onto the street. His hands were wet with blood and shaking. He looked down. His cloak was covered with blood. He couldn't go to Tate looking like this! The man would hang him without a trial. But he had to find the sheriff before the killer got too far.

Fox walked back up Peach Street as casually as he could, and stopped at the first rain barrel. He glanced up and down the street to be sure no one was about, and then broke the ice on the top of the barrel. He sank his hands into the frigid water.

His hands clean, he pulled off his cloak and balled it up. In the alley beside Simon's Boardinghouse was a trash barrel. It reeked of rotten vegetables. Fox dug with a stick under some of the refuse, threw in his cloak, and then covered it. He felt guilty for cleaning up like this, but he'd be damned if he'd let Tate get him lynched for a crime he didn't commit.

Back on the street, as chilled by the sight of the dead girl as his fear that it had been Celeste, Fox stood for a moment to get his bearings. He was only a little surprised to discover that his hands were still shaking. He stuffed them into his pocket and stood in indecision. Should he go to the sheriff's office where Tate slept in an upstairs room, or did he try looking for him in Sal's first? It was only midnight, and early for Tate.

Turning grimly on his heels, he decided to check Sal's first.

It was nearly three in the morning by the time the woman's body was carried off by the undertaker, and Sheriff Tate had released Fox on his own recognizance.

After an hour of questioning that sounded more like badgering, Fox was relieved he'd washed his hands and disposed of his bloody cloak. Sheriff Tate was so hell-bent on finding a killer, that Fox had no doubt the man would have locked him up, had there been one smear of blood on his person. Tate was so obsessed with nailing someone for the crimes that Fox feared it was more important to the sheriff that he pin the murders on someone, than it was to actually catch the real killer.

It was close to three when Fox stepped out onto the icy street. But instead of heading for his boardinghouse and his warm bed, he found himself wandering down, first Peach Street, then Plum. The woman's name had been Sarah Mae. She'd been sixteen.

Fox wiped his mouth with the back of his cold hand, but he couldn't wipe away the evil taste in his mouth. There was no way he could sleep. Every time he closed his eyes he knew he would see that poor, butchered girl. Every time he closed his eyes, he knew he would be afraid. Not for himself, but for Celeste.

The killer had changed his method. Young Sarah Mae was not a whore, but a maid in one of the new saloons. She had lived with her brother in a shack out on the miner's claim. The killer had either made a mistake, or had broadened his circle of victims to include women of merely shady reputations. And the killing hadn't taken place in a whorehouse, but on the street. The girl had been headed home after washing whiskey glasses for Mr. Gloakem, the saloon owner.

Fox glanced up and found himself in front of 27 Plum Street. The house was still dark, and quiet. He stared up at Celeste's window. He considered banging on the door, or going back to the boardinghouse for the key to the front door. He had an overwhelming desire to see her, just to be certain that she was safe. But Fox knew he was being overly apprehensive. The killer had never struck more than once on a single night. Celeste wasn't even really a target. She'd not slept with a man for payment in close to a year.

Would that matter to the killer?

Fox sat on the upper step of the porch, shivering. He thrust his hands into his pockets for warmth. It would be dawn in a few hours and then Celeste would be safe. He'd just wait it out.

Celeste woke early, then tossed and turned in bed, hoping she could go back to sleep. Though she'd gone to bed before ten, she didn't feel rested. Several times during the night she knew she'd reached for Fox in her sleep, only to find he wasn't there.

After lying in bed for another ten minutes, she gave up and rose to add coal to the fire. She missed having Fox here to warm the house before she got up in the morning. She missed waking up to the whistle of her teakettle, too.

She missed Fox.

Throwing on her flannel wrapper and wool mules, she shuffled to the coal stove to stoke it. She wouldn't add coal because she wouldn't be upstairs the rest of the day, but even a little warmth from the turned coals would be welcome.

Celeste stirred the dying coals wearily. She was beginning to have second thoughts about Fox. Maybe he was right; maybe she *was* asking too much. Maybe to have him care about her, to have him make her happy, should be enough.

She leaned the poker against the stove and closed the door. She knew one thing. She was certainly miserable without Fox. Could living with him without love make her any more unhappy than she already was?

Wrapping her arms around her waist for comfort as well as warmth, she walked to the window and peered out. Dawn was just beginning to light the winter day and radiate its heat. Absently, Celeste tugged on the curtain and drew a heart on the frosty window. She added her name and Fox's inside it.

If only Fox had argued with her that morning. If only he'd begged her to go with him to California. If only he'd come back later and tried to compromise. If only he'd shown some sign that there was a possibility he could come to love her someday . . .

With a sigh, Celeste wiped the cold window with the heel of her hand to smear their names, and turned away, letting the curtain fall.

Fox waited patiently on Celeste's step until the first streak of dawn peeked over the snowy mountain tops. Then, he rose off the step, cold and stiff, walked down her sidewalk, and turned onto the street. He dared only one glance back at the house. Was that Celeste's bedroom curtain he saw move? He watched for a moment, hoping to catch a glimpse of her pretty, sleepy face in the window glass. After a moment, he gave up, turned away, and headed back to his lonely boardinghouse room for a couple hours of restless sleep.

Chapter Twenty-four

Celeste lifted her skirt to allow the warm air to drift under her woolen knit petticoat. At her insistence, Petey had added coal twice to the stove this morning, but she was still cold. It seemed as if she hadn't been able to get warm in weeks—not since Fox left.

Celeste reread the list of equipment and supplies that needed to be ordered and shipped from Denver. She'd checked the list twice already, but couldn't concentrate enough to know if it was correct. With the coming of winter, the trains weren't running as regularly, and it was imperative that the necessary supplies be available to keep the mine operating.

Instead of checking the list, though, Celeste idly sketched a grape leaf and wondered what Adam would think of the idea of moving to California to live in a vineyard.

But, who was she fooling? The offer had come and gone. Fox had said nothing more of going with him to California since he moved out of her house three weeks ago. He seemed perfectly content with the new arrangement. He'd not once tried to see her, except here at the mine. Then he was all business—charming, but cool.

Celeste heard Fox's rich-timbered voice and dipped her pen into the inkwell and added something to the list. His voice grew louder as, talking to a miner, he entered the equipment room. They finished their business and Fox walked over to her desk, Silver trailing him.

"Did you add that extra order of timber to the list?"

"Mm hm." She didn't look up. To talk to him without seeing that twinkle in his eyes that had once been for her was agonizing, so she tried to avoid eye contact.

At his silence she glanced up from the desk. He apparently had something else to say, or he would have left by now.

"Yes?" she finally asked. "Something else to be ordered?"

He massaged the back of his neck with one broad hand, and she felt her own neck tense. What she wouldn't give to have him touch her like that right now . . .

"Um . . . no. I—" he said awkwardly. "I was thinking I would set up a meeting with Trevor next week to um . . . talk about selling my share of the mine. I thought you should be there."

"Fine." She pretended to concentrate on the list again, but suddenly felt light-headed. All she could think about was that Fox was definitely planning to leave Carrington. He was leaving her. She'd known it would happen. So why did it still hurt so much? "I'd like to meet with him," she heard herself say as if they were speaking of the weather. "I might be interested in selling as well."

"Oh. All right." He stood silent again. "Going to Sally's party tonight?" he asked after a minute.

"Wouldn't miss it." She glanced up and smiled as she would have smiled at any of the miners who'd come to ask a question. "Say, I meant to ask you, could you take Silver for a few days? I have to go somewhere."

She could have sworn he glowered, but then he flashed that boyish grin of his. "Want me to take him tonight?"

"If you would."

"Not a problem."

"Thank you." This was the most personal conversation they'd had in weeks. Dismayed, Celeste lowered her gaze.

Fox stood a moment longer in front of the desk, as if he wanted to say something, but then he walked off briskly, leaving Celeste alone with the supply list and a heavy heart.

Filth. Nothing but filth, those who think they're reformed. They are falsely led to believe that forgiveness is so easy to come by. They think they are forgiven simply because they ask for forgiveness.

But how can they truly be exonerated for such a sin?

There is only one way. Death. Blood. Only the blood poured out for Him can wash the soul clean. Only in death can forgiveness come.

She must die.

Celeste stood outside Kate's Dance Hall, listening to the raucous music that filtered through the walls and into the street. Tonight was Sally's farewell party, and tomorrow she and Noah would take a train to Denver and then on to St. Louis, where they intended to be married by his uncle.

Celeste tried to gather her wits before she walked into the dance hall. She was so happy for Sally, and yet at the same time she felt a deep sadness for herself and what she now knew she would never have.

Celeste knew Fox might attend the party, so she had dressed carefully in an emerald green watered silk gown with a white muslin canezoe trimmed with Valenciennes lace. She'd spent an hour in front of the mirror, taking a hot curling rod to her freshly washed hair. Then she'd added a hint of color to her lips and cheeks, too subtle to be recognized as paint, but attractive to the eye.

Celeste intended to go into Kate's and have a wonderful time. She wouldn't let Fox know how much he had hurt her, how much she had allowed herself to be hurt. She would laugh and chat with her friends, share in a good luck toast to the happy couple, and she would pick up the valise she'd left at the train station and take the midnight train to Denver.

Adam wasn't expecting her until Christmas, but she felt the need to be with him. Seeing Adam would remind her that in losing Fox, she'd not lost everything. She still had her son, who she loved dearly. As long as she had Adam, she could make a life for herself.

With that determined thought, Celeste pasted on her prettiest, most beguiling smile, and walked into the dance hall.

Kate's was alive with music and laughter and bright with glittering lantern light. Kate had surprised everyone in Carrington, including herself, by closing for the evening in Sally's honor. Only friends of the bride and groom had been invited, and other would-be patrons were sent down the street to Sal's.

The moment Celeste entered the dance hall, her cloak was swept away and someone passed her a glass of wine. As she sipped the dry vintage and nodded greetings, she spotted Sally.

Sally was dressed in her wedding gown of white satin, its skirt trimmed in white tulle, with a square-cut bodice and elbow sleeves with ruffles. Her hair was pulled back with a pink ribbon in a mass of curls; and without face paint, she appeared as virginal as any cloistered bride on her wedding day.

"You look beautiful," Celeste said as Sally approached in a swish of white skirts.

Sally laughed girlishly and held out her arms to hug Celeste. "I feel beautiful. And oh!" Her eyes shone. "You have to finally meet my Noah." She looped her arms through Celeste's and led her across the dance hall's main room past the painted mural of naked dancing women. They wove around two men doing a jig.

"I swear, I didn't think I'd get him off that claim," Sally told Celeste. "But here he is. Noah, honey."

A giant of a man turned to Celeste and Sally.

Noah was over six feet tall and nearly as wide. He had a great scraggly red beard, wild red hair, and the merriest blue eyes Celeste had ever seen.

"There you are. I thought you'd gotten away without me."

Noah grabbed Sally in his arms and pulled her against him. "And this must be the Miss Kennedy I've heard so much about."

Celeste curtsied and then offered her gloved hand. "I'm so pleased to finally meet you."

The apples of Noah's cheeks reddened as he accepted Celeste's hand and bowed cordially. "It is indeed my pleasure, Miss Kennedy." The man was as paradoxical as Sally, with his scruffy beard and impeccable manners.

Sally giggled behind her fingers and then smoothed the sleeve of Noah's new black wedding waistcoat. "I think Noah's more nervous about getting hitched than I am. First he kept checkin' the train schedule, fearing we'd not make St. Louis in time. Now he's got it in his head that I shouldn't sleep here tonight. He wants me to come back to his place. He says he's worried about the murderer,"—she cupped her hand around her mouth—"but I think he just wants *a piece.*"

Sally and Celeste laughed.

Noah blushed, his apple red cheeks turning crimson. "That's not true, and you know it. I'm just worried about you, sweetie pie. If something happened to you, they might as well bury me in one of those worthless mines out there."

"I think it's nice that Noah is concerned about your safety, Sally." Celeste smoothed the lace on one of Sally's sleeves. "Perhaps you should go with him and give him peace of mind."

"Aw, no. I've held out this long. If I go back to his place, one sweet word, and I'll spread my legs wide."

"Sally!" Noah admonished playfully. "You're embarrassing the hell out of me."

Sally laughed and rose on her tiptoes. Noah leaned over to accept her kiss.

Celeste sipped her wine, beginning to relax. She hadn't caught sight of Fox. Maybe he hadn't come after all. "Well, if it would make Noah feel any better, you could stay at my place tonight."

"With you?" Sally hung on to Noah's arm. "That might be fun."

"Actually, I intend to take the midnight train to Denver, but you could stay in my house anyway. I could give you my key."

Sally glanced up at her bearded fiancé, who towered over her. "What you think, sweetie pie? Would that make you sleep any better?"

He wrapped his arms around her tiny waist. "I'd sleep better with you in my arms, but I reckon that will do."

"All right. Celeste's place it is." She struck his chest with the palm of her hand. "But you'd best come for me in the morning, you big bear."

He squeezed her tightly against him. "Don't you worry, this man will be there. I've been waiting my whole life for you, Sally Ann. A stampede of runaway ore wagons couldn't keep me away." He kissed the top of her head.

Celeste glanced down at her wine and took a long sip. She was jealous of Sally and embarrassed to admit it, even to herself. She wondered if Sally realized how lucky she was to have a man like Noah love her.

As Celeste took another sip, she heard a painfully familiar male voice near the door.

Fox.

She wished she could hide behind Noah's broad back, or slip out the back door.

Fox stood just inside the doorway, dressed in the pinstriped suit she'd had made for him. He looked so damned roguishly handsome. He'd brought Silver with him, which didn't really surprise her. John had taken the dog everywhere he went, too.

Celeste averted her gaze before Fox caught her staring at him. She thought she was prepared to see him tonight, but just the sound of his voice made her knees weak. God, she loved him. She loved him with every ounce of her being.

"You all right?" Sally whispered. She released Noah's arm and took Celeste's.

"I'm all right. Just stay with me, will you?" Celeste lowered her head. "I don't want to make a fool of myself and beg him to take me back or anything ridiculous like that."

Sally held Celeste's sweaty hand in her cool one. "Let's get you another glass of wine and a dance partner."

The next couple hours passed in a blur for Celeste. She drank champagne, but was careful not to overindulge. She danced. She talked. She laughed with her friends and exchanged stories about Sally. When Kate raised a glass in toast to the new couple, Celeste joined in, truly happy for them.

As Kate spoke, Celeste glanced around the room. She knew she was fortunate to have such good friends; Kate, Titus, Petey, Sheriff Tate. Even Joash had shown up for the going-away party. And no matter how far from Carrington Celeste went, she knew the people in this dance hall would always be her friends and always care for her.

Everyone in the room toasted Sally and Noah and drank up. Then one of Noah's friends stepped in and began another toast. Celeste slipped behind Sally and wrapped her arm around her waist. "I have to go. Here's the key. Leave it under the loose brick on the front walk."

Sally kissed her cheek. "Thank you."

"You're welcome. Have a good life. Let me know where you settle."

"You too." A tear slipped down Sally's cheek as the two women embraced.

Celeste stood on her tiptoes and gave Noah a kiss on the cheek. "You take care of her, will you?"

Noah squeezed Sally around the waist. "Will do."

"Goodbye," Celeste whispered. Quietly she retrieved her cloak and hat and went out the front door, unnoticed, in the midst of another toast. All she could think about was Adam. Once she saw Adam again, she'd know she was doing the right thing letting Fox go. She was sure of it.

Fox watched Celeste say goodbye to Sally across the room and then leave. He kept a whiskey in his hand and pretended to laugh with the others as another toast was made, but his thoughts were on her.

She was going to Denver. He was certain of that.

But what if she didn't come back? The idea was inconceivable. Life without Celeste was inconceivable.

So what could he do? She'd told him she wouldn't go to California. She'd told him to leave her house. Now she was going back to her man in Denver.

Fox knew he was at a crossroads that would affect the rest of his life. Twice already he'd given his love to the wrong woman. Would he be making a mistake here, too? Should he let Celeste go?

The answer hit him hard. He gritted his teeth.

Hell no. He'd stop being a coward, and he'd fight for her.

But first he had to know what he was up against. *Who* he was up against.

"Come on, boy," Fox said to the dog as he gave him an obligatory scratch behind the ears. "We've got a train to catch."

Fox took the same train to Denver as Celeste, taking care to remain two passenger cars behind her, even when they had to switch trains. He had a little bit of a disagreement with the conductor about taking Silver, but several greenbacks had persuaded the young man to simply pretend he didn't see the yellow dog.

After several stops during the night, the train screeched into the Denver station mid-morning. Fox slept little and he was fatigued, but determined. He watched Celeste disembark and then followed her. She hired a coach to take her to midtown where she entered an expensive hotel.

Fox waited a suitable amount of time and then checked into the same hotel. Once again, the power of money persuaded the hotel clerk that dogs were, indeed, permitted in The Morris Hotel. Fox ordered bread and cheese in his room, shared the meal with Silver, and then stretched out on the bed to take a nap.

Fox slept longer than he had intended and woke late in the afternoon. Leaving Silver in the room, he went downstairs where he found the hotel clerk to be quite helpful. Miss Kennedy had indeed checked in, but was currently out, the young man had enthusiastically offered. She'd be returning this evening though, because she had dinner reservations for two in the hotel restaurant. Did he care to leave Miss Kennedy a note?

Fox declined to leave a message and went out onto the street. The late afternoon was cold and snowflakes dimpled the gray sky. He found a small mercantile store to buy a clean shirt, a comb, and some toiletries.

Back in his hotel room, Fox cleaned himself up, fed the dog more bread and cheese, and waited. As the time passed agonizingly slow, Fox tried not to think too much about what he was doing. If he thought too hard, he would rationalize his way out of this whole crazy idea.

No, his instinct was to follow his heart.

Fox pulled a piece of paper from inside his waistcoat, unfolded it, and read it. The letter was nearly illegible, the grammar poor. It spoke of his brief illness and of the woman who had come into his life. He read the entire letter from his father twice, before he read the last line.

Marry my angel, it simply said.

He refolded the letter, taking care not to tear it at the creases, and put it back inside his coat. He checked his pocket watch. Time to go. Time to face his dragons.

His plan was simple. He would go downstairs to the dining room, walk straight up to the table where Celeste and her man sat, and then he would . . . punch him in the mouth.

Silver cocked his head and stared at him as Fox laughed aloud at the thought.

Fox crouched and scratched the yellow hound behind the ears. ''Nah, I'm not going to hit him,'' he said aloud. ''At least I probably won't. I'm just going to tell him that he can't have her. That she's mine. That I can't live without her. Hell, I'll tell him I love her.'' He patted Silver's back. ''What would she say then, huh, old boy?''

The dog hung out his tongue and panted contentedly.

''All right. You stay here. I'll be back soon, hopefully with Celeste on my arm.''

Fox glanced in the mirror, pushed his hair off his forehead, and left the room. Downstairs, he addressed the maitre d'. At first, the man was hesitant to show him to Miss Kennedy's table. Apparently he knew her and knew she liked her privacy. But Fox once again found that a greenback could be persuasive.

"Is the gentleman with her?" he asked the maitre d' as the mustached gentleman led him through the candlelit dining room.

"He is."

Fox stiffened and fought the fear that crept up his spine and threatened to paralyze him. Who was this man that had such a hold on Celeste. Did he love her? Could he give her what Fox was unsure he could give her?

"There." The maitre d' stood in the shadows and pointed.

Fox glanced across the dining room. He immediately spotted Celeste, her back to him, seated at a small, round table. She was dressed in an evening gown of sapphire blue satin, her shoulders bare.

She was as beautiful as—Fox's gaze settled on the figure that sat across from her. The sight so startled him that he drew in his breath.

The gentleman Celeste entertained could not have been more than ten years old . . .

Chapter Twenty-five

"Celeste?"

Fox spoke so softly that she wondered if she merely imagined his voice. Had she subconsciously wished so ardently for him, that she was now hearing him? But the look on Adam's face revealed that there was, indeed, a man behind her.

She felt a firm, warm hand on her shoulder and knew that it was Fox in the flesh.

"Celeste."

She turned in her chair. "Fox," she whispered. She didn't ask him how he had found her. Obviously he'd followed her. The question was: why?

Adam rose politely from his chair. Holding his hands stiffly at his sides, he said, "Good evening, sir," in his most intelligible voice.

Celeste felt a surge of pride. She knew how hard Adam worked to speak clearly.

Fox bowed. "Good evening."

"Adam," Celeste said. "This is Mr. MacPhearson. Fox Mac-Phearson." She felt her heart flutter; she avoided eye contact with both of them. "And this is Adam Kennedy, my . . . son."

There. She'd said it. She'd told Fox her terrible secret. Her wonderful secret. She waited for his reaction, her skin prickly with fear.

If Fox was surprised by her announcement, he never showed it. His face was as serene as she had ever seen it. *Thank you,* she thought. *Bless you, Fox.*

"It's very nice to meet you, Adam."

"And you, sir." Adam spoke slowly, his hands wiggling at his sides as if he was fighting the urge to speak with his hands. "Would you care to join us?"

Fox glanced at Celeste. His dark eyes were filled with uncertainty, yet there was an intriguing sparkle in them. One of promise. "May I?" he asked her.

She smiled. It felt so odd to be dressed as they were in this fancy dining room, speaking cordially as if she and Fox were mere acquaintances rather than lovers. "Please." She indicated the space to her left at the table, between her and Adam. "We were about to order."

Fox signaled to the maitre d', who must have been lurking behind a crimson drape. He appeared instantly with an upholstered chair.

"Something to drink, sir?"

Fox glanced at Celeste's wineglass, filled with a rich red wine.

"A merlot," she said softly. She couldn't tear her gaze from his. He had come all the way from Carrington looking for her. Perhaps it was just a business matter, but she knew that wasn't likely. The look on his face told her it was personal . . . very personal. A part of her was angry that he had found her out this way, but a part of her was greatly relieved.

"I'll have the merlot."

"Very good, sir."

The maitre d' disappeared, and Celeste found herself alone with the two men she loved most in the world. Now what did she do with them? What did she say?

Fox and Adam studied one another with equal interest.

Fox seemed as at home in this elegant setting as he had in

the mine shaft. But of course he would. Though this was not the world she knew him from, this *was* his world.

"I'm a business associate of your mother's," Fox said, beginning the conversation casually. "Has she told you?"

He looked directly at Adam, and for that Celeste was thankful. She wouldn't have to tell Fox, in front of Adam, that her son was nearly deaf. Fox must have been able to tell by the way Adam spoke that he had difficulties hearing.

Adam wiggled in his chair, obviously excited by Fox's attention. "No, sir. My mother has been very secretive about her new business, but she said she would tell me soon."

Fox glanced at Celeste meaningfully, then back at Adam so that he could read his lips. "Will she, now?"

"Yes, sir."

"You don't by chance go to school here, do you, Adam?"

"Yes, sir." Adam beamed. "Miss Higgens's Academy."

"And you live there?"

The boy lowered his gaze. "Yes, sir." He glanced up quickly. "But I'm thinking of changing schools and living with my mother. She needs me. My father is dead, you know."

Celeste trembled as Fox once again met her gaze. She was awash in emotional turmoil. Then Fox gently placed his hand over hers where it lay on the table, and she knew that no matter what happened next, she was going to be all right.

After a fine dinner of roasted beef and apple tarts for dessert, Fox suggested that the three of them go for a walk in the city to get some exercise after such a plentiful meal. They parted in the front lobby to go to their rooms, and agreed to meet in ten minutes.

Celeste didn't know who was more delighted when Fox reappeared with Silver at his side, her or Adam.

"How did you get that dog in here?" she murmured in his ear.

Fox strolled beside her through the lobby in a wool great

coat, his bowler hat in his hand. ''My persuasive personality.''
He grinned.

His smile made her feel warm and tingly inside, as if they
had just met and he was courting her.

''Wow!'' Adam exclaimed, kneeling in front of Silver. ''This
is the best dog I ever met.'' In his excitement, his words were
a little garbled, but both Celeste and Fox understood.

Silver licked Adam's face and the boy laughed.

''Come on,'' Fox said, taking Adam's arm. He raised him
to his feet and buttoned the top button of his overcoat. ''Let's
get out of here before someone realizes that's a dog and not a
guest.''

Adam laughed and ran ahead out the door with Silver right
behind him.

On the street, lit by oil lanterns, Fox and Celeste walked
behind Adam and the dog. They walked half a block before
Celeste got up the nerve to speak. ''You followed me. Why?''

''I wanted to see who I was up against.''

The cold wind blew loose strands of hair across her mouth,
and she brushed them away. ''Up against?''

''Who I'd have to fight to win you back.''

Her heart hammered in her chest. She didn't know what to
say. He wanted her. Was he going to ask for a compromise?
Surely he knew she couldn't; she wouldn't. Did that mean he
had changed his position? Did she dare hope that perhaps he
could find a small place in his heart for her?

Fox took her gloved hand in his and slipped them both into
his large pocket. ''And now that I've met Adam, I'm really
scared, Celeste.'' He looked straight ahead at the boy and dog
frolicking. ''He's steeper competition than I had anticipated. I
don't know if I can beat that.''

Tears clouded Celeste's eyes and she blinked them away.
That was the most romantic thing Fox had ever said to her.
''He's a good boy.''

''Smart,'' Fox added. ''Delightful. Is he completely deaf?''

''No. He hears certain lower tones. He reads lips very well.''

''His speech is excellent.''

"He's worked very hard at speaking. Just in the last few months he's stopped relying on sign language."

The two of them watched Adam and the dog stop, look both ways for oncoming traffic, then cross the street to a small park.

"He's Gerald's, isn't he?"

"Yes. But I don't want him to know—not ever. Gerald hurt me enough. I won't have him hurt Adam, too."

"I wish you had told me."

"I don't know why I didn't. I suppose I didn't know what you would think—a whore being a mother."

"You're a good mother. A good woman."

"I'm very proud of Adam, and I want what's best for him."

Fox squeezed her hand inside his pocket. "You should be."

"I love him more than life."

He stopped on the edge of a patch of snow and met her gaze, his dark eyes troubled. Adam and the dog continued.

"Then you can't leave him here, Celeste."

The strength of the emotion in Fox's voice disturbed her. He was nearly in tears.

"What do you mean? Is he in danger?"

"Yes." He took both her hands and held them tightly. "Grave danger. Danger of feeling abandoned. In danger of believing no one will ever really love him—that no one will ever really care. He's in danger of believing that everyone he loves will leave him sooner or later."

Celeste sensed that Fox was not just speaking of Adam . . . but of himself. "I don't understand."

Ten paces away, Adam and Silver rolled on the ground in the snow. The dog barked wildly and Adam was laughing, his sweet, childish voice echoing in the dark, cold night.

"You can't leave him in a boardinghouse."

"It's a school," she corrected. "A school where he learned to speak."

"He speaks now. He needs to come with you." Fox swallowed, his eyes clouding with tears. "He needs to come home with us, if you'll still have me."

She searched his teary gaze for understanding. "If I were to take Adam home with me, it would have to be to a real home, to a man who loves me and could learn to love him. I would have to be wed.''

He pulled off his glove to brush her cold cheek with his warm hand. Snowflakes drifted through the air and fell cold on her face.

''So marry me. Let me be your husband and Adam's father, if he'll allow me.''

''Oh, Fox,'' she whispered as she threw her arms around his neck. ''Do you mean it? Are you certain, because if you're not—''

''I'm as certain of this—more certain—than I've ever been of anything in my life.'' He hugged her. ''When you walked out of Kate's last night, I knew I couldn't live without you. I knew that no matter how afraid I was to love you, that it was too late. I already love you. I've loved you since the day you opened your front door to greet me when I arrived in Carrington.''

Celeste was so choked with happiness, with relief, with disbelief, that she didn't know what to say. ''I love you, too.'' The words seemed inadequate.

He pulled back a little, but still held her in his arms. He adjusted her hat that must have gone askew when she'd hugged him. ''Let's take him back to Carrington. We'll sell the mine and go to California. Tonight.''

She laughed. ''We can't go tonight! It's Adam's bedtime.''

Just then the boy and dog loped over. Adam stopped beside them and look curiously at his mother. ''You said Mr. Mac-Phearson was your business partner, Mama.'' He signed the word Mama as he spoke it. ''Is there something else you didn't tell me about him?''

Celeste glanced at Fox, feeling as if she would burst with happiness. ''Actually, Adam . . .'' She released Fox and crouched to pull Adam's hat down further over his head. ''There's a lot I haven't told you. Why don't the three of us,''— Silver shoved his head under her hand to be petted—''*the four of us,* go to our room, call for hot chocolate, and talk.''

Adam nodded. "Good idea. Can Silver have chocolate, too?"

Fox laughed. The tears in his eyes had faded, and he appeared as happy as Celeste had ever seen him. "Dogs don't drink chocolate." He grabbed Adam's hand and took care to look directly at him. "Race you back to the hotel."

The boy and the man darted off, with the dog barking at their heels. Celeste just stood for a moment under the lamplight, watching them retreat, thinking that she was so happy at this moment, that her heart might burst.

Much later, when hot chocolate had been shared, and Celeste had explained to Adam that she and Fox were intending to wed, the two tucked the tired boy into bed. With Silver stretched out at his feet, Celeste kissed Adam on the forehead, tucked his quilt over his shoulders, and left him to sleep.

She found Fox by the blazing fireplace, seated on the floor on a blanket he'd laid out for them. He had poured two glasses from a wine bottle he'd had sent up with the chocolate.

"I think he likes you," she said as she sat beside him on the floor. Suddenly she felt shy. It had been weeks since they'd been alone like this.

"The dog?"

She elbowed him. "Adam. He likes you. But he says you're a slow runner."

Fox laughed and handed her a glass of ruby wine. "I think we should toast to my finally coming to my senses."

They entwined arms and drank. "To Fox MacPhearson's good sense," she teased. "And to my good sense for knowing a decent man when I see him."

She took another sip of her wine and set the glass down. Then she drew up her knees and stared into the blazing fire. She and Fox had so much to talk about, yet there was one thing that she had to ask before they discussed their future.

"Fox?"

He stared dreamily into the flames.

"Um hm?"

''What you said in the park tonight about Adam, you weren't just talking about him, were you?''

He took a long moment to answer. ''No.''

She stroked his arm, savoring the heat and strength of it. ''Want to tell me?''

''No.'' He turned his head to gaze into her eyes. ''Yes.''

She kissed his shoulder and threaded her fingers through his. ''I'm listening.''

He spoke so softly that she had to lean closer to hear him.

''He . . . he put me in a boarding school. John . . . my father. He said it was the best place for me. He said they could provide what he couldn't—a stable environment, an education. He said men like him didn't belong raising children.''

''He must have believed that was best, or he wouldn't have done it.''

''At least he came to visit. He brought me gifts and took me places, but she—''

She noted a bitter tone in his voice. ''She?''

''My mother.'' He spit out the words as if they tasted bad. ''She just abandoned me. She gave birth to me, handed me to my father, and left. She went back to work . . . in the whorehouse where I was born.''

His words so shocked her that for a moment Celeste couldn't find her voice. She had guessed that Fox had been born illegitimate, but thought his mother had died, probably birthing him. Never in her wildest dreams had she imagined that his mother had been a prostitute. Why hadn't John told her?

''Fox,'' she whispered, squeezing his hand tightly. ''You should have told me.''

He shook his head. Tears glistened in his eyes again. ''All those years in the boarding schools, I imagined she would come for me someday. I thought she would clean up, that she would marry my father, and that we would live as a family. But she never came. Not once.''

Celeste knelt and drew Fox into her arms. ''I'm so sorry,'' she whispered, rocking him as she would a child. ''I understand now. I understand it all.''

"I'm sorry," he whispered. "I'm sorry I was so mean to you. I did love you. I loved you from the first day. I was just afraid to admit it, even to myself."

Then he glanced up, meeting her gaze with the darkest, saddest black eyes she had ever seen.

"Can you forgive me? Can we start again? I need you to love me, Celeste."

"I love you. I'll love you forever." She brushed her lips against his, their tears mingling. "And I will be your wife."

He kissed her back. "Good. Because my father told me to marry you."

"What?" She gave a little laugh as she wiped away his tears with her fingertips.

"I'll show you later. Now, how about a kiss for a weak, foolish man?"

"A kiss?" She glanced across the dark room to be sure Adam was sound asleep, then back at him. She curled her arms around his neck and drew close. "I can do even better than that . . ."

Chapter Twenty-six

Two days later, Celeste, Fox, and Adam rode the train into Carrington.

"Cali-fornia," Adam bubbled as they walked off the train with the other passengers. "I can't believe we're going to California!"

"Now, it may take a few weeks," Fox warned. "We have to sell the mine and the house, though the house could go with a broker."

Adam hopped up and down as they passed through the aisle between the train seats. "I know. But we can take Silver, right? Dogs can live in vineyards."

"Best place for a dog is a vineyard."

Fox disembarked first, then reached up to give Celeste his hand. He winked at her.

She smiled. Fox and Adam were getting along wonderfully. Fox really did love her, and everything really was going to be all right.

I love you, Fox mouthed as she walked down the steps.

She brushed his cheek with her hand as she descended. "And I—"

''Mr. MacPhearson?''

Celeste gazed over Fox's shoulder to see one of Sheriff Tate's burly new deputies standing on the loading platform. She knew him because he had often frequented Kate's Dance Hall. He had been one of Sally's best customers before he turned lawman.

''Mr. MacPhearson.'' The deputy clamped his hand on Fox's shoulder. ''You'll have to come with me.''

Celeste grabbed Adam's hand protectively and led him off train. The dog followed. ''What's this all about, Larry?''

''Sheriff Tate told me to meet every train 'til he came back.'' He glared. ''If'n he came back.''

Adam's eyes grew round with astonishment as the deputy took Fox's arm.

''Come on, now.'' Larry threw back his burly shoulders. ''I don't want no trouble, but I got no qualms about using this thing if I have to.'' He tapped the ancient oak-handled pistol he wore on a belt around his hips.

''Larry!'' Celeste stepped up to the deputy. He smelled of chewing tobacco and sour sweat. ''What are you talking about? What does Tate want with Fox?''

''Questioning.'' He jerked his head. ''Come on.''

Larry tried to pull Fox after him and Fox shoved him.

''I'll come, but of my own accord,'' Fox said. ''You don't have to treat me like a criminal.'' He smoothed his sleeve. ''Now let's get this over with so I can go home.''

Celeste held tightly to Adam's hand and followed the men into the street, the baggage forgotten. ''Larry! Tell me why Sheriff Tate wants Fox. What's happened? Has there been another murder?''

''Murder?'' Adam echoed, trying to watch his mother's mouth so he would know what was happening. ''Who got killed?''

''Celeste, take Adam home,'' Fox told her. ''I'll be home directly. I'm sure this is just more of Tate's nonsensical questioning.''

She ignored him and hurried to catch up. ''Larry! I want to

know why Fox is being brought in for questioning again. He told you everything he knew about that girl he found in the alley.''

"Yes, well, we found another,'' Larry shot over his shoulder.

Celeste felt her heart skip a beat. "Who?"

"The sheriff said I wasn't to tell anybody anything. Just bring Mr. MacPhearson in, and that's what I aim to do.'' As they walked down the sidewalk, Larry glanced over his shoulder at her again. "Mr. MacPhearson's right. You best go home, Miss Kennedy.''

"I'll do no such thing.'' She marched up the steps into the jail house with Adam and the dog in tow. "Not until I know what the he—'' She glanced at Adam. "What's going on,'' she corrected herself.

"What's going on?'' Tate met them in the front receiving area of the jail house. "I'll tell you what's going on. Surprised you haven't heard, Celeste.''

She tightened her grip on Adam's hand, sensing she didn't want to hear what Tate would say next. "What? Heard what?''

Tate hooked his thumb into the waistband of his pants. "I'm sorry to be the one to tell you this.'' He looked down at the floor, seemingly genuinely upset. "I know how close you two were, but—''

Celeste placed her hand on an old table for support, gripping Adam's hand with the other. *No. No.*

"But Silky Sally's dead. Killed. Murdered right in your front yard.''

Celeste felt her heart plummet. She yanked her hand off the desk and brought it to her mouth, afraid for a moment that she would be physically ill.

"No,'' she whispered.

"Celeste.'' Fox tried to reach her, but Tate grabbed him by his arms and pulled him back. It took the sheriff and his deputy to hold him.

"Keep your hands off that woman!'' Tate threatened.

Celeste tried to take a deep breath and keep her head clear.

Her vision was blurry. She couldn't breathe. *Sally, sweet Sally was dead . . .*

"Wh . . . when?" Celeste asked numbly. "She . . . she was supposed to leave with Noah. She . . . she was getting married."

"It was the night of her party. Poor girl never had a chance. He cut her down on your front walk."

Celeste glanced up through a veil of stinging tears. "You . . . you don't think Fox had anything to do with Sally's death?" she managed.

"I'd be a fool not to. A man's got to look at the evidence. He walks nights in the town when all decent folk are in bed."

"That doesn't make a man a killer," Celeste retorted.

"And then there's that business with the dead woman in California. Bet you didn't know about that."

"He was questioned and released."

The sheriff pulled a coat from behind a desk. "And then there's this that we found in a trash heap behind Simon's Boardinghouse."

Celeste stared at the coat. It was Fox's . . . and covered with blood.

She met Fox's gaze. She knew there was an explanation for this. She knew he didn't kill anyone.

With his eyes, he silently thanked her for trusting him.

"Fox didn't kill that girl, and he didn't kill poor Sally," Celeste said, pushing through the blinding pain of her friend's murder. "You've certainly not done a good job of investigating. He couldn't have. He was with me in Denver!"

"That right?" Tate lifted a bushy eyebrow.

"The coat's mine," Fox admitted. "The night I found the girl, I picked her up to see if she was still alive. I got the blood all over my coat. I knew what you'd think if I came to the jail house looking like that, so I just got rid of the coat." He ran his hand over the back of his neck. "It was a stupid thing to do." He glanced at Celeste. "I'm sorry. I was so worried about you, about us, that I didn't think I could deal with any more complications."

Tate frowned. "Sounds like quite the story."

"Check with the train station," Celeste said. "Find out when he boarded the train to Denver. You knew he left, right? Why didn't you have the sense to find out *when?*"

"I'm lookin' into that now." Tate dropped the bloody coat on a chair. "But you best go home, Celeste. We won't need you to talk to Mr. MacPhearson."

Fox interrupted her protest. "He's right," he said. "You need to take Adam home."

Celeste glanced down at her son. The boy was afraid. Everyone was talking so fast that he probably couldn't follow the conversation, which at this point was just as well. But she knew how disturbing it was for him not to know what was happening. It was in a group of people like this that he lost his confidence.

She smoothed Adam's hair and squeezed his hand. "You're right. I'll take him home, but I'll find someone to stay with him, and I'll come right back."

"Celeste, you stay with Adam," Fox instructed. "It will be easy enough for Tate to check the written records of when I boarded the train, now that he knows to do so." He glared at the sheriff. "So go home and wait for me." He managed a bare smile. "Why don't you whip your menfolk up something decent to eat."

She forced herself to smile, because she knew that Fox needed to know she was all right. Of course she wasn't all right, but she was strong. She could be strong for Adam and Fox . . . even for poor Sally.

"I'll be back," she said determinedly, and left the jail house.

At home, Celeste took the time to show Adam the house. He was worried about Fox, but she brushed over the whole jail incident as a mistake and told him Fox would be home tonight or tomorrow, once the train records were examined. Though he questioned her about the murder, she didn't give him any details; she didn't want to scare him.

After leading him through the house and showing him the room that had been Fox's, which would be his until they left for California, Celeste escorted boy and dog to the kitchen and fed Adam bread and cheese. It was the only thing she had in the house to eat, but Adam seemed content with the meager meal.

She lit the kitchen stove, and then sat beside Adam at the table. As she held her warm teacup between her palms, finding comfort in the heat, she wondered what was happening at the jail house. Had Fox been able to reason with Tate? Had someone located the train ticket records necessary to prove that Fox had boarded the midnight train?

As Celeste sipped her tea, she tried not to think about Sally. When she'd walked up her front walk with Adam, she'd kept her gaze fixed on the door ahead, careful not to look for bloodstains. Right now Celeste couldn't allow herself to be distracted by that which she could not change. First she had to get Fox safely home, and then she would grieve.

Celeste lowered her head to her hands, warm from the teacup, and tried hard to think with her head, not her heart. What she needed most now was a level mind and her dependable logic. Sally had been murdered the night before she was to leave Carrington. Did that mean the murderer knew she was leaving, and didn't want her to get away? And how did the murderer know to look for her here, rather than at Kate's? Sally had never slept in her house. The decision was made by Celeste and Sally only hours before her murder. How could anyone have known that's where she was going?

Unless . . .

Celeste lifted her head and stared blankly ahead, thinking. Adam sat with his bread and cheese, preoccupied with feeding crumbs to the dog.

Unless . . . the murderer had been at Sally's party, Celeste concluded.

She slapped her hand on the table. "It has to be someone who was there," she said aloud, raising out of the chair. "Someone who knew her . . . knew her well."

A friend. It had to be one of Sally's friends who had murdered her . . . one of Celeste's friends. Perhaps this friend had even meant to kill Celeste and taken Sally's life when Celeste went to Denver instead of home.

"Adam." Celeste touched her son's arm so that he would look up at her.

"Get your coat. We have to—"

Silver's head popped up and he barked.

The echo of the bark was followed by a knock on the front door.

Celeste hurried to the door, hoping, praying it was Fox, who couldn't get in because he didn't have his key.

"Oh, Fox—" She threw open the door. Her hopes tumbled. "Joash . . ."

"Celeste." He nodded, his pale hands poised as if in prayer, as usual. "I heard you came in on the train. I wanted to offer my condolences. I know you cared a great deal for Sally. Mrs. Tuttle would have come, too, but she was feeling poorly— tripped on the steps and banged herself up. May I come in?"

Celeste stepped back to allow him inside the front foyer. This wasn't the time for visitors; she had to get to the jail house. But Joash . . .

Celeste grabbed his black frocked arm. "Joash. Could you do me a favor?" She spoke quickly. The killer was still on the loose, and she had to tell the sheriff what she knew. "Could you stay here with my son?"

"Your son?" His black eyebrows shot up and his protruding Adam's apple bobbed. "You have a son? An illegitimate son!"

She glanced at Adam, who peeked around the doorway. "I'll explain later, Joash," she said, facing him so Adam wouldn't know what she was saying. "You can preach to me then. Right now, I just need you to sit here with him and be sure he's safe."

She didn't give Joash time to reply as she smiled at Adam, turning her head so that he could easily read her lips. "Adam, this is Reverend Tuttle, and he's going to stay with you for a short time while I fetch Fox."

Adam's lower lip quivered. *I don''t want to stay here with him,* he signed with his hands.

"I need you to do this. You'll be fine. Joash is my friend."

"Please, Mama," he said aloud. "Please don't make me stay."

"Just trust me, Adam. You need to stay here." It tore at Celeste's heart to see Adam upset like this, but she knew it was best if the boy stayed safely inside with Joash. As Adam's mother, it was her responsibility to see that he did what was best for him, not necessarily what he wanted. *You'll be fine, Adam,* she signed.

She turned to Joash. "Adam has a little difficulty in hearing, Reverend, but if you'll simply look at him when you speak, the two of you will get along just fine." She grabbed for her cloak. "You'll be fine here with the reverend, Adam."

She threw her cloak over her shoulders and went to kiss Adam. As she did, Silver thrust his head under her hand and looked up expectantly.

"No, you stay here, Silver, and keep Adam company."

The dog followed her to the door and whined as she drew it open. "Silver? What's gotten into you? I said, stay." She motioned to him, but the dog followed her onto the porch. It was almost dark and there was an unseasonably cold wind blowing out of the mountains.

"You've never been disobedient before," she mused aloud. Her first impulse was to make the dog go back inside, but she stared at him for a moment. Was he trying to tell her something with those big, brown dog eyes of his?

She sighed. "Oh, all right. You can come." She glanced up at Adam in the doorway with the reverend. "You'll be fine here with Joash." She smiled. "All right?"

He nodded. She could tell he was trying to be brave. *God, she loved her son.*

She waved to him. "Thank you, Joash," she called over her shoulder. "I'll be back as soon as I can."

Celeste hurried up Plum Street with the dog on her heels. It was so cold that she drew her hood over her head. She wished she'd worn her hat with the long woolen black scarf that tied beneath her chin. It was so cold.

She turned onto Peach, headed into town.

As Celeste walked, she noticed how desolate the street was. Of course it was a weekend, and most of the miners were on their claims. Those who lived in the boardinghouses were probably working the mines or asleep in their beds, depending on which shift they worked. The bitter cold and the snow flurries must have kept everyone else inside.

Celeste walked faster, spooked by the darkness and the cold and the empty street. Something didn't feel right, but she didn't know what. She looked behind her. No one was there. She could hear nothing but the whistling wind, her footsteps, and the dog's nails scraping on the wooden sidewalk.

She took another step forward, still glancing over her shoulder, and struck something hard. ''Oh!'' she cried and stumbled back.

Startled, Silver gave a yipe and trotted backward.

As she lifted her head, she gave a little laugh at her foolishness. She'd been so busy looking behind her that she'd run into a rain barrel.

''Scare you too, boy?'' She laid a shaky hand on Silver's back and stroked the yellow dog. ''You're quite the fierce mutt to be scared of rain barrels.''

They circumnavigated the barrel and walked on. Half a block ahead, she could see the jail house lantern light spilling from its tiny windows.

''Here we go. Almost—''

Someone stepped out of an alley directly in front of her so that she collided with him. He was covered from head to toe in a heavy, black hooded cloak.

Celeste's instinct was to run, but the specter took her unaware. She stopped so suddenly that she lost her balance.

Silver snarled.

Celeste opened her mouth to scream, but the cloaked figure was too fast. He clamped a leather-gloved hand over her mouth. At the same time, he yanked her into his arms by a handful of her cloak.

She kicked wildly and struggled to escape.

The hand covered her mouth and pinched her nose. She was suffocating . . .

No! No! No! Celeste screamed in her head. *I won't let you do this. After all these years, I've finally found happiness. You won't take my son from me! You won't take my Fox.*

Silver barked and snapped at the cloaked figure. He kicked the dog as he dragged Celeste into the alley.

She drew up her knee and kicked backward hard, hitting him in the shin.

Her attacker grunted, but didn't relinquish his iron grip.

Celeste was dizzy from lack of air. Her heart was pounding, her lungs exploding.

No! No! No! She told herself. *He won't win! Not this time. Not with me.*

So light-headed that she was on the verge of fainting, Celeste drew her energy and focused on escape. The attacker had her by her mouth and her cloak. If she could slip out of the cloak . . .

She could hear the faceless killer panting as he struggled to subdue her.

Celeste threw her head forward and slammed it backward, taking him by surprise. He cried out with pain as she struck his face.

Celeste lifted her feet off the ground, forcing the attacker to hold her entire weight. He dropped her and she rolled, pushing away, gasping for air.

She screamed as she tumbled. From the corner of her eye, in the shadowy darkness, she saw something fly through the air and hit the attacker full in the chest.

Silver! It was Silver!

The shimmer of the steel blade the killer drew was unreal in the murky darkness.

"No!" Celeste screamed.

Silver gave a scream that was nearly human as the killer sank the knife into the dog's yellow chest.

Celeste scrambled to her feet. "Help!" she screamed. "Help!" Then she added what she knew would bring results. "Fire! Fire on Peach!"

Because the killer blocked the alley to Peach, Celeste turned on her heels to run the other way. She couldn't see or hear Silver. The bastard had killed her dog.

"Fire! Fire!" Celeste screamed.

"Bitch! Whoring bitch!" the killer shouted after her in an unearthly voice. "She who sins must die! You must all die!"

Celeste could hear the pounding footsteps behind her, but she didn't look back. No time.

Celeste had nearly reached the end of the alley and Cherry Street when she felt an iron hand fall on her shoulder.

"No!" Celeste screamed as she spun around. She was so angry, so damned angry!

She shoved the killer backward, hard against the sideboards of the building. She had no idea where her incredible strength came from.

The killer lashed at Celeste with his knife. She saw a slash of light and then felt an agonizing burning in her arm. The killer's limbs tangled with hers. Celeste kicked and swung her fists in rage.

"You won't do this to me!" she screamed.

She heard male voices approaching from down the alley in the direction of Peach Street.

"Help!" Celeste screamed. "Help. It's the killer! The killer!"

The sound of the running men startled the killer, and he released his hold on Celeste's hand, shoved her forward, and ran.

Someone seized Celeste's shoulder from behind and she screamed. How could the killer have gotten behind her, even in the darkness?

She screamed again and whipped around to face him.

The hands clamped down on both her forearms.

"Celeste?"

"Fox? Fox?"

"Celeste." He shook her.

For a moment her eyes were unseeing. She still thought the killer had come for her in his faceless cloak.

"Celeste, it's me. It's Fox, sweetheart."

"He ... he ..." She couldn't breathe. She couldn't speak. She pointed in the direction the killer had escaped.

Sheriff Tate and two deputies ran past them.

"That way!" Fox hollered. "Black cloak. Don't let him get away, boys."

"You all right?" Fox gripped her shoulders and forced her to focus on his face. "Celeste, are you all right? Are you hurt?"

She lifted her arm lamely. "A scratch, I think." Finally realizing that she was alive and unhurt, she threw her arms around Fox. "Oh, God. Fox. Fox."

He held her tightly. "It's all right," he crooned. "They're going to catch the bastard."

Gunshots cracked in the air, sounding almost unreal. One, two, three shots.

"We got him! We got him!" one of the deputies called.

Arm in arm, Fox and Celeste hurried out of the alley and on to the Cherry Street side.

In the center of the snowy street lay a black-cloaked figure, facedown and motionless.

"You stay here," Fox said. "I want to make sure he doesn't jump and run."

"No." Celeste grabbed his arm. "Don't leave me here. I want to see. I have to."

Sheriff Tate and the deputies surrounded the body and, weapons drawn, cautiously walked closer. Still the killer didn't move.

Tate gave the body a nudge with the toe of his boot. "I think he's dead, boys."

A butcher knife gleamed in the moonlight, still locked in the killer's hand.

Celeste stepped closer. "Who is it?" she whispered. She knew it was someone she knew well, but who? Ace? Titus?

Tate kept his pistol ready as he rolled the body over with his foot. Obviously the sheriff wasn't taking any chances. He stared at the killer. "Yeah, he's dead all right."

Tate reached down and drew back the hood of the black cloak. "I'll be damned," he murmured in obvious shock.

''Who?'' The word was barely out of Celeste's mouth.

''The preacher's wife,'' Fox murmured.

''Mrs. Tuttle?'' Celeste stared at the round German face and the tight curls that framed it. Her eyes were mercifully closed. Her cloak had fallen open to reveal a round red splotch of blood in the center of her chest.

Celeste couldn't believe it, and yet she had no choice. There was Mrs. Tuttle with the knife in her hand, Celeste's and Silver's blood on the knife. To add to the evidence was what the preacher's wife had shouted at her in the alley about sin. It had to be her. It was her all along . . .

''Silver!'' Celeste looked suddenly at Fox. ''She stabbed Silver. I think he's dead, but I'm not sure.''

Fox grabbed her arm. ''Show me.''

Hours later, Celeste lay stretched out on her white iron bed and stared at the moon that shone through her window. Adam was asleep. The doc had taken Silver home with him to stitch him up, saying there was a good chance to save him. Joash was home in his musty parlor, where he wanted to be alone with his wife's body. Poor Joash; he was devastated.

Fox walked into the dark bedroom. ''Adam's fine. Sound asleep.''

She rolled onto her back and sat up as Fox sat down on the edge of the bed.

''I can't believe Mrs. Tuttle was capable of such a thing.''

He lifted one shoulder as he reached around her and caressed her hip with his hand. ''She was a big woman, so Tate thinks that's how she was able to physically subdue the women.'' He smiled grimly. ''Apparently Sally put up a hell of fight, because Mrs. Tuttle was bruised and battered.''

Celeste shook her head. ''She told Joash she'd fallen and that was how she'd gotten the bruises.''

''As for Mrs. Tuttle being mentally capable of such atrocities,'' Fox continued, ''someone as sick in the mind as she was can find justification in anything.''

Celeste arranged the folds of the flannel dressing robe she wore. "I'm tired." She rested her head on Fox's shoulder, and he wrapped his arm around her waist.

"How's your arm?"

She rubbed the place where Doc Smite had bandaged it. "Aches a little, but it's all right."

"Well, you best get some sleep, then." He drew aside one edge of her dressing gown and kissed the swell of her bare breast. "Because you've a wedding to go to tomorrow, and you want to look your freshest."

"A wedding?" She was so exhausted by emotion that she couldn't think clearly. "Who's getting married?"

He gazed into her eyes. "You." Then he kissed her gently on the mouth, a kiss that would seal their love for all of eternity.

Epilogue

Napa Valley
California
Eight years later

"Maria, could you please ring the dinner bell again?" Celeste asked in exasperation. "I know they hear me; they just won't come. Your enchiladas and my corn bread will be ruined."

"*Sí, señora.*"

Celeste stood in the open-air archway of the kitchen and watched the servant walk to the black wrought-iron dinner bell and ring it enthusiastically. "Dinner, *mi hijos, señor!*" She rang the bell again, and Celeste smiled. Maria loved the power of the dinner bell.

Celeste walked out onto the Spanish-style courtyard on the stones that had lovingly been laid by Fox, Adam, and Maria's husband, Joaquin. The sun was just beginning to set over the hills, and it cast a red gold light over the rows of grapevines that fanned out from the home she and Fox had built.

This was Celeste's favorite time of day here in California, when the sun was just setting and the wind held the scent of the grapevines. Here in the young vineyard, Colorado seemed a world away . . . a lifetime. Sometimes, Celeste even wondered if all that had happened there had been a dream.

She spotted Fox coming up the hill and laughed aloud. On each shoulder he balanced one of their twin daughters. Sally and Meg giggled uproariously at some nonsense their father had no doubt fed them.

Behind Fox walked Adam, no longer a boy, nearly a man. He was trailed by old Silver, whose gait was a little slow, but who could still keep up. Across Adam's strong shoulders, he bore a pole with a bucket on each end. Her men, inseparable, were dressed in grape-stained cotton workpants and shirts open at the chest. They wore identical beaten straw hats woven by Maria's capable hands.

Celeste lowered her hands to her hips, trying to look stern as they crested the hill and walked into the grass that led to the courtyard. "Maria's been ringing for you for ten minutes."

"Look what we've got, Mama!"

Fox lowered first the red-pigtailed Meg to the grass, and then her identical sister Sally.

"Grapes, Mama," five-year-old Sally piped in. "Peanut . . . *Pinot Noirs!*"

"Wait until you see them, Mother," Adam said, lowering the buckets to the ground. It had been two years and one young lady since Adam had called her Mama. He was growing up so fast. "I know the plants are young and the grapes will only get better as the vines mature, but Joaquin says the texture is nearly perfect."

As her family drew closer, Celeste realized that the girls were covered in splatters of dark purple . . . again. "Sally! Meg!" she admonished, but not too harshly. "You just dressed for supper! I told you to stay off the ground when you went with your father to check the vines."

The girls burst into laughter. "We stayed off the ground, Mama. It was Papa's fault!" Meg said.

"He threw the grapes at us, didn't you, Papa?" Sally added.

Celeste eyed Fox.

He tugged off his hat and whistled, glancing away to the amusement of his daughters and son.

"Told you," Meg laughed.

"Guilty," Sally accused.

"Fox MacPhearson!" Celeste lit into the expected litany. "How am I ever going to teach these girls to be young ladies if you're going to get into grape fights with them?"

The girls giggled behind their fingers, their cheeks rosy.

Adam laughed. "Come on, girls. Let's find Maria and get you cleaned up."

Celeste left her hands balanced on her hips. The children passed her and then she settled her attention on her dear husband, who looked like one of the workers they'd recently hired. Fox's skin was tanned a dark brown, and he'd probably not shaved in two days. His hair was too long and fell over his eyes when he pulled off his straw hat. He was as handsome, no, *more* handsome than the first day he'd walked into Carrington and her life.

"Suppose I need to change for supper, too?" he said sheepishly as he caught her around the waist with one arm.

She dropped her hands to his shoulders and let him twirl her around. She tipped back her head and the vineyard and the house whirled by. The air smelled of rain, of fresh grapes, and of her husband.

"I suppose you should."

Their gazes met.

"The harvest going to be as good as Adam says?"

"Better." Fox grinned. "Better than we imagined, Celeste, better than we dreamed."

She held his gaze with hers. "Nothing can be better than this."

"What, this?" He ran one hand over his dirty, purple-stained shirt.

"Yes, this." She tapped his chest. "And this." She gestured to the vineyard. "And this." She kissed his mouth.

"Told you we could do it, Celeste." He danced her in a circle, caught her hand, and let her twirl away from him.

Celeste released his hand and scooped some grapes out of the split oak basket. She rolled a black *Pinot Noir* grape between her fingers, and then crushed it to study the pulp.

They had come to this land knowing nothing of viticulture. She and Fox still had a great deal to learn, but with Joaquin and Maria's help, their vineyard was going to be successfully productive.

"Excellent color." She glanced up at Fox, who stood three feet away. On impulse, she tossed the squashed grape at him.

"Hey!" He threw up his hand, but it was too late. She struck him in the chest, making a dark purple splotch.

Fox dove for the basket. Celeste squealed, throwing grapes over her shoulder at him as she ran.

She felt the thump of grapes hitting her back, and laughed harder, running into the grass.

Fox pelted her with grapes and they split as they hit her, staining her sunshine yellow gown. "Fox!"

"You started it." He chased her.

She ran, but he caught up to her and wrestled her to the ground. Their laughter mingled as he lowered his mouth to hers.

He tasted of grapes.

"The children, Fox. Dinner."

"Yeah, yeah." He kissed her again and then lowered his head to her slightly rounded belly. "Hello in there? Can you hear me?"

She rolled her head in laughter, and threaded her fingers through his clean, silky black hair. "Fox!"

"Attention. Attention, this is your father. I just want you to know that your mother started that grape fight. Not me."

Still laughing, she gave him a push and he rolled over and pulled her on top of him.

Celeste's hair fell loose in a curtain of red-gold around their faces, and she stared into Fox's black eyes. "Thank you," she whispered.

"For what?"

"For saving me."

He stroked her forehead with his grape-stained hand. ''Thank you,'' he said.

''For what?''

''For saving me.''

Celeste closed her eyes and lowered her mouth to his. The sunshine was still warm on her back, and warm in her heart where she knew it always would be.

Please turn the page for
an exciting sneak preview of
Colleen Faulkner's
newest historical romance
Once More
on sale at bookstores
in October 1998

Prologue

Julia closed her eyes and felt the bitter wind against her face. It tore at her unbound hair and whipped at her new wool and ermine cloak, a costly gift from her betrothed.

She felt numb. Was it because of the teeth-chattering cold, or because, as she stood here on the precipice, she felt her hopes, her dreams, dying? All these years, through the wars, she had imagined that one day she would be rescued from her father's decaying house by a handsome lord. His lordship would marry her, take her away to a foreign land, and love her more than life. She knew it was just a dream, a girlhood fancy, but it was difficult to let go of that dream just the same.

Steadying herself with one hand on the crumbling wall, she hesitantly slid one foot, and then the other, forward, until the toes of her kidskin slippers hung off the edge of the tower floor. Chunks of deteriorated mortar fell and hit the rocks below. She did not hear them splash as they made their final descent into the ocean far below.

Julia held her breath and imagined that she was one of those ill-fated bits of mortar. She wondered how easy it would be to let go of the disintegrating wall and drop into the cold depths of the waves. Did the mortar feel terror—or dull acceptance? Was there, at the last moment, a certain sense of relief before death?

The ermine lining of her new cloak ruffled in the wind, brushing the sensitive flesh of her throat. Instead of feeling soft as it should have, it felt as abrasive as spun steel. She hated the cloak. She hated he who had sent it. She hated her mother for making her wear the cloak. She hated her mother for making her marry him.

"I would miss you if you went away to our Lord Jesus . . ."

The sound of her younger sister's voice startled Julia, and she gripped the wall tightly. Fearing she might lose her balance and plummet off the tower ruin, she took a step back and opened her eyes. "Lizzy! What are you doing up here? You'll catch your death in this cold!"

Lizzy drew her patched brown woolen cloak tightly around her shoulders. "You wouldn't do it, would you, Sister? You wouldn't leave me."

Julia had always wondered how Lizzy had the innate ability to read others' thoughts. Her mind damaged since early childhood, she barely had the sense to get in out of a hailstorm, yet she was exceptionally sensitive to the feelings of others. Sometimes she seemed to understand Julia's thoughts better than Julia understood them herself.

Julia offered her sister her cold hand. "I just came up here to think . . . to say goodbye."

She narrowed her pretty eyes. "Not to jump into the ocean and go to Lord Jesus?"

Julia thought a long moment before she replied. Had she climbed the crumbling tower steps to contemplate suicide? Had she actually considered the choice of death over marriage to the Earl of St. Martin? Had she thought herself willing to abandon her sister and mother to the perils of poverty, rather than marry a man she did not like?

Julia lifted her lashes and gazed into Lizzy's blue eyes, eyes as blue as the heavens. "Silly chick." She squeezed her sister's petite hand in her own. "I wouldn't leave you."

"Not ever?"

"Not ever. I just came to say goodbye to the ocean. There's no ocean in London, you know."

"London? Is that the house?" Lizzy's yellow blond hair fluttered in the wind, framing her oval face.

How Julia envied her sister's perfect blond hair. Her own hair had too much red in it; her father had called it strawberry. "No. London is the place, the city. Bassett Hall is the house. That's where we'll be living, you and I."

Lizzy thrust out her lower lip. She was strikingly beautiful, even when she pouted. "But you'll no longer sleep with me. St. Martin will sleep in your bed, and I will have to sleep with Drusilla and her cold, bony feet."

Julia laughed and hugged her sister as she turned her around. "Better to sleep with Drusilla and her feet than Mother and her snoring."

The sisters laughed in unison, Lizzy's voice the higher pitched of the two.

"Race you down the steps," Julia dared.

"And ruin my slippers? I think not!"

But the moment Julia darted down the winding, stone steps, Lizzy bolted after her.

"Mother says the coach is ready," Lizzy called. "Race you to London."

Running her hand along the cold stone wall, Julia descended the steps as fast as she could, her heart pounding. It was time to say goodbye to the disintegrating walls of the home of her childhood, the home of her father's childhood, and of his father before him. She was bound for London and a new life, bound for Bassett Hall and her new husband.

Julia's grandfather, now dead and buried in the churchyard, had always said that in life, each time a door closed, another opened. She prayed feverishly that he was right.

Chapter One

Bassett Hall
London, England

The Earl of St. Martin stood at the window of his new gallery overlooking his gardens. He watched intently as two young women followed a stone path toward a fountain. Both wore heavy cloaks to ward off the October chill, but strands of hair escaped their wool hoods and silk bonnets and fluttered in the wind.

Annoyed by the vexatious sounds of chewing saws and banging hammers, Simeon glared at the carpenters. He clamped his jaw tight and ground his teeth. Didn't these maggot brains realize they were disturbing his concentration?

He considered ordering a halt to the construction, just so that he might better enjoy his picturesque winter garden, but instead, he chose to take a deep breath. Inhaling the chilly air, he slowly exhaled warm breath, forcing himself to be calm. With this great control, he was able to block out the noise so that he might better enjoy the vision of the sisters.

His eyelids fluttered at the sight below. He crossed his arms over his chest and brushed his lips with his perfumed fingers.

One woman was quite an ordinary blonde, but the other, Julia, his betrothed, was simply exquisite. In all his worldly travels, Simeon had never seen hair the color of his beloved's. It was like spun fire, as golden and red as the setting of a Caribbean sun, a sparkling jewel in the midst of the dead winter garden. Now, that fiery hair was his. Those sparkling blue eyes were his. Julia, heart, mind, soul, and body were his. All his.

He let out a small sigh of satisfaction and felt his hot breath on his fingertips. He was glad he had agreed to honor the betrothal agreement signed many years ago with the wench's father. Though she was now poor, this connection with her family name would be advantageous. Her father had fought for Charles I and lost most of his lands and possessions to Cromwell. In Charles II's court, her father was a hero. A woman of Julia's distinction could only add to his own importance.

Simeon slid one foot forward to take a closer look, mesmerized by the way the wind ruffled strands of his Julia's hair. His hand ached to tuck the locks into her hood. He liked nothing out of order, not even his betrothed's hair.

A coarse figure moved between him and the window, blocking out the sunlight and his vision of beatitude, and Simeon shouted in rage.

A yellow-haired, filthy-faced mason yelped in surprise and attempted to scurry by, a small pallet of bricks propped on one shoulder.

Simeon cuffed him hard against the back of his greasy head as he slipped past. "Haven't I told you not to step so near me?" he exploded. "Haven't I?" He struck him a second time.

Knocked off balance, the workman fell headlong to the floor, his stack of bricks scattering as he went down.

"Get away from me, you filthy turd!"

The mason scrambled to his feet and darted off, leaving the broken brown bricks in a crumble of dust where they lay.

Simeon inhaled again, breathing in calm, exhaling anger, as he returned his attention to the window. He removed a handkerchief from his sleeve and wiped his hand where it had touched the mason's dirty hair. Now he would have to return to his bedchamber and wash with strong lye soap.

Simeon folded the handkerchief carefully so that the soiled part was inside and returned it to his sleeve. With his clean hand, he smoothed his gray wool coat with the black velvet garniture as his gaze fell upon his betrothed once more.

Julia and her sister sat on a stone bench facing him. As the women arranged their cloaks around their knees, he took a step closer to the windows that ran the length of the gallery under construction. Julie was laughing now, as was her dim-witted sister. He wondered what had amused her so. He wondered what he himself could say that would be clever enough to make her laugh with him and purse her rosy lips in such a provocative manner.

The clacking of heeled shoes on the Italian marble floor caught Simeon's attention. Who dared interrupt him now?

It was his cousin Griffin; no one else would be so bold. He was dressed in his usual abominable fashion, this morning in lime green and yellow striped breeches with a matching lime green great coat with yellow looped ribbons hanging from his shoulder. The heels of his shoes were lemon yellow, as was the hat perched on his black Stuart's wig.

Behind him trotted a Moor close in age to his master, his skin as dark as ebony against his white turban and flowing robes. Griffin had never voiced his relationship to the man, but Simeon guessed that like many of the fops of Charles's decadent Court, Griffin retained him as a sexual plaything as well as a personal servant. The thought disgusted Simeon, but he liked Griffin, so he tried not to think about it.

"Good morning, Cousin," Simeon offered.

"Good morning, my villain with a smiling cheek." Griffin removed his befeathered hat and bowed deeply, striking a pretty leg.

Simeon drew back his lips in a near smile. His cousin was impertinent, but at least he knew his place. He liked a man who knew his place, especially when it was below him. "And where are you bound this morning? I hadn't thought you drew your shades before noon."

Griffin chuckled as he replaced his ridiculous hat and took his silver-tipped cane from the Moor. "I've a call to make at

Whitehall in high chambers. Care to join me?'' He buffed his polished fingernails on the sleeve of his coat.

"No, thank you. I've better matters to attend to than our King's tattletales.'' Simeon nodded to the window. "Have you seen her?''

Griffin lifted a plucked eyebrow. *"Her,* my lord?''

"My latest acquisition. My betrothed, of course. She's in the garden. Come see.'' He waved his cousin toward the window.

"Ah, the blessed Virgin Mary, of course.'' Griffin drew to the window, his Moor a step behind.

The men leaned on the unfinished sill and gazed down. At the same moment, Julia looked up toward the gallery. For an instant her face was without emotion, as it had been for the three days since her arrival from Dover, but then, to Simeon's delight, it lit up with the most angelic smile.

Simeon felt his heart flutter. The smile was for him. So perhaps she didn't dislike him after all, but was simply playing coy, as women sometimes did.

Simeon turned his head to speak to Griffin, and his smile turned to a frown. His cousin was staring intently at his betrothed, too intently, a strange light in his blue eyes. Simeon looked back down into the garden and came to the unpleasant realization that Julia's smile was not for him, but for his foppish cousin.

A quick anger bubbled up inside Simeon. *Witless female,* he thought. *Fickle.* And worse . . . *untidy.*

"And yet I love refinement, and beauty and light are for me the same as desire for the sun,'' Griffin whispered.

For an instant, his cousin's comely face appeared different to Simeon; the light in his eyes reflected a depth in the man he was certain didn't exist.

Simeon scowled. His cousin was always babbling something from obscure literature. "God's teeth, I don't know what *you're* staring at. Everyone knows you prefer the rod!''

Griffin blinked and the strange light in his eyes disappeared so quickly that Simeon wondered if he had imagined it.

"A might dimber wench,'' Griffin commented lightly. "But

by the stars, that hair. Looks like she just tumbled from your sheets, my lord. Do let Monsieur De'nu see what he can do with her coiffure.'' Once again he was his silly self.

Simeon took Griffin's comment as a compliment to his manhood and smiled again. ''Pleasant tart, isn't she? Nice, firm teats, but then you wouldn't really appreciate that, would you?'' He eyed the Moor.

Griffin fluttered a perfumed handkerchief he pulled from his coat sleeve like a magician. The man couldn't be insulted.

''God rot my bowels, you're lewdly bent.'' Griffin laughed, and Simeon laughed with him.

Simeon liked Griffin for his wit. That was why he tolerated his vices and was willing to keep him in cloth and coin. Simeon liked to keep such men under his thumb. They added to his own notability.

''Well, I should be on my way. I ordered your coach and four. You don't mind do you, Cousin?''

''Take it.'' Simeon gave a flip of his hand, feeling generous. ''Keep it all night.''

''Very good, my lord.''

Griffin bowed as deeply as a man bowed to the king. The impudent monkey behind him stood stock-still, staring as if he were blind. Because he was in good humor, Simeon chose to ignore the slight.

''Good day.'' Simeon nodded his head.

''Good day.'' Griffin backed away, then turned, and made his exit from the gallery.

Julia stared at the man in the window. His hat was so preposterous that she wanted to laugh, and yet there was something about the face beneath the feathers that enticed her. His gaze met hers and she felt light-headed, the way she did when a coach went over a bump and remained airborne for a moment. It was the strangest feeling, not bad, just different.

Lizzy glanced up and giggled. ''See the man in the funny hat?'' She covered her mouth with mitted hands and laughed behind them. "They wear silly clothes in London, don't you think, Sister? I see men in face paint and women hanging their bosoms out of their gowns until you can see their nippies."

Julia didn't answer. She couldn't tear her gaze from the stranger's. She knew St. Martin watched as well. She knew he would think her stare inappropriate, and yet she couldn't help herself.

It was the stranger who glanced away first.

Julia lowered her gaze to her lap. Her stomach fluttered. Who was that man? Surely not a servant in such flothery? A friend? Another distant relative? There were so many members of her betrothed's household that she still had not met them all.

"Sister, I said I'm cold." Lizzy spoke in a tone that implied she'd been forced to repeat herself.

Julia blinked. "Oh, I'm sorry, Lizzy. Let's go inside then and warm ourselves with a cup of chocolate." She rose from the bench and took her sister's hand. She didn't know what on earth possessed her to stare at the stranger like that. Perhaps Lizzy was right, perhaps it was just his preposterous hat.

Julia led Lizzy back up the garden path, beneath a bare arched arbor, and through double doors into the rear of the great, sprawling London house. As they entered the dim hallway, a man approached. To her dismay, Julia realized it was the stranger in the hat.

"Morning, ladies," he called gaily.

Lizzy giggled. "The feathers of his hat are yellow as a daffodil," she whispered.

"Shhht!" Julia reprimanded softly. Once again, she couldn't take her gaze off him.

Like many other men of the king's court she had met here in Bassett Hall, his lips were rouged, his high, handsome cheekbones dusted with rice powder, and his chin was decorated with a half-moon-shaped face patch. His head was covered in a monstrous wig, the same coal black hue that the King's hair was said to be. He looked the part of every dandy she'd met in the last three days, but there was something different about this man . . . something different about his eyes. They were not

vacant like the other fops, but filled with a glistening light . . .
a secret.

"Out early this morning are we?" he asked. His outrageously
high-heeled shoes clacked on the flagstone floor. "Is it chilly?
Shall I need my muff?" He swaggered oddly as he walked on
tiptoes, his arms slightly extended.

Never in her life had Julia seen such a theatrical man. She
found her voice. "Not . . . not too cold, but windy."

He touched his manicured hand to his breast, still
approaching. His well-cut doublet was a most hideous lemon
yellow and lime green. *"That time of year thou mayst in me
behold when yellow leaves, or none or few, do hang upon those
boughs which shake against the cold."*

She turned as he passed her. "Shakespeare, a sonnet, I
think." She smiled to herself, pleased she could recall.

He met her gaze, a flicker of surprise on his face. "A woman
who reads? Gads." He struck his chest again. "Another wonder
of the modern world?"

Julia lifted one eyebrow and lowered her hand to her hip.
"I beg your pardon, sir, but of course I can read."

He raised his palm to her. "No offense meant . . ."

"Julia," she offered, too intrigued to be insulted. "Lady
Julia Thomas."

He struck a leg and bowed, sweeping his hat off his bewigged
head. "My profuse apologies, Lady Julia. You are, of course,
his lordship's intended."

She dipped a curtsy. Lizzy just stood behind her and stared.

"Baron Archer, cousin to the Earl of St. Martin, at your
service. Griffin, I am called to friend and foe." He straightened
and replaced his hat.

"Oh, and this is my sister, Lizzy." Julia sidestepped to
present her.

He bowed again. "Lady Lizzy."

Lizzy giggled and curtsied. "My, sir, that is an ugly hat you
wear. I hope you did not pay a great deal for it."

Julia sucked in her breath, shocked that her sister would dare
say such a thing. "Lizzy!"

But instead of being offended, the baron threw back his head and laughed. He whipped off his hat and stared at it. "God rot my bowels, 'tis ugly, isn't it?"

Lizzy nodded, wide-eyed and frank. "Ugly, indeed. The ugliest I believe I've ever seen."

Footsteps sounded in the hallway and Julia saw a dark-skinned man approach. She had only seen a blackamoor once before, and had to force herself not to stare.

"Jabar! Where did I get this atrocious hat?" the baron called.

"Paris, my master." The exotic man with chocolate brown skin spoke in a liquid-soft voice that was mesmerizing.

"And why did I buy such an unsightly beast?"

"Because you liked it, my lord." Jabar's English was impeccable.

"Well, Lady Lizzy doesn't like it, nor do I." With that, Griffin sailed the hat into the air, over Julia and Lizzy's heads.

Lizzy burst into another fit of giggles.

"Good morn to you, ladies." The cousin to St. Martin bowed again and, before Julia could think of anything reasonable to say, he and his blackamoor were out the door.

"Funny man." Lizzy picked up the discarded hat and placed it on her head. She blew at the feathers that dangled over her face and watched them flutter with amusement. "Do you think he lives here with the dark man?"

Julia stared at the empty doorway, utterly perplexed by the exchange that had just taken place. Lizzy was right, the man was funny, and utterly ridiculous, and yet there was something about him . . . something . . .

Julia wrapped one arm around her sister's waist and led her down the hall. "I don't know if he lives here, but it wouldn't surprise me." She glanced over her shoulder. "Nothing would surprise me at this moment."

That evening Julia dressed carefully in one of the gowns her betrothed had presented to her upon her arrival. She tried not to feel hurt that his lordship did not find her own country gowns appropriate for her to wear while she served as his hostess. Instead, she wrestled down her pride and donned the gown he requested she wear. She would have preferred the green velvet, but he had been specific in the note he sent by way of his secretary.

The dress was a magnificent piece of work, far finer than anything her mother had been able to provide for her. The underskirts were a heavy azure brocade trimmed in fur, the bodice and overskirt sewn of the same azure in silk. The neckline of the bodice was fur-trimmed and scooped low over Julia's well-rounded breasts. Her hair was dressed from the center, parting into wide side ringlets and a single shoulder ringlet which Drusilla—with the aid of her trusty iron-curling rod— had worked long and hard.

Julia stared at herself in an oval free-standing mirror framed in gold gilt. Her grandmother's pearl earrings swung in her ears. She smoothed the bodice of the gown, feeling a little uncomfortable with the way it revealed her breasts. "I suppose I'm ready."

" 'Bout time," Drusilla, the woman who had been her nurse since birth, complained. After all these years Julia had grown used to Drusilla's grumpiness. In fact, here at Bassett Hall, it was a comfortable reminder of home.

Before pushing out the door of the apartment, Drusilla rubbed rouge on Julia's lips and pinched her cheeks hard.

"Ouch!"

"Try not to look like you're bound for yer hangin', eh?" Drusilla warned.

In the doorway, Julia glanced over Drusilla's hunched shoulder to wave goodbye to Lizzy. Although Julia's mother Susanne had been invited to sup with the earl's guests, Lizzy had not.

Lizzy grinned and waved, not understanding that she was being snubbed by her new male guardian.

Julia gathered her courage and took the hallway toward the grand staircase and her awaiting betrothed.

Halfway down stairs that were wide enough to ride a coach and four, Julia heard footsteps behind her. "Lady Julia . . ." someone called, then softer, "Lady Julia."

The voice was familiar.

She halted and turned, her crackling skirts bunched in her

fists. It was Baron Archer . . . Griffin. He was dressed in another ludicrous outfit, this one of pastel blue and pink silk.

"Lady Julia." He fluttered a long pink handkerchief. "Do allow me to escort you below."

Julia watched with fascination as the man tottered down the staircase in his heeled shoes. The height of the platforms added to his own tall stature, making him a rather imposing figure.

She smiled and curtsied as best she could on the stair tread. "Good even', my lord."

"S'death, please, call me Griffin." He took her hand.

"Then call me Julia."

He nodded, his gaze meeting hers. "Julia," he said softly in a voice that didn't quite seem his own.

They paused for the briefest moment, then broke the mutual gaze and started down the steps again.

"I wanted to apologize for my comment in the entry this morning. Anyone will tell you my mouth runs day and night, but I mean nothing by it." It was Griffin's slightly effeminate voice, and yet it wasn't. "I never meant to infer you lacked intelligence."

His arm was warm beneath her grasp. Comforting. "No offense taken. I swear it. In truth few country girls are educated beyond household responsibilities and needlework. As luck, or God's intervention, would have it, my father was a man who believed learning was for all noble families, even the *inferior* females."

He chuckled, seeming not only to catch the tone in her voice when she said "inferior," but to agree with her sarcasm.

"Well, I wanted to welcome you to Bassett Hall and tell you that if you need anything, I offer my services."

She dared a sideways glance at Griffin. His offer was of course nothing but a formality, and yet there was something in his tone that made her believe he was entirely sincere.

"This Hall, London, and my cousin for certain, can be intimidating." Griffin halted at the bottom of the grand stairs. "I wouldn't wish to see you frightened or unhappy."

Their gazes met a final time, and Julia was amazed to see not the man in the ridiculous clothing, but the man beneath the genuine smile and sparkling eyes similar to her own shade of blue. Her grandfather had always said a person should not judge a man by his cloak, and she was beginning to understand the wisdom of his warning.

"Ah! There she is, my prize," the Earl of St. Martin called from the nearest chamber. "Come, my dearest, and meet our guests."

Julia's gaze flickered from St. Martin back to the man who still held her tightly on his arm.

"Your servant, my lord," she bid formally as she pulled away from Griffin and curtsied to him.

"Your servant, madame . . ." Griffin bowed deeply. "Forever."

Julia lowered her lashes and turned away. The warmth of Griffin's touch still burned her fingertips as she greeted her husband-to-be.

ABOUT THE AUTHOR.

Colleen Faulkner lives with her family in Southern Delaware. She is the author of eighteen Zebra historical romances, including *Fire Dancer*, *To Love a Dark Stranger*, *Destined To Be Mine*, *O'Brian's Bride*, and *Captive*. Colleen's newest historical romance, *Once More*, will be published in October 1998. Colleen loves hearing from her readers and you may write to her c/o Zebra Books. Please include a self-addressed stamped envelope if you wish a response.

BOOK YOUR PLACE ON OUR WEBSITE AND MAKE THE READING CONNECTION!

We've created a customized website just for our very special readers, where you can get the inside scoop on everything that's going on with Zebra, Pinnacle and Kensington books.

When you come online, you'll have the exciting opportunity to:

- View covers of upcoming books

- Read sample chapters

- Learn about our future publishing schedule (listed by publication month *and author*)

- Find out when your favorite authors will be visiting a city near you

- Search for and order backlist books from our online catalog

- Check out author bios and background information

- Send e-mail to your favorite authors

- Meet the Kensington staff online

- Join us in weekly chats with authors, readers and other guests

- Get writing guidelines

- AND MUCH MORE!

**Visit our website at
http://www.zebrabooks.com**